MESSY, WONDERFUL US

CATHERINE ISAAC

LARGE PRINT

First published in Great Britain 2019
by
Simon & Schuster UK Ltd.

First Isis Edition
published 2020
by arrangement with
Simon & Schuster UK Ltd.

A catalogue record for this book is available
from the British Library.

ISBN 978–1–78541–885–3

Published by
Ulverscroft Limited
Anstey, Leicestershire

Set by Words & Graphics Ltd.
Anstey, Leicestershire
Printed and bound in Great Britain by
T. J. International Ltd., Padstow, Cornwall

This book is printed on acid-free paper

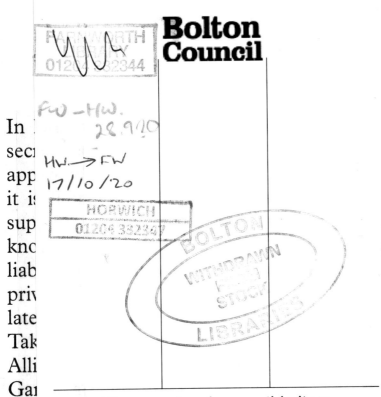
In ... aining
sec ... away,
app ... later,
it i ... s ever
sup ... ng she
kno ... truth
liab ... ires a
priv ... to her
late ... born.
Tak ... entist,
Alli ... Lake
Gai ... ut the
sec ... they
wer ... age to
con ... be her
futu

For Sheila Crowley, with enormous gratitude

Prologue

There were certain scents that could whisk her back to that sultry night at any moment. It would happen for months afterwards. She'd be getting on with her life, trying to keep her head down, when she'd breathe in and a rush of memories would follow. Of hot skin and the spike of perfume. The fug of cigarette smoke and hairspray. The musky aroma that had clung faintly to his neck, as he'd slipped his hand around her waist and whispered to her. And the pollen-rich grass that infused the darkness as she'd followed him, until the boom of music grew faint and they were out of sight, heading towards a tangle of woodland.

She hadn't set out to be reckless that night. But then, she hadn't set out to tell all those lies so she could be with a boy — no, a man — she shouldn't have been with. In the preceding weeks, she'd found herself floating towards this point, unable to stop herself. Unable to think about her betrayal and the pain she had the capacity to inflict on the one man who really loved her.

From the moment this stranger had swept into her life, everything about him had bewitched her. The lilting way he spoke, in an accent that captured the intrinsic beauty of words. The muss of hair around the nape of his neck. The way he looked at her, as if every other girl was invisible. She'd glanced up at the shadows on his face as the moon glowed behind him, trying to pretend she was more experienced than she was. But he can't have failed to notice that she was trembling.

His features were unusual, striking rather than handsome. But this wasn't about his looks. It was about what she saw behind his eyes, the antidote to every humdrum thing in her life, a world of adventure, a foreign land. He was leading her to a new place inside herself, away from the person everyone thought she was.

They followed a secluded path beyond the trees and found a spot where the air had stilled. Nobody could see them or hear them. She knew what was about to happen and it made her chest burn. His lips felt like velvet as his mouth travelled along her jaw, her temple, the stretch of her collarbone. Bark scratched through her dress into the damp flesh on her spine and her hem rose to the top of her thighs. All she could do was abandon herself to the exquisite ache in her belly. The weightlessness of the moment. The sky-high feeling of being a woman.

CHAPTER
ONE

THE PRESENT DAY

Allie

The lobby is uncompromisingly fashionable, with a glass staircase that sweeps onto an airy mezzanine, a gleaming grand piano and an architectural approach to flower arranging. I stand amidst a sea of tuxedos and cocktail dresses, of chatter and clinking glasses, and seek out a familiar face.

"Would you care for a rosemary-infused martini?" A waitress appears next to me with a tray of drinks, her slender frame neatly contained in a black minidress.

"Thank you," I reply, taking one. I sip the drink, wondering if it's the floating twig that distinguishes it from a G&T, and crane my neck over the crowd.

I know there are others here from the university: Petra, my boss Alistair and his wife Maureen, all work alongside me in the department of Cellular and Molecular Physiology. I know I shouldn't, but part of me hopes that I've been seated next to one of them, rather than a stranger. It's not that I'm incapable of small talk, on the contrary. But I enjoy being surrounded by like-minded people, even if it's just to gossip about the affair between our new senior lecturer and the Ukrainian postdoc.

Wherever I end up sitting tonight, a glitzy charity ball is, undisputedly, a change of scene from my last few Friday evenings, which I spent in the lab looking down a microscope, taking photographs of fluorescent proteins. Given that Petra likes telling me this is not how a thirty-three-year-old single woman *should* spend her weekends, this will at least satisfy her.

"Well, don't you scrub up well? *Love* the heels." I turn around to find Petra grinning at my feet. "They *can't* be comfortable."

"I'm not exactly walking on air, no," I confess.

The round apples of Petra's cheeks are enhanced by a complicated, serpentine up-do and she's wearing a pretty yellow dress I can already tell she regrets bitterly, judging by her determination to tug her pashmina over her cleavage.

"That's a beautiful gown," I say.

"Do you really think so?" she replies, hoisting up the front a little higher. "I bumped into the vice chancellor on the way in and I don't think he was a fan."

"Well, I'm not sure it would suit *him*, but on you, it's a winner." She snorts.

But I'm telling the truth, and not simply because in the days when we were working on our joint project about CFTR protein abnormalities in airway smooth muscle, I was more used to seeing her arrive at the lab brushing Coco Pops out of her hair. It was an important and high-profile piece of work, which meant constantly working late and, while this is no terrific

4

sacrifice to me, I know Petra hated missing bedtime for her two young daughters.

Still, research is the most rewarding part of the job, for both of us. It's what took me halfway across the UK, then boomeranged me back to the Russell Group university that has been thriving in my home city since 1881, leading the way in key areas of scientific research and turning out nine Nobel prize winners. It's also the focus of this evening's festivities. Every penny of the money raised tonight will go to cystic fibrosis research, and at least some will be channelled into my area of work. So I definitely *should* prepare myself for small talk.

"I see your friend Ed is doing the keynote speech," Petra says. "I get the impression that there's a lot of money in this room, so I hope he's persuasive."

"I hope so too."

"From what I hear, the CFA love him," she continues. "So we can only hope he dazzles the crowd."

I smile at the thought, not because I don't think Ed can be dazzling. I've seen with my own eyes the effect of his presence on both sexes, the way the most unlikely admirer will soften around him. Yet, no matter what my friend achieves, to me he's still the skinny kid I'd sit next to on the top deck of the 86 bus, its windows misted with condensation as we doubled up with laughter.

"Couldn't you tempt Simon out tonight?" As I say it, it strikes me that I can't remember the last time Petra brought her husband to an event like this.

"Couldn't get a babysitter. Besides, he can't stand work dos. There's a reason so many scientists marry other scientists, you know. We bore everyone rigid."

"Speak for yourself." She laughs.

The toastmaster calls for attention and invites everyone to take their seats. It's a large room, atmospherically lit with a rosy glow pooling on each table centrepiece. I take my seat next to a man who immediately offers me his hand to shake. "Good evening! I'm Teddy Hancock." I'd place him in his early sixties, American, with a jovial face and heavy-lidded eyes.

"Oh, I think I recall Ed mentioning your name. I'm Allison Culpepper."

The corner of his mouth turns up, betraying his satisfaction. "We're trying to put a deal together right now. Do you work for him?"

"Oh God no. I'm sure he's a lovely boss, but we're just old friends. I work at the university, as an academic research scientist."

"So, you're *Professor* Allison Culpepper?"

"Doctor." Blowing my own trumpet has never come easily to me and I sometimes have to remind myself that I earned that title and the authority that comes with it, so I really shouldn't be shy about it. "But give me time."

"What do you specialise in?"

"Physiology," I reply. He makes an expression of vague recognition that reminds me a little of my six-year-old nephew, who remains convinced I am undertaking vital work in the field of fizzy drinks.

"You have some connection with the charity?" he continues.

"They funded a research project of mine a couple of years ago — my primary interest is in the pathophysiology of the airway associated with cystic fibrosis. Also, it was me who persuaded Ed to get involved. He ran the London Marathon for charity a couple of years ago, so I thought I'd twist his arm into devoting his energies to this instead. Keeps me in honest work."

His eyes narrow momentarily. "You know, you don't *look* like a scientist."

"Really? Well, between you and me, they let scientists wear lipstick these days. At least on our days off." He guffaws with laughter.

Truth is, I'm wearing more lipstick than I ordinarily would tonight. A small gap in my teeth earned me some character-building nicknames at school so it's still rare that I draw attention to my mouth, but this felt like a suitably grand occasion on which to change that policy. And somehow it compliments my dark hair and the emerald green dress that pulls in my wobbly bits and made my heart soar a little the second I saw it.

"Ladies and gentlemen, may I have your attention please." The marketing director of the charity is at the lectern. He has a slight face, with thinning ginger hair and a surprisingly basso profundo voice.

"The man I am about to introduce is someone many of you know professionally and some of you know personally. His company, Spark, was a success story of the dot.com boom and became one of the UK's fastest-growing business-to-business retailers. We were delighted to announce earlier in the year that he and his wife Julia are now official ambassadors for our charity and have since worked tirelessly to raise both funds and awareness for cystic fibrosis. Without further ado, please put your hands together for Mr Edward Holt."

Applause cracks through the room, as I spot Julia at the top table, not far from where I'm sitting. Her cool beauty is unequalled tonight. She is a goddess in Valentino, the pale blue fabric of her dress cinched at her slim waist. Her blonde hair is swept into a soft chignon, drawing all the attention to her face, with its slender nose, faintly dredged with freckles and wide, ingénue eyes. She glances up and we exchange a friendly smile as a hush descends on the room. Ed steps up to the lectern.

Despite being a child with plug ears, permanently bloody knees and filth that clung to him like treacle, he grew into a striking adult.

He has strong cheekbones, but there's a softness to his mouth. He keeps his light brown hair closely cut and his skin retains the ghost of last summer's tan. But it's his eyes that are the most arresting: ocean blue and framed with black lashes, with straight brows that make him appear more intense than he is.

"If I'd known I'd get a reception like that I'd have spent longer on my speech," he says. Then he smiles that smile, the one caught somewhere between charisma and self-deprecation, and that's all it takes. He already has the audience in the palm of his hand.

CHAPTER
TWO

"How much did the event raise?" Granddad Gerald takes off my coat and hangs it on the bannister of the narrow hallway, before wrapping me in one of those bear hugs that grandfathers do best, all love and fabric conditioner.

"They're still totting it up, but *a lot*. Ed wrote a hefty cheque himself, though, so I'm not sure if that counts as cheating."

Granddad shakes his head as he loosens the collar of his maroon jumper, his bald patch still shining from the heat in the kitchen. "He's done well for himself that boy, hasn't he? Mind you, I still can't believe I've got a granddaughter who's a *doctor*. Speaking of which, will you just take a look at these bunions for me . . ."

I laugh, as ever, at his standing joke; last time he asked me to check his temperature. Granddad never changes and neither does this house. There's still the same Christian Aid collection box on the sideboard, the family photos fighting for space on the textured walls, the blue carpet with tiny Fleur de Lys emblems that I thought were ducks when I was little. It's always spotlessly clean and often smells of new paint, though the fundamental look of the place hasn't been updated significantly since my mother lived here.

"Gerald, could you come finish setting the table?" Grandma Peggy pops her head around the kitchen door. "Oh, hello, Allie. I didn't hear the doorbell."

I walk towards her and give her a kiss on her cheek. "Lovely perfume, Grandma," I say, breathing in the scent that clings to her blouse.

"It's just lotion," she protests, waving me away, as if she'd never bother with anything as frivolous as perfume.

Grandma Peggy is not a frivolous woman. She is generally intolerant of nonsense, loudmouths, cold callers, people who leave lights on around the house and anyone who sings hymns in church with a two-second delay. Still, she's also the woman who knitted my favourite jumpers as a child, gave me my prized jewellery box from Paris that she'd had since she and Granddad briefly lived there, and relinquished a coveted slot in the local bowls team to take me to ballet classes when I was seven. I also reserved a special admiration for her more recently, after she scolded her friend Dorothy for being "a silly bigot" when she blamed her Indian GP for everything from a rise in unemployment to the stubbornness of her haemorrhoids.

"What's for dinner?" I ask.

"A feast," she replies. "We'll have leftovers until Easter at this rate."

"Sounds wonderful."

"I can't claim credit. Your dad's done everything except the roast potatoes."

Dad and Grandma join forces to cook for the whole family one Sunday a month. This is usually at her house, where there's a slightly bigger dining room and the boon of a hostess trolley, though it's Dad who does most of the cooking.

"As long as he left the roasties to you. He knows better than to encroach on your domain." She purses her lips into something that resembles a smile. Grandma's skin has slackened with age, but she retains her classically handsome features, even if she does virtually nothing to enhance them. There is never a hint of lipstick, nor a whisper of eye shadow; her slate-grey hair has been cut into a short elfin crop for as long as I remember.

I step inside the kitchen, a neat and functional space in which everything is tucked away behind stained pine cupboards with brass knobs, except a collection of Delia Smith cookery books next to the spice rack.

Dad is at the hob, stirring one of three bubbling pans with a look of intense concentration on his face. He's wearing the apron I bought him for Father's Day, with the words "Executive Chef" on the front.

He looks up and wipes his hands on a tea towel, "Hello, love," he says brightly, pausing to give me a kiss, his skin warm from the heat of the stove.

"How have you managed all this, Dad? I thought you were at work this morning."

"I got most of it done during the week." My dad is big on batch cooking. It's how he seems to spend most of his days off, stuffing the freezer, so that by the last Sunday of the month he's always ready to serve some posh starter — little salmon soufflés or a watercress soup — followed by a huge, traditional roast complete with a selection of spiced accompaniments and home-made sauces. "It was a good job as well. I didn't get out until late today."

"Nothing serious I hope?"

He shakes his head. "One of the staff at the Royal left the toast on too long and set off the fire alarm."

Being a firefighter was the only job my father ever wanted and he had joined the service soon as he was old enough. He spends most of his days dealing with house fires, traffic accidents, dogs locked in cars and, in one recent case, helping to rescue a thirty-four-year-old man who'd got his backside stuck in a child's swing. He's also had some close shaves in his time, including one incident last year in which he was caught in a flashover in a disused warehouse. The room flooded with flames and melted the shield on his helmet, leaving him with a second-degree burn that still puckers the freckled skin on his neck and gives me the odd sleepless night.

I head to the dining room and find Granddad laying the cutlery.

"Let me help you with that," I offer, taking a handful of forks to the other side of the table. "Oh, while I've got you . . . You know it's Grandma's birthday in a couple of weeks? I'm thinking of buying her a jacket, what do you think?"

He gives me a blank look. "I've no idea, love. I tried to ask her what she wanted the other day and she said she's too old for presents. She'll end up with a pair of roller skates if she can't be any more help."

"The one I've seen is lovely, really chic."

Granddad's forehead crinkles. "You don't need to buy her designer things, Allie. She's seventy-six."

"Being seventy-six doesn't mean you don't deserve nice clothes."

"She'll tell you off for wasting your money."

"Tough," I declare. "Any idea what her dress size is?"

He looks up from under his eyebrows and hesitates. "Eighteen?"

I tut. "Oh, Granddad, she's much smaller than that. Fourteen surely, maybe even a twelve?"

"I wouldn't have a clue. It's been years since she let me buy her clothes. She said the last cardigan I gave her made her look like a sheepdog. Why don't you sneak up and have a peek at the labels in her clothes?" he suggests. "She's got a wardrobe full up there."

CHAPTER
THREE

It feels strange entering the bedroom where Granddad and Grandma sleep, even if it was his idea. I haven't ventured in here since I was a little girl, when I'd creep in to play with Grandma's soaps or hide under the candlewick bedspread.

It could be a bright room but the big mahogany dresser that sits in the window blocks out much of the light. The carpet is in a faded shade of pink and on either side of their high double bed are two small cabinets, with a Robert Ludlum novel and a tube of denture glue on one; a book of crosswords and a silver-framed photograph of Mum on the other. It was taken when she was in her early twenties, not long before she became ill.

I quietly pad across the floor, wondering how they sleep in such a chilly room, with two windows wide open. Letting in "fresh air" is a constant preoccupation of Grandma Peggy's, as if there is a limited amount of it on offer.

The sound of laughter drifts upstairs from the kitchen as I gently open her wardrobe door, releasing a faint scent of lily of the valley. The interior is tightly packed with dresses and suits, all in muted fabrics, some still covered with plastic from the dry cleaners. I take out a dress and examine the label. It's a size 16, which surprises me, so I put it back and check out some of the others. Only, there's a whole array of sizes, ranging from 12 to 16, and no indication as to which might be the most accurate.

I close the door and decide to look in her chest of drawers instead, where I'm more likely to find a top that I know she's worn recently. I work from the bottom up, opening the first drawer to find a stack of sweaters and the cashmere cardigan she had on when I saw her a couple of weeks ago. I take that out and check the label: size 14, much more what I was expecting. I want to leave the clothes as neatly as I found them, so I remove the pile to refold each item. But when I attempt to straighten the drawer liner, I realise there's something underneath. I slide my fingernail under the edge and carefully lift it up. It's then that I find the envelope.

It's dry and faded with age, ripped open at the top. I don't know what it is exactly that compels me to pick it up, slide out the letter and unfold it, carefully unfurling the old newspaper page concealed inside. I do it almost without thinking, stroking my fingers against the grey print before I can even contemplate the ethics of my intrusion.

It's the date that I register first — 11 June 1983 — before I cast my gaze over a spread of pictures from a summer party held at Allerton People's Hall to celebrate its centenary. There are two rows of photographs, some of austere-looking men in cricket whites, others of women in pleated skirts and batwing sleeves. There are teenage boys in Ray-Bans and polo shirts with popped-up collars, girls in crop tops and lace, looking sticky under the dying heat of the day. Then I spot the name on one caption: Christine Culpepper.

When my eyes settle on my mother's face, at first I don't think beyond the tug in my chest, a jolt of something sad and indefinable. But as I take in each detail, a creeping realisation begins to take hold. Something doesn't add up.

My mother is holding hands with a young man I don't know, someone I've never even seen before. Her mouth is curled up in a mysterious smile and teenage infatuation shines brightly in her eyes. The name of this unknown person, according to the caption, is Stefano McCourt. He looks to be older than my mother by a couple of years and has dark eyes, a full mouth and a gap in his teeth. I look at the date again, trying to reconcile each contradictory detail, but one in particular: the photo was taken nine months before I was born.

"*Five minutes until dinner,*" I hear Dad shout from downstairs. I don't answer, ignoring the rapid thudding in my chest as I turn my attention to the handwritten letter. It is addressed to my Grandma Peggy and dated December 1983. There's no address from the sender.

Dear Mrs Culpepper,
   I write to respectfully ask you not to contact Stefano, myself, or my husband Michael again via his office at the Museo di Castelvecchio.

While I understand that you are in shock about Christine and Stefano — we all are — no good can come of us continuing to maintain contact. I am particularly upset about you writing to my son about his supposed responsibilities to his "flesh and blood". This kind of emotional blackmail is very wrong when he already made his decision not to have anything more to do with your daughter before our family left Liverpool. The fact that he moved back to Italy with us should have made this very clear.

From what you said in your letter, Christine has now made amends with her boyfriend. He will no doubt make a good father to the baby. So why rock the boat by trying to bring Stefano back into the equation when nobody needs to know the truth?

He is not going to change his mind and he has absolutely no intention of returning to the UK. I am deeply sorry if this sounds harsh under the circumstances, but I'm sure you appreciate that it is not just you who has been upset by events.

Yours truly,
Signora Vittoria McCourt

I look again at the photograph on the newspaper cutting. At the date. At my mother's enraptured smile. But most of all, I am drawn to the young man with dark hair and a gap in his teeth that's so identical to my own that it makes my breath catch in my throat.

CHAPTER
FOUR

There are eight of us for dinner once my uncle Peter, Dad's younger brother, has arrived with his wife Sara and their two young sons, Oscar and Nathan, aged four and six. While everybody else chats happily as they thread into the dining room, I am unable to concentrate on anything but the buzzing in my head, the thrum of my heart against my chest wall.

"Is this a new toy?" Dad asks Oscar, as a remote-control car hits him on the back of the ankles.

"Yes, I got it because I filled up my sticker chart."

"Well done! You must've been a good boy," he says, taking a seat at the table.

"I wiped my own bum every day for a week."

"Congratulations," Dad replies.

"Will you teach me how to play a song on your guitar again, Uncle Joe?" Nathan asks.

"Oh, sorry, Nathan, I haven't brought it with me today. It's at home."

Dad looks more disappointed than my nephew that he's missed the opportunity to get his old Gibson guitar out and play a tune. It's his prized possession — crafted in 1979 and *"just like BB King's"*, as he never tires of telling us.

The table is technically too small to accommodate eight people and the amount my dad has cooked, but we squeeze round it, before Grandma says grace. "For food that stays our hunger, for rest that brings us ease, for homes where memories linger, we give our thanks for these. Amen."

Everyone tucks in enthusiastically, while I find myself gazing at the table wondering how I'm going to stomach anything.

"You've surpassed yourself, Joe," Aunt Sara tells Dad, as she spoons some carrots onto Nathan's plate. "This is tremendous."

The talk around the table involves the kind of minor family dispatches I'd ordinarily join in with: what the kids are up to at school, Sara's plans to extend their kitchen, the fact that Grandma and Granddad's Golden Wedding Anniversary is coming up at the end of the year.

"Oh, you'll have to do something special," Sara says.

"Hmm. We'll do . . . *something*," Grandma replies, the unspoken implication being that there will not, under any circumstances, be any *fuss*.

"Why don't you go on a cruise?" Sara suggests, unabated.

"Muriel and Bobby put us off," Granddad tells her. "They went on one last year and weren't keen. Bobby lost his dentures down the toilet in the first week and he was stuck without them for the rest of the trip."

Dad chuckles into his wine.

"Don't laugh," Granddad continues, though he's absolutely laughing himself. "Muriel stuffed herself at the buffet, but poor Bobby had to eat soup while his teeth were floating somewhere in the mid-Atlantic."

"Everything all right, love?" Dad asks and I look up sharply. My eyes are drawn to his fair hair and the way it curls around the pale skin on his neck. Then the face of another man altogether tears through my head.

"Fine. Sorry. Just a bit tired. It's been a busy week."

"What are you working on at the moment, Allie?" Sara asks.

"Um . . . gene-editing technology," I mumble. "We're trying to find a cure for people with cystic fibrosis, basically."

"Gosh, isn't Aunty Allie clever?" she says to Nathan.

"Do you still study fizzy drinks?" he asks.

As Dad and Uncle Peter begin chatting about the football results, my mind drifts to the Christmas before last, when my father sat in that same spot where he's seated now. Grandma Peggy and I handed over a gift about which we had both been apprehensive but in complete agreement: a subscription to a dating website. I held my breath as he opened the envelope, his expression changing as he read the voucher.

"We all thought it was about time," Grandma Peggy had said, in her usual matter-of-fact way, yet the monumental implications of this gesture were clear to all.

He lifted his eyes and pressed his lips together into a smile. "Did you now? Sounds like a conspiracy to me." I think we all knew nothing would come of it.

20

To be absolutely fair, he did eventually go on a couple of dates, including one with a woman in Hull. He drove all the way over there, only to find out that she bore about as much resemblance to her profile picture as I do to a Victoria's Secret model. She'd told Dad regretfully that she didn't really think it was going to work out between them. Nevertheless, she'd be prepared to give him a go on the basis that he was an Aquarius and she was a Leo, which meant though their chances of compatibility and communication would be poor, sex would be passably good. He finished his cappuccino and left. So we all gave up again, just like we'd done nearly a decade ago when he split up with Sarah, a nurse he'd technically been seeing for years, but who always felt more like a companion than his girlfriend. We all know the reason why he's still single and it's not because there's anything wrong with him. He's no Calvin Klein model, but he's honest, practical, caring and he makes an exceptional roast dinner.

The real issue is that he doesn't believe he'll ever love someone like he loved a woman who died nearly three decades ago. My mother, the woman in the newspaper photograph that's hidden upstairs, along with a whole load of secrets it's very clear that Dad and I were never supposed to know about.

I get tipsy over dinner. Not falling down drunk, but infused with enough of a wine buzz to agree to teach Nathan how to use his pogo stick in the street in my tights. When we return inside for dessert, Granddad appears at the table with the cake that he's tried to convince the children was all his own work, even though they saw him taking it out of a Tesco box. He cuts a piece and hands a plate to Sara first, before I notice him glance at Grandma anxiously.

"I hadn't realised it was lemon cake," Granddad replies.

Grandma says nothing, but even Nathan senses that something in the room has shifted, as if the air circulating around us has suddenly become denser.

"What's the matter?" he asks her.

She smiles at him defiantly and pats his hand. "Nothing at all. The cake looks delicious. Lemon was my Christine's favourite so it always reminds me of her, that's all."

My mother's name silences us all. It still has an ability to do that, all these years later.

"All right, Peggy?" Aunt Sara asks.

"Of course," Grandma replies. Then she looks up at Granddad. "Come on now, Gerald. There are two hungry little boys waiting patiently here."

As Granddad hands him a plate, Nathan tugs my sleeve. "Is Christine the one who died? Your mum?"

"That's right." I nod.

"That must've sucked. Your mum dying I mean."

"Yeah. It was a long time ago though."

"And at least you've still got your dad," he says, as I look up and feel my heart flare.

CHAPTER
FIVE

Watering my house plants always takes a little time. They sit on every shelf in the kitchen, a tangle of green leaves that spill over the bare wood surfaces and white metro tiles. But today I feel slower than usual, at this and everything else.

Six days after my discovery of the letter and newspaper cutting, my chest feels tight and acidic, the manifestation of repeated episodes of insomnia. The whole thing has become such a preoccupation, or an obsession, that by the weekend I know I'm going to have to do something about it. I put away my watering can and throw the dregs of my tea in the sink before washing the cup and turning it upside down on the drainer. There's nobody to silently disapprove of me not putting it away before I leave the flat anymore.

I spent four of my nine years in Cardiff living with my ex-boyfriend, Rob, a soft-spoken Geordie with gentle eyes and a love of football, Vietnamese food and science. We met while I completed my PhD and collaborated on two concurrent projects, which meant long hours in the lab, gathering data and listening to Etta James on a portable speaker.

Our relationship was never a grand passion in the *Gone With the Wind* tradition, but it survived us being apart for six months during my MRC training fellowship in the United States, at Chapel Hill in North Carolina. He didn't merely understand my ambitions to lecture and have my own lab, to work independently and make discoveries. He shared them. But with hindsight, I accepted my current job in Liverpool before I thought through what would happen to our relationship, assuming that it'd all just work out like it had after my stint in the US. Only he ended things, which felt like a punch in the gut, even before I discovered that he'd spent the night with an Argentinian researcher at a CF conference in New Orleans the previous year.

Since moving back to Liverpool, I've lived by myself but don't have time to be lonely. I have a full and rich life, with my family nearby and several sets of friends with whom I go to pub quizzes, play tennis, or just share a cup of tea. It's been less fruitful on the romance front, except for a purple patch last autumn when I tried Tinder. I was on it for three and a half months, before giving up, fatigued and empty, much to Petra's disappointment as she no longer got to hear all the details on our tea breaks. At thirty-three, I'm not altogether deaf to the ticking of my biological clock but it's on snooze. My parents had me so young that I was brought up with the words *there's no rush* being drummed into me. Perhaps I'll still be telling myself that when I'm on HRT.

24

I head to the bathroom and unzip my make-up bag, before looking in the mirror. I mean, really looking. At my thick, dark hair. The honeyed undertone of my complexion, which looks nothing like the pale skin of either my mum or dad. And the distinctive gap in my teeth.

I pick up my phone and click on the picture I'd copied from the newspaper cutting. Stefano McCourt has all of those features but his resemblance to the face in the mirror goes beyond that. The arch of his eyebrow follows the same pattern as mine. The almond shape of his eyes are set the same distance apart. It's as if the lines and curves of his face have been traced over mine with translucent paper and a pencil. I take out my mascara and force myself to think straight.

Did my mum lie? Did she have a baby — me — by another man and let my father believe that I was his? If that turned out to be true, if his entire family was built on deception, it would quite simply ruin his life. These issues boil inside me, until the moment I zip up my make-up bag and realise this comes down to one single, inconceivable question. Is the man I've called "Dad" for thirty-three years really my father?

Grandma Peggy is on a small stepladder washing the window frame on her front porch when I arrive at her house. She's not tight with money, but of a generation that wouldn't dream of paying a stranger to do a job like this simply to make life easier. Instead, at seventy-six, she stands three feet from the ground, pumping her arm back and forth, until not a spec of dirt remains.

"Why don't you let me do that, Grandma?" I ask, peering up at her.

"No, no," she says dismissively. "I'm nearly done."

"Are you sure you're all right up there?"

She frowns down at me. "Why *wouldn't* I be?"

My Grandma hasn't sat still since she retired a few years ago from her job as a secretary at Belsfield, a fee-paying secondary school far posher than the comprehensive I went to. Her refusal to relax goes back longer than that though. If there's something to be cleaned, or organised, you can guarantee she'll be on her feet doing it. Eventually she climbs down and snaps off her rubber gloves, dabbing a faint sheen from her forehead with the back of her sleeve. "To what do I owe the pleasure?"

"I just thought I'd pop round for a cup of tea. That's all right, isn't it?"

She looks so pleased at the idea that I wish I'd done this more often, in less difficult circumstances. "Of course. Come in."

In the kitchen, she refuses to let me make the drink, instead flicking on the kettle and taking out two gold-rimmed china mugs, painted with turquoise leaves and pink camellias. I sit down as she brings over the tea, trying to remember exactly how I'd planned to broach this subject.

"Is everything all right, Allie? You're very quiet."

"I . . . yes, I'm fine. I've just been thinking about Mum."

The light in her eyes seems to change and she sinks into her seat. "About anything in particular?"

"A few things, I suppose." I feel the edge of my teeth biting against the inside of my cheek as I try to just come out with it. But it feels easier to skirt around the issue first. "Do you think Mum regretted having me so young?"

She looks surprised. "Of course not. You might not have been planned, but you were the best thing that ever happened to her. It meant that she got to be a mother before she became ill. She wouldn't have had it any other way."

"It must've been a shock though," I reply. "When she found out she was pregnant, I mean."

"I can't deny that. She was only seventeen, after all. But if anyone thought it couldn't work, her and your father proved them wrong. They had a wonderful life together."

"So they *were* happy?"

She looks confused by the question. "You know they were. They brought out the best in one another and your dad was her rock. He made her last months bearable."

"And did . . ." But the words dry up in my mouth. "What?"

I feel my neck redden. "I just wondered if Mum ever had any other boyfriends, apart from Dad."

There is a subtle alteration of her demeanour. It's barely perceptible beyond the slowing of her movements, the stiffening of her jaw, the gradual whitening of the skin on her knuckles. "A couple of adolescent romances, but nobody you'd call a boyfriend. Nobody like your dad."

I take a sip of tea. "They never had a break?"

She blinks once, her expression steadfastly blank, before she picks up her handbag and begins rustling inside, for what I'm not sure. "Why are you asking this, Allie?" The words come out in a half-laugh.

I think about lying. I think about continuing this discussion in this same low-key, conversational manner, as if these are issues about which I'm mildly intrigued at most. I think, in the words of the letter, about not rocking the boat. But this isn't something I can just forget.

"Grandma, I need to ask you something." My words are clear and deliberate, but my heart is fluttering in my chest like a trapped skylark. "Or at least, tell you about something that I found. Something for which I need an explanation."

She swallows slowly. "Go on."

"On Sunday, I went into your bedroom. I wasn't snooping about deliberately. I'd wanted to buy you a jacket for your birthday, only I didn't know your dress size, so Granddad suggested I go and find something in your chest of drawers to check it."

The faint glow that had bloomed on her cheeks when she came in from the cold seems to drain from her face.

"I'm sorry," I say quickly. "I didn't mean to intrude, but I found something that I just can't explain."

Her jaw seems to grind slightly, but she refuses to fill the silence.

"It was a newspaper cutting and a letter. They were in your bottom drawer, under the lining paper. The cutting showed a picture of my mum with someone who looked . . . well, he looked like he was her boyfriend. It was taken nine months before I was born. And the letter was from someone called Vittoria McCourt. The mother of the boy in the picture."

Her eyes dart to the table and she fixes them on the grooves in the wood.

"I read the letter and I don't understand some of the things that it says. Because it gives the impression, the strong impression, that . . ." My voice trails off and I wonder if I can actually say this out loud. "Grandma, is that boy in the picture — Stefano McCourt — is he . . ."

"Is he what?" Her features have hardened into silent, stubborn shock.

"My father?" The two words come out in a croak and the tiniest, loaded hesitation follows.

"What?" she asks, incredulously.

"Is he my father?" I repeat.

"Absolutely not. You've got it *completely* wrong."

I wait for her to continue but she says nothing. Instead, her eyes blaze with some undefinable emotion and I can't decide whether it's fear or fury.

"Okay. Well, that's a relief," I say, steadying my voice. "But can you explain it to me?"

She scrapes back her chair and walks away to one of the drawers, which she starts busily rearranging with her back to me. "There's nothing to explain."

"But, Grandma, there is. What's the letter all about? Who was the boy in the picture? I need to know. I've got a right to know."

She spins around furiously. "A *right?* Don't talk to me about rights. I suppose you think you had a right to go through my private things?"

"I never meant to snoop, I swear. But, Grandma, you're changing the subject. Who's the boy?"

Her jaw clamps together as she fixes her eyes on me. "He's nobody."

"He clearly isn't."

"No, Allie. Listen to me, lady. You're putting two and two together and making five."

"Then . . . tell me the truth," I blurt out.

Panic seems to race in her eyes. "The truth is simple — there's nothing to it. So please just forget this nonsense. Stop jumping to ludicrous conclusions and, for God's sake, give it a rest with these questions."

"How . . . how can I, Grandma?"

"You can. You *must.* I don't have anything to do with the McCourts any longer and, whatever you think you read or saw in that picture, you got it wrong. Your father is your father. Joe. Nobody else."

"But my mum and that Stefano boy were obviously *together* in the photo," I argue. "They look like they're in love, Grandma."

"Of course they weren't in love! This is ridiculous."

I sit silently for a moment. But I just can't leave this. "Has Granddad seen the contents of that envelope?"

Her lungs seem to inflate with air, her eyes widening. "Do *not* say a word about this to him, or anyone in this family. Especially Joe. I'm not saying this for my sake. I'm saying it for his."

I press my spine into the back of the chair, feeling winded. When she next speaks, her voice is lower, calmer. Somehow it has twice the impact. "I mean it," she warns. "Do not mention this again, to me or anyone else. I'll never forgive you if you do."

CHAPTER
SIX

There is only one day I spent with my mother that I recall in any kind of detail and that's when she married my father. Every second of it feels so vivid, part of me thinks that my imagination must've filled in the gaps, because no six-year-old could remember all those details. The memory fixated me as I grew older. I'd day-dream about it as I gazed through the mottled windows at school, replaying conversations as sleep enveloped me each night.

"You make a very pretty bridesmaid, Allie," Grandma Peggy told me, as she fixed a pale, yellow rose in my hair and straightened my dress. I was a tomboy when I was little, the kind of kid whose eyes lit up at the sight of an unclimbed tree and who asked for an electric guitar for Christmas after seeing The Bangles on *Top of the Pops*. But I couldn't deny it. That dress was awesome — the colour of sunshine with a bow that bloomed out of the small of my back. I'd even been allowed to wear it with my jelly shoes, which I'd been surprised about. I'd seemed to be getting away with a lot lately.

"Let me just fix a safety pin into the back," Grandma said. "It's a little big for you."

"Why didn't we find one in the right size?"

"If we'd had more time we would."

Time. A child's perception of it tends to be distorted. Weeks feel like months, months like lifetimes. Even so, I remember thinking that this whole thing was definitely sudden. When my friend Sally had been a bridesmaid, she'd gone on about it for two school terms, telling us about endless dress fittings and trips to the shops to find the perfect pair of patterned tights. But Mummy and Daddy had only told me about this a week earlier.

"Come on, missy. Let's go and see if Daddy's ready."

Grandma took my hand and led me to the living room, where Daddy was standing in a posh grey suit and looking out the window. When he turned around, the first thing I noticed was that the flower on his lapel wasn't straight. The second thing was that his eyes were puffy and red. His face broke into a huge smile.

"You look like a princess!" he said and, although I'd have preferred to look like Suzannah Hoffs, I graciously replied: "So do you."

He laughed. "I hope not."

"I *mean* Prince Charming."

"Oh good. That's more the look I was going for. So, are you ready to go and be a bridesmaid?"

"YES!" I replied. "Are we going in a special car?"

"Well, no. We're going in my car," he replied.

"Oh. Are we going to throw confetti when we get outside?"

"Hmm. Probably not."

"Are we going to have a disco afterwards?"

"Mummy's not well enough for that, sweetheart."

None of this sounded anything like the wedding Sally went to. "She will be able to walk down the aisle of the church with me behind though, won't she?"

He glanced at Grandma Peggy then knelt down in front of me and took my hand. "No, Allie. She's going to still be in hospital, sweetheart. She's too poorly to go to a church."

"There is going to be a priest though. Father Daniel will be present," Grandma Peggy said.

"Oh. Okay." I felt bad for even admitting this to myself but I was disappointed. Her room in the hospital was horrible, full of machines and beeping things. I had no idea how they were going to fit all the guests in.

When we arrived, it became apparent that there were, in fact, no guests. None of their friends were there — and they had loads. There was just Mummy and she was asleep. And although the nurses were all beaming and fussing around with flowers and she was wearing a wedding dress, she didn't look as beautiful as brides were meant to. She didn't even look as beautiful as she had only months earlier, with thick eyelashes that I'd ask her to flutter against my cheek and lips so full that it took me ages when she let me put lipstick on her.

The grown-ups talked about her having *aggressive ovarian cancer*. They said she'd become ill so quickly that one of her lungs had collapsed. None of that sounded good and the watermelon that seemed to have grown in her belly looked even less good. She had a hosepipe that went up her nose and she was connected to a machine by her finger. It wouldn't shut up. It was like our house alarm when the battery had run out and Daddy would run around looking for a spare and getting cross when he couldn't find one. The dress didn't fit right at all. It was too big, except for across her tummy, where it stretched violently.

Before the ceremony, Grandma Peggy took me to the toilet even though I didn't really need it, like they made me do when we had a long journey ahead of us. I recall washing my hands, when all of a sudden, quite unexpectedly, a rush of sadness tore up my neck. The room seemed to close in on me and heat shot to my face as I looked down at the sink to see Grandma turning off the tap. The water stopped but my tears splashed onto the enamel in its place.

Grandma Peggy turned me gently by the shoulders and took me in her arms, hugging me softly at first, then so tight it felt as though she would squeeze the breath out of me. "Please don't cry, Allie," she whispered frantically, stroking my hair. "Please, *please* don't cry."

She wiped my sticky red cheeks with a tissue and I tried to uncrumple my forehead. "I can't help it."

Her face contorted with despair as she nodded and said: "Allie, this is going to be very hard for you. But for your mummy's sake, we *have* to stay strong. All of us. We've got to do everything we can to let her have one happy day. If she sees you crying . . . I don't think she could bear it. So no tears, sweetie. Please."

The ceremony was short. All the nurses clapped when the man in a suit said Daddy could kiss his bride. Then Grandma handed Mummy a piece of paper, words she'd said earlier and asked her to write down. But she didn't really need it, because when she delivered her speech, she didn't move her eyes from Daddy.

"You've spent the last few weeks tearing yourself apart about the unfairness of this, as have I. But today isn't a day for dwelling on that. Today is when I want you to know what you mean to me."

Her voice was quiet but, for all her pain, full of strength. "When we met, other girls dated boys who broke their heart and took them for granted. By sheer dumb luck, I got the boy who took me to watch *Flashdance*, when really he wanted to see *Scarface*. The boy who once waited an hour in the rain to pick me up after my Saturday job ran late. The boy whose sweetness and generosity shone through in everything he did. And still does. You taught me that real love is not about the passion of new attraction. It is about seeing each other stripped bare, in our ugly moments as well as our beautiful ones, and still feeling certain that you are better together.

"We started out together as teenagers and, sooner than we'd both imagined, you had to become a father. Others wouldn't have stepped up to the mark. But you did. My devoted friend and boyfriend became the man who made sandcastles with the lovely little girl who'd come into our lives. The man who introduced her to *Winnie the Pooh* and *Peter Pan*. The man who would rush into her room and hold her hand when she had a nightmare, stroking her hair until she fell back to sleep. The man who showed her how to catch a ball and spent hours trying to teach her to swim, finally coaxing her in after she'd been terrified. All of that made you the best daddy any of us could've asked for.

"There are still times when I look at the two of you together and feel like my heart will burst because I love you so much. So, today, I refuse to dwell on the unfairness of it all. I'm going to dwell on what a privilege it is to love you. And how proud I am to call myself your wife."

Daddy couldn't really talk then. He just leaned in and mumbled: "I love you too."

Afterwards, I went over to give Mummy a cuddle, when something occurred to me about the bump on her tummy.

"Is that a baby in there?"

"No, sweetheart, it's not a baby. My tummy's like that because I'm poorly. That's what the doctors have told us."

I narrowed my eyes. "Doctors don't know everything. That's what Grandma Peggy says to Daddy."

"In this case, the doctors are right. I'm very sick."

I patted her hand because she looked terribly worried. "It's okay, Mum. You don't need to be upset. You'll get better. I'm going to get you some of my pink medicine."

She hesitated. "I'm not going to get better, Allie. This isn't like when you had a sore throat."

My mouth suddenly felt dry.

"Are you going to die?"

The beginning of a smile appeared at her lips and she said softly: "Yes, sweetheart. I am."

It felt like my chest was on fire. My face ached and something pulsed behind my eyes. But even as I felt the weak grip of her fingers around my hand, I was absolutely determined I was not going to let her down. And I didn't. I did not cry.

CHAPTER
SEVEN

There are four students around the table in my office, all first years. Winning a place on an oversubscribed course like this involves not just hard work but a high degree of intelligence, so you might think that a reasonable excuse for failing to submit a final piece of coursework was not beyond any of them.

"My girlfriend found out she was pregnant."

Lewis Hornby announces this news in a manner that seems very matter-of-fact, leans back onto the windowsill that overlooks the Georgian university quadrangle, and awaits my response.

"Shit." Jennie Hamilton, a mature student of twenty-eight, has beaten me to it, proving that, as well as rockabilly hair and a fine collection of Doc Martens, she also has a better grasp than Lewis on the significance of impending fatherhood.

"It's okay," he reassures her. "It was a false alarm."

She raises her eyebrows briefly. "Nice one."

"Yeah. Turns out it's someone else's."

From the way he returns my gaze, I must look perplexed at this exchange. "Sorry but . . . how does your girlfriend being pregnant — but not with your baby — prevent you from submitting your lab report?"

He straightens his back. "Well, it's been very stressful."

The other two students, Liam O'Callaghan and Anja Pollit, turn to me, eager to see how I'll respond. But I catch a glimpse of the clock and realise that it's gone five. Although ordinarily I'd stay behind long past this, Ed and I have decided to make the most of the recent spate of good weather to meet for a run in the park after work.

"All right, Lewis. You can have an extension until Monday, but make sure it's in my inbox before then, okay?" I turn to the others. "So any final questions before your exams?"

They shake their heads, murmuring that there are none. I hope this is a promising sign, but part of me thinks that some of them look a little too relaxed. Certainly more relaxed than I ever was in their shoes; not nervous, as such, but there was never any room for complacency. I close my A4 notepad.

"Well, good luck, you lot. You know where I am if you need me."

Anja hangs back as the others begin to filter through the door.

"I just want to say thank you for all your support this term, Allie." She removes a box of Roses chocolates from her bag and hands them to me self-consciously.

40

Anja was suffering from severe anxiety at the start of the year. She'd skipped lectures and, after seeking help from the student counselling service, a support plan was set up to help her find her feet on the course.

I've spent every Thursday evening for the past month with her, going over the work she'd missed. It genuinely wasn't a big deal. She's immensely bright, if a little intense, so there was no way I was going to let her fall so far behind that she'd have to withdraw from the course entirely. But she never seems to stop thanking me for it.

"Anja, you really didn't need to."

Her expression softens and I realise she looks emotional. "I mean it, Allie. I don't know where I would've ended up without you. Thank you." A film of liquid begins to form on her eyes. "I realise I've never really told you what happened. I'm sure you must have wondered."

"No, no," I say, and she blinks, surprised. "Sorry. I just meant that you don't need to share that kind of detail with me. That stuff is private. You're better off talking to a friend. But I want you to know that I'm here for you, to help you with anything regarding your work. Any time of day or night." This is the nicest way I can think of to say that heart to hearts are really not my thing.

She sniffs. "Thank you, Allie."

"Any time at all," I smile, gently guiding her towards the door.

I would never describe myself as a keen runner, but I am keen on the fact that running means I can eat cheesecake and not have hips the size of a small caravan. Consequently, I try to get out with my old school friend Ruth, who's slightly slower than me, a few times a week.

We usually choose a circuit in Sefton Park, not far from where I live. I enjoy the ease of the wide, flat pavement that ribbons around its irregular perimeter, shaded by gnarled horse chestnut branches. Occasionally, we venture inside where, as well as an expanse of green space, waterfalls, caves and lakes, there is a wealth of features that were clearly designed to tickle Victorian fancies: a bandstand, Eros fountain and the Palm House, a three-tier domed conservatory that houses a collection of oversized botanicals.

This evening, though, Ruth has an alternative engagement.

"She's gone to see a plastic surgeon after work," I tell Ed through laboured breaths as we jog along the iron bridge that spans the Fairy Glen. "She wants to spend some of the money from the divorce on breast surgery. It's all turned nasty with Andy apparently."

"Not the 'conscious uncoupling' she was hoping for then?" Ed asks.

"No, that hasn't quite worked out. Still, I can't tell you how glad I am that she seems to be moving on."

He suppresses a knowing smile; Ed is well aware that I'm no use to anyone during a romantic crisis. It's not that I'm unsympathetic. I do listen and make all the right noises. But I can't stand seeing people upset and weeping into their Earl Grey. I just wish we could skip to the bit where we start talking about movies, politics or neuronal signalling again.

We reach the section of the road next to the boating lake and Ed begins to head up the gentle slope away from the water. Which reminds me of the other thing I love about running — going home. Only, I've now been puffing and panting for thirty-five minutes and this is showing no signs of drawing to a conclusion.

"Do you want me to slow down?" he asks.

"I'm fine," I insist, then: "Oh, go on then."

We head back to the car while discussing the usual incidentals of our lives — what we're both doing at the weekend, how our families are, what we're reading. Ed and I have similar taste in books, so I know if he recommends something that I'll love it, with the exception of *The Dice Man* or poetry, neither of which I can abide.

"I started *The Blind Assassin* by Margaret Atwood a couple of days ago," I tell him.

"Any good?"

"It is. Though I'm struggling to concentrate at the moment."

A little boy on a bike comes hurtling towards us and we dodge out of the way at the last minute. "This business about the letter you found at your grandma's has really got to you, hasn't it?"

"Wouldn't it you?"

"I guess it would."

My legs suddenly grind to a halt and I bend over breathlessly. He turns and walks back to me as I straighten up.

"They could've just been friends, Allie."

"They're holding hands. She looks besotted with him. And what about that letter? And the fact that he *looks* like me. He's even got my gap . . ."

"Hmm." We break into a jog again, gentler this time.

"What shall I do?" I ask him.

"I don't know." This silences me momentarily because Ed always knows what to do. When I dropped my school bus pass down a gutter at the age of fourteen, he knew what to do. When I was selling my first apartment and a survey revealed a bloom of hitherto-concealed rising damp, he knew what to do. I've always felt that, if we were stuck in a hot-air balloon with ten other people, he would know what to do.

"I can see that this throws open a lot of questions, I'll give you that much," he continues. "But there could be an explanation."

"Like what?"

"I don't know."

Twice in one conversation. My heart clenches.

As he clicks open his car, my mind turns again to the picture. How carefree and happy and *young* my mum looks. I can't begin to imagine what must have been going through her head only a few weeks after it was taken, when she realised the catastrophic mess she'd got herself into.

CHAPTER
EIGHT

The changes in her body had been barely perceptible at first. A pimple or two at the top of her back, a film of grease that slicked her skin like it hadn't done since puberty. Her joints seemed to soften and ache and she felt as though she was coming down with something, a sickness that never materialised.

And she was tired like never before, a fatigue so crushing that sometimes it felt like an enormous physical effort just to raise her eyelids to the rims of her skull. She prayed for it to pass, but as the sun rose each morning, nothing and everything changed. A dull pain throbbed in her breasts and belly, the same as she'd fleetingly known at the time of the month. Now, they were accompanied by a spidering of veins that led to her nipples, blue and pumped with blood.

And that time of the month still hadn't come.

It'd been weeks and there was still no sign, while her anxiety grew, filling the corners of her bedroom like black smoke. Her circumstances were impossible. How was she going to tell anyone this without ruining absolutely everything? So she continued to clutch to the hope that there would be nothing to tell and that she'd wake one morning to find a dark pool on the pad she'd been wearing at night, in the hope that just putting it there might encourage her body to respond how it should.

She occasionally found herself drifting past the surgery at the bottom of their road, glancing at the door as if there might be a solution inside. But it was small and Dr Jennings had been the family doctor since she'd been a little girl. He'd given her injections and treated her for whooping cough and her mother still gave him a jar of home-made chutney every Christmas.

She thought about going in, but was plagued with the idea that one day her mum would be in there and Dr Jennings would let something slip. And all she'd be able to think about was how her daughter was going straight to hell. How all those prayers she'd uttered in church had been for nothing because her daughter had let her and everyone else down.

The thought made her cheeks tingle and her chest pound. She didn't have it within her sphere of comprehension to picture a resolution to all this. And the knowledge that she was loved was not a consolation.

Quite the opposite. The girl everyone loved was only one version of her, the version they assumed she was. Someone loyal and honest and fundamentally good. Nobody wants to lay bare another side of themselves, one driven by lust and a capacity to put her own temporary, selfish desire ahead of everything else.

Yet, she was going to have to tell someone soon. Her shape was subtly changing and it was only a matter of time before her clothes started to stretch beyond their capacity. She knew all this, but panic froze her into inaction and she continued to say nothing on the grounds that she didn't have the words to explain any of it. She didn't understand it herself.

CHAPTER
NINE

Two full months after my conversation in the park with Ed, I wake up to a plumbing emergency in the form of a nasty-looking liquid slowly emerging from the radiator in my bedroom. It's left a stain the shade of Marmite on the carpet and when I phone Dad for his advice, he insists on racing over.

"No, don't! I can call a plumber," I reply, cursing myself for not doing that in the first place.

"Let's just see if I can fix it first," he says cheerfully.

"But aren't you at work today?"

"I'll pop in on my way. It's really no problem."

I should've known he'd do this. My dad loves DIY and will turn his hand to anything after a glimpse in his Collins manual. Fifteen minutes after our phone call, he is on my doorstep, toolkit in his hand, smile on his face. "Shouldn't take long," he says, before striding to the bedroom, removing his jacket and kneeling down next to the radiator.

I hover above him as he examines the chrome plug on its side and glance at my watch. I'm not proud that

I'm in my thirties and still haven't accumulated enough home improvement expertise to resolve this matter myself. In that sense, I'm glad he's here. The problem is that I urgently need to be somewhere else.

"Why aren't you at the university today?" he asks, tilting his head as he takes a spanner to the valve.

"I've got a day off."

He looks up, surprised. "Really? Mid-week?"

"Yes! I'll be doing some lecture planning from home later on but . . . Dad, this is awkward, but I've got a hair appointment. Then I was due to have lunch with Ruth."

"Your old friend from school? It's fine, Allie — you go. I'll let myself out when it's done. Just get me a bowl first so I can drain out some water."

I grab a cereal dish from the kitchen and hand it to him, pricking with guilt. "Are you sure you don't mind?"

"No, go on, run!"

Half an hour later, I arrive at St Michael's Business Centre, a former church converted into offices in a fairly down-at-heel part of town. I am buzzed in and greeted by a receptionist who also looks after clients in hired rooms throughout the building. The others include a cognitive behavioural therapist and a financial advisor. I suddenly wish I were here to discuss my pension provision. I flick through my Facebook feed while I'm waiting, when it occurs to me that I haven't heard from Ed for a while. I sent him a text last week, but he hasn't responded. I pause briefly to message him.

All okay with you? The silence is unnerving!

"Allie?" Ged McKenzie is wearing a checked blue and white shirt with a polyester tie, layered with a navy V-neck jumper and grey slacks. He is very tall and looks about seventy, but is slim and sprightly for his age. "Come on up. We've made some progress."

Until recently, I had no real grasp of the kind of person who hires a private detective. The fact that it turned out to be *me* is something I can't fully anchor to real life. It still feels like the sort of thing that belongs in an American crime thriller or pulp novel.

I didn't know where to start looking at first and simply began with an internet search. Despite the glossy websites, there was something vaguely sleazy about some of them, not helped by one of the most prevalent services on offer being "honey trapping", along with a pick 'n' mix of phone tapping, debugging and investigations into employees who are off sick.

This all leads to the impression that there's an unsuspecting victim somewhere down the line, albeit one who could well be spending Friday nights with his floozy and not at a conference like he told his wife. Does the fact that I'm looking for Stefano McCourt make him a victim? Does my doing this behind my father's back make *him* one?

As I follow Ged up a set of metal stairs, every step produces an echoing clank, as if we're inside a shipping container. We reach the second floor and he invites me into his small office, which smells of freshly laid carpet tiles and the tang of marker pens. On one wall there is a small picture of him shaking hands with the Home Secretary when he retired from Greater Manchester Police. I've been here once before, but this is the first time I've noticed the photos on his desk — one of a St Bernard and another of three little girls, his granddaughters I presume.

"Very cute," I say.

"He is, isn't he? Though old Tyson is getting on a bit these days."

"I meant the girls."

He smiles. "I know. Just joking. Can I get you a coffee before we start? Or a Hawthorn tea? I've got tons of the stuff. My wife saw something on *This Morning* saying it'll improve my blood pressure but I can't stand it. I've got a secret stash of Nescafé."

"I'll pass, but thank you." I'm paying by the hour and I'd rather he wasn't boiling a kettle while the clock is ticking.

I told Ged everything I knew last time I was here. He took a copy of the newspaper cutting and my birth certificate, while I filled him in on what I'd found from the internet, Facebook and LinkedIn. This amounted to almost nothing, though I did find a Stefan McCourt serving six months at her majesty's pleasure for fraudulently claiming £35,000 in invalidity benefits. A break-dancing routine posted on YouTube put an end to this particular source of income. Regardless of that, he was too young to be the man in my picture.

Ged sinks into the seat opposite, leans across the desk and clasps his fingers together. "So, I have some news."

"Okay."

"I need to warn you that I don't have all the answers you're looking for, but I do have some background information and a solid start. Obviously, I'm aware of your financial circumstances and that you want to cap your spend."

"It's a question of necessity, I'm afraid." I earn enough to live in a nice apartment, drive a three-year-old Peugeot and go on holiday twice a year, but there's certainly not enough spare to authorise an unlimited bill for this.

"Well, I'll talk to you about the money after I've told you what I know. But, don't worry, I'm not here to try and twist your arm to spend more. That's not what I'm about and I'm jam packed with cases anyway."

I swallow the tension in my throat and nod. "Okay. Tell me what you've found."

CHAPTER
TEN

"I started with the electoral roll in 1983 and, while there is no mention of either Vittoria or Stefano, there is one Michael McCourt registered — Stefano's father."

He opens his brown folder and takes out a thin stack of A4 pages. "The family's address while they were in the UK was 47 Bamford Avenue in Aigburth. It's now owned by a private landlord and rented out to some young professionals."

"My mother grew up in Mossley Hill, where my grandparents still live. It's not far from there." I shift forward in my seat.

"I could find a birth certificate for Michael but not Stefano, nor his mother Vittoria, whom we can presume was born in Italy. The time they spent here as a family seems to have been relatively brief — about a year as far as I can tell, when Stefano would have been nineteen. As the letter you found indicated, Michael McCourt had been a curator at the Castelvecchio museum, until 1983, when I discovered his name in some of the acquisitions catalogues from Liverpool Museum. It appears that the two institutions had a partnership that allowed him to transfer there."

He takes out another piece of paper. "As well as looking at the documentation, I also made contact with the chairman of Allerton People's Hall to see if he remembered anything about Stefano. It felt like a long shot, but my phone call turned out to be remarkably fruitful."

"Oh?"

"Both Stefano and his father made a mark on the club's cricket team in the short time they were in the UK. Michael had been a keen batsman and passed on his skills to Stefano, who won a Player of the Year award. The chairman vaguely remembered that he'd worked as a porter at the Royal Hospital, but spent a lot of weekends at the club in the summer of 1983. I asked him if he'd left suddenly or if he had any idea why but he just couldn't recall, it was too long ago."

"So he had no idea where they ended up back in Italy?"

"He didn't," he replies. "However, one of my counterparts in Italy has found you an address."

I lean forward.

"I subcontracted the work to a PI based in Rome called Virginia Boldrini. She has discovered an address on the Italian equivalent of the Land Registry — until four years ago the property was owned jointly by Michael and Vittoria McCourt, when ownership was then passed to their son."

He pushes a piece of paper with a typed address towards me. "It's in Sirmione, in Lombardy, Northern Italy."

I stare at the paper, not touching it. "So what now?"

He leans back in his chair. "Well, you need to decide what it is you want, Dr Culpepper. If money were no object and all you wanted to do was find out more about Stefano McCourt, Ms Boldini could take on the case. She could follow Stefano McCourt, knock on doors, interview people."

"How much would that cost?"

He flicks through to the bottom of his pile of papers and removes an envelope, before handing it to me. My eyes skitter to the figure at the bottom of the letter and I try not to choke.

"I've no reason to think she wouldn't do an excellent job. But the money isn't *really* your issue."

"I think it is at that price."

"What I mean is . . . we can try to find out anything about Stefano McCourt from his tax affairs to his shoe size. But the one thing we *can't* find out is whether he really is your father. There are only two people who could know that for certain. Unfortunately, one of them — your mother — is no longer with us. You definitely couldn't ask the man who raised you to undertake a paternity test?"

My chest contracts. "No. I couldn't do that. He can never find out about this. It'd be . . . terrible for him if he ever found out she'd deceived him. That he'd brought me up all these years thinking he was my father and . . ." My voice trails off and I look up at him, before stressing: "He can *never* find out."

"In which case, there are only two other options open to you. The first is that you learn to live without ever knowing."

I feel a sudden wave of nausea. "What's the second?"

He clasps together his hands. "You could go and ask Stefano McCourt yourself."

CHAPTER
ELEVEN

Ed

Ed lies in bed on a bright Thursday morning, staring at the ceiling. A pale sun shears through the shutters and the light hurts his eyes. He feels like he's getting the flu, though he hasn't even had a cold in years.

"You're going to be late. It's nearly six forty-five," says Julia gently, as she kneels next to the bed.

Her slender nose is crinkled, the rims of her eyes are tinged pink, yet she's still a vision of poise and beauty. She's dressed in a pale grey, softly tailored suit that compliments her gym-toned legs. A delicate diamond necklace spills into the notch where her clavicles meet and the nails on her pretty hands are neatly painted in a glossy shade of nude. Everything about her exudes breeding, quality and class.

Ed, on the other hand, feels tired today. And old. There is a sickly knot in the pit of his stomach.

"You haven't been for a run again this morning. That's the third day in a row," she says, but it's not a criticism. He started running in his early twenties, when he was completely broke and joining even the grottiest of gyms wasn't an option. Now, the need to start his day outdoors, to work up a sweat, is as much a part of him as the blood that pumps through his veins and the swirl of skin on his fingertips.

"I'll go for a long one tomorrow," he says.

She turns and walks to the dresser to pick up a bottle of perfume, which she spritzes on her wrists. The scent floats upwards, drifting across the room and filling his face. He wants to sneeze but he can't.

"Do you want some coffee?" she asks.

"No," he murmurs. "Thanks."

She walks to the bed and bends down to stroke his hair, as if he's ill. "Ed, is everything all right?" she sighs.

He looks up at her, but doesn't need to say that it isn't. She already knows. She must. Suddenly, she looks frightened by the silence and he wants to say something to reassure her that everything between them will be okay. But the words don't come. He reaches out and clasps her fingers briefly, before letting go.

Physically, she is still the same woman that captivated him from the moment he met her. Yet today, he looks at those Tiffany-blue eyes, the subtle curve of her cupid's bow, and is numb to them. What she turned him into at the beginning, Superman reinvented, is a part of his personality he can no longer access.

"Well, listen. I had an idea," she begins. The cheery note in her voice hangs between them like a spiderweb, threatening to break under the slightest pressure. "Could you spare me an hour today?"

"What for?"

"I thought we could go for a romantic lunch. My treat. Just like at the beginning. Then . . . we could see where the afternoon takes us." The corner of her mouth turns up playfully as she slides her hand under the sheets, reaching for his skin. He sits up and she withdraws.

"I've got a big meeting at one," he says, and it's the truth. "It's likely to go on for the rest of the day. Sorry."

He can see a shimmer of new tears in her eyes and his stomach twists. There was once a time when all he wanted was to make her happy. When every song he listened to had some relevance to her. When a single text from her had the ability to transform a terrible day into a magnificent one.

"Okay," she manages.

She bends down to kiss him on the forehead. Her lip gloss feels sticky on his skin as she walks to the door. She pauses before turning around. "I love you, Ed. So much," she whispers.

He opens his mouth to speak, but his throat closes up.

"See you later." She slips out of the door.

When he hears her Range Rover crunching out of the drive, he picks up the remote control and turns on the television. There is a news story about events in Aleppo; a child on the screen, who can't be older than three years old, covered in rubble and blood, his eyes glazed with fear and shock. The newscaster explains that he is one of the few survivors of a barrel bomb attack on a nursery school in the Saif al-Dawla district.

Ed is hit by a wave of repulsion, at the world we live in, at *himself*. So he has a marriage that has not lived up to his lofty expectations, that isn't as solid as everyone around him thinks. So what? His are pathetic, first world problems compared with what that little boy has endured.

He reminds himself to be grateful for everything he's got. Not just the things. The *things* have never been what motivated him. They're just garnish, though he'll admit that he got a schoolboy buzz out of buying the car. He'd dreamt of driving something like that since he was eight years old and got a Scalextric for Christmas, neither noticing nor caring that it was second-hand and blew the fairy lights every time he took a sharp bend.

The things he really values though — they're there. He has a mother and father who are still alive, healthy and together. He has friends, some just the kind you'd go for a pint with, one or two for whom he'd lay down his life. And he has his work — his passion and purpose. The fact that he didn't always feel this positive about the business gives him hope. That, no matter how miserable something makes him, it always passes. Ed is a man who makes the best of things. He always has.

He closes his eyes momentarily before grabbing his phone and clicking on his emails. Three hundred and forty-seven unread messages load on the screen and his eyes blur. Then he pulls the covers off the bed, sits up and draws air into his lungs before making a decision. Tonight, it's time for him and Julia to talk.

CHAPTER
TWELVE

Allie

By the end of July, the university campus has the air of a ghost town. The limestone slabs that stretch between science buildings are empty, the clusters of students reclining on the grass of Abercromby Square gone. Only academic staff linger, so few of us comparatively that it's almost as if the world outside my office has stilled, become idle and drowsy in the heat. Yet, the pace of my working life hasn't slackened and turning on my out of office leaves me with a familiar, uneasy feeling.

I eat the last of the Roses in my desk drawer, grab the new edition of the *Journal of Physiology* and head over to the lab, in a recently constructed building adjacent to my office. I push open the door to find Khalid with his head down, one eye pressed against a microscope, his tattooed arms and Guns "N" Roses T-shirt — because it's always a Guns "N" Roses T-shirt — concealed beneath his white coat.

"Knock, knock," I say brightly, but when he lifts his head he appears unsurprised to see me.

"I'm beginning to think you don't trust me to look after this project while you're away."

"Of course I trust you. Besides, it's only the legwork left to do." He flashes me a look. "*Crucial* legwork, obviously. What are you up to?"

"Just checking the culture. The cells are looking really healthy."

"That's what I like to hear."

When Khalid was employed as a post-doc researcher to support my work after he'd finished his PhD, I don't think either of us could've predicted that we'd soon be on the brink of a breakthrough as significant as this.

For the last two years, I have been collaborating with a group at the University of Chapel Hill in North Carolina on a novel gene-editing technique known as CRISPR-Cas9. The potential for this technology is both massive and widely known within my field; researchers all over the world are currently investigating ways that it might ultimately lead to the golden egg, a cure for cystic fibrosis. Now, our little group — Khalid and I in the UK and three other researchers in the US — is so close we can almost touch it.

The technique works through its ability to repair the defective gene responsible for cystic fibrosis known as CFTR. What our group has done is design a method that delivers the CRISPR machinery directly into primary cells grown in the lab which have been taken from the lungs of CF patients. Until now, nobody has achieved this degree of success at reaching the target in this type of cell, in this environment. Once there, we've also demonstrated that it successfully repairs the defective gene and results in a normally functioning protein. What we're now trying to prove is that it can do this more efficiently than any method that's ever been developed before.

If this is the case, this technology has the potential to correct literally *any* of the thousands of mutations that cause CF. So it's big. We may, just may, be working on what will ultimately see the end of a disease that currently affects more than 70,000 people worldwide, drastically limits life expectancy and presents the kind of daily challenges to those affected that most of us can't begin to imagine.

"So when do you fly off to Portugal?" Khalid asks.

"Sunday morning."

"Shouldn't you be packing?"

"I've done most of it already. I just thought I'd pop in and see if there was anything to report before I leave."

"Not since you last popped in . . . ooh, four hours ago." He smiles impishly.

"Just so you know," I continue, ignoring the comment, "I've put my out of office on, but that's only for everyone else — not you. I *absolutely will* be responding to emails from you."

"Okay, I get it. So, who are you going away with?"

"It's . . . a singles holiday," I reply and a gap appears between his lips, as if he's viewing me in a new and unexpected light.

"*Really?*"

"Yes, why?" I say, feeling a bloom of heat on my neck.

63

"Well, I just didn't have you down as the kind of person . . . I mean, if I'd known you were in the market for . . ."

"For what? Charming nineteenth-century architecture and the castle ruins of the Duoro Valley? Absolutely. I can't wait."

The following day, I go for lunch at a new place in Lark Lane with Petra and another colleague, Gill, who last week announced that she's pregnant. The tiny cafe is different from our regular haunts near the university, with a bohemian, relaxed vibe.

"We've got my scan tomorrow," Gill tells us, sipping her mineral water.

"Are you going to find out if it's a girl or boy?" I ask.

"Oh, they don't do that at the *first* scan, Allie," she tells me, with the air of a woman who's read a hundred baby magazines and can't fathom why everyone else on earth wouldn't know this. "This one is to find a due date, check the baby's development and measure the nuchal fold, to identify potential Down's Syndrome. There's only a very narrow window in which that can be done, between eleven to thirteen weeks, so they won't do it after then. You only find out the sex at twenty weeks."

"Ah. Now I know," I say, glancing at Petra, who smirks into her couscous.

The rest of the lunch is spent discussing morning sickness, epidurals and some unusual gastrointestinal symptoms that make me fairly relieved to return home to clean my flat and finish packing. I travel quite

64

regularly; cystic fibrosis conferences are held in both the US and Europe every year and I always attend, even if I'm not presenting. I've been on holiday with Ruth for the last couple of years, and before then it was Rob. We always had a nice time, but he had such ferocious prickly heat on the last trip that my overriding memory is of being indoors, rubbing calamine lotion on his back.

The singles holiday to Portugal is a smokescreen I'm starting to regret. Even Dad's eyes widened slightly when I told him I was holidaying alone, as if it involved sitting on a coach next to strange men in brown macs, fingers poised on my rape alarm.

Still, it's easier than the truth, that I'm going in search of a man who could be my birth father. *Could be.* That's as far as my thinking will stretch, because I am still hopeful that, even if something *did* happen between my mother and Stefano McCourt, my father could still be the man I've always thought he was. Perhaps I'm imagining the physical similarities between Stefano and me. Perhaps they're coincidence. One thing is certain though: I'll get no more information out of Grandma Peggy, even if I was brave enough to try again. And I wouldn't dare ask Granddad after the warning she gave me.

Aside from Ged McKenzie, there is only one person who knows what I'll actually be doing for the next two weeks and that's Ed. But he's been noticeably un-opinionated about it, so wrapped up in work recently that he's become a virtual stranger. I did consider telling Petra about it over lunch, but one of the things I've always loved about our friendship is that it never strays into territory I'd consider difficult. We don't burden our relationship by sharing innermost secrets or troubles, we simply enjoy a bottle of wine together, have a laugh and a good gossip about work.

I stuff the last of my toiletries into my luggage and lay out my passport, along with the budget airline tickets that had seemed a bargain, until I realised they charged extra for checking in a bag, checking in yourself and failing to bring your own air to breathe.

My phone rings and Julia's name flashes up, to my surprise. The only previous time I can remember her calling me was when she wanted my help in contacting Ed's old school friends for a birthday party last year. I call Julia a friend, but the unspoken truth is that our relationship would probably not exist independently of him. But I remind myself that our mutual respect and enjoyment of each other's company still amounts to something significant and worthwhile, even if it's not cocooned by the same easy familiarity as my relationship with Ed.

"Hi, Julia. How are you?"

A broken response follows, her voice intermittently silent as the signal falters. "Sorry, Julia, this is a terrible line. Can I ring you back?"

"I'm outside your flat," I make out. "Have you got five minutes?"

I open the door to find Julia in slim white jeans and an oversized cashmere sweater that reveals the creamy curve of a single tanned shoulder. The soft strands of her golden hair cascade down her back and, except for her eyes, which are pink and anxious, she reminds me of a model in a White Company catalogue.

I invite her in and move a stack of laundry from the sofa so she can sit down. I clear away a glass from the table and notice a faint circle of tea, staining the wood like ink on blotting paper. Compared with Ed and Julia's house, my flat feels scruffy and haphazard, something I can't explain away by the money they've spent on it. Their home is the manifestation of exquisite taste, attention to detail, expert use of colour and fabric.

"Sorry I haven't got any wine to offer you. The fridge is empty. I'm going on holiday tomorrow morning," I tell her.

"It's fine, honestly, Allie."

"I can get you some coffee though. Or peppermint tea?"

She gives me a little nod. "That would be lovely."

I make my way to the kitchen and dig out the tea I opened last time she came here, realising it's now out of date. I'm midway through sniffing it when Julia appears at the door.

"Sorry, would coffee do? I've only got instant," I say, realising this is the second time I've apologised.

She's not listening though. Instead, she lifts her fingers to her forehead and begins to gently rub it as her expression crumples.

"Julia, what's the matter?"

She begins to sob. I step towards her automatically, then freeze, panic billowing up in me. She wipes away tears with the flat of her hand. "Ed is threatening to leave me."

"What? I mean . . . why?"

She shakes her head. "I'm still trying to work that out."

"Are you *sure*, Julia? Ed adores you."

As she lowers her eyes, a tear that has been clinging to the rim of her eye escapes and slips down her cheek. "You probably think it's odd that I came here. Forgive me if this is an intrusion. I know you and I . . . we've never really been close."

Guilt prickles under my skin. It's true that Julia isn't the kind of person to whom I'd automatically gravitate. I can't ever imagine her family dinners being the noisy affairs ours are, with Granddad telling jokes and Dad playing blues on his guitar, nor getting drunk with her on a Friday night like I do with Petra or Ruth. But I could have tried to get to know her better, spent time with her without Ed, and I didn't. Instead of making an effort, I actively avoided it.

"There's just no one else who knows Ed better than you do. He admires and trusts you, Allie. Can I . . . can I tell you what's been happening?" she continues.

I feel a rush of cold moisture under my arms, already out of my comfort zone. But it isn't just that I owe it to both of them to listen. I'm astonished and, above all, worried about Ed. I invite her into the living room and, after sitting down opposite me, she begins to talk.

"He won't recognise it, but Ed is under a huge amount of stress from the business. You know how driven and single-minded he is. He acts as though there's no problem on earth that he couldn't deal with. But the pressure has really started to affect him. He's always been so lovely . . . *is* so lovely," she says hastily. "But he's changed."

Her words make me realise that something has been tugging at the back of my mind lately, like a puppy that I've failed to pay enough attention to. Ed hasn't been himself, she's right. I'd told myself that he was simply busy, focused on a big deal or a new venture. It's clearly more than that and I feel ashamed that I didn't realise it.

"Part of me wonders if he's having some kind of breakdown. I made the mistake of suggesting he get some professional help, but instead . . . he thinks that everything's gone wrong between us. He's blaming me."

"Why would it be *your* fault?"

Her smooth forehead puckers. "We *have* had rows, Allie." The pain of this confession glitters in the film on her eyes. And it is a confession. To admit that they're not the perfect couple everyone assumes takes bravery on her part, one I feel a new admiration for.

"A few rows are normal in a relationship," I reassure her. "I've been part of a family for long enough to know that. Plus, Ed doesn't want a Stepford wife."

She sighs. "I just have a horrible feeling that I don't make him happy anymore, Allie."

Julia is one of the most capable women I've ever met. I don't only mean that she has a high-flying career as a lawyer and sits on the board of two charities. She's simply one of those women you know would never use the wrong fork at a dinner or lean in to kiss someone on the cheek and end up smashing noses. You could put her in any given situation, any crisis, and she would handle it with grace. Yet, now, as she sits opposite me, she looks as vulnerable as a lost child. Unexpectedly, I feel a rush of sympathy, followed swiftly by overwhelming concern about Ed.

"I *used* to make him happy," she continues. "I know I did. There was a time when he'd light up when I walked into a room. I'd text him and he'd respond straight away, desperate to see me. But Ed needs excitement. He gets bored. And, after three years, the gloss has worn off. I ought to have known it would. He hasn't said it, but right now I think he honestly believes he'd be happier alone."

"No," I say automatically. "I can't believe he thinks that. Because he wouldn't."

She looks at me, as if I'm missing the most obvious point. A fact so big and unavoidable that as soon as she says it, it takes on a greater volume than that at which it was uttered. "Ed could have any woman he wants, Allie."

"But he's never wanted anyone else. Not since he met you."

I still recall the intensity in his eyes on the day he told me about Julia. The way he spoke about her, the mystery of her, was almost poetic. It was as if, by stepping into his life she had shone a bright and beautiful light upon him. He was captivated, incredulous at his luck.

70

"I'm convinced that the problem is not with his marriage, but with himself," she continues, forcing herself to take on a practical tone. "I truly believe he simply needs to learn to love himself again. To not take on the burden of so much work. But I don't know how he's going to do that. Not when he's moved into Jeremy's flat."

I feel my lips part. "He's moved in with *Jeremy*?"

"I got home from work tonight and he told me he needed space to think. He packed his bags and he's there now."

"Now I really don't believe it."

I notice for the first time that her hands are trembling. "Do you think I've lost him, Allie?" she asks.

The truth is, I don't know what to think. I don't understand any of it. "You *can't* have, Julia. Look, I don't know what's going on with Ed at the moment, but I do know he loves you."

"I feel as though he wanted this perfect woman. Then he quickly realised that I'm not perfect and I never could be. Now he feels robbed."

In the ensuing moments of silence, I notice a shift, not just in her position, but her entire demeanour. She leans forward on the sofa, as if everything she's told me has been building up to one question.

"Will you talk to him for me, Allie?"

My ribs tense. "Me?"

She nods, her eyes fixed on me. "*Please*. Nobody is closer to him than you. I truly think you're the only person capable of getting through to him."

CHAPTER
THIRTEEN

It's difficult to pinpoint exactly when I met Ed because I knew of him long before we actually came into contact. His family swept into school one golden September, arriving with the crunch of leaves and the glare of chilly sunshine. Ed was eight and one of four; his brother Mike was in the year above us and they had two little sisters, Michelle and Kim, aged four and two.

Until then, juniors had felt small and uneventful, with little to disturb the ebb and flow of harvest festivals, spelling tests and British Bulldog. We didn't see much of his dad at first, but his mum, an Avon lady, added a rare touch of glamour to the school gates, where she'd wait with her beauty queen hair and frosted lipstick, radiating Skin So Soft.

Despite being in the same year, Ed and I were not drawn to one another in any way. I was conscientious and hardworking. Ed was not. He didn't need to be. He was a child with an unequalled memory and hunger for information that appeared unsated by the national curriculum. The books in the school library, aimed at our age group, failed to hold his attention and he was bored by the work taught in maths and English classes. He was often in trouble, out of bounds or bending the rules, which unsettled me, long before I entered secondary school and I felt that way about virtually everything.

I started my first year at Cherryfield Community Comprehensive having lost all my friends. I'd been separated from the small group of girls with whom I'd learnt to jump rope and play rounders, after they won places at a highly regarded, oversubscribed Church school. This hadn't been an option for me: after Mum died, Dad quietly became an atheist, so there was no way we'd have fulfilled the school criteria — having a parent with five years of church attendance behind them.

So I ended up at Cherryfield, a sprawling and undistinguished institution that had received a boost in spending in a bid to improve student attainment and reduce expulsions. Five years later, it had some impressive facilities and had produced two trampolining contenders at the Commonwealth Games, but no great rise in exam results. All in all, it felt like a strange and dangerous city, in which I was entirely lost.

Puberty didn't help. I was surrounded by girls experiencing the more glamorous elements of adolescence — sprouting breasts, starting periods — whereas I just developed a chin pebble-dashed with acne. I didn't want to discuss these changes, current or pending, with either Dad or Grandma Peggy, despite their excruciating efforts. There are some things you just don't want to talk about, and the fact that everyone around me was changing at a rate I couldn't keep up with was one of them.

Still, I eventually made a friend. Gail was an aspiring beautician with an electrifying home perm and who carried an inhaler, not for medical reasons, but because she said it made her "get high". I was so relieved to finally have someone to hang round with that I became a willing subject for the fake-tanning experimentations she inflicted on me at every sleepover.

We weren't what you'd call kindred spirits though. One afternoon I caught her looking at the bookshelf in my bedroom, her eyes narrow and wary. I had a large collection of novels, some gifts, some from the charity shop, the odd one — such as *The Wolves of Willoughby Chase* — that had been on loan from the library forever.

"All these books clutter the place up," Gail told me, a curl appearing on her top lip. "You want to get rid of them and go for a minimalist look. That's what my salon's going to be — minimalist. White walls. White chairs. White . . . bog paper."

I noticed, to my alarm, that she'd taken *A Wrinkle in Time* by Madeleine L'Engel from the shelf. She flicked it open with a crunch of its delicate spine, and the pages splayed open like a rolodex.

"You wouldn't be interested in that," I said, prising it from her, before folding my hands tightly around it and clutching it to my chest.

The book had belonged to my mother. Grandma Peggy told me that she used to read it under the necklace of apple trees at the bottom of their garden. I'd read it so many times I could've recited it from cover to cover. The knowledge that my mother's fingers had turned the same pages as mine, her eyes had fallen on the same words, used to leave me with the most wondrous feeling, like I was swimming in a pool of warm, silky water.

This was more than sentimentality. It was a genuinely brilliant book, with a main character, Meg, who I'd idolised. When I was really young I'd liked to imagine that, had my mum still been around, our family would've been just like hers — with a beautiful scientist mother with whom I'd go on adventures through time and space in search of the Tesseract or similar threats to humanity.

It's little wonder really that it took me a while to find my feet at school. And at Cherryfield, if you were clever, the last thing you wanted to do was shout about it. This left me in the tricky position of desperately wanting to achieve, but having to do so as inconspicuously as possible. I'd deliberately keep my hand down in class even when I knew the answers. I'd hide my exercise books, glowing with secret pleasure when I opened them and found an A plus inside. But everything changed when I was moved up to the top set in science, and found myself seated next to Ed.

He smelled of boy, though not in the same way the others did, that rot of ripening boxer shorts. His boy smell wasn't unpleasant, but dry and warm, almost like biscuits when he hadn't overdone the Lynx. Paradoxically, the fact that he smelled nice was one of many reasons I was more comfortable around Gail, even when she was cackling an anecdote about her mum's friend's breast implants exploding on a flight to Bulgaria. I also hadn't forgotten the trouble he'd got in at primary school. That put me on edge. Because, for all that I was desperate to fit in with the other kids — I was a natural-born conformist who rarely challenged authority — my overriding desire was to work hard and do well academically.

We barely spoke for the first few lessons — simply sat side by side, tolerating each other's presence. So when I took my place behind the desk in preparation for biology one afternoon, I was surprised when he said: "Is this the lesson when we have to dissect a frog?"

I registered a sheen of perspiration on his skin and how his complexion looked white and waxy.

"I think so," I mumbled.

"Well . . . I . . . ugh."

I turned my head to the front of the class and pretended not to have heard him. But I became aware that he was swaying.

"Is something the matter?" I whispered.

"I just . . . might have a problem with this." He grasped the edge of the table to steady himself and his knuckles whitened.

"Not as much of a problem as the frog." I grinned hopefully, but my wit fell on deaf ears. "Seriously, are you okay?"

He nodded tightly.

"If you don't feel up to it I'm sure they'll let you off," I suggested.

But he turned to look at me in a way that made one thing absolutely clear. He was not the kind of kid to just give up. "I'm fine."

He *wasn't* fine. But he did go through with the exercise. It was only when the teacher instructed the class to open the stomach to see what the frog last ate that it all became too much. He began swaying again and a rivulet of sweat made its way down his temple. I could hear my own heart racing through my ears and I glanced up, realising that Mr Kegg's back was turned.

Ed puffed out his cheeks, closed his eyes and the scalpel fell out of his hands onto the table.

I checked Mr Kegg again, picked up the scalpel and made the incision.

I nudged Ed and he opened his eyes. Then I placed the scalpel back in his hands as he looked at me in silent disbelief, as Mr Kegg appeared and said: "Well done, Edward."

CHAPTER
FOURTEEN

I discover from the address Julia gave me that Jeremy's flat is in an exclusive development in the city centre, a giant, mirrored totem pole of superpads that rises up into the sky. When they first went on sale, the local press made much of their eye-watering price tags, the roof terraces and walk-in wardrobes, providing a glut of publicity that the developers must have loved. The seductive message was clear: this is not just an apartment for sale, it's a statement. But statements don't always have the desired effect and I've never been able to walk past them without thinking of a balding man in a lipstick-red Ferrari.

The thought that Ed has fled to Jeremy in his moment of crisis, as opposed to me, his oldest friend, sits like a blister on my pride as I drive through torrential rain and try to work out where to park my car. I could've understood if it had been his friends Aaryan or Charlie, both of whom are married with kids and therefore at least qualified to discuss what's wrong. Ed seems to like Jeremy, but I can't look at him without recalling his excruciating attempts to chat up a waitress at his wedding, when it was patently clear that all she wanted to give him was a teriyaki beef skewer. If he's a better confidante than me, I really must be bad.

It takes me twenty minutes to find a parking space, followed by a short walk through plastering rain and hardy party-goers refusing to let the biblical weather ruin a Saturday night. I announce myself to the twenty-four-hour concierge, who invites me to stand in a gleaming lift, where I drip on the floor until I reach the penthouse with a small lake under my feet.

Ed opens the door and I step in, shaking myself off as I remove my coat. "Hello there," I say tentatively, hanging it on the rack.

"Hi," he replies.

The apartment is large and unforgivingly masculine, a showroom of polished surfaces and contemporary *everything*. I follow Ed to the sofa and sit opposite him on a marmalade orange chair, an angular construction that looks as though it's designed to be installed in The Tate rather than actually sat on. As I silently scrutinise him, my first instinct is that he seems fine. But there is something behind his eyes that makes me question the integrity of that word. When does fine ever really mean fine?

"Do you want to talk?"

The sentence does not come easily to me. It never has. Yet I've never been more acutely aware of my failing than tonight. He leans back on the sofa, pressing his neck against the cushion.

"Julia told me that you're thinking of leaving her," I continue. "She wanted me to come and speak to you. If I'd known any of this was going on, I would have . . ." But the truth is I don't know what I would've done.

He doesn't respond.

"Clearly, it's up you whether you want me to push off and mind my own business." I glance at the window, the rain snaking down the glass. "Although it'd be good if you didn't throw me out in this." The sentence begins as a laugh but barely gets started.

A clock chimes somewhere. A flash of lightning illuminates the sky. I hear voices in the corridor outside, that quickly fall silent.

"Should I go? I should, I think. Yes, I'll go," I decide. I stand up and walk over to collect my soggy coat, slowly in case he changes his mind. I pick it up and drape it over my arm, turning around. "I hope you're all right, Ed."

I have my back to him again and my hand on the door latch when he speaks.

"Don't go, Allie." I swallow and return my coat to the rack, before making my way back to the orange chair. He raises his eyes to me. "Sorry." His voice sounds dry and raw.

"No worries." I smile, hopeful that it's somehow catching. "You *can* talk to me, though."

He nods. "Thanks. But I'm fine, honestly."

"I know I'm not usually . . . good at this sort of stuff. But I want you to know that I'm here for you, Ed. Whenever you want. I'm off on my trip to Italy in the morning, but you can phone me at any time of the day and night while I'm there. Well, after ten would be ideal obviously . . ." The joke does not raise a smile.

"Thanks."

I cross my legs and try to settle my hands on my lap, but no position feels comfortable. "It might help you to try and talk now. How do you feel?"

He shifts forward, elbows on his knees. "Like shit."

That, it appears, is that.

"Listen, Ed," I continue gently. "Julia told me you're under pressure at work. It happens to the best of us. Even you."

"It's not about work. It's about me and Julia. Things aren't . . . like they were at the beginning."

"But what made you think they would be?"

He shrugs. "Perhaps I didn't mean that. Things just aren't working between us right now."

"Can I ask why?"

"I don't fully know the answer to that, Allie. And I don't know how to make it right. That's why I'm here."

I glance around the place, at the geometric wallpaper and glossy black kitchen units. "Do you really think Jeremy might be able to offer you clarity on this?"

"He's in Chicago. He's letting me stay while he's away."

This is at least a small relief. I try to think of something wise and useful to say. "Ed, relationships change. It's surely normal that feelings in the first flush of love aren't as intense after a few years. But you've got other exciting things on the horizon. Kids, for one thing. It won't be long for the two of you, I'm sure."

Ed has always seen himself as a family man. Even in the days when he had an inexhaustible supply of girlfriends, he'd liked to think that wasn't the most authentic version of himself. What he really wants is to live in a house full of kids and dogs and books and, above all, love. Something he had in spades as he grew up. Yet here he is, about to throw it all away because "things aren't like they were in the beginning". It seems so illogical.

"Even the strongest relationships have patches of trouble," I argue. "Especially when you're under stress. But, Ed, you don't just bail at the first sign that things aren't perfect."

"I know, Allie. That's why I'm not sure what to do."

"You still love her, don't you?"

"Yes. No. I don't know."

My heart clenches, followed by a wave of desperation to say and do the right thing. "If you love her, Ed, you need to keep hold of her. Fight for her. You've probably given the poor woman the shock of her life by saying you are leaving."

"I said I needed some time to think, that's all. And I do."

My mind turns to Jeremy returning from Chicago. I have a hideous thought that his strategy to "help" Ed will probably involve taking him out on the pull. "When's Casanova back?"

"Tomorrow."

"Then you definitely need to go home." I smile, but I mean it. "What are you going to do otherwise? Where are you going to go?"

"I honestly don't know yet."

"You could always stay at my place while I'm away. That'd be better than checking yourself into a hotel. We don't want you turning into Alan Partridge." I realise from his reaction, or lack of, that my attempts to cheer him up by joking are not working, but I still can't stop myself. "Well, the only other option is that I put you in my suitcase and take you to Italy with me, but frankly I had to sit on it to get the zip up as it is."

He looks up and blinks, his blue eyes settling on me. "I could always get a flight though."

I feel my chest brace. "I was only joking, Ed."

"I know. I *could* though."

I shake my head. "No. Absolutely not. You couldn't do that."

"But why?" He is now more certain, more animated than I've seen him since I got here. "I speak Italian. You'd have someone with you to support you on your search for this Stefano guy. That's not something you should be doing on your own anyway. Besides, who the hell wants to go on holiday alone?"

"It's not a holiday."

"Whatever, Allie. I should come. I *definitely* should come."

"You *definitely* shouldn't. What would Julia think? It looks terrible." Whatever is going on between him and Julia, I know he wouldn't want to humiliate her. He contemplates this for a second, long enough for me to assume I've persuaded him of the madness of his idea.

"How about this then," he says finally. "I'll speak to Julia and explain why I need to get away and have a little time to think. I'll promise her that when I return she'll have a straight answer about our future. One I haven't been able to give her so far."

"What if she says she wants you to stay and make that decision here?"

"I don't know, Allie. Under the circumstances I think, or at least hope, that she'll understand where I'm coming from."

CHAPTER
FIFTEEN

As Julia stands at the doorway of their house, painted tastefully in a Farrow and Ball shade of blue, she somehow looks smaller than usual. The magnolia tree that dominates the front garden was in spectacular bloom last month, but now its silky raspberry-ripple petals are brown and wilting.

"I suppose, if this is what it takes to get him thinking straight again, perhaps it's a good idea," she says.

Ed discussed the trip with her at length on the phone before I left Jeremy's flat and went to collect his passport. He assured me that she understood and agreed. I don't know if that's true, or how it *can* be true. And while my primary concern in this situation is for my oldest friend, I can't help looking at Julia and imagining how I'd feel in her shoes. Completely broken.

"Are you *sure* you're all right about this, Julia?"

She sighs. "Obviously, if it was up to me, he wouldn't be going anywhere. But he's clearly made his mind up that this is something he needs to do. And who knows, perhaps if he feels the sun on his skin again, clears his head a little, it *could* make the difference." She's saying the words as if trying to convince herself, to find a positive in a sea of negatives. Perhaps it's even her way of proving to herself she has some control over what's happening. But it feels as though she's chasing a kite in the wind, its ribbons just out of reach.

"Are you sure you don't mind him tagging along?"

I feel uneasy at the question, unsure of the right answer. "It's absolutely fine."

"I'd understand if you did. He's hardly great company at the moment."

"Well, hopefully he'll be a bit more like the old Ed by the time he returns." I smile and she tries to return it but falters.

"He's very lucky to have a friend like you, Allie. Look after him for me, won't you?"

The first leg of the flight, which disembarks in Amsterdam, is full, noisy and we are surrounded by women in neon pink T-shirts, with "Mandy's Hen Party" emblazoned across the front. Ed is quiet, almost sullen, in contrast to his neighbour, who doesn't allow the 7.30a.m. departure to deter her from downing two miniature bottles of red wine with a vodka and Pringles chaser.

Part of me is glad of the circus around us, that it temporarily absolves me from having to address the issues that are clearly burning Ed up. But this recognition is followed by a stab of frustration, a reminder that that's precisely why he's here. To talk about his problems. To open up. Not just to anyone, but to *me*. A shiver makes its way down my spine.

"Did I tell you about what happened last time I was on a plane, when I was going to that conference in Berlin a few months ago?" I say, flicking open my in-flight magazine.

Ed glances at me sideways. "No?"

"Someone passed out. When the flight attendant saw my name on the passenger list, she assumed that the word "doctor" in my title qualified me to provide medical assistance. I had to confess that the last first-aid training I had was when I was in the Brownies."

The hint of a smile appears briefly on his lips, but his mind isn't on my small talk. I flick over the page onto a retail section, glancing through endless blingy watches, lip gloss collections and other whimsy.

"Were they okay?" Ed asks.

I look up. "Who?"

"The person who passed out."

"No idea. But there was a cardiothoracic surgeon on board, so they would've stood a better chance with him than me trying to copy something I'd seen on *Call the Midwife*."

When we reach Verona airport, I wait at the carousel, watching everyone else collect their luggage with an augmenting sense of dread until, half an hour after landing, only a pushchair and a suitcase in the shape of R2-D2 are left. After a lengthy wait at the baggage enquiries counter, I am greeted by a young man with a bun, beard and yellow knitted tie, which hangs begrudgingly from his neck. I fill him in on my predicament while he taps silently on his computer and finally looks up at me.

"Good news. We have located your baggage. Fill this in please." He pushes a pink form across the desk.

"Oh, that's great," I say, relieved. "So where is it?"

"On its way to Budapest."

CHAPTER
SIXTEEN

As the first weeks passed, her nausea subsided but isolation began to consume her. The father of her child, who'd captivated her first with his self-assured smile and then his sheer persistence, was now gone — away from Liverpool, from her, from their baby.

When she'd first tried writing to him, she couldn't find the right words. Every version of her letters felt surreal, as if it were a stranger speaking, a girl other than herself. But after a few attempts, she was finally able to put one vaguely lucid word in front of the other.

I hope things are going well over there and that life is rewarding you with all you deserve. I think about you often, about all those dreams of yours, and wonder how close you are to fulfilling them. You opened my eyes in that sense. Until we met, I hadn't given much thought to anything beyond my own doorstep. You reminded me that there's a whole wide world out there.

Now, when I think of you, it's under a canopy of bright sunshine. Which probably has something to do with the fact that it's been raining here in the UK for what feels like weeks! I can't imagine what it must be like to be living in a place where it's never really cold, that horrible, biting cold that gets into your bones.

Still, it brightened up at lunchtime and I went for a walk by myself in Sefton Park. The problem was, everywhere I looked, there were young mothers pushing prams or holding hands with their toddler. I got a bit upset, which is silly because I don't need to see that to be reminded of the mess I'm in. I know it can't go on, all this deceit. But I just can't think of a way of telling everyone without ruining everything.

Part of me doesn't even know why I'm writing to you. I suppose I'm hoping a solution might come to me, though so far I've singularly failed to find one. I don't blame you for any of this, by the way. I want to make that absolutely clear. I knew that you wouldn't be in England forever, you'd told me that on the first day we'd met.

I wonder sometimes if that had anything to do with what happened between us — why I did it, I mean. It is surprisingly easy to be reckless with someone you know won't be around forever. That sounds dramatic, doesn't it? I don't mean it to, but I'm sitting here crying again like a total sap. In truth, I have nowhere to turn. I am entirely lost.

He never responded. She'd never expected him to. Yet, her dispatches started to become strangely comforting, an invisible thread that ran between the tiny heart beating inside her and the man who, with her, had put it there. Because, for all her despair, something else had started happening to her, frequently and at random.

It would often occur in the mornings, just before she fully woke, when she placed her hands on her belly and felt the first sign of a lump that protruded when she lay flat on her back. Or when she'd dress in the morning and her zip would snag, her disappearing waist preventing further movement.

The reminder that there was a baby secretly growing inside her prompted an unexpected rush of joy that filled her up from her shoes to her chest, warming her insides. It was fleeting at first, a thunderclap of light in the darkness, but when it happened it was so powerful that she started to believe, or at least hope, that there was some supernatural force at work that could somehow get her out of this mess.

Her secret was a blade with a double edge. On the one hand, she was unable to see a way out. On the other, she marvelled at how blood rushed through her body like a waterfall after a storm, how she alone was capable of supporting another life. It was an unequalled kind of elation — a clean, dizzying warmth that, each time she stopped and thought about it, could keep her going for hours afterwards.

The day after she wrote that letter, she was sitting on the bus, half-listening to a conversation the two women were having about Ken Barlow's new woman in Coronation Street, when she felt the flutter of tiny limbs inside her. She'd thought she'd imagined it at first. But then she slid her hand inside her coat and waited until another one came. Her neck inflamed with heat as she sat, astonished by how distinct it was.

When the bus reached the end of her road, she scrambled down the steps and raced home, letting herself into the house before pounding up the stairs to the mirror in her mum's bedroom. She drew the curtains and took off her coat, peeling away each item of clothing until she was down to her knickers and blouse. She turned sideways, lifted up her top, and examined herself. She hadn't really looked at the mound between her hips before; she'd only glanced at it as she wrestled on her tights each morning. Now she was mesmerised by it. She smoothed her hand over the skin and felt another kick, this time so sharp that it made her splutter with laughter.

"You'll leave me black and blue," she whispered.

The creak of the door made her head snap up and a bolt of adrenalin coursed through her body, nearly making her legs give way. There was her dad, staring at her naked, swollen belly, his face drained of colour.

CHAPTER
SEVENTEEN

Allie

Ed has always been the type of person who refuses to acknowledge that a problem is insurmountable and the fact that my luggage is currently en route to another country has clearly not altered this.

"You'll be fine," he says, dismissively. "I've got shower gel and toothpaste you can use."

"I presume you're not carrying any spare mascara?" I reply. "Or moisturiser? Or *knickers*?"

"Left those at home," he deadpans. "Look honestly, we'll find you some shops as soon as we get to Sirmione."

I do hope so, because my entire worldly belongings now consist of a passport, half a bottle of Evian, a copy of *The Quiet American* and a pot of lip balm. From the airport, we head to the station in Verona and from there we'll go on to Peschiera del Garda, a short taxi ride from our final destination. I sit opposite Ed on the train and drink in the view, as the industrialised buildings and freight containers unfold into resplendent countryside.

There's something soothing about the thrumming rhythm of wheels against track, as we pass green olive groves and vineyards moulded into the landscape. Dry-stone walls are tinged pink in the sun, like a blush, and the cherry trees and cypresses, all canopied by a luminous blue sky, hint at the riches that await us at the shores of Lake Garda.

I warned Ed before we arrived that the accommodation I'd chosen was fairly basic and away from Sirmione Old Town, the famously beautiful peninsula that inspired the ancient poetry of Catullus. The place I'd booked for the first couple of nights — but no more in case I need to move on — is close, but nowhere near as expensive. I refuse to splash out as if I'm here for a holiday, something this trip resolutely is not.

If Ed is disappointed when we pull up in front of a B&B on the main road, with sausage-pink walls and a two and a half star TripAdvisor rating, he is gracious enough to hide it. We step out of the taxi into fierce sunlight and head in to reception, where we're greeted by an elegant woman in her seventies, wearing high wedge heels and scarlet gloss on her nails.

"*Buongiorno*," she smiles.

"*Buongiorno*," I echo, instantly wishing I knew more of the language. I glance at Ed, who steps forward to check us in, and after filling out various forms, she slides a Yale key towards us. "Your husband speak nice Italian," she tells me in faltering English.

"Oh, we're not . . ." I feel a shot of heat on my neck. "We're just friends. It is a *twin* room, isn't it?"

Ed repeats the question in Italian and she nods. "*Si, è una doppia. È già pronta. Ti accompagno.*"

As she shows us up to the room, I notice how Ed's face changes when he makes small talk, how creases appear around his eyes as he smiles. He stops at the door and turns, making me blink, feeling caught out. "There are a couple of clothes shops in the old town. She's not sure if they're open though because it's so late on a Sunday."

The room is sparsely decorated and functional, with two low, creaky beds pushed against plain painted walls and made up with clean sheets and thin pillows. There is a shared bathroom along the corridor, while the view overlooks the busy road and a faded billboard for a "Sexy Shop" in Desenzano. I can't see evidence of any air conditioning but decide not to highlight that.

"I think the two and a half stars are a bit harsh personally, don't you?" I say.

He makes a "hmmm" sound. "I'm going to get a cold shower. Or do you want to go first?"

"Well, I'll probably take longer than you, so perhaps I should. Can I borrow that deodorant?"

"Help yourself," he says, throwing his leather wash bag onto the bed.

I pick it up, along with the thin towel folded on top of the mattress, before heading down the sweltering corridor towards a claustrophobic bathroom that smells intensely of mildew. I balance Ed's wash bag on the toilet cistern and open it up. It contains a handful of basic toiletries, half a bottle of aftershave, and a blister pack of tablets called Fluoxetine, from which only one has been taken.

The water from the shower makes up for a lack of pressure with its temperature, which remains consistently volcanic. I leap in and out of a scalding trickle, like I'm auditioning for *Riverdance*, before emerging flushed and light-headed, my skin still sticky. I put my pants on inside out and dress, before letting Ed go next while I text Dad.

Arrived safely, but sadly my luggage didn't — it's lost! Fortunately they tell me that it'll be sent on asap (not sure when that is though). Still the sun is shining so all's well. How are things? x

He responds immediately.

What a nightmare. Hope it turns up soon. All fine here — off for a pint with your granddad shortly x

Have fun — but don't let him have too many. Grandma would not be impressed! x

I place the phone on the bed next to me and begin attempting to style my hair with my fingers, when Ed returns to the room. I glance up to see the towel hanging low on his waist, his bare chest and muscular arms still damp and glistening.

"I forgot to take my shorts with me," he explains, stepping past me to the bag on his bed and beginning to find some clothes. "Shall we go and see what Sirmione has to offer when I'm dressed?"

96

"Why not?" I reply, fixing my eyes firmly on the bedside lamp.

Golden light spills upon the pale walls of the thirteenth-century castle at the entrance to Sirmione's historic centre. A drawbridge leads us across a stretch of clear, turquoise water, its rails dotted with lipstick-red geraniums and climbing lilac. There is a clutch of pretty cafes on the other side, some with creamy, buttermilk walls, others with rough stone that has weathered centuries.

We enter a labyrinth of narrow streets lined with elegant shops, wine merchants and tiny art galleries, passing several gelaterias, where children and adults struggle to choose between the creamy swirls of ice cream, lined up in colourful rows.

Sirmione is a place well suited to wandering; there are lots of people but nobody is in a rush to be anywhere other than here. It's also impossibly stylish, where the women gracefully negotiate cobblestones in skyscraper sandals and the men are effortlessly cool in cotton shades of sand and sky blue.

The streets open out onto a main square flanked by al fresco restaurants, each of them packed with families and romancing couples. I look down at my own clothes and hastily styled hair and feel as though my shower never even happened.

"Why don't you go and get a drink somewhere and I'll go and see if I can buy some clothes?" I suggest.

"Do you want me to come with you?"

"I'm not going to inflict a shopping session on you, Ed. Just make sure your phone is on so I know where to find you."

We part under the bell tower of a tiny, ancient church and I head back to one of the boutiques I'd spotted earlier. The shop window displays only two dresses, but they're both beautiful, with soft, brightly coloured fabric and just the right amount of va-va-voom. I head inside and, despite the eye-watering price tag, lift up the sleeve of one of the dresses, wondering if I should try it on. Then the door opens and I look up to catch the briefest of glances — of a middle-aged man with dark hair. Something inside my chest jumps.

It takes me a moment to realise that he's too old to be Stefano McCourt and another moment to tell myself that *of course* he isn't Stefano McCourt. He's hardly going to be the first person I bump into. But the awareness that I could now be close to him boils inside me, as I quickly open the door and step out into the dry heat.

CHAPTER
EIGHTEEN

"You didn't find anything *at all*?"

We are seated at a table outside a lively restaurant, as the convivial sounds of laughter and clattering plates rise above the main square. A group of small children make street theatre on the cobblestones as their parents look on, while couples stroll in the direction of the lake as the last drop of sun glows on the horizon. We are sheltered by a canopy of rampaging honeysuckle and, even in the dusky light, the air is warm around my shoulders.

"Well, I got some mascara," I reply.

"But no clothes?" Ed asks.

"All the shops are designer boutiques. They're ridiculously expensive and far too fancy for an emergency purchase. I'm sure my luggage will arrive tomorrow."

"I can buy you something," he offers.

"Absolutely not," I reply, my thoughts instantly turning to Julia. It's bad enough that he's away with another woman, I don't want to add insult to injury by accepting gifts from him — even if this is only me we're talking about. "I've got all I need for now. I did get some clean underwear." In fact, the single pair of lacy Brazilian pants cost more than I was hoping to spend on an entire outfit.

We drink Aperol and dine on pizza that tastes only as it can under a topaz Italian sun, with a hot, thin base that yields to the soft, tangy topping. But I can't help noticing that Ed does not eat as much as he usually would. This bothers me enough to suggest a dessert — twice — and when he declines, wonder if this is the time to try and talk about him and Julia.

But the conversation instead drifts to wine and travel, to a funny Tweet I read earlier, and the fact that Shakespeare chose to set *Romeo and Juliet* in nearby Verona without ever having set foot in it. Eventually, as the light fades on the bustling square and is replaced by the collective glow from dozens of candle-lit tables, I tell myself that if Ed wants to talk, he'll do so when he's ready. He doesn't need me to prompt him. He's decisive enough without that.

"So what's your plan in the morning, Miss Marple?" he asks, as he gestures to a waiter for the bill.

"What do you mean?"

"Well, what happens if you knock on the door and this Stefano guy answers? How are you going to spring it on him that you've got this mad idea that he might be your father?"

I fortify myself with a sip of my drink. "Do you really think it's a mad idea?"

He pauses, his blue eyes softening in the candlelight. "I just hope it is, Allie. For your sake."

"Well, logic tells me that all I can do is come straight out with it and introduce myself as Christine's daughter. Every time I think about meeting him and announcing what I found in Grandma Peggy's drawer though . . . God, I am dying inside, Ed. How am I going to just come out and say: 'Hi, I'm Allie Culpepper. I have reason to believe you slept with my mother and — guess what — I could be your daughter.'" I shudder.

"What are you going to do if someone else answers and he's not home?"

"I thought perhaps I could tell them I'm a solicitor working for Christine Culpepper's estate and that I'm trying to track down Stefano regarding her will. Does that sound believable?"

"Yes, I suppose so. Though he might hope he's about to inherit a mountain of cash."

"Well, whatever happens tomorrow, I need to stay flexible about how I handle this."

He fixes his eyes on me. "You mean you might wimp out of it altogether?"

I shrug. "Maybe."

Total inaction is becoming an increasingly attractive prospect. Yet I couldn't live with myself if I leave Italy knowing nothing more than when I arrived. If there's an innocent explanation behind what I found in Grandma's house, I need to know what it is, for my sake and for Dad's.

A rush of heat behind my eyes takes me by surprise and, as I blink it away, my throat begins to ache. I take another sip of my drink, feeling mute and self-conscious, aware that Ed is looking at me. He reaches across the table and fastens his fingers softly onto my forearm. The gentle pressure of his palm pulses underneath my skin as I lower my eyes onto the dark sweep of hair on his tanned arms, the way it disappears into the soft lines inside his elbow. I swallow hard as a text arrives on his phone. At first I assume it's another from Julia, from whom he's received a few since we arrived, but "Mum" flashes up on the screen. A second passes before he withdraws to pick it up. He reads it briefly and starts to compose a response.

"Does your mum know what's going on between you and Julia?" I ask.

He shakes his head. "No. She thinks I'm away on business. She'd be distraught if she knew. The happiest day of my mother's life was when she got to wear her insanely proportioned hat to watch someone make an honest man of me."

I smile into my drink. "It was big, that hat."

"The size of the Death Star."

"She looked *lovely* though," I add.

"She did," he concedes fondly, through a smile that quickly disintegrates.

After dinner, the town is still busy as we step through a set of ancient colonnades and make our way along the pale stone cobbles towards the lake. The tiny peninsula has a timeless beauty that seems all the more special from the fact that it's so alive today. That in the shadow of a fortress and ancient Roman villa, *la dolce vita* seems to carry in the air, along with the uninhibited laughter of friends and the intensely sweet fragrance of Italian woodbine.

The water lies muted and still as we stroll back to the hotel via the wide promenade that runs alongside the lake, the lights from the opposite shore twinkling under an eerie, moonlit sky. After a few hundred metres, the bustle of the town gives way to the hot, gentle sounds of night, of lapping water and chirruping crickets.

"I realised after I'd given you my wash bag that you probably saw the tablets in there," Ed says suddenly.

I glance at him briefly and continue walking, focusing on the gecko scuttling ahead on the dry stone wall beside us.

"That's your business, Ed," I say, then catch myself. "But, of course . . . if you want to talk about it, that's fine. I'm all ears."

We take several more steps in silence. The only sounds are the soft thud of my sandals on the ground and the sway of the high palms above us. My eyes drift to the pillows of lantana that tumble from the rocks and I breathe in their faintly sharp, botanical scent.

"Julia suggested a few weeks ago that I should go to the doctor," he says. "She thinks I'm under stress."

"Are you?"

His jaw tightens in the shadows. "You could say that."

We pass a bench on which a couple in their fifties sit closely, talking in whispers. Their hands are entwined with such casual affection that it's as if every crease in every digit of his has found the place where it's most comfortable in hers.

"He prescribed anti-depressants." Despite Ed's matter-of-fact tone, I am totally floored by this. Maybe part of me suspected that that's what they were when I saw the pills, but I simply couldn't correlate that idea with the man I know.

"Are you taking them?"

He shrugs. "I tried. They didn't work."

I feel wrong-footed to learn that a medical professional has deemed Ed's mental state to be this bad when, I, his best friend, hadn't even realised. I am annoyed with myself, determined to make up for my failure.

"You've surely got to give these things time, Ed," I say.

"They *won't* work."

"They work for other people," I argue. "What makes you think you'd be any different?"

"Because stress isn't really the problem, Allie. I only got them to keep Julia happy."

I am contemplating my next sentence, when I become aware that he's looking at me. "Anyway, they give you wind." He smiles, clearly determined to lighten the conversation, but I purse my lips.

"They do!" he insists. I just shake my head.

"I think you could live with the odd fart if it stops you throwing away your marriage, don't you?" I reply sternly, and he doesn't really have a response to that.

When we arrive back at the B&B, I stop at reception to see if my bag has arrived and discover to my increasing concern that it hasn't. Ed heads up to the room as I sit on a bench outside, trying to find enough signal to phone the twenty-four-hour helpline on the form I was given at the airport. Heat rises from the tarmac as I wait to be put through, the Sexy Shop sign blinking intermittently, lighting up the street and the odd car that passes. I am on hold for twenty minutes before finally reaching someone who tells me to try again in the morning because he's just the security guard.

I return to the room to find it thick with heat and moisture, with Ed fast asleep. I drop my bag on my bed and pause momentarily, watching the tiny trembles of his face as he sleeps, the way his shoulders gently rise and fall. I creep to the window and push it wide open, deciding that the odd traffic sound is preferable to suffocating heat. I return to my bed as he stirs lightly and turns over onto his back. As the silver light of the moon rains on his face, my insides soften.

I get ready for bed in the bathroom, finding Ed's shower gel to be an effective if abrasive make-up remover, before returning to slip off my trousers and slide under a thin sheet, quickly submitting to a plunging sleep. When I wake in the dead of night to find someone walking round the room, I'm gripped by an electrifying panic. I sit bolt upright and fumble for the light, beading with sweat as I am confronted by a semi-naked man opening the door. It turns out to be Ed.

"What the hell are you doing?"

"Sorry, couldn't sleep. I'd just gone to the bathroom," he says. "It must be thirty-five degrees in here."

I click off the light mutely, allowing my adrenalin to subside as I curl onto my side. He treads past me and silently sits on the edge of his bed, gazing out of the window. The last things I see before I close my eyes are the bare contours of his back, the freckle just below his shoulder blade, the angles of his triceps.

I sleep like a baby for the rest of the night and, when I wake the following morning I stretch out, feeling luxuriantly relaxed and rested. Then I roll over and do a double take. Ed is still gazing through the window, in exactly the same position as he had been hours earlier.

CHAPTER
NINETEEN

A few weeks after the frog incident in science class, we discovered that Ed lived on the same bus route as me. Our houses were miles apart, his in an area I'd never set foot in. But on the odd afternoon, he took to hanging back after school so we could walk to the bus stop together, before climbing to the top deck, where we'd sit at the front. I was unnerved and suspicious about this at first. I'd never have been brave enough to seek out a *boy* and couldn't work out why he'd want to be around me. But I liked it all the same.

"Aren't you worried about people getting the wrong impression about you and me?" I asked him one day.

His nose wrinkled in such a way that made me embarrassed for asking. "No. I've got a girlfriend. At least . . . I think so."

"You mean Bernadette?"

He nodded, looking troubled. Bernadette McGovern had a reputation as a man-eater, which is quite an achievement when you're only thirteen.

"She's asked me to take her to see a Jennifer Aniston movie."

"Which one?"

"I don't think she's fussy. She can't be if she wants to go out with me." I laughed. He was always making me laugh.

Ed was an unusual breed in our school. Academically, he sailed through everything, but managed — at least at first — to keep the company of a select group of friends who were far cooler than mine. They were the kind of kids who wore the right trainers, said the right things, even *walked* the right way, with a swagger that underlined one indisputable fact: they were awesome and they knew they were.

But he was part of that group, without ever being central to it. It felt as though they were on a glittering carousel that he only ever ran alongside, without fully leaping on. And there was the odd occasion when he was subtly ostracised altogether, such as after the school signed him up to a government scheme to promote modern foreign languages, meaning he took thirteen GCSEs instead of nine like everybody else. In our school, this was the opposite of cool and he found himself adrift from them, something I knew bothered him more than he was prepared to admit.

Whatever their opinion though, personally I found him to be rare and stimulating company. He talked about books and movies in ways I'd never encountered, deconstructing them in a manner that I hadn't the breadth of thought to consider. He broached questions of science that went beyond what we learnt in the classroom: the ethics of animal testing, genetic editing, whether humans have the right to colonise other planets. His opinions were bold but carefully thought out. He was prepared to accept he didn't know all the answers.

By the time we were fifteen, Ed had dated several girls. It felt as though I'd blinked and overnight he'd become a heart-throb, the boy everyone wanted to go out with. His blossoming love-life cemented my suspicion that I was lagging horribly behind and the only way to handle all the fuss around him was to pretend to be entirely blind to his attractions.

It was true that when he started coming over to my house to revise for exams, it wasn't only because of the warm feeling we had when I'd light a joss stick on my dressing table and we'd pontificate about the periodic table or the new Verve album. The simple fact was that nobody else was prepared to devote as much energy as either of us to studying.

"Is Ed your boyfriend these days?" Grandma Peggy asked once. She'd popped in while I was making us a peanut butter sandwich after school and the question nearly made me drop the Sun Pat.

"Grandma!" I hissed.

"What?"

"It *is* possible for two people of the opposite sex to have a purely platonic relationship, you know," I lectured her, under my breath. "There's nothing romantic going on between me and Ed. Not now. Not ever."

"The lady doth protest too much," she said, raising her eyebrow archly, as my face flared.

But there were occasions when he'd sit on the end of my bed, and the way his lips moistened when he concentrated on something would elicit the same flutter in my belly that only Leonardo DiCaprio had been capable of previously. I never thought anything would happen between us though. I wasn't deluded.

The closest I got to my own romantic action at that age was a single humiliating fumble at a house party with a boy called Adrian Graves. He wasn't what you'd call a hunk, but he had a pleasingly unremarkable face, with ears that protruded slightly and mousy hair that fell into his eyes. Nobody else fancied him. I wasn't sure I did, but that night he paid enough attention to me to make me think it'd be convenient to reciprocate.

Our kiss, and the brief wrestle that followed, happened in a downstairs toilet when he was drunk on Cinzano Bianco. It was underwhelming, yet for reasons known only to him, when it became common knowledge at school on Monday, he decided to tell everyone that I had "tits like fried eggs". The comment was flippantly made, a cheap laugh, but salacious and public enough to spread like wildfire. The school I'd never loved suddenly felt like a more noxious enemy than I'd ever considered it, my mortification all the more intense from the fact that it was true: I barely filled an A cup.

I told Dad I was sick the following day and I wasn't lying: I actually *was* nauseous. I couldn't eat. Anxiety gnawed at my bones as I lay in bed, cocooned under the quilt, rising only late in the afternoon after the doorbell rang. It was Ed, who followed me up to my room and sat on the end of the bed, while I tried to maintain the gastroenteritis story I'd spun.

He listened to me silently, processing the lies, before saying, in a voice I didn't recognise: "I heard what happened." His jaw pulsed and anger radiated in his eyes. "Adrian Graves is a dickhead. I'm going to say something."

"Don't!" I hissed.

"Then I'm going to *do* something."

"Like what?"

"I *feel* like fucking killing him."

The ferocity of this sentiment excited me, but he misinterpreted my reaction.

"You know . . . you *can* cry, Allie. It's okay to cry."

I blinked up at him. "I never cry."

It was true. I hadn't cried when I'd broken my arm on a trampoline. I hadn't cried when I watched *E.T.* I hadn't cried when my mum died. So I certainly wasn't going to cry over Adrian Graves.

I went to school the following day. I straightened my back and wore an expression of defiance that made my face ache. And, after a torturous morning, I made it to the queue in the canteen, preparing myself for a deluge of abuse from the other kids. But Ed appeared by my side.

"Would you like to go and see a movie with me this weekend?" he asked loudly.

A ladle of baked beans sloshed onto my plate and I became aware of a dozen jaws dropping. "Yeah. Okay."

He took me to a Saturday morning showing of *Casablanca* at the art house cinema in the city centre, a film I'd doubted would appeal to any of the girls at school he'd dated. I'd been slightly put out by that at first, that they'd been worthy of *The Matrix*, when all I got was some ancient, crumbly movie that only cost a pound to watch. But just under two hours later, we both left the theatre spellbound by the suspense, the tenderness, the wisecracks. And Humphrey Bogart's final, iconic words: "I think this is the beginning of a beautiful friendship."

CHAPTER
TWENTY

Wearing an overpriced thong and dousing my armpits with Ed's deodorant, unsurprisingly, does not alter how grubby I feel in the same jeans, top and Converse as yesterday.

"I think we need to move to a hotel with air con tonight," Ed says, as we emerge from a bicycle hire shop a few minutes away from the B&B.

"But I've already paid for another night at this place," I reply, wheeling my bike to the side of the road. "I realise it's not five-star luxury, but you don't think it's that bad, do you?"

He ignores the question. "I saw a hotel up the road that looked nice. I'll give you any money you lost."

I tut. "Don't be ridiculous. I don't need you to spend your cash on me."

"Fine. Why don't you just humour me on the other hotel, then?"

I purse my lips. "Well, I hope it's got a view over a busy main road and a Sexy Shop sign. That's all I'm saying," I tell him haughtily, as I pedal off onto the road, leaving him behind.

We're not on the main drag for long, instead finding a route on the wide promenade along the shore of the lake. We slip along a tree-lined path in the whispering breeze, dodging dog walkers, children on skateboards and the odd gecko that scurries out of our way. The heat is dry and pleasant, the water a milky shade of blue as it laps onto the rushes at the edge. But the peaceful scenery is at odds with my mood as we close in on our destination.

"It's the next turn off, Allie," Ed says. I slow down and feel my pulse racing as I wait for him to scrutinise the GPS on his phone. We take a left down a quiet residential street, heat shimmering on the tarmac as we freewheel in silence, listening to the purr of our tyres on the road and the hiss of sprinklers on front lawns. To my foreign eyes it's hard to place the kind of area this is. There are middle-of-the-road cars parked in driveways of neat, modern apartment blocks and houses that are neither grand nor shabby. We finally arrive at the address, 36 Via Esposito, to find a house that is detached and compact, surrounded by clipped hedges. The walls are painted butter-yellow and there is a thin veranda above the front door, room for a clutch of flowerpots but no chairs.

"You okay?" Ed asks. He takes a mouthful of water from his bottle and offers me some. I shake my head as the door opens. A man emerges. I feel my knees go weak.

"It's not him, he's too old," Ed whispers quickly.

I balance my foot on the pedal of the bike and think about just turning around, but by now the occupant of the house has seen us.

"*Posso essere d'aiuto?*"

Ed looks at me briefly, but when he sees that I'm mute, he steps forward. "*Salve — stiamo cercando un certo signor Stefano McCourt?*" Ed says. I feel heat rise to the surface of my cheeks.

He shakes his head, looking confused. Then he says: "*Ah! É il padrone di casa. Non l'ho mai conosciuto. Ho solo avuto a che fare con il suo ufficio. Ma la sua famiglia una volta abitava in questa casa, quindi Elisabetta, la vicina, lo conoscerà di sicuro. Lei vive qui da sempre.*"

Ed turns to me. "Stefano is his landlord but he's never met him. His neighbour could be our best bet as she knew the whole family when they used to live here."

I nod at the man self-consciously. "*Grazie,*" I say, then I turn to Ed. "Can you ask him if he's got the contact details for his office?"

Ed translates and he disappears inside, before emerging with the name and address of a Verona letting agency, scrawled on a piece of paper.

After we've thanked him again and he's retreated into the house, we lean the bikes against a low wall and make our way next door, to a slightly bigger building with terracotta walls and the odd weed sprouting from cracks in the paving. The woman who answers looks to be in her late fifties, with a delicate face and short auburn hair.

"Um, *buongiorno*," I say falteringly, then look to Ed to step in.

"*Salve. Ci scusi se la disturbiamo*," he continues politely. She is soon deep in conversation with him. As they talk, her expression unfolds into a smile. It's clear, even in a language incomprehensible to my ears, that she knows Stefano McCourt.

CHAPTER
TWENTY-ONE

I let them talk at first, forcing myself to hold back until there is a lull in the discussion. "I take it she knows Stefano?" I ask Ed.

"Yes. This is Elisabetta. She says he lived with his parents here for many years after they returned from England. He moved out when he got married, but he must have been in his early thirties by then. She thinks his wife was called Rosa."

"What about Vittoria and Michael?"

"They moved to a smaller home soon after Stefano married. It had always been Vittoria's ambition to open a *pasticceria* and she thinks they wanted to put money into that."

Ed continues the conversation, turning to me to translate intermittently. "They were a very private family. But Vittoria absolutely adored Stefano, she was so proud of him. He was a *mammone* . . . a mother's boy. Every time they chatted, the conversation would turn to what a good boy he was to her, how loyal and clever. She lavished him with affection."

The woman says something else and laughs. "She says, it's little wonder that she didn't loosen the apron strings until his thirties," Ed explains.

"What about Stefano himself?"

"He was a polite young man, a respectable boy. She'd often see him outside cutting the grass or doing chores. We never saw him much during the summer though; he'd spend those with his uncle who had a boat yard. She says he changed after they came back from England. He'd grown up a lot."

Adrenalin snaps through my chest. "What did he say? Did the family talk about their time in the UK and why they'd returned?"

He asks the question and she replies, before Ed says: "Probably just homesick."

"But what about now? Has she got any idea where he is these days?"

I can tell from her expression that I'm not going to get far. "She doesn't know where any of them ended up. She says she used to bump into Vittoria in Peschiera or Sirmione every so often, but hasn't for years. She assumes they moved away. Last time she went to the *pasticceria* in Peschiera it was run by another lady."

"Can she tell me anything else? Anything at all?"

Ed asks her again and she shakes her head.

"Sorry, Allie. I think we've hit a dead end."

As we're returning the bikes to the hire shop, Julia phones. I leave Ed to go inside to collect the deposit, while I hover in the car park and take the call.

118

"How is he, Allie?" she asks urgently, discernible strain in her voice. The question is reasonable, probably inevitable, but I feel a sliver of discomfort at the idea of discussing Ed when he's only a few feet away. Or even at all.

"Well, I'm honestly not sure yet."

"Oh." She is clearly disappointed at my lack of insight.

"It's early days, isn't it?"

She sniffs. "Yes, you're right. Sorry. It's all I can think about. I should have left it a few more days before phoning."

"Oh, don't be silly!" I reassure her, feeling bad. "It's really fine."

There's a pause as she breathes in and says: "So is it lovely there?"

"Well, the weather's nice and Sirmione's gorgeous, but it's fair to say that the place we're staying in probably isn't the best Lake Garda has to offer."

"He's responded to a few of my texts but only briefly," she continues, as if she hasn't heard me. "He seems so distant, Allie. Maybe I'm imagining it. Do you think I've lost him already?"

"No, of course not." Ed emerges from the bike shop and pauses to put his wallet back in his rucksack. "Listen, Julia, it's a little difficult to talk at the moment."

"Oh, I'm so sorry. Maybe we can have a chat in a couple of days — would you mind Allie? I just want to know he's okay, that's all."

"Of course. And try not to worry too much," I add gently.

When we return to the B&B, my luggage has arrived. I'm pleased to be reunited with my own pants, but it's slightly embarrassing to have to try and explain to the lady on reception that we are leaving today when the room's already paid for.

"Was she offended that we were going?" I ask Ed anxiously, as he lifts my luggage into the boot of the taxi and we slide in to the back seat.

"She couldn't have cared less."

"So where is this "far nicer place" you've found us?" I ask.

He leans forward to our driver. "Villa Cortine Palace Hotel, *per favore*."

Cars are not ordinarily allowed into Sirmione old town. But as soon as the guard at the entrance to the historic centre learns where we're staying, we're waved through. The car slowly negotiates the narrow streets, so close to the vanilla-coloured walls of the shops and galleries that it feels as though there's barely an inch either side.

"How long have you booked us in for?" I ask.

"Four days."

"I'm not even sure what the point is anymore," I sigh. "Do you think there's any way that letting agency could be persuaded to change their mind about giving us his contact details?"

"It didn't sound that way."

Ed phoned the agency as soon as we left Elisabetta's house, but they said if I want to get in touch with

120

Stefano, I'd need to do so via email, explaining who I was and what I wanted. Then they would forward it on to him. This might end up being my only option but having a discussion about something as big as this via email is a long way from ideal.

The taxi emerges from the labyrinth of streets into a wide turning circle in front of an imposing set of wrought-iron gates. The driver speaks through a security intercom and, after a brief moment, they click open.

A steep driveway snakes through terraced parkland abundant with oversized conifers and palm trees. Neoclassical statues of angels and warriors line our route, with street lamps from a bygone age and stone urns weathered by centuries and patterns of lichen. We pass a large, circular pond thick with lily pads, and a steep rockery dotted with rampaging myrtle and soft pink hydrangeas.

At some point as I take this all in, I become aware of the heat from Ed's gaze on me. I glance up.

"Okay, you win. It's very nice."

He smiles to himself. "I'm not trying to win. I'm glad you like it though."

"How much is it?

"It was my idea to move, so I'm footing the bill."

"Don't be ridiculous."

"I'm not. Don't argue."

"But —"

"Allie," he interrupts, smiling. "Just enjoy it. It'll save a lot of time."

We find ourselves high on a hill, crunching onto a gleaming stretch of gravel where sports cars in kick-ass shades of red and yellow line up in rows. A uniformed doorman clicks my handle and invites me to step out. The air up here is so clean and pure that it feels different just to breathe, as I gaze down to the brilliant blue of the stretching lake and the hills that dazzle in the sunlight.

"Welcome to the Villa Cortine Palace Hotel."

I raise my eyes to the colonnaded entrance of a spectacular, three-storey villa with walls the colour of fresh linen and high windows carved with intricate stonework. Three steps lead into a cool reception area, with a patterned marble floor, Murano chandeliers and subtle pieces of modern art. I hang back as Ed checks us in and log onto the Wi-Fi to look at my emails. They consist largely of the usual dross, but one catches my eye, entitled "Your bill" from Ged McKenzie.

Hello Allie,

Sorry it's taken a few weeks, but I'm finally attaching my invoice for the work completed on your search for Stefano McCourt. Also: a little bonus for you. When I contacted Virginia Boldrini, the investigator in Rome I'd mentioned, she'd apparently completed a brief search. She didn't come up with much, but she has forwarded this cutting. Not sure it helps, but you're welcome to it. Good luck with it all — and you know where I am if you need me.

Ged

I'm tempted to reply, pointing out that Stefano doesn't live at the address he gave me — though it strikes me that he'd never actually said he did, just that he owned the place. I open the attachment to find a copy of a colour picture from a local magazine, a slightly amateurish publication, judging by the jumbled layout of the pictures and text. The date on it is last September and it features five people, standing outside a restaurant, raising their glasses to the camera. I can't read the headline, so when Ed is finished checking us in I ask him to translate. "'Torri to host new wine festival'," he tells me. Then I look at the list of names in the caption and see that the middle-aged man second from right is Stefano McCourt.

CHAPTER
TWENTY-TWO

I lie on my belly with my toes draped over the end of a lounger, sunshine soaking into the back of my legs. I had considered going for a walk this afternoon, or hiring bikes again, to explore some of the pretty harbour towns dotted along Lake Garda. But instead, we climbed down the steep hill steps to the water, where a slender bathing jetty cuts into the lake, lined with seashell-white furniture and parasols that cast yawning shadows on the water.

There are two men opposite us, a glamorous couple in their mid-forties, one reading a spy thriller from behind his Ray-Bans, the other fast asleep. A little further along is a woman in white shorts and a navy halter top, holding the hand of a toddler, who laughs in breathless disbelief as he takes a couple of jerky steps.

As she scoops him up, I'm reminded of a video clip from when I was tiny, not much bigger than the little boy on the jetty. Someone had burned it onto a DVD for Grandma Peggy and, though it was only four minutes long, she'd watch it over and over again. I'd been one of a clutch of children allowed to attend my second cousin Anthony's wedding to his long-term girlfriend Harriet and, despite being nearly two years old, still hadn't taken my first steps.

"Your mum had tried everything to persuade you to put one foot in front of the other, but you only wanted to shuffle around on your bottom," Grandma told me. "She got fed up of people asking why you weren't walking. Someone even told her she should see a doctor in case something was wrong with you. 'Nothing's wrong,' she'd insist. 'My girl will walk when she's good and ready.'"

In the clip, the opening bars to "It Must be Love" by Madness pounded out, as Mum sashayed onto an empty dancefloor with me in her arms and gently lowered me to the ground. Then she swept back the pale waves of her hair, bent to hold both of my hands and laughed in delight as I began to swing my hips from side to side. We danced together for most of the song, but as it neared the end, a smile spread to the corners of her mouth and she began to back away, until my fingers gently slid from hers. Wide-eyed and wobbling, I was literally standing on my own two feet for the first time in my life, clearly certain that catastrophe loomed.

Then my mother said something to me. I don't know what it was, but those private words of reassurance seemed to convince me that I didn't need her right there in front of me, holding my hands, to know that she'd still be watching out for me. It remains true to this day that the biggest cheer I ever raised in my life was elicited by my first four, precarious steps, a performance that ended with a flourish, on my backside. The next thing I knew, Mum had swept me up and was spinning us around, planting kisses in my hair as I laughed until I could hardly catch my breath.

"*Bravo!*" I'm snapped from my thoughts as the Italian woman begins to clap her little boy as he toddles along the jetty.

It's an adorable sight and I can't help but smile, before turning over to see Ed sitting on the adjacent lounger, glaring out onto the horizon. He's been doing that since we got here, occasionally glancing at one of the dozens of texts that ping on his phone, most from Julia, some from his office.

"So, what do I do with this?" I ask, gesturing to the cutting on the decking in front of me. "Any ideas?"

"What?"

"I just wondered if you had any ideas about what I do with this magazine article?"

"I'll have a think," he replies, his mind clearly elsewhere.

Our silences have always been the comfortable kind over the years. Ed is one of the few people with whom I'll happily share time without puncturing it with noise. But this doesn't feel like that. This feels sultry, almost oppressive.

I pick up my phone and decide to check in with Khalid.

All okay with you? Anything to report?

He responds immediately.

Nothing major, still all good. In fact, a couple of the results from yesterday are slightly better than previously. I'll email the data to you today 😊.

Something approaching hope billows up in my chest but I push it away. I'm an optimist by nature, but nothing is certain until *all* the results are in and I won't be drawing conclusions until then. Still, as I tuck the phone under the lounger, rest my cheekbone on my arm and close my eyes, my mind has other ideas.

My thoughts turn to the next big CF conference in Baltimore. I imagine myself on stage, presenting to an audience from a whole spectrum of scientific discovery, clinical research and healthcare provision. Anyone in the room would be able to see how passionate I was about my work, but there would be no need for hyperbole. The results would speak for themselves. The excitement would begin as a ripple, one that would swell and surge into a wave of enthusiastic applause.

The fantasy quickly disintegrates as I think instead about little Rowan Archer, at five years old the youngest boy in a clinical trial in which I've been involved at Alder Hey Children's Hospital. It's separate from our gene-editing project, something I've been helping with for the last five months, during which time I've become familiar with his repertoire of knock-knock jokes and still melt every time his brown eyes glitter when he giggles.

When he arrived in the trial room at Alder Hey for our last round of testing before I came to Italy, his mum Dawn took me to one side to tell me that it'd been a bad morning, with an hour of coughing fits before she'd managed to get him dressed, and give him his meds and nebuliser.

You'd never have guessed it to look at him, as he leapt on the edge of the hospital bed, full of good cheer, as he waited for me to attach an electrode to his wrist to begin the procedure.

"So, how is my favourite patient today?" I asked him.

"I've got some news," he told me, looking like he might burst.

I stepped back and mock gasped. "You're getting married?"

He burst out laughing. "NO!"

"Okay, let me guess. You've just passed your driving test?"

"NO!"

"You're actually not a five-year-old kid . . . you're a spy?"

He shook his head and grinned the biggest, cheesiest grin he could muster, before pointing at a gap where one of his lower incisors had been wobbling since Easter.

"No way! You finally lost it. Well, congratulations," I said, shaking his hand. "That tooth has been on the verge of coming out for as long as I've known you. I think you deserve a sticker. In fact, I think you deserve ALL the stickers," I added, offering him not one, but three full sheets, as he released peals of laughter. I looked up and saw his mum smiling too, widely and emphatically, despite the pink rim around her eyes.

"Time to simmer down now," the consultant Mr Atkinson said gently.

"Sorry. That was all my fault," I said, but he flashed me a grateful smile for helping to relax a patient who couldn't be persuaded to leave his mum's knee the first few times he came here. This time, Rowan lay down without hesitation and stayed perfectly still while a probe was inserted into his nostril to send a series of different solutions down the back of his throat, which he then had to swallow.

Over the next twenty minutes, I sat next to his mum, chatting to both of them as I glanced at the readings on the equipment next to me, entirely underwhelmed by Rowan's rate of improvement, considering he's been on this trial drug for the past five months. Afterwards, as we sent him on his way, clutching his stickers, I remember being swept up in a tide of determination. *This* treatment might not be able to help him. But, one day, mine will.

I wake with my cheek stuck to the pages of my book, having not registered that I'd drifted off to sleep. I have no idea how long I was out cold, but when I sit up, Ed is no longer beside me. I take a sip of mineral water and find it unpalatably warm, before scanning the jetty. There's no sign of him either in the water, or along the promenade or beach. His belongings are still on the lounger next to me. And although I'm keen to go back to the room to freshen up, something makes me want to wait for him first.

I start reading again, but I'm woozy from sunshine and can't really concentrate. I try ringing him and only then realise that he's left his phone under his towel. I open my book again and try to settle down, but after twenty minutes he's still not back. Instead, I get up and walk to the couple a few metres away, before employing my best in pigeon Italian to work out if they saw Ed leave.

"*Scusi . . . mio amico . . .* he went where?"

I accompany this with an emphatic shrug of the shoulders and bemused look, feeling as if I'm taking part in some sort of pantomime. They point across the line of the beach, to the foot of a craggy rock that rises up on a jagged slope.

"*È andato lassù,*" the man says. "A . . . path. *Un vecchio sentiero dietro a quegli alberi. Non so se sia sicuro però.*"

"*Grazie,*" I reply, grabbing my bag and stuffing Ed's phone and other belongings into it.

I crunch towards the cliff as children splash in the shallows of the lake and ribbons of light rain across the sky. The outline of an old footpath winds upwards from the side of the rocks, lined with wild flowers and fragrant herbs. It's precariously steep and my footwear is far from ideal, but when I reach the top the view is heart-stopping, a verdant landscape dotted with elegant stone buildings in ice cream shades and cypress trees that rise like feathers sprouting from the ground.

Then I see him. Standing at the edge of the cliff, his silhouette opaque against the sunlight, his broad shoulders pulled back. It occurs to me that Ed hasn't only got a head full of troubles. It's full of something else too. Secrets.

CHAPTER
TWENTY-THREE

Ed

Ed lowers his eyes to the water as the faint ring of giggling children drifts up from the bay. The sound reminds him of Allie, the way he used to feel when they'd laugh together as kids. Warm and happy and high. Yet, it's not even a *high* that he's looking for. Right now, he just wants to bear to think about his future without nausea taking hold around his throat.

He still can't precisely work out when his feelings started to change. The question he's asked endlessly — why? — is never going to be answered. But something shifted in him on the night of that first big row with Julia. There had been others before but nothing like that. It could have been just another spat at first, but what it turned into that night shocked them both. He became a man he no longer recognised.

He walked around for days afterwards, with a knot in his stomach, asking himself: is *this* who I am now? A man who went from hearts and flowers to *this* so soon after the wedding? Ed is not self-absorbed enough to look in the mirror and try to claim it was all her fault.

Yet now, he is struggling to be around Julia, a woman he thought he loved enough to bind himself to forever. He didn't take that decision lightly, on the contrary. It was no shotgun wedding, rushed into for the wrong reasons. To him, she was the *phantom of delight* of Wordsworth's poem — a perfect woman, *nobly plann'd*. There had been no room for doubt.

That thought fills him with a numbness, a blur of misery that's starting to take on a life of its own. There are times recently when he's been unable to gain pleasure from the things he usually loves. Running and books and wine and friends. At night he gazes at the ceiling listening to the thrum of his heart and asking himself the question: what would those loyal friends of his make of him if they knew the truth? When he thinks about Allie trying to do her bit to cheer him up he doesn't know whether to laugh or cry.

Julia, unbelievably, maintains that there's nothing fundamentally wrong with their relationship. She seemed genuinely surprised when he said he thought there was. How? How can she still think that? He's beyond looking for answers because he can't think straight about it any longer.

"Is everything okay, Ed? Do you want to talk?"

Ed turns around and is surprised. Both at the sight of Allie, standing with shards of sunlight in her hair and the faintest wrinkle between her eyebrows, and by the question itself. It takes a lot for Allie to offer to have a *talk*.

"Sure," he shrugs and the wrinkle deepens.

This is not because she lacks empathy, on the contrary. But for all his friend's warmth and goodness, stoicism runs through her core. She has a stiff upper lip. She *pulls herself together*. None of these things are considered positive attributes these days, in an age when feelings are to be dissected and analysed like complex organisms under a microscope.

They sit side by side on the dusty ground and Ed's eyes blur onto the horizon, the outline of the pine trees and the ridge of the mountains on the other side of the lake.

"I wondered where you'd gone," she says, sounding unsure of herself. Her skin smells of sun cream and tiny beads of sweat glisten on the bridge of her nose.

"Just for a walk. I needed to do some thinking."

"Did you . . . work anything out?"

"Not really." He feels himself smile at her, but she doesn't return it.

"I'm worried about you, Ed." As the words emerge from her mouth, emotion shines in her eyes and he almost can't bear it. Not from her, of all people. He edges towards her and wraps an arm around her shoulder, squeezing her into his side. She tenses at first, but as she relaxes into him, warmth spreads through his body. Reflexively, he bends his head towards her, breathing in the clean, herby scent of her shampoo as he briefly presses his lips against her hair.

"Sorry. I don't like to worry anyone," he says.

She turns and looks at him and for a spark of a moment he feels as though he has no idea what's going

134

to happen next. She brushes dust off her feet and sniffs. "Why don't we go and get ready for dinner?"

They sit on the veranda in Ed's room after they've eaten, breathing in the night while they chat, as piano chords drift from the other side of the building. Ed asks a lot about Allie's work; partly because he's interested, but mainly because he likes the way her eyes light up when she tells him about it. And of course it's easier than other topics.

It's late when Allie looks at the time on her phone and stiffens, as if she's been reminded of something important that she was supposed to do.

"We still haven't really discussed what's happening with you, Ed," she says, twisting her bracelet around her wrist.

"No," he says.

"Well, I think you should talk about it, with someone. I mean, I don't want to pry, I hope you know that that's the last thing I'd want. But it's not normal to keep things bottled up."

He can't help but smile.

"What?"

"Nothing. It's just that you're not really one to open up and talk about your feelings, are you?"

Her spine lengthens as she sits up, defiant. "This isn't about me."

"I know, but you're speaking sense," he says gently. "Yet, I don't think in all the years I've known you I've heard you talk about your mum, for example."

"I have!"

"No, I mean really talk about her, the impact of her death when you were so young. And now all this stuff with your dad and this Stefano guy . . ."

"I'm sure we were discussing *your* issues, not mine."

"Oh, I'm not saying you've got issues . . ."

"Good."

"Not many, anyway."

"Very funny. Well, it's up to you. But maybe I'll surprise us both and turn out to be a great shoulder to cry on."

"Maybe." She picks up her clutch bag, ready to leave. "So whose shoulder are *you* going to cry on, Allie?" he can't help but ask.

She holds his gaze defiantly. "I never —"

"You never cry. Yes, I forgot."

"Truth be told, I have been thinking about my mum a lot lately."

He leans forward, interested, but she just shrugs.

"I don't mean just the woman she became after I'd been born, but the girl she was before. I mean . . . she was only a teenager, yet found herself in what must have felt like an impossible situation. What *does* a seventeen-year-old do when she has to announce to her devoutly religious mother that she's unexpectedly pregnant? Let alone when the father might be a man who isn't her boyfriend?"

CHAPTER
TWENTY-FOUR

As her father fixed his eyes on her swollen, naked belly, she felt as though all the air had been sucked out of the room. She pulled her blouse down sharply, clasping her hands around her bump, as if her stupid, pale forearms could conceal what he'd already seen. He hadn't even moved, or said anything, when she heard the slam of the front door downstairs.

"Only me!" her mum called. The cheerful, sing-song of her voice sliced through the air.

Their eyes locked. Father and daughter. And she'll never forget the look on his face, one that said everything without saying a thing: *you aren't the person I thought you were.*

"Dad . . . I need to explain," she mumbled, but of course she couldn't explain. There wasn't an explanation, at least not one that would make any sense. So she started talking, filling the air with words in the hope that they were at least better than the acrid stench of shock that hovered between them.

"It's not what you think. I mean, it IS, obviously but . . . the thing is, it was all a mistake. An accident. It's . . . such a mess." A statement of the obvious if ever there was one.

The ensuing silence nearly cracked her eardrums. Even from the other side of the room, she could see petals of fierce heat blooming around his temples.

"Does he know?" he managed.

She opened her mouth to respond, but something stopped her.

There was only one person her parents could think was the father.

But they were wrong. The real father was by now miles away, in a different country, his identity unknown by anyone. It wasn't as if she'd been sneaking off for dozens of illicit trysts for months on end. It had been once. Just once. That was all it took.

These thoughts and a dozen others were thudding in her head, when she became aware that her father had given up on her responding and had left the room. She scurried to the door to see him walking down the stairs in shock, to intercept her mother as she was still taking off her coat in the hall.

She hung it up on the bannister, her movements slowing as she looked at her husband then followed his gaze up the stairs. "What's the matter?"

She felt as though the breath had been ripped out of her throat. Hot tears rose from somewhere inside her and teetered precariously on the rims of her eyes.

And a dozen possible sentences brushed her lips, until she realised that all she was capable of now saying was: "I'm sorry. I'm so very sorry."

CHAPTER
TWENTY-FIVE

Allie

A few months before Ed and I took our mock GCSE exams, I'd rushed out in the morning to catch the bus and left my key on the cupboard next to the stairs. I only discovered this when Ed and I, intending to revise for Sociology — a subject neither of us loved — battled torrential rain on my doorstep as I frantically emptied my bag.

"Where are we going to go now?" Water snaked down the skin on his face and droplets of rain hung like tiny crystals on the tips of his eyelashes.

"We need a coffee shop," I replied. "Somewhere quiet and atmospheric."

So we went to McDonalds, where we spent an hour and a half pontificating over a Haralambos & Holborn textbook and small fries, before eventually we were asked to make another purchase or move on.

"It's going to have to be your place," I said, heading outside.

"Fine. But there'll be no peanut butter. Mum's joined Weight Watchers again."

Fifteen minutes later, I stood behind him as he let us into a small terraced house with a blue door and a single bay window. As we stepped in, someone shouted from the front room: "Is that you, Brian?"

"No, it's me, Mum." Ed hesitated before pushing the door, releasing a lush cloud of boudoir scents, of heavily fragranced creams and potions and soaps.

"Mum, this is Allie." I smoothed down the rat ends of my hair and followed him in.

We found Ed's mum on the floor, surrounded by invoices, cosmetics and a stack of Avon magazines, as a game show flickered on the television behind her. She leapt up and welcomed me with a whoop of, "*At last!*"

"Hello, Mrs Holt. Pleased to meet you."

Mrs Holt, or Jackie as she invited me to call her, was in her dressing gown, a short, pale blue terry towelling item with a diamante teddy on the pocket. She had long, slim legs and slipper-socks topped with pom poms. She was fully made up, her features painstakingly enhanced with a tawny palette of eye shadow and peachy blush on the apples of her cheeks.

"I wish he'd told me you were coming," she told me, starting to tidy up the room, as Ed went into the kitchen to get some drinks. "What must you think of me?" She paused and lit a Silk Cut, blowing a ribbon of smoke into the air before she turned back and caught me looking. "Disgusting habit, I know."

"Oh no, I —"

"So, what are you studying tonight, love?"

"Sociology."

"*Ooh*," she said approvingly, before falling silent. This felt dangerously close to being the end of the conversation. "Is that like politics?"

"It's connected," I explained shyly. "But it's more about how society is organised. We look at issues like crime and poverty."

"I can't stand politics myself," she told me, conspiratorially. "I never vote. Doesn't seem to matter who gets in, they're all the same."

I disagreed with this, but wasn't going to be impolite.

"That's a very good argument for proportional representation," I said instead. "Lots of people think that would be a fairer way of producing a more representative legislature and faithfully translating votes into seats won." I realised how pompous this sounded and I added, self-consciously: "I like your pom poms."

She laughed. "Aw, thanks."

"And also your make-up. It must be lovely to know how to do it like that."

She lowered her cigarette and softened her gaze on me. "You know . . . you're a very pretty girl, Allie." I must have turned the colour of a beetroot. "Sorry. I didn't mean to embarrass you. Here — why don't you take some samples, for you and your mum. I've got a lovely new Colour Rich lipstick for you. And your mum . . . perhaps she'd like a little bottle of Imari? 'A fragrance to fire the imagination' apparently."

She stubbed out her cigarette and opened a little bag, into which she started to put bottles, before handing it over. "There you go."

"Thank you," I said, breathlessly, peering into it. "Um . . . perhaps I should leave the perfume though. My mum's no longer with us."

She blinked. "Sorry?"

"She died," I said.

I'd tried to come up with a low-key way of telling people that over the years — something that didn't unleash a torrent of fuss — but judging by Jackie Holt's reaction I'd failed.

"I'm so sorry. I didn't . . . Ed didn't —"

"It's fine. I just don't want to waste your perfume."

She glanced at the bag, then up at me again. "It's not a waste. *You* can have it, Allie."

"Are you sure?"

"Absolutely. *Abs-ol-utely*," she repeated. Then she grabbed an eye shadow, a mascara, a blusher and some peach-coloured lipstick, all of which she added to my little bag of treasure.

"Let me know if you need me to show you how to use any of them," she added gently. I could tell that she meant it, that Jackie Holt was the type of woman to help a girl with no mother on this small but important matter.

In fact, I'd have asked her for a full makeover there and then if Ed hadn't appeared and suggested we adjourn to his room.

"If it smells like beef and tomato Pot Noodle in here, blame Mike," he said as we traipsed up a narrow staircase with a threadbare carpet.

"Oh, it doesn't smell," I said as we entered, but he marched to the window and shoved it open anyway, unleashing a loud hiss of rain.

It struck me as a tiny room for two big teenagers, particularly as they didn't get on. On Ed's side of the room there was a Salvador Dali print, a framed *Private Eye* cartoon, a black and white picture of Bob Marley and another of Juliette Lewis. On Mike's side there were fourteen posters of Melinda Messenger and Kathy Lloyd, all in various states of undress.

"Sorry about the . . . you know," he said, gesturing to the wall full of nipples.

We sat at the end of the bed and I opened my folder, then looked up.

"Your mum's really lovely," I said. "Is your dad still at work?"

He nodded. "You can't take a day off when you're self-employed."

"What's his firm called?"

"B. R. Holt & Sons," he said. "Not very original, I'll admit."

I laughed momentarily then felt it trail off as something occurred to me. "So, is he hoping Mike will take over the business when he retires?"

Ed snorted. "I seriously doubt it."

"Then who will —"

But the door flew open and Mike burst into the room. "KNOCK KNOCK! Shagging are we?"

"We're revising," Ed replied, through gritted teeth.

"All right, Mastermind," Mike added, before farting, flopping onto his bed and peeling off his socks to start applying some athlete's foot cream.

144

CHAPTER
TWENTY-SIX

After a tortured night's sleep, I wake sharply at nine-thirty. I reach for my phone and find a text from Ed:

Found us a table on the terrace for breakfast. See you downstairs when you're ready. It's a lovely morning.

I shower and tie back my hair, picking out a yellow dress with tiny black polka dots in a soft fabric that skims my knees. I pick up my sunglasses and wide-brimmed hat, before heading downstairs.

The heavy scent of potted lemon trees leads me onto a terrace constructed from thick slabs of marble. Vines twist around the colonnades that surround it and palm trees stand in neat rows, with marigolds and blue-green grasses planted at their roots. I find Ed at a table overlooking the glittering blue of the lake, in front of a row of clipped hedges. He is drinking from a cappuccino cup, with a silver tea spoon and a glass of orange juice in front of him.

"Morning," he smiles sleepily, as a waitress arrives to lay out my place setting. She is in her early twenties, with raven hair, plump lips and skin as clear as mountain water. Ed is polite but seems not to notice her beauty, nor the bloom of pleasure on her cheeks when he looks up and thanks her.

I breakfast on miniature sweet buns and cream-filled brioches, on snow-white yogurts topped with juicy pieces of fruit, but he eats nothing. He simply downs his coffee, ignoring the plume of steam from it, as if he hasn't even realised it's scalding.

"I was happy about getting my clothes back but I suspect I won't fit in any of them soon," I say, taking a sip of my americano. "Problem is, I'm not yet at the point at which another one of these pastry things make me feel guilty. There's something about Italy that makes you not feel guilty about anything. You just feel . . . *decadent*."

"I think that's why people love this country," he replies, raising his hand to capture the attention of the waitress. He orders another coffee.

"When did you last come to Italy?"

"Must be five or six years ago," he replies.

"Where did you go?"

"Tuscany."

"Was it nice?"

"Very."

I wonder if we're going to have one of those conversations again, the ones that finish before they've even started. But, after a pause, he continues: "I went to the Palio di Siena. You know the big horse race that runs around the town square?"

"Oh, I remember you telling me about that. It must've been amazing."

"It was. You should go and see it one day."

I take a sip of orange juice and look out to boats dotted on the water, before my eyes are diverted by a tiny house martin hopping along the cast-iron railing.

"I've been thinking about the next stage in your hunt for Stefano," he says.

"Oh?"

"Couldn't we just get the Italian PI to go and find him for you?"

"It would cost a fortune."

"Then I'll pay it."

I pull a face. "Absolutely not. You have already put me up in a *palace* and I refuse to allow you to spend any more money on me. And, on top of all that . . . I think I'm changing my mind about this whole thing."

"Surely not after you've come all this way?"

I don't answer. The fact is I don't know what I want.

"Well, I had another idea anyway," he continues. "That picture from the magazine that she sent you. The caption says it was taken in Torri Del Benaco."

"So?"

"I looked it up this morning. It's only a boat ride away. It wouldn't do any harm to go and check out that bar."

The ferry takes longer than it looked like it would on the map. This is partly due to the sheer scale of this great lake and its multitude of ports, each with its own captivating features: medieval castles, citrus groves, rocky cliffs mossed with greenery. Our boat pulls into each quayside in the most leisurely fashion, refusing to be rushed as visitors empty out and others climb on, carrying cold drinks and smelling of sun cream.

It's possible, of course, that my perception of time is distorted by my anxiety. The thought of getting warmer on the trail of Stefano seems to bubble under my skin, even if I know logically that that picture in the magazine is nearly a year old, that he was merely a guest at a bar, nursing a glass of wine in the sun like scores of others before and since. There's no way anyone will remember him now. This will be another dead end, I'm sure of it.

Despite this, simply knowing what the young man pictured with my mother thirty-three years ago now looks like adds a new level of reality to this endeavour. Imaginary scenarios jostle in my mind, of bumping into Stefano in the cobbled streets of Torri. Of a dramatic family reunion that I absolutely don't want.

The idea nudges my thoughts to Dad, the man who'll always be my father, no matter what. As the ferry approaches a new harbour, I look at my phone and realise that the signal is strong enough to text him. The town, Garda, is at the foot of a mountain that is thick with vegetation and rises above a string of pastel-painted buildings. Our boat hugs the pale bricks of the old quay and I compose a message:

Hi Dad, all okay there? Hope my flat is still in one piece? x

It doesn't say much because it can't. I'm too concerned about giving away where I really am.

He responds within a few minutes, before the boat departs.

All fine here. Post picked up, plants watered and still alive (promise). How is Portugal? I've been looking on Facebook for some pictures but you haven't posted any. Dad x

He and everyone else are still under the impression I'm on a singles holiday. God knows what he'd think if he knew the truth. I turn to take a selfie that captures a corner of water, which is blue enough under the cornflower sky to pass for the Mediterranean.

"Let me take one for you," Ed offers. He has a better phone than me, a new device capable of far superior pictures than mine. He clicks on it and shows it to me for approval.

"Much better," I say. He texts it to me and, when it lands in my phone, I forward it to Dad, with a vague update about the weather and nice food, plus a note of thanks for looking after my plants. Then the engine shudders and our ferry purrs away. I take off my hat, close my eyes and let the breeze whisper against my hair.

"Everything all right?" Ed asks.

When my eyelids lift, I find him looking at me. Something about the way his gaze settles on my skin makes my heart flare in my chest. "I'm fine." I look at the timetable. "I think the next stop is ours."

Torri Del Benaco is a town of concentrated beauty. The dominating feature is a Roman castle that rises above the clear water, dotted with yachts and painted rowing boats. We follow the crowd off the ferry past a shock of pink oleander trees that lace through the streets, passing a medieval church with frescoed walls and a lemon garden.

"Where are we going to start?" I ask as we emerge next to a series of buildings with terracotta facades and wrought-iron balconies.

If we were following a trail of clues on a TV show, I'd have a friend who conveniently worked in the police, who'd be able to tap a few numbers into a computer and a mug shot or address would appear. But I'm not an expert in surveillance. I'm not a private investigator. And where Ged McKenzie and Virginia Boldrini led me suddenly wasn't nearly close enough.

"Let's look at your cutting again," Ed says, as I click on my phone photos and hand it to him. "We can just ask a couple of people, see if anyone knows where this place is."

"Really?" I feel self-conscious at the idea.

"Yes, we just need to bypass the holidaymakers and go for people who live here. You can spot the tourists a mile off."

The first guy he stops is from Munich. Then he hones in on a man in his thirties with slightly receding

150

hair and high cheekbones, striding purposefully across the square with a box of fruit hooked under his tattooed arms.

"*Scusi?*"

They talk for a minute or so, before the man disappears across the square. "It's back by the harbour," Ed says.

"It can't be. We walked along it when we got off the boat and nowhere looked like the place in the picture."

"Well, he was a local and he was certain."

"But . . ."

But Ed is already on his way down a narrow side street. He turns a corner and I follow him until we reach the harbour, retracing our steps along the neat slate cobbles, past the colonnades of the Gardesana hotel and the tiny pink flowers that tumble over its balcony.

We pass each of the adjacent cafes and bars slowly, scrutinising elements of every building, the facades painted in soft shades of yellow and red, the creamy parasols shading tables from the sun, the striped canopies and creeping vines that sweep across the walls. Eventually, Ed draws to a stop.

"It's here."

I lift up my sunglasses, shielding my eyes from the sun to get a better look.

"Imagine it without the canopies and a different paintjob. Look at the window frames." He's right. It's had a refurbishment but this is the place.

★ ★ ★

We find a table on the edge of a large al fresco dining area, shaded from the fierce sun under a series of vast canvases. It's busy, and the service brisk and friendly, as visitors and locals alike take refuge in the shade with a strong coffee or a cold glass of Moretti. The waiter who arrives to take our order is older than most of the others, with a compact moustache and a head buried under black hair, flecked with grey.

"*Un'informazione per cortesia: stiamo cercando uno degli uomini in questa foto,*" Ed says, holding out the picture on my phone. "*Sa per caso come possiamo rintracciarli?*"

He leans in briefly and looks blankly at the image. They talk in Italian for a few moments, before he disappears into the bar.

"What did he say?" I ask.

"He asked if we wanted ice with our Cokes," Ed replies. I roll my eyes. "He also said he didn't have a clue what the event was or who any of the people were."

"Did he have a clue about anything?"

"No."

I sigh. "Well, I didn't hold out much hope."

The drinks arrive and as I take a sip I feel someone looking at me from the adjacent table. There are eight or so people deep in animated conversation, but it's an infant boy of about eighteen months, perched on his mother's knee, who is gazing at me with wide hazelnut eyes, apparently mesmerised.

I smile automatically and his face breaks into delighted laughter, displaying a set of tiny pearly teeth.

He claps his chubby palms together and I mouth: "*Ciao!*" before nudging Ed. "Look at this little guy."

But Ed is already smiling. "You're really great with kids, Allie."

"It's my immature streak."

He chuckles. "Yes, that'll be it." Then, after a momentary pause he adds, "You'd make a great mum, you know."

I glance up.

"Well, I'm hardly in a position to even contemplate that at the moment," I reply, but to my surprise the thought spreads through my chest like a warm drink.

He's about to say something else, when another waiter appears, thinner and younger than the first one. "My father said you asked about one of our events. We don't have many but when we do, I coordinate them. Can I help?"

"Perhaps you can," I say, taking the opportunity to have a conversation of my own with an English speaker. I pick up the phone from the table and show him the picture. "We're trying to find this man. He's an old friend of a woman whose family I represent. Do you remember anything about the party — or him?"

"That was at an event to try and launch a new wine festival. The attendees were mainly merchants from different vineyards. I never had a copy of the guest list and I do know that he wasn't the person who booked the event."

"Can you put me in touch with who did?"

He hesitates. "I'm not sure. I'll . . . see what I can do," he says vaguely.

He walks away and we finish our drinks, unsure of whether the waiter is planning to help us or not. A few minutes later, Ed is waving to the little boy when the waiter returns to give us our change on a plate.

"No, you can keep it," Ed says, offering him a tip.

"*Grazie*," he replies, taking the money. Then he pushes the plate towards me again, before disappearing to attend to another couple. I realise he's left a business card on it, which I pick up and turn over. There, in scrawled handwriting, is a name and address.

CHAPTER
TWENTY-SEVEN

Seeing that little boy with his mum and their extended family makes me wonder about how my dad managed by himself sometimes. Life can't be easy for any single parent, but particularly a grieving one, still empty from loss and forced to take on the role of both mother and father.

He was out of his depth for a while. All the packed lunches, the school assemblies, the dress-up days, the PE kits, the sleepovers . . . he was a modern enough man, but I suspect it would've been Mum who'd taken the reins on such matters had things panned out differently.

Two years after she'd died, despite his valiant efforts to organise home and work life smoothly, on the afternoons when he was on a day shift, I was always the last to be picked up from after-school club. He'd arrive out of breath, his hair still wet having hastily showered away whatever carcinogens, chemicals, blood or bed bugs he'd had to deal with.

I remember one evening when Mrs Edwards, the after-school teacher, looked at her watch and said through pursed lips: "Five thirty-four p.m. We're not allowed on the premises after five-thirty. Our insurers won't have it." Then she told him he had to pay an additional charge to cover the cost of her staying behind late.

He rustled in his pocket and pulled out a couple of pounds, before handing it over and saying: "Thanks a million, Mrs Edwards. There was a big chemical spill off the M6, quite nasty. I won't bore you with the details."

Mrs Edwards didn't want the details, she just wanted the two pounds.

"Thank you, Mr Culpepper," she said snippily, and he clearly decided not to correct her that he and I had different surnames.

When we stepped outside, he gave me the biggest hug, as if having his arms around me was the best thing to have happened to him all day. He gave me a piggy back and we galloped to the car, where I sat next to him in the front.

"Why isn't my last name Hudson, the same as yours?"

"Because your mum and I hadn't married by the time you were born," he said, starting the ignition. "After she'd done all the hard work of carrying you round in her tummy, we thought it only fair that you took her surname, not mine. Besides, Culpepper is a very pretty name, isn't it?"

"But it's not fair because Grandma and Granddad are both called Culpepper and so am I and that means you're all on your own with nobody else to share your name with."

"I don't mind. Besides, Grandma wasn't always called Culpepper. She was Smith before she married Granddad."

Then I remembered something. "Oh! I got a lunchtime detention today."

"What? Why?"

"We had music and my recorder wasn't in my bag."

He winced. "Oh . . . sorry, sweetheart. I forgot. You should've told your teacher it was my fault."

"He wouldn't have believed me. I sat at the back behind Debbie Johnson and played my blue felt tip with my fingers instead, but Mr Jones spotted me and told me I was insolent."

He frowned. "That's a bit uncalled for."

I liked the sound of this. "I thought so. Why don't you go in and get him sacked?"

He laughed. "I'll just send in a note apologising about the recorder." He glanced at me. "Why have you taken your braids out?"

"Oh . . . they fell out when I did PE so I thought I'd tie it in a ponytail."

This was a lie. In fact, I'd taken them out as soon as he'd dropped me off that morning, to avoid another humiliating day as *the girl with the worst hairstyle in school*. Dad had been practising braids for two years and still hadn't mastered it. But I wasn't going to hurt his feelings. And I hoped he'd improve, like he did when it came to painting my toenails with Mum's polish. My feet looked like they'd been mauled by a dog the first time he had a go, but he'd greatly improved recently.

"That's a shame. They were really good this morning, too."

"Hmm," I said, wanting to change the subject. "Oh, you need to sign the letter saying I can go on the end of term museum trip. And provide one pound fifty for the coach. We're also allowed a healthy snack — Peperami aren't allowed so Mrs Hastings says you're not to send me in with one again."

He sighed.

"Also, they need helpers to accompany the children on the coach — can you do it?"

"I can't, sweetheart. I can't move my shift."

"Oh yes." I looked out of the window. "Dad?"

"Yes?"

"Can you buy me some bigger gym knickers? Every time I do a cartwheel my legs turn blue."

"Yes, I'll do that."

"Also, can you cut my sandwiches in the shape of roses tomorrow?"

"What?"

"Madeleine Brown's mum makes her packed lunch sandwiches in the shape of flowers. Some days she has daffodils, other days she has roses."

"I'm not sure I'm as artistic as Madeleine Brown's mum."

I thought about this. "Could you manage a boat?"

"Probably not."

"Stars? Teddy bears?"

"How about triangles?" he offered.

158

"Great!" Then I frowned. "But I have triangles already."

He sighed.

"Dad?"

"Yes?"

"I love you."

He glanced over and ruffled my head. "I love you too. Shall we get fish and chips on the way home?"

Fish and chip nights — when Dad hadn't had time to go to the supermarket — were my favourite. They summed up everything about our messy, wonderful existence. We'd arrive back home an hour after the central heating timer had kicked in and would snuggle up on the sofa next to each other before unwrapping the paper, unleashing the mouth-watering smell of vinegar and salt. When we'd finished, he'd pick up his guitar and play a song that I only discovered years later was "Ain't No Sunshine" by Bill Withers. He didn't sing and, in those days, I didn't know the lyrics to that aching, melancholy tune. I just knew that I loved the way Dad's fingers gently picked at the strings, filling the space around us with music while the rain pummelled the windows outside.

It was only later on, as I got a bit older, that I became aware that Dad hardly ever went out anymore, not for fun anyway. When Mum had been alive they were always at concerts together; she'd loved music and, according to Grandma Peggy, had had a vast and precious collection of records, which burgeoned after she got a Saturday job in a chemist and spent all her money on everything from Prince's first album to The Cure's *Seventeen Seconds*. She and Dad had seen dozens of bands live — The Smiths, Erasure, Transvision Vamp — and, in between those concerts, simply had lots of friends who they'd go to the pub with; Sally and Tim from over the road, Uncle Peter and Aunt Sara.

Grandma Peggy still looked after me every so often so Dad could go out, but it was nothing like as much as before as they'd largely socialised with other couples. Grandma said it wasn't as enjoyable for Dad anymore. Besides he preferred to spend the money on paying the mortgage and saving up for our holidays.

He did occasionally see his friends Steve and Mark, with whom he'd previously spent each Friday night when he was off duty playing cards and drinking beer at the pub down our road. Every couple of months or so, they would arrive carrying plastic Thresher's bags filled with lager cans and a Yorkie bar for me.

I liked those nights, even though they kept me awake because they were always shouting at the football on the TV. Although they would never swear in my presence, as soon as I got upstairs they'd start using all kinds of words that I knew Grandma would call "choice language", while Dad tried to tell them to shush so I couldn't hear. But I could hear — and expanded my vocabulary quite significantly during those nights. Mainly though, I liked those Friday evenings because it put Dad in a good mood for days afterwards, as if he'd remembered what it was like to be the real him.

It took until the age of nine though before I really became aware of how little back-up he had. Whenever he was sick — just a cold or whatever — there was nobody to take over. Parents work in a tag team, stepping in when the other can't. But in Dad's case there was just him and my grandparents. Grandma Peggy was always keen to help, leaping in at a moment's notice. But she had other things on her plate, not least the fact that my great-grandma — her mum — was in a nursing home slowly dying of Alzheimer's and she would visit most days after work. And Dad only ever conceded when he was desperate, as if doing so made him less of a parent.

It was at about that time when he sat me down gently and asked if I knew anything about the Facts of Life.

"Yes, I know *everything*," I replied confidently. He looked alarmed.

"Okay," he swallowed. "Well, would you like to start by telling me . . . *everything*? Then I can fill in any gaps."

"Okay. Well, the largest land-based mammals on earth are elephants."

"What?"

"Also, unlike humans, cows and horses sleep while standing up."

"I don't think that's quite —"

"The Amazon rainforest produces half the world's oxygen supply."

"Allie, when I said the facts of life, that wasn't really what I meant."

"Why? They're all true. I'll show you my *Amazing Science Facts* book if you like."

But it wasn't just the touchy-feely stuff for which he had to step up. There was one incident I recall when the PE teacher, Mrs Benson, thought I'd broken my jaw after Louise Watson had done a handspring without checking the vicinity for other pupils. Her foot clipped me on the mouth and the resulting blood loss made Serena Ahmed pass out.

There was a lot of fuss and they called and called Dad at work, but couldn't reach him so they had to leave a message while Mrs Benson drove me to hospital. We arrived at the reception desk at exactly the same time as Dad, looking even more flustered than he did on the after-school club nights. Mrs Benson was midway through explaining the situation when the receptionist looked at Dad.

"Are you the father?" she asked.

Dad was in such a state that he couldn't even answer the question. "Sorry?"

"I was just asking you to confirm that you are the father?" the receptionist answered.

"Oh. Sorry." Then we all waited for Dad to actually answer the question but he didn't say anything.

"Yes, he is," Mrs Benson finally replied and put us all out of our misery.

CHAPTER
TWENTY-EIGHT

We stroll along the neat cobbles of the promenade towards a clutch of fishing boats tied up at the edge of the water, as I look up the address given to us by the waiter on my phone. Ed pauses to take in the view of the castle, a behemoth of a construction that demands to be looked at, with its honey-coloured medieval ramparts and brooding, mountainous backdrop.

"It's a few miles outside Verona," I tell him, as I search for the best way to get there. It turns out not to be a straightforward journey. "We'd have to find the station here, to get a train to Peschiera. From there, we'd travel to Verona, then it's quite a long walk to the house itself."

Ed appears to be deep in thought, his eyes fixed on the chestnut trees on the horizon. "Let's look for a taxi," he says.

We make our way through the town, navigating narrow streets with crumbling pastel walls and balconies that tumble with flowers. We find a cab on the outskirts, and settle in to the back seat, taking quiet refuge from the heat. The car winds up a series of gently rising hills, towards the main road and it's when we are half an hour away that my phone rings. I reach into my bag and, when I see Julia's number, silence the handset and slip it back in. "Just Petra, probably wanting to fill me in on the gossip at work."

He looks out of the window as the driver turns into a dusty road, and I text Julia back:

With Ed. I'll phone soon. x

A message lands shortly afterwards:

Is everything okay? How is he right now? xxx

I bite the skin on the inside of my mouth, feeling increasingly uncomfortable at the idea of discussing him with her. Then I remind myself what she's going through, that she's clearly desperate for some reassurance.

He seems to have perked up a little today x

I feel Ed's eyes on my hands as I tuck the phone back in my bag.

"Tinder," I lie.

He raises an eyebrow. "You're choosing *now* to check out the local talent?"

"There was just someone there who seemed nice. Quite a catch actually."

164

He fixes his eyes on the road. "Now I know you're lying."

When the driver's sat nav says we're less than half a mile away from our destination, I spot a sign for a shopping centre. I unscrew my bottle of water and down the final third of it. "Could we pull in here to get something to drink?" I ask. "We've run out."

Ed leans in to talk to the driver, who flicks on his indicator. "I'll get us some," he tells me. "You wait here."

He steps out of the car and, as he walks away, I dial Julia's number. She answers after a single ring.

"Allie, thank you so much for phoning. I can't stop thinking about you both."

"It's fine, Julia. The least I can do."

"You said he was a little brighter today?"

"Kind of. A little up and down, really. One minute he's his old self, the next he's a bit quiet."

"That's been building up for weeks. I know how difficult it is to deal with, Allie. You're a real saint."

"I've got a long way to go to sainthood, Julia."

She makes a "hmm" noise, halfway between a smile and a murmur. "Have you visited many places? I love Northern Italy. We used to go there when I was a child."

"We went to a place called Torri del Benaco today."

"Oh, beautiful," she sighs. "I bet he loved it. I so wish I could've been there with him myself." An uncomfortable silence hangs between us, until her gentle sobs become audible.

"I'm so sorry, Julia," is all I can think to say.

She sniffs. "Thank you, Allie. Has he talked to you about what caused this yet?"

"Not . . . really, to be honest."

"So, he hasn't told you about what has been happening between him and me?"

"Julia, that's *your* business," I tell her. "Ed and I are close but I'd never intrude on what goes on in your marriage and he'd never be anything other than discreet."

"Okay," she replies quietly. There's something about the way she says it, as if all hope is lost, that makes an urge to comfort her swell up inside me.

"So you know, Julia . . . I've made it clear to Ed that if he's not careful he's going to throw away the best thing that's happened to him."

"Thank you, Allie. I mean that. We've had our ups and downs. We've both said and done things we regret. But, no matter what's he's done . . . I still love him. I can't help myself."

CHAPTER
TWENTY-NINE

The address on the business card takes us to an uninspiring neighbourhood on the edge of Verona. I realise that this is probably an unfair assessment; virtually anywhere would look uninspiring compared with the Villa Cortine Palace Hotel. We make our way through the car park of a boxy apartment block with balconies overlooking a sparse but well-kept garden, and find ourselves at a faded green door shaded by a plastic canopy.

My heart feels tight in my chest as Ed knocks on the door and a woman answers. She's in her late fifties, dressed in a pencil skirt, cardigan and orange flats, with a waved bob that frames her face.

"*Posso aiutarti?*" she asks.

Ed shows her the picture and begins to talk. I follow little of the actual conversation, but her body language shifts enough through the course of it to make me realise that the photograph means something to her. Eventually she opens the door and with a convivial smile, invites us in.

I glance at Ed. "Stefano is a friend of her husband's," he tells me, following her inside. But he pauses at the threshold and adds quietly: "She's asked me twice about why we're tracking him down, whether Christine has left him some money. What would you like me to say?"

With a bolt of anxiety, I fix my eyes on him. "Just say . . . at this point we, um . . . can't divulge that. Really, it's not about the money. I'm sure when he hears her name, he'll be wondering what had happened to her. That's why they're so keen to find him. That and other reasons."

Ed's brow wrinkles at this trail of nonsense and it's clear he won't be bothering to translate it. The woman invites us to take a seat on one of two small sofas arranged around a coffee table. The room is tightly packed with furniture and a sewing machine sits in the corner, surrounded by a mountain of fabric.

"*Mia figlia si sposa tra quattro mesi,*" she says, before settling her gaze on me and delivering a long and detailed story in Italian, none of which I understand.

"She's making her daughter's wedding dress," Ed explains.

"Ah, wonderful! *Bello!*"

"*Complimenti,*" he adds.

For half an hour, Ed translates and our host talks and talks, furnishing us with a glut of information for which we don't even have to ask. Stefano, she says, has been friends with her husband Gino since they worked together at an award-winning seventy-acre vineyard, La

Cavalletta, producing wine from Lugana grapes. Gino was a logistics coordinator until he retired early last year with ambitious plans to start up a wine festival in his spare time. Sadly, it didn't work out. Her until now congenial expression changes as she launches into a tale of betrayal, back-stabbing and financial ruin for which she blames several individuals, judging by her liberal hand gestures and repeated use of the word "*bastardo*".

Ed gently guides her away from this tangent by asking her how often Gino sees Stefano. She says that they get together infrequently these days, but Stefano always makes time to visit Gino when he's in the area. She vaguely remembers him saying he was half-British, but can shed no more light on his time in Liverpool.

"*È una brava persona,*" she concludes.

"He's a good man," Ed translates.

"Is she saying that Stefano doesn't work at the vineyard any longer?" I ask.

Ed puts the question to her and she shakes her head, but as she begins to reply, she is interrupted by the crank of a key in the door.

"Ah, Gino!" She stands up to greet her husband, before starting to make some introductions.

Gino steps forward silently, his eyes fixed on Ed as she continues talking, explaining who we are. He offers an unsure hand for Ed to shake, but when his wife mentions Stefano's name, the curiosity knitted on his brow darkens into something else. He pulls away his hand and turns to his wife furiously: "*Cosa diavolo ti viene in mente di parlare alla gente di Stefano? Non ti rendi conto di cos'hai fatto?*"

169

I can follow none of the ensuing conversation as it billows up like a mushroom cloud into a full-blown argument. But we stand in silent, redundant astonishment, as Gino yells at his wife and she yells back, until Ed finally tries to interject, to protest strongly to something. Gino does not want to know. He simply opens the door, ordering us both out.

"He thinks we're up to no good," Ed explains as we shuffle outside.

I spin round and try to explain, but the door closes in my face while the muffled sounds of marital discord vibrate through the windows.

My first instinct is to get out of there as fast as we can so I quickly make my way back to the road. But as we turn the corner into the street, something makes my legs slow.

"We're getting nowhere fast here," I say, more to myself than Ed. I sit down on a low, concrete wall as heat rises from the tarmac on the road and my eyes blur onto the dusty bonnet of a Fiat Panda. The thought of returning to the UK with no more answers than those with which I arrived lies heavy in my stomach. "Maybe I need to be braver."

"What do you mean?"

"I mean . . . they *know* Stefano. They know him personally and are in touch with him. Getting hold of a current address clearly isn't going to be easy, so perhaps the only way I'm ever going to resolve this whole thing is by trying to make contact, either through this couple or the letting agency."

"They didn't seem too inclined to help," he points out.

"No," I murmur. "But I can't bear leaving them with the conclusion that we're just a pair of charlatans. Have you got a pen?"

I take a notepad out of my bag and tear out a page. Then I pass it to Ed and ask him to write a message in Italian for me:

"Hello, I am sorry for the misunderstanding earlier, but our search for Stefano McCourt is for entirely honourable reasons. I am from the UK, representing the family of an old friend of his called Christine Culpepper. If you are in touch with him, I'd be very grateful if you could please pass on my email address." I hesitate. "And . . . also my phone number. Thanks, Allie."

"Sounds a bit informal. No surname?" Ed asks.

"I don't want them to know I'm Christine's daughter. Not yet."

While Ed orders a taxi on his phone, I return to the apartment. My footsteps are rapid and so is the fluttering inside my ribcage, but I'm relieved to arrive at the door and find it in silence. I bend down and place the note on the floor, pushing it under the threshold. But before it disappears completely I pause and breathe. Then I nudge it inside, far enough that there's absolutely no going back.

CHAPTER
THIRTY

In our final year at school, Ed and I had to apply for university. My first choice was Physiology at Cardiff, at their highly regarded department, which is ranked in the UK top ten. I'd fallen in love with the place at an open day during the summer, when I'd struck up conversation with a research associate in their neuroscience division and walked away feeling an almost magnetic pull back.

In the meantime, Ed's mum and dad had been contacted by the head teacher, who arranged a meeting at their home. He felt strongly that Ed should sit the entrance exam at Oxford, to study physics, and he wanted their full support. If he got in, he'd be the first boy in the history of the school to go.

I couldn't help but imagine my own dad's elation if we'd found ourselves in a situation like that. His fierce determination to grasp every opportunity possible for me was partly instinct, but partly the fulfilment of my mother's wishes. She'd never measured her own life as a series of stunted opportunities, but the twists and turns of history had snatched a great deal from her and she'd been determined to ensure the same would not happen to me. As a girl, she'd been bright, ambitious and focused. She'd wanted to be a journalist and would no doubt have ended up at university if she hadn't fallen pregnant in her final year of A levels.

"She loved how clever you were," Dad once told me. "The fact that you always had your head in a book and could count before all the other kids at playgroup. She wanted to give you the world. When she knew she wouldn't be around to do so, she made it clear that it was up to me."

Ed's mum and dad would have wanted to give him the world too. But a parent's means don't always match their hopes, no matter how fiercely held. And I always suspected money might be an issue for them.

My own dad had been squirrelling away a small amount of cash for me each month for years and the fact that he was a single father on a firefighter's income meant that I was eligible for a small grant. While anyone could see that Ed's family weren't rich, the fact that they weren't so poor that they all starved wouldn't go in his favour if he applied for financial help. Their combined family income fell just above the threshold required, so his only option was a loan, for a sum quite simply beyond his parents' comprehension.

I don't know how I knew all this, because Ed and I never openly discussed this indelicate subject. I just did. I knew it from years of being in his house, lying on his bed studying, or sitting in the living room while his mum gave me a manicure. The signs were all there in his sisters' complaints that they needed new shoes. In the growing patch of damp in the hallway that had never been addressed. Or the raised voices after his mum returned from the supermarket empty-handed, her card having been declined.

Still, he submitted his application, took the exam and went for an interview. I thought about him all day while he was there, stepping inside the privileged realm of those dreaming spires, centuries' worth of learning and excellence. I hoped and prayed with every cell of my being that he'd get in.

"How did it go? What's Oxford like? Is it like being in *Inspector Morse*?" I asked excitedly when he returned.

He breathed in, before exhaling slowly. "It's . . . incredible."

"And?"

"And I'll just have to wait and see what happens."

That October, we found ourselves in the unusual position of attending a lavish Guy Fawkes party, held in the grounds of Belsfield, where Grandma Peggy was a secretary. She hadn't always been employed in a school. Her first job was in the box office of The Empire in Liverpool, which eventually led her to Paris for a short stint, working backstage in theatres there. She'd always been hard-working, hence her drumming up support for that evening, even from those who weren't pupils at Belsfield, such as Ed and me.

The school was set in three sites on opposite sides of an oak-lined road, with a grand gothic building dominated by a large tower and stained-glass windows. A poster at the entrance promised fireworks, dancing and a fairground. There was even a champagne tent for adults and sixth formers with ID.

"I can't believe this has been organised by parents," I said. We stood in the smoky glare of the bonfire, transfixed as it roared and hissed against the night. "Has our school even *got* a PTA?"

"It had one once. It disbanded after a coffee morning when all the attendees caught salmonella from the custard tarts."

I realised he was looking at me.

"What is it?"

"Nothing. You look really pretty tonight. That's all."

There were fireworks later on, a mesmerising display accompanied by the Upper School orchestra's performance of Stravinsky's *Firebird*. As the sky flared with colour, the flicker of the Catherine Wheel was reflected in Ed's eyes and hot blood rushed to my neck. He turned and caught me looking but, instead of asking why, he just smiled and turned back. I could feel a pulse throbbing somewhere deep inside me as a thought pushed itself to the front of my head. For the first time I remember asking myself a question I'd never fully articulated before: did I have feelings for Ed that went beyond friendship? I held my hot chocolate to my lips and wondered if the same thing had ever occurred to him.

"I know what you're thinking." He turned to look at me as the whispers of our breath mingled in the space between us.

"Do you?"

He hesitated, as if something significant was dancing right there on his lips. "Yes. We need to get in the queue for the waltzers before it gets any bigger."

We span in the teacups and fell about, literally, in the house of fun. Ed bought candyfloss that we ate until our fingers stuck together and our stomachs ached. As we headed for the helter skelter, he grabbed me by the hand. I turned around and could see the faint shine of perspiration in his clavicle.

"Maybe I should apply to Cardiff."

My heart jumped. "Instead of Oxford?"

He hesitated, then nodded. For a sweet moment I indulged myself in the fantasy.

"Ed, no. You've got an incredible, unmissable opportunity. Don't blow it. Your parents would never forgive you." I was saying the right words, but wanted him to protest, to stick to his guns. To come with me to Cardiff.

"Maybe it's not about my parents." I felt his fingers tighten around mine and would later think a lot about that subtle application of pressure and the meaning behind it.

"What's it about then?"

"Maybe it's about being away from you," he whispered. "I don't think I'd like it."

I tried to protest again. I knew it was the right thing to do. But instead I heard myself say: "I don't think I'd like it either."

"You both made it then!" Grandma Peggy approached, clutching a strip of raffle tickets and I

176

pulled away from Ed's hand. Her face dropped. "Oh, sorry, did I interrupt?"

"No, not at all!" I protested.

"Not at all," repeated Ed.

But I wondered for a long time afterwards whether she actually had.

I didn't see him for the rest of the weekend. It was Dad's birthday so we'd spent two days in the Lake District, walking up the Old Man of Coniston, where we sat at the top and ate our packed lunch like we used to do when I was little.

"You look deep in thought," Dad said.

"Sorry, miles away," I shook my head. "I was taking in the view, that's all."

I unwrapped the cling film from my cheese sandwich. "I never did manage to make them into the shape of a rose," he said.

"What?"

"You used to want me to make sandwiches in the shape of flowers for your packed lunches when you were little."

I laughed. "What a brat."

"You were lovely," he protested, as I rolled my eyes and my thoughts turned to Ed again. There had never been any suggestion that our relationship wasn't simply platonic. But, as we both hurtled towards a future in separate universities — separate cities — I wondered if something beyond friendship was crystallising between us. I was starting to miss him before I'd even gone. He seemed to feel the same.

"How did you know you were in love with Mum?" I asked and Dad lowered his sandwich as he thought about the question.

"Because she was the first person I'd think about when I woke up in the morning and the last person I'd think about when I closed my eyes to go to sleep. And I don't just mean at the beginning, when things were exciting and we'd never had anything to test us. It never changed." He glanced at me briefly then lowered his eyes and said: "It still hasn't."

When I went into school on Monday I felt as though someone had tied a ribbon around my chest and was pulling it in tightly. Selfishly, I wanted Ed to repeat what he'd said in the radiating heat of the bonfire: that he would come to Cardiff with me. But when I sat next to him on the bus that evening, he was quiet. I dared to think that perhaps this meant something.

"My dad's thinking of retiring," he said finally.

"Oh, really? Cool. He's quite young though."

"Yeah. His knees are giving him trouble."

"Is he going to sell the business?"

He looked out of the window. "I'm not sure. He doesn't want to, after the years it's taken him to build it up."

I was about to ask more, when he started talking about some political debate he'd seen on TV, followed by an album he'd heard was good. I didn't think any more about the conversation and its implications until the following year, long after Ed received conditional offers from several universities, including Cardiff and

Oxford. The latter had been so impressed with his interview that their conditions were unusually generous. He could've achieved the grades they wanted in his sleep.

But as green shoots appeared in the ground and the creep of spring took us closer to exam time, I started to feel an odd and uncomfortable disconnection from him. He no longer wanted to revise together and was non-committal when I talked about what university life was going to be like. Then each paper came and went and when I asked how he felt he'd done, his response was the same every time: "I can only do my best."

We travelled to school together on the morning our results were released. I remember walking up to the gates on a cool Thursday in August, as grey clouds scudded across the sky in defiance of summer. Envelopes containing our marks were waiting in the head's office.

"You go first," he said and I swallowed and opened up the envelope to find I'd got two As and a B. I was furious with myself about the B, but at least it was enough to get onto my course.

"Well done, Einstein."

"Go on then," I replied, nodding at his envelope.

He ran his finger along the top and took out the thin white paper. He read it with an inscrutable expression, before lowering it and closing his eyes in despair.

"Didn't you get what you wanted?"

He handed it to me silently and I read it out. "Three As and a B. Ed, *YOU'RE IN!*"

I went to hug him, but his body was stiff and unreceptive. I felt his breath in my hair and smelled the washing powder on his shirt, as I pulled back to see the impossible sadness in his eyes.

"What's the matter? They're brilliant marks. And *you can go to Oxford!*"

"I'm not going to Oxford, Allie," he replied.

My heart swelled in my chest. "You're coming to Cardiff instead?"

He shook his head. "I'm going to take over my dad's business."

I didn't feel my jaw lower but became aware suddenly that my mouth was hanging open. I was appalled.

"But that's . . . *mad*. You can't do that, Ed. You've got the chance to go to *Oxford University*. Not some poxy college. Whose idea was this?"

"Mine," he fired back, as if I'd implied something terrible by even asking.

"And your parents think this is a good idea?"

"They want to support whatever decision I want to make," he replied defiantly. "And I've already told them that this is what I want."

"Well, I'm sorry, but I *just don't get it*. I know it's expensive and —"

"It's insane, Allie," he interrupted furiously. "The money I'd need is insane."

"I know it'd be a struggle. But you'd get a job afterwards. You could pay back the loan. Ed, *you could do this*."

His jaw tightened and it crossed my mind momentarily that it must have been his dad's idea, but I dismissed that as quickly as I'd thought it. If Ed had told them how much he'd wanted to go, his mum and dad would've done everything within their power to make it happen, even if it meant selling the house and living in a squat.

But he wasn't going to let them do that. He'd made his decision and he'd wanted my support and reassurance that he was doing the right thing. But I'm afraid I couldn't give it to him.

CHAPTER
THIRTY-ONE

I meet Ed for dinner outside as the light casts a golden filter on the cypress trees and pines that stretch to the lake. I spot him at a table, gazing at his phone and wonder if it's Julia, though she's already texted him a few times today. He looks up and clicks off as I approach. We take an *aperitivo*, while the sky fades to black and stars hang above the water like dewdrops.

He seems looser tonight and, when we eat, he savours it. The food is just the right side of fancy, gourmet dishes made with simple ingredients: ribbons of fresh pasta and grilled lake fish, followed by *piccola pasticceria* that frankly isn't all that *piccola*.

"I feel like we've hit a brick wall on the Stefano trail," I tell him.

"I don't know about that," he says. "We could go and take a look at Peschiera."

"Why, what's there?"

"The bakery Stefano's mother used to run. That's what her neighbour said, wasn't it?"

"She also said she'd left years ago. I can't see that helping."

His eyes soften on me. "Okay. I understand."

"What do you mean, 'you understand'?"

"It's fine," he replies.

"*What's* fine?"

"It's fine if you're having second thoughts about doing this."

"I'm not saying I'm having second thoughts . . ." I sigh. "Oh, look, fine. Let's go to the bakery in Peschiera. I'll never say no to cake. How far away is it exactly — will you Google it?"

He picks up his phone to unlock it, as I peer over his shoulder to look at the screen. And before he can click away, I catch a glimpse of what he'd been looking at when I arrived. It's the picture he took of me, as the sun blazed behind me on the ferry to Torri.

The following morning, we borrow bikes from the hotel and pedal along the shoreline pathway for just over an hour until we reach Peschiera. The little town is dominated by the thick walls of a fortress and a network of canals in which mallards bathe in the silky water and speedboats line up under stone arches. There are two *pasticcerias*, though we have no idea which one Stefano's mother owned, so simply head to the place that came up first on our internet search.

The shop, Dolcezza, is tucked away in a narrow, cobbled street with an elaborate window display, shaded under a red canopy. Elegant chocolates and pastries are arranged in trays, like jewels in a treasure chest. There are tiny domed candies glistening with syrup and strands of caramel and cheesecakes topped with cherries and hazelnuts, or miniature leaves of dark chocolate. We step inside to find rows of hand-made sweets, wrapped in colourful papers.

"*Buon pomeriggio.*"

The woman who greets us is in her early fifties, with a narrow waist, glossy hair swept into a loose bun and huge eyes the colour of chartreuse. If she gorges on the contents of those trays every day, it certainly doesn't look like it.

"Can I help you?" she asks, and I wonder what makes us so easily identifiable as English. It's not as though we're wearing bowler hats or carrying Marks & Spencer carrier bags.

"Um . . . *si.*" I cast my eyes over a tray of cream dessert cups, miniature strawberry tarts and sweet cannoli oozing with lemon ricotta. I eventually point to some choux pastries and little biscuits, which she places in a pretty patterned box and begins to tie it up with ribbon.

Ed gives me a meaningful look, as if to imply I'm procrastinating. I look away, refusing to acknowledge that he's right.

"*Vorremmo anche dei dolci, ma c'é qualcos'altro con cui ci potrebbe aiutare,*" Ed says.

I hang back while he talks, pretending to browse as I gradually become aware that she is responding positively. She disappears into the back of the shop and returns with another woman who introduces herself as Ava, the owner. Her age is difficult to place. I'd guess

184

mid-seventies, though her honeyed, voluptuous skin could be that of a much younger woman.

"Allie, have you got a minute?" Ed says, beckoning me forward as he addresses her again and I nod and smile in that slightly excruciating way I tend to when I haven't a clue what anyone is saying, beyond the names Christine Culpepper and Stefano McCourt.

"Sadly, Vittoria passed away three years ago," Ava tells us. Her English is broken but significantly better than my Italian. "She was my business partner until she got sick. Cancer. So very sad. But I haven't seen Stefano since the funeral. *Mi displace* — sorry."

"Oh, I see," I say. "He moved away soon after I believe?"

The lines etched above her nose deepen. "I have recollection . . . that he went to live somewhere at the coast with his father, Michael. I expect his mother death must be hard, and for Michael too. Stefano was very close to her. It was probably a good time for a change."

"You knew Stefano well then, before he moved away?" I ask.

"*Ah, si! Almeno* . . . when he was a small boy. Vittoria was a young mother, like me, and she was good company. We would meet at the beach in summer. Stefano was a lovely thing, always happy and full of mischief. Vittoria called him '*il mio angelo*'. He had no brothers or sisters . . . so a little spoilt. But in a nice way."

"Mamma, *ma che gliene importa?*" tuts the younger woman, but Ava ignores her.

185

"Do you know why the family moved to Liverpool when Stefano was nineteen?"

"Liverpool had been his father's, that is Michael's, home as a child. He'd come to Italy to study history at Verona university and it was in his time as a student that he fell in love with Vittoria. For years afterwards, they had ... *discussioni* ... rows about if to stay in Italy or return to UK. She got her own way, until Stefano was grown up and Michael was offered a transfer to a good job in England. Also, his mother — Stefano's Nonna — was still there and was ... um, *malato* ... sick. But, in the end, they only stay for one year. It didn't surprise me Vittoria won!" she laughs. "Though Stefano ... he'd wanted to stay."

"Really? I wonder why he didn't?" If he was nineteen or twenty by then, he was surely mature enough to work and live in the UK if he'd wanted?

"He probably didn't earn enough to be on his own. Plus, was some ... *girlfriend trouble.*" I wait for her to expand on this, but she offers nothing. "Anyway, I wasn't surprised they came back. And she could fulfil her dream to open this place with me. It brought her a lot of joy until she became ill."

Ed decides to cut to the chase. "Do you know where exactly on the coast Stefano lives?"

She shakes she head. "Perhaps Genova, or somewhere close. I don't have Facebook — my daughter says I should. I tell you who will know though — he worked for years in La Cavalletta, the vineyard. His friends and former colleagues are probably still there. I'm sure they'll put you in touch."

CHAPTER
THIRTY-TWO

She'd once heard her mother use the phrase: "A problem shared is a problem halved". But she couldn't recall many examples of that in practice — both her parents kept themselves to themselves and weren't the kind to discuss what went on beyond the teak-panelled door of their 1930s terrace. Her mum would stay behind for tea and Digestives at church on a Sunday — every opportunity to be there was enthusiastically welcomed — but conversation rarely strayed from the dry rot in the belfry or the tremendous job Geoffrey Byrd had made of the reading. It was chat, not talk.

Indeed, the fact that her particular problem had now been unceremoniously shared with her parents did not halve it, quarter it, or make it better in any way. On the contrary, it augmented her shame and revitalised her guilt, which spread through her until it almost began to suffocate her. The delusion that she might magically make this work was now gone. Admittedly, her parents still didn't know the full story. They hadn't a clue who the real father was.

Sometimes she tried to look at her dad, just to catch his eye and see if she could create a moment of connection. But it quickly became apparent that he simply couldn't bring himself to do it. She'd thought at first that things were better with Mum, that the air around her was less oppressive. But one day after her mother had gone into the kitchen to put the tea on, she spotted her leather-bound edition of the *King James Bible* on the arm of the settee, the frayed edges of a bookmark poking out of the top. She idly picked up the book and ran her fingers along the embossed lines of the "B", the dimples of red and gold ink. When she carefully opened the saved page, there at the bottom was a passage neatly underlined in pencil. Hebrews 13:4. "Let the marriage bed be undefiled, for God will judge the sexually immoral and adulterous."

She managed to conceal her shape until fairly late into the pregnancy. Before she reached seven months, anyone could have looked at her and simply concluded she'd been too fond of the biscuit tin. But eventually, she handed in her notice at work, telling everyone vaguely, laughably, that she had another opportunity she couldn't turn down. She withdrew from friends and found refuge in her bedroom, hidden from the world but unable to escape the thoughts that boomed in her head.

Then the day came that she went with her mother on the train, to a place not far from Liverpool, but far enough. Her dad didn't join them, a small mercy for which she was immensely grateful. She hoped her mum

188

was exaggerating when she'd said the stress would've killed him. So, she gazed out of the window at a blur of blond fields and warmed herself with a thought that she could never say out loud. That, despite the impossibility of it all, she loved the child growing inside her, more than she loved herself.

Nightingale House was a Victorian mansion, with white gables around the windows and a large garden at the front filled with sycamore trees. Despite the pretty name and nice grounds, it didn't feel like a welcoming place, although nowhere really did anymore. At least the woman who opened the door had smiled at her. She felt as though nobody had smiled at her lately.

Her time there passed faster than she'd anticipated and she kept busy, like everyone else there, with daily church services, reading and chores. Everything felt easier when she didn't stop to think for too long and, who knew, maybe scrubbing the staircase did have some miraculous capacity to recover her moral standards. She'd have polished the bannister till she could see her face if she'd thought it would work.

Mum came to visit every few days. Sometimes she'd bring egg sandwiches and a home-made gooseberry tart, which had always been her favourite. She liked to think that this meant a small part of her mother had forgiven her. But her favourite thing about those weeks was making the baby box. She wanted to fill it with more than the standard twelve nappies and handful of matinee jackets, although she wasn't a natural when it came to knitting. She'd always considered it old-fashioned and she hadn't the patience. Yet, there was something about crafting those little booties and hats in those final weeks of her pregnancy that soothed her soul.

When one of the other girls gave her a pattern for a pram blanket, she'd known it was trickier than anything she'd attempted before, with scalloped edges and a ring of stars in the centre. She came to be slightly obsessed with it, as if her fitness as a mother was innately connected to the successful completion of this delicate item. The stars were the hardest part; her first few tries resulted in a tangle of knots and she repeatedly ended up unravelling the wool and starting again. But she was determined to finish it, even if it made her fingers bleed.

Her waters broke on an unseasonably cool evening in June, when the sky was thick with clouds and drizzle. She'd been doing the laundry at the time and carried on until the taxi arrived to take her to hospital. She travelled alone. There weren't enough staff on that night to send anyone with her.

The first nurse she encountered there was pretty and young, with a pinched nose and frosty demeanour. "Let's show you to a bed, shall we . . . miss," she said, in a manner that made her immediately hope she wasn't going to be stuck with her for the whole thing. She needn't have worried. The next few hours were spent entirely by herself, while her body ripped in two.

She felt certain she was dying. She had to be. Nothing normal could have felt like this.

But after all the pain and fear, when her baby finally came into the world, bloodied and coated in grease, there was just the two of them. He was absolutely perfect, with a mop of soft, dark hair — the darkest she'd ever seen — and cheeks like velvet when she brushed her fingertips over them. His toes were somehow already miniature versions of hers, but that was the only resemblance she could identify.

She did not place him down in the crib next to her all night. Even when she went to the toilet she took him with her. If she was going to move, he was going too. But most of the time she just stayed in bed, stroking his soft limbs and kissing his new skin. It was heaven.

She called him Christopher. As the other mothers around her were visited by family and friends arriving with presents and flowers, nobody congratulated her. She told herself she didn't care.

His face was so beautiful her insides melted when he clasped his tiny fingers around her hand and suddenly the world made sense for the very first time. And she knew one thing. If this boy was the result of her weakness and her immorality, then she'd have done the same again a hundred times over.

On the day when they were due to leave, she wrapped him in the soft white wool of his blanket of stars and took a fortifying breath. That day, she didn't think about the past, or the future. All she could think about was finally walking out of the ward with the most beautiful baby in the world nestled in her arms. All she had to do first was sign her name on the discharge form and write the date next to it: Peggy Smith. June 29th 1963.

CHAPTER
THIRTY-THREE

Allie

The following morning, as the sun burns in a sky mossed with white clouds, my mind drifts to Grandma Peggy. I dread to think what she'd say if she had any idea I was here, on a hunt for the answers to a mystery she steadfastly refuses to shed any light on. I hate lying to her. I hate lying to anybody. But what am I to do given that she's determined to keep these bewildering secrets about the past hidden in her drawer?

"I phoned La Cavalletta vineyard this morning," Ed says, taking a sip of his hot, fragrant coffee. "Their wine tours are running at this time of year, but they're fully booked today. They've got two spaces tomorrow afternoon though."

"Oh. Okay."

"I assumed you'd want to go?"

"Yes, of course," I say, though the truth remains that my feelings about every step of the search for Stefano are conflicted. "Let's hope our reception there is a little friendlier than our last experience."

Later that morning, we head down the steps that cut into the cliffside and find a couple of loungers on a jetty a little walk along from the hotel. A high sun slants through the branches of the trees, the rocks smooth and blond in the brilliant light. It's so peaceful that the silence hums as a soft breeze drifts in from the water.

While to me it feels like the perfect way to relax after such a busy day yesterday, Ed can't get comfortable. When he's in the shade, he shifts into the sun. When he's in the sun, he's hot and sticky and irritated by the heat. He opens his novel, but quickly abandons it.

"Is the book no good?" I ask.

"I can't really get into it."

I take out some sun cream and hand it to him. "Want some? You don't want to add skin cancer to your problems."

He takes it from me and starts applying the cream like only men do: as if he's de-greasing a pan with a Brillo pad, rubbing it first on his cheeks and then across his forehead, over the long, thin scar above his right eye. He got it when he fell during a half-marathon a few months after his wedding.

"Your running injury has almost completely faded now," I tell him.

"Yeah. Almost."

"You're lucky given the mess it was. How many stitches did you need?"

"Ten or so. It wasn't a big deal. It certainly didn't put me off going for a run."

"Hey, that's an idea," I say. "Why don't we get up early and go for one tomorrow?" I've never experienced anything comparable to what Ed is going through, but I do know whenever I've had a bad day, it helps to get the blood pumping round my body. "What do you think?"

"About what?"

"Going for a run in the morning."

"Yes, okay. Possibly."

"Have you got your running shoes with you?" He doesn't answer at first. It's almost as if the thoughts converging in his head are so distracting that there isn't room for anything else.

"I'm not sure, Allie."

I shuffle further down the lounger and decide to just keep my mouth shut for a while. Then I realise he's looking at me.

"I'll have a swim though," he says, out of nowhere.

"Oh. Okay good."

"Why don't you come in with me?"

I let out a spurt of nervous laughter. "Swimming is not my forte, as you well know."

"You *can* swim though."

"I can paddle."

This is a slight exaggeration. It's not that I can't swim *at all*. Dad repeatedly tried to teach me and we were forced to learn at school, in a pool shallow enough to put your feet down when the teacher wasn't looking. Consequently, the most I ever passed was my ten-metre badge, which I achieved while holding my breath the whole way across. As a result of all this, I have successfully avoided all invitations to pool parties or skinny-dipping sessions, not that there have been many of those.

"Allie, everyone should learn to swim." I don't think for a moment that the preachy tone is serious but his expression is deliberately opaque.

"I'd only need to swim if I went near any water, which I'm not going to."

He laughs. "What if you fell off the side of a ship?"

"I will be very careful not to."

"Well, how about we don't take that chance." At that, he stands up, peels off his T-shirt and offers me his hand.

Ed's hard, muscular physique has softened a little in the couple of days since we got here. It suits him, as does the colour of his skin which, even below his neckline, somehow doesn't look as pale as previously. I follow him along the jetty as a dewdrop of sweat makes its way slowly down my temple. I lower myself onto the edge and dip my toes in the cool water with a shiver. When I glance up at him, my eyes land on the hair on his stomach, at the point where it feathers beneath the waistband of his shorts.

"I'm only going to spectate."

"You said. Sure you can't be tempted?"

"Quite sure."

I shade my eyes from the glare of the sun and crane my neck to see him smiling at me. Then he turns and dives in, generating a rush of white surf and bubbles. I wait for him to reappear, watching as the ripples flatten to a soft undulation. I lean forward to try and see below the water. "Ed?"

196

He emerges from the surface with his elbows aloft, pushing hair out of his face as the burnish of his shoulders glistens in the sunlight.

"What is it?"

"Just wondered what kept you."

He dives away, as arcs of light soar across the sky. I close my eyes briefly, feeling the heat against my lids. But when I become aware of him swimming towards me I flutter them open to find his tanned forearms on the edge of the jetty, his chin resting on top.

"I'd look after you," he says.

A soft thudding inside my chest feels like the wings of a hummingbird. "What do you mean?"

"I mean, if you were to come in the water I'd look after you."

"Oh. No, I don't think so."

"Allie, do you really want to go your whole life without feeling what it's like to swim in a beautiful Italian lake, with the sun beating down on your back?"

"I do if it means staying alive."

"*I'll* make sure you stay alive." Ed's expression has been taut and troubled since we got here, but now a smile spreads across his face like a sunrise.

"Just for a minute, all right? In fact, twenty seconds."

"Twenty seconds it is."

I slip off my sandals and slide my T-shirt over my head, breathing in to flatten the exposed flesh below the blue and white stripes of my bikini top. I shuffle to the edge, gazing anxiously at the water. He holds out his hands.

I'd love to say I glide elegantly into the water, but that would be some way from reality. Instead, I crash on top of him, arms flailing, and, when I feel myself slipping, end up using the top of his head to try and keep myself afloat. I am aware that I am drowning — possibly murdering — my best friend, but that knowledge does nothing to persuade me to deviate from this strategy and I continue thrashing as if beating off a school of piranhas.

"Allie, I've got you." I can feel his breath against my ear, as he holds my waist with one hand and pulls us into the wooden post with the other. "I've got you."

He waits until my grip around his neck loosens, before taking my hand in his and gently guiding me away from the jetty. He slides an arm beneath the bones of my hips, until I can feel the stretch of soft skin under his forearm against my belly. My legs begin to kick instinctively.

"There, that's okay isn't it?" he whispers, almost sleepily. But through my shallow breaths an answer fails to form on my lips. Because this, this whole thing, is so much more and so much less than okay.

It's not simply the absolute knowledge that I am safe, in a situation in which I'd ordinarily feel vulnerable and exposed. Or indeed a feeling that he's the only person ever capable of making me feel like that. It's something else, a series of exquisite observations that pulse into my head like the clicks of a slideshow. Sunburnt lips. Glistening skin. Damp eyelashes. And the colour of the water reflected in his eyes, as if the sole purpose of this

198

entire lake's existence was to converge with them and create the most vivid blue on earth.

We stay in the water for far more than twenty seconds. While I no longer worry about imminent death, there isn't a single moment when I'm at ease. I try to convince myself that I stay for so long merely to appreciate what Ed highlighted: the beautiful Italian lake, the sun on my back.

I want that to be true. But it isn't, not even slightly.

CHAPTER
THIRTY-FOUR

Ed

There are times when Ed is laughing with Allie and he forgets everything except the immediate feeling of release, the lightness in his limbs as he watches her. But when he goes back to the room, he lies alone in the darkness and it all rushes back.

Sometimes "it" amounts to no more than a gritty unease, like grains of sand under his skin. Still, there has been an imperceptible change since he got to Italy, as subtle and sheer as gossamer. The ache in his bones isn't there every morning when he wakes up. He no longer hates the feel of his own body, the way his joints grind when he moves. His stomach does not burn with acid and there have been nights — not all, but some — when he has slept for more than three hours, and woken feeling rested.

The question of why he is now thinking like this is a difficult one to answer. Why does he now have a sliver of the impossible — optimism — running through his veins? He could put the answer down to nostalgia, but that word is hopelessly inadequate to describe the layers of how he feels when he's around Allie.

His mind drifts to Julia. To her exquisite face and clear voice, her intelligence and poise. When did he become immune to those things? The answer is, he hasn't. He still recognises them all and that, whatever has happened, his feelings for her have not switched off like a light.

But it's complicated. Both their relationship and Julia herself. He used to find her mysterious and undiscoverable; when they met he relished the idea of glimpsing the real her. He'd assumed he'd like what he found.

It is impossible to pinpoint a day when things went wrong. When he started to find Julia's wit cruel, not funny. Her moods unpredictable, not enigmatic. Her strength of character merely aggressive and unpleasant. She says she never changed and it's possible that she's right. Maybe it's only him.

Yet, he'd never considered himself the sensitive kind. He used to let the little things slide and not allow anything to get on top of him. He is an optimist. A pragmatist. He is a man with backbone. At least, he used to be. He doesn't know who he is anymore.

So why should it have bothered him when, at her friend's dinner party, his wife clutched his hand under the table and whispered: "Don't eat so fast. It's embarrassing." It was hardly a big thing, yet he was silently mortified at the idea of giving her cause to be ashamed of him. Why should it have prickled under his skin when, on her mother's birthday, she sighed at the expensive handbag he'd bought as a present, and asked:

"I hope you kept the receipt?" Or at the wedding when a fellow guest asked about his business and she leant over and laughed, "You're boring everyone *rigid*, sweetheart."

The trouble was, the insignificant moments that had begun as a handful, soon multiplied to dozens and eventually happened so frequently that he might as well have laid down on his back and attempted to count the stars.

Ed refused to become fixated with them; he was not some delicate flower, wounded because his wife didn't idolise him. So why did he start to feel like a failure, as if his lack of refinement was causing the most dazzling woman he'd ever met to slip through his fingers?

For the first time in his life, his background bothered him. With good reason; Ed discovered a few months ago that Julia's father, a stable, honourable, family man — exactly the kind of man Ed himself wants to be — had repeatedly tried to persuade her *not* to marry him as he'd be the first family member in generations who'd never even been to university.

But there was nothing to be gained in dwelling on this or any other criticisms. And gradually he started to think they might have a point.

CHAPTER
THIRTY-FIVE

Allie

I take my time dressing for dinner, picking out a dark blue dress in a soft fabric that falls off my shoulders, which have deepened in colour since we got here. My phone beeps and I open a text from Ed.

Booked us into a nice restaurant for 8.30.

I type my response:

What's the dress code?

Fancy dress. Tarts and vicars.

I don't own anything tarty.

You're the vicar.

I slip on a pair of wedge sandals that show off the rose gloss on my toes, and give my hair one last spray before heading downstairs. As the last trace of sun glows red on the lake, I find Ed at a small table on a circular balcony made of centuries-old stone that juts out of the rocks. It sits high above the lake, with tall columns covered in lichen and its floor dotted with pots that tumble with white and orange flowers. He looks up from his notebook as I approach and an airy smile appears at his lips.

"You look lovely, Allie Culpepper."

I feel a shot of heat in my cheeks as I pull out the ironwork chair opposite him and lower myself into it, pretending I haven't noticed his eyes settling on my skin. "Thank you."

His phone beeps and he glances at a text, before switching it onto silent. "Jeremy," he explains. "He's holding the fort brilliantly. I know you're not his biggest fan but my timing for this isn't great and he hasn't complained once."

"What about Julia? Have you spoken to her?"

He begins rubbing his thumb into the dry knuckles on his other hand. "We've had a couple of conversations."

I search his face. "Do you want to talk about it?"

His lips part as if we are finally going to do this, but he simply says, "Maybe. But not tonight."

I feel as though I should say something profound here. I want to. But the words jostle for space in my head, then a waiter appears to offer us some drinks and the moment is gone. We stroll down to the town and dine in a lively restaurant on the outskirts of the old quarter, under a canopy of greedy honeysuckle. The food is exquisite, home-made pasta filled with duck, and rack of lamb with creamy green peppers, potatoes and figs. I'm contemplating a coffee, when an elderly Italian couple who've been sitting on an adjacent table pause to say good evening before they leave. I'd guess they were in their eighties and, although her face has lost the glow of youth, she retains a beauty in her smile as she clutches her husband's hand.

"*Siete proprio una coppia perfetta*," she says.

Ed smiles and replies in Italian before she nods and they disappear into the street.

"What did she say?" I ask.

He hesitates. "That it's going to snow tomorrow."

"Very funny."

Most of the shops are still open after dinner and it's still so warm that my sweater is redundant. We head down a narrow street to a busy gelateria, with a long, glass-fronted counter. There must be a hundred flavours of gelato lined up in a kaleidoscope of muted colours — deep berry reds, soft greens and pale lemon, all served using flat metal spades. We are greeted by a handsome man in his mid-twenties, with a smile that suggests he's very aware of his own sex appeal. "*Buonasera, bellezza.* You like a recommendation?"

"Hmm . . . yes, okay."

"Let me see, for you, something sweet. *Sesamo e miele*, sesame and honey. I think you'll like it," he says, and as he holds my gaze it occurs to me that he might be flirting.

"Um, *grazie*," I mutter after he's handed me the ice cream. We step outside into the glow of the street light and Ed shakes his head, half amused, half something

205

else I can't put my finger on. Indignant? "I can't believe that," he says.

"What?"

"Your admirer."

"He was only selling me an ice cream," I shrug.

"He could've kept his tongue in while he was at it. I'm embarrassed for him."

I chuckle into the gelato, before taking a bite, its grainy sweetness cold on my tongue. We start strolling towards the main square before Ed says: "Did you ever regret taking the job in Liverpool after your break-up? Rob was a nice guy."

"No," I reply immediately. "Especially not after I'd found out about what happened at the New Orleans conference."

"God, I'd forgotten about the Argentinian researcher. Rob was a *dick*," he says emphatically, correcting his earlier statement.

I suppress a laugh. "He wasn't *The One* that's for sure."

"So why did you stay with him for so long?"

I think for a moment and try to come up with a satisfactory answer. "Why does any couple stay together when they're not head over heels in love? Because they assume it's enough to appreciate someone's company? Or they don't like change? Honestly, I'm not even sure. It felt like more than habit at the time, but . . . maybe not."

"You did have lots in common too. Work-wise, at least."

"That's very true. It was good to have someone to talk to who actually understood what I did all day."

"Good . . . but not everything?"

"No, not everything," I reply, briefly lifting up my eyes.

He smiles. "It's not easy finding the right person to spend forever with, is it?"

"No, it's not."

"I think as human beings our system can be pretty flawed: if someone ties your stomach up in enough knots, you leap to the conclusion that you're capable of spending the rest of your life with them."

By now we are in the shadow of the fort, where the pools of light from within its turrets cast a pearlescent gleam on the water. We cross the cobblestones until we reach a small stone well in the centre of the square.

"I once asked my dad how he knew he was in love with Mum," I tell him. "He said it was because she was the first person he'd think about when he woke up in the morning and the last person he'd think about when he went to sleep."

"It's definitely part of it, the good part."

I press my hip against the curve of the well. "What's the bad part?"

"When the person you've fallen in love with isn't who you thought they were. Then you discover *you're* not the person you thought you were either."

I swallow. "Well, let's try my dad's test. Is Julia the person you think about before you go to bed?"

"Yes," he replies, without missing a beat. The eruption in my chest is followed by a helpless wave of guilt and the knowledge that it's time for me to step up and do the right thing.

"But the thing is —"

"Ed, listen," I interrupt. "You *have* to go back to her. Not for her sake, but for yours. I don't want to know the details of what happened. I'd never intrude. But all relationships need work, you know that. Some of them aren't worth it. Others are. And what you and Julia have is worth it."

A small pulse appears in the side of his neck. "What makes you think that I didn't just get it wrong?"

"Because I've known you for most of my life, Ed, and you were *so* happy when you met Julia. You were talking about the future, about kids, within weeks of meeting her."

He reaches into his pocket and takes out a coin, handing it to me. "Make a wish," he says, gesturing to the well.

I rub the coin between my fingers and toss it into the water. It plinks onto the surface before sinking into the murk.

"I hope it was something good."

"Lottery win," I joke. He doesn't need me to say that all I really want is proof that the man I call Dad is my father. "Go on, your turn."

He flicks a coin into the water and gazes after it with a frown etched on his forehead. And it occurs to me that, these days, Ed simply doesn't know what to wish for.

CHAPTER
THIRTY-SIX

Ed

When Ed was small, he'd thought of his father as a powerhouse. Physically strong, dominant, a man's man, with an angular jaw, thick hair and beefy shoulders allowed to peel in the sun. On the days when they'd go to the park as a family, his dad would play fight on the grass with him and Mike and it felt like they were wrestling a wolf.

His mother would sit on a blanket looking after Michelle, just a gurgling baby then, as she'd tuck her slim legs underneath her and wince if the high jinks went too far. Then sometimes they'd all go to the pub, where Mike and Ed would muck about in the car park and the drifting eyes of other men reminded Dad what a head-turner his wife was. He'd throw his arm around her shoulder and kiss her hard on the lips, until she'd playfully bat him away and Mike would stick his fingers down his throat and pretend to puke.

It was about that age that Ed had started to become curious about what happened each morning after his dad drove his van off to work. But it wasn't until he was thirteen that he was allowed to tag along on the weekend jobs he used to take in an attempt to address the family's ever-present financial pressures.

Watching his father solve even the most complex of electrical problems had felt like witnessing a kind of magic at first. But Ed soon came to think of it as better than magic. His dad had an analytical brain, he was a brilliant trouble-shooter and an instinctive mathematician. He knew exactly which wires to splice, join and connect, and seemed to safely and efficiently solve any problem put in front of him. Ed was never let loose with a set of long nose pliers before he'd earned his stripes officially, but long before the tests, he had an encyclopaedic knowledge of earthing and bonding, circuit breakers and fuse enclosures.

Ed found his mind drifting to this when, a decade after his first weekend shift with his father, he was celebrating the fifth birthday of Spark. In the years that preceded it, Ed had been overcome by an almost superhuman drive to build, progress, grow. It was an intoxicating, euphoric period, when he worked sixty-hour weeks and slept for five hours a night but had still recently managed to beat his own personal best when he'd run a half-marathon. He never took drugs but he felt like he was on something: addicted to success.

The party had been a glitzy affair, held at an upmarket, if slightly self-aware, hotel. Ed found himself buzzing at his father's presence, like a small child in his classroom, proudly showing off the stick drawings he'd produced last term.

210

"What are these?" his dad asked, stopping a waitress with a tray of canapés. He'd been dressed in a polyester suit that looked like he'd last worn it to attend a magistrates' court hearing. Ed wished he'd had the foresight to buy him something nicer.

"Lobster with pink grapefruit mayonnaise," she replied. "I believe they're delicious."

He took one, placed it in his mouth and gave her a thumbs-up. Ed laughed.

"How's your hotel, Dad?"

"Swanky. No tea and coffee facilities in the room, though."

"You just need to phone room service and they'll bring you a coffee if you want one," Ed told him.

"Your mother wouldn't want to drag someone all the way upstairs for a cup of tea. You'd pay through the nose for that."

"The bill's covered, Dad. You don't need to worry."

"It's the principle," he said, then he smiled. "We're very proud of you, son."

"Learnt it all from you," Ed said and his father snorted.

"Hardly."

But it was partly true. It was Ed's father, after all, who'd shown him how rewarding running a business could be. In fact, he had enjoyed it so much so that B. R. Holt & Sons was still tootling along, owned by Ed, but with his father as managing director, in charge of three employees. Being the boss was remarkably easy on the knees, he found, though he still couldn't resist rolling up his sleeves and stepping in when someone phoned in sick.

"So will we get to meet Annabel tonight?"

"Er . . . no. We're not together anymore," Ed said.

His dad raised his eyebrows. "What happened?"

"Nothing. We just weren't right for each other."

He gave him a knowing look. "I understand. You play the field, son. Get it out of your system while you're a young man."

"It's not that," Ed protested, hoping that this wasn't a common perception, the idea that he was some would-be playboy. He didn't date for dating's sake. He'd met a lot of nice women. Intelligent, attractive, sexy women. The fact that none had progressed into a serious relationship was simply because he hadn't found the right person. "Anyway, *you* didn't play the field, and you and mum managed to stick it out," Ed continued, at which point his father coughed and a little bit of champagne fizzed out of his nose.

"Well, I can't pretend it's *all* been a bed of roses. Things were difficult when we had a few money worries — and when Michelle went through her rebellious phase. I don't claim to be any great harbinger of wisdom, son, but I do know this. When you finally meet someone special and your head's in the clouds, just be aware that things get tough for the best of us. The only trick is riding the storm."

CHAPTER
THIRTY-SEVEN

Returning to Nightingale House was lovely. Until then, she'd wondered if she'd been biased about how beautiful her baby was, but everyone adored his shock of dark hair and the expressions on his little face. Christopher never cried. When other mothers were *traipsing up and down corridors in the dead of night, desperately trying to settle their babies, Peggy would lean over and tuck in the blanket she'd knitted for him, letting her eyes settle on the face of her angel. She could watch his tiny eyelids flicker with unknown dreams for hours on end.*

Over the next six weeks, she revelled in every new expression of his. He was only five weeks and a day old when he first smiled at her, as they sat under the huge, ivory blooms of the magnolia tree on the far side of the house. That moment of connection made her heart flare and she wished her mother could just see him and fall in love like she had. But when her mum visited, she refused to meet the baby, insisting that while she was there the staff should look after him.

"Who was he, Peggy?" her mother asked once, out of the blue. "The father, I mean. I think you owe us that much."

Both her parents had initially leapt to the assumption that it was poor John Astley, the boy next door but one with whom Peggy had played in the street as a little girl. He'd repeatedly asked her out through the course of their teenage years and, despite her politely declining — she just didn't feel that way about him — her dad remained permanently suspicious that he was up to no good. Peggy had put the stoppers on the theory that he was the father immediately and John's subsequent engagement to a girl who worked in the Pavilion bingo hall forced her parents to accept that she was telling the truth.

"It might make things a bit better if your dad and I knew," her mother persisted.

But it wouldn't have. 1963 might have been the year when four lads from Liverpool — mere streets away from where Peggy lived, in fact — were taking the world by storm, but the cultural revolution that the Beatles represented never made it past the doors of Peggy's house. In fact, it never would.

He'd been an actor, with a small part in The Pirates of Penzance, which ran for two weeks at The Empire in the summer of 1962. Although the cast rarely mixed with the front-of-house staff, Peggy had been tasked with helping out backstage when a tummy bug led to several crew calling in sick. It was as she was handing out refreshments during rehearsals that he'd first come to talk to her.

"What on earth are they thinking getting a girl like you to make the tea?" he'd said as she'd offered him a cup.

A blush rose from somewhere inside her. "A girl . . . like me?"

"You're too pretty to be backstage. You should be the leading lady."

"I just work in the box office." She shook her head, cursing the quiver in her voice.

"So you're pretty, clever and good with people?"

"Well, I try my best."

He was posh, from somewhere down south, and called himself Jack Newman, though that was a stage name, a combination of two of his heroes, Jack Lemmon and Paul Newman. He had a mop top like Paul McCartney — the kind of hair her dad thought heralded the downfall of society. She considered him exotic and worldly wise, though everyone who wasn't from Liverpool fell into that category at the time.

He took to seeking her out every afternoon before the matinee and hovering about between rehearsals as she worked. "He's like a lost puppy around you," her friend Barbara had said, although that wasn't how it felt to Peggy. She was flattered by his attention and went to sleep each night replaying his brazen advances.

"I hope you're coming to the end of show party," he'd said, the day before the final performance. "You're part of the team now." The entire production company was moving on to Birmingham afterwards, though Jack's ambitions went far further afield — all the way to Hollywood.

Although her heart soared at the invitation, the first thing she'd thought of was her parents. Other twenty-two-year-olds might not have hesitated, but she couldn't imagine even suggesting it to them.

"Not your thing?" he'd teased.

"Oh, no it's not that," she protested. But, as the heat of his eyes warmed her skin, she didn't feel like protesting about anything anymore.

The first lie she'd ever told her mother was surprisingly easy. She casually informed her that her boss had insisted she do overtime on Monday evening, when the party was taking place in the garden of the local theatre impresario, Peter Crewe. She couldn't have looked at her father and said it; she'd have crumbled under the pressure of his glare. She loved her dad unconditionally, but she couldn't help wishing he'd been a little less strict and a touch more modern. He didn't approve of parties. He considered them the domain of foreigners and their rowdy neighbours, the ones he tutted at through the net curtains on New Year's Eve when they sang "Auld Lang Syne" in the street.

The event was held on an Indian Summer evening in early September after daytime temperatures had soared to eighty-three degrees. After a damp, dismal couple of months, this was a shock to the system, as her mother's wilting hair testified when Peggy left the house after tea, just as Juke Box Jury was starting.

216

As she stepped through the wrought-iron gates of the Victorian mansion, she was a bag of nerves, and thoroughly dissatisfied with her appearance. The other women looked like Jackie Kennedy or Bridget Bardot; sophisticated, fashionable, confident. She felt drab and pedestrian. She glanced down at her blouse, which she'd been happy with before she left home, and realised with a crunch of despair that she'd dressed like her mother. She almost turned and ran to the bus stop there and then.

"Hello there!" Jack was beckoning her in, glass in one hand and a smile as soft and sweet as peaches. "Let me get you a drink."

The heat and the Babycham went straight to her head. It made her limbs fuzzy and giggles escape from her lips like bubbles in the bath. Everyone else seemed to feel the same, bare arms sizzling with sunburn from earlier in the day. It was as if the whole world was on holiday. She was not the first one to sneak off into the woodland behind the house as the light began to fade.

But she can't claim he seduced her. She'd seduced him too, gazing at him with Elizabeth Taylor eyes and deliberately brushing the sleeve of her arm against his. The man with the beautiful, warm accent. A muss of hair around the nape of his neck. The man who would later follow his dreams to Hollywood, to try his luck as an actor there. She'd hoped to find a forwarding address from someone at the theatre but, despite her efforts, none was ever forthcoming, so the letters she subsequently wrote all went unsent. Of course, he'd always told her America was part of his grand plan. She couldn't claim she hadn't known. All of which meant that, after that fateful evening, she never saw Jack Newman again.

Ten and a half months later, the day came that she would try for the rest of her life to erase from her memory and fail entirely.

The doctor had been along first thing that morning to give her some medicine to calm her nerves and, after that, her sharp waves of anxiety settled into a blurred sense of otherworldliness. She was oddly, unpleasantly calm, sleepwalking almost — a feeling that she tried to fight but simply hadn't the strength.

She did as she was told, bathed Christopher, dressed him in one of the little outfits she'd made and carried him with his little star blanket draped over her shoulder in case it turned chilly. He was lovely and alert, his eyes shining with new, innocent life, his little hands furled into fists as if he was ready to take on the world.

Peggy was surprised to see her father arrive in a taxi with her mother. He didn't say much, but she registered his eyes darting to Christopher every so often as the car bumped along the road. When Peggy had been a little girl, she'd thought she'd never love anyone like she loved her dad. He might have been stern and impenetrable, but all she wanted — all she'd ever wanted — was his attention and approval. On the rare occasions she got it, when he'd let her sit on his knee or listen to her read, she felt herself light up.

Only now, as they sat in the taxi and Christopher gurgled on her lap, for the first time in her life she realised that another human being existed whom she loved more. A million times more.

When they arrived at the agency, Peggy's mother took the baby while she stood in front of the desk and a stack of papers was presented to her. She was handed a pen and told to sign her name. She thought about asking to read them, but by now her heart was thrashing and nothing came out of her mouth. She felt the heat from her father's frame against her back as he moved towards her and smelled the tobacco on the fabric of his jacket when he said: "Go on."

His fingers squeezed her shoulder, hard enough that she couldn't work out if he was reassuring or threatening her. Either way, she did as she was told. Because, for all her muddled thoughts, she always had.

Peggy was invited into a waiting room, where she sat on a chair and clutched Christopher close to her body as she stroked the warm skin on his face, the ghost of the tiny milk spots that remained on his cheeks. It was then that the noise began building in her ears; a thudding, a pulsating. She felt, surreally, as if someone was knocking on the door trying to press upon her the most urgent message of her life.

She wasn't going to let this happen.

She couldn't agree to it, no matter what she'd signed. Her chest rose and fell and she tried to clear the fuzz from her head and come up with a plan. But the medicine was making her confused and woozy, so the only idea she could come up with was to go along with it until the right moment, when she'd do something to stop this. She could wait until when it was time to say goodbye and then spring into action and make it all end.

Then the lady arrived and took Christopher from her arms, leaving the room temporarily as Peggy waited for her to return and for the pivotal moment to happen. But as she looked between the door and her parents, recognition seeped through her and she felt a warm patch of liquid puddle in her seat. She looked down at the chair next to her and realised that the blanket of stars had been left, crumpled in a heap, and the tiny cries in the next room were his.

She started shaking. Violently trembling, every bit of her body: her hands, her legs, her jaw.

"Is that it?"

Her mother lowered her eyes.

Peggy ran for the door and had it half open, until her father's hand pushed her out of the way and slammed it shut. "NO!" She grasped at his hair, pulled at his tie, scratching at his face with her fingernails until he slapped her down.

"I need to say goodbye," she sobbed, gasping for air, suffocating. "I didn't . . . realise. I need to say goodbye."

Her mother knelt down next to her and stroked her hair. "It's for the best, Peggy. You can get on with your life now."

Then the social worker came in again and told them they weren't to move until the baby's new parents had left the building with him. So she huddled in the corner, clutching the blanket around her knees, until the tiny cries on the other side of the wall faded to silence.

CHAPTER
THIRTY-EIGHT

Allie

I'm roused by gentle birdsong, sunlight slanting through the gap in the curtains and thoughts of little Rowan Archer, with his brutal cough and missing tooth and mum who has to stop herself from crying every time she walks into Alder Hey Hospital.

I think about him bouncing onto the hospital bed and laughing at my jokes, unaware of what his future might hold. I feel a stab of impatience, wishing I could fast-forward to some sweet future moment when I and the team at Chapel Hill could definitively declare our gene-editing project a success.

I slip out of bed and head to the balcony, resolving to email Khalid again today to see if there's an update, as I click open the glass-panelled door and breathe in the intense smell of the morning, pure air and pollen, picked up by the cooling wind when it blows in with each sunrise. The sky is painted a rich blue, blurring to incandescent yellow and orange. I suddenly wish I were only here to enjoy the scenery and that Ed and I could carry on like we did last night, savouring icy mouthfuls of gelato and every easy moment in each other's company.

Instead, I contemplate what we've got to embark on today and a knot pulls in my stomach. My phone beeps and I return to the plug by the bed, assuming it's Ed telling me that he's up and ready to meet me downstairs. Instead, it is a text from Julia, which confuses me at first as we are an hour ahead of the UK, so it's only 6.30 a.m. there.

Can we talk ASAP?

As I scroll up, I register that she'd sent another message last night but I'd entirely missed it.

We are overdue an update! Let's talk tonight! xxx

It must have arrived while we were out eating and I hadn't even noticed. I dial her number and she answers after one ring. "Allie."

"Julia, is everything okay? It's so early."

"I was worried because you didn't phone last night," she says.

"Oh, I'm sorry. I hadn't realised you'd texted. We went out for dinner and I didn't look at my phone until this morning." When she doesn't reply immediately, I pull the device away from my ear briefly to check we haven't lost the connection. "Julia?"

"I'm here."

"So, you wanted an update. Actually, he does seem better." For the first time this feels like I'm telling the truth, not spouting some vaguely optimistic words designed to reassure her. There was a sparkle in Ed's eyes last night that I haven't truly seen since we arrived.

"Has he said anything about what's going to happen when you come home?"

"We haven't really got onto that yet."

The hum of silence that follows makes me wonder if she's crying again and my mind flickers with comforting words that I might offer. But she responds before I get a chance, in a tone quite unlike anything I've heard her use before.

"I feel like I'm being kept out of the loop here, Allie."

She sounds snippy and irritable, her usually soft inflections cold with annoyance.

"Uh . . . what?"

"I'm here alone, while you two are gallivanting around Italy and my mind is working overtime. Whose wouldn't be?"

I feel awash with adrenalin; shocked and, above all, defensive.

"We're not *gallivanting*, Julia. You're surely not suggesting —"

"I'm not suggesting anything." She elicits a long sigh. "I'm just saying . . . look, Allie, you *must* phone me when I ask you. That is non-negotiable."

My mouth falls open. I didn't know I was negotiating. "How many women do you know who would be comfortable with something like this?" she continues. "I'm being more than understanding. Do remember that."

I am perplexed and mildly resentful about this contradictory speech, the turnaround in Julia's attitude. But while my heart races as I work out how to respond, the ghost of a sensation whispers against my skin, as if I can still feel Ed's arms against my body when we swam together. The warmth on my neck becomes a couple of degrees hotter. Maybe *gallivanting* is closer to the truth than I'm prepared to admit.

"Julia, I hear exactly what you're saying," I say, with an air of gentle authority. "I know you're upset at the moment. All I can say is, I'll make sure I stay in touch."

"Okay." She takes a breath to gather her composure. "Sorry if I sounded . . ."

"It's okay."

"Look, you do understand, don't you, Allie?" she says softly. "You're my only real point of contact. I realise I need to give Ed space, so I don't want to be phoning him every five minutes or it'll just make everything worse."

"Of course. And yes, I understand."

"Thanks, Allie. Thanks *so* much."

I end the call with a feeling of unease, as if the equilibrium between Julia and me has been nudged out of place, like the edge of a jigsaw piece that no longer sits flat. Then I remind myself of what she's going through. And how the curious effects of love can derail any of us when we fear it slipping away.

CHAPTER
THIRTY-NINE

The idea of leaving for university while Ed stayed at home could have made me miserable, if I'd allowed it. But I reminded myself that I'd had plenty of time to prepare for our separation and the prospect of being in the same city as my best friend for our university years had never amounted to more than a throwaway line, whispered in the smoky glow of a bonfire. The summer before I went to Cardiff, Dad tried to raise the matter with me a couple of times, as if he sensed some suppressed anguish. But there was really nothing to talk about. I had everything to look forward to, not least a hotly contested place at my first-choice university. So I was not going to mope and that was doubly true once I arrived in Wales.

"You've signed up for *what?*" Dad asked when I telephoned him at the end of my third week.

"The Capoeira society."

"What's that when it's at home?" he laughed.

"A Brazilian martial art combining kicks and acrobatic movements to music and song," I said, reciting the line I'd heard at Fresher's fair.

"Blimey."

"I'm very much a beginner. I nearly knocked myself out trying to do a headstand the first time, but Olivier the instructor says I've got natural talent."

I didn't mention that I had actually slept with Olivier the instructor. I got talking to him after a class, we adjourned to a bar and ended up at his place, where he popped an E and we had positively gymnastic sex until six in the morning.

"Well, it certainly sounds like you're getting lots of exercise," Dad said.

"What? Oh. Yes."

"And the course lives up to all your expectations?"

"Oh, Dad, it's fantastic," I gushed. The societies and the sex of my first term were merely side shows, what I felt a fresher *ought* to be doing, rather than what I actually wanted to be doing. I didn't want to be one of those obsessives who were all work and no play, after all. "I love everything about it. It's just the right balance between data interpretation and time in the lab. And some of the research my tutors are working on is so inspiring."

"At this rate you're not going to want to come home at the end of term."

"Oh, I am. I miss your cooking."

He laughed. "Is Ed still coming to see you at the weekend?"

My heart began to thud uneasily. "No, he postponed. He's too busy."

On the day Ed eschewed the opportunity to go to Oxford, a hairline crack had appeared in our

227

relationship and I'd felt it widening the slightest bit every day. It wasn't that he had ignored me since I'd arrived in Cardiff, nor my regular, two thousand-word emails. But it took him days to reply and his responses were short and perfunctory. I suspected there was a new woman on the scene. The fact that he was working towards turning his apprenticeship into full accreditation before taking over his dad's business didn't seem a sufficient explanation.

Either way, he never did come and visit me that term. I didn't see him at all until I returned home in December, when we arranged to meet early one evening at a posh hotel in Liverpool's business district, a far cry from the student venues to which I was now accustomed, pubs with sticky floors and political graffiti on the toilet doors. I stepped into the bar in my vintage 501s and CND T-shirt, to find most of the clientele in business attire, sharp suits and chignons. I couldn't decide if I felt self-conscious or defiant, but then I saw him at a table and all such frivolity emptied from my head. He was writing in his notebook, the swift, light movements of his pen contrasting with the intensity of his concentration.

When he looked up, my entire body rushed with blood, at nothing more or less than the sight of his smiling face. I tucked my hands in my pockets and casually walked towards him. He stood as I approached and leaned in to kiss me on the cheek, a movement that seemed so natural to him and so alien to me that I pulled away, frowning. I wondered, rather pompously, if this had been what he'd been doing instead of setting

Oxford University alight: mastering the conventions of *networking* — a concept to which I'd never given a moment's thought, until now, when I took an irrational dislike to it.

"How are you?" he asked.

"Very good thanks. Can I get you a beer?"

"I'll get it," he replied, which was a relief because I remembered that I only had fifty-four pence in my pocket.

It struck me during that first drink that anyone bored or nosy enough to be watching us might have concluded that we were on a blind date. It felt as though we were strangers weighing each other up, reserving judgement about whether we liked what we found.

"How's life in the cut and thrust of electricals?" I asked, blushing at the question, anxious that something in my tone might reveal what I really wanted to know: whether he regretted his decision.

"Good, actually," he said brightly. "I won't bore you with the details, but I've got a few irons in the fire."

"Go on."

He shook his head dismissively. "I'll fill you in when I'm a millionaire."

"Oh, come *on*. Don't be coy."

His idea was simple, as all the best ones are, and had occurred to him as a result of some supply issues he'd had with wholesalers. He was going to create a website to sell parts direct to the electrical trade, quickly, cheaply, easily. He talked animatedly about channels of distribution and discounting, capital expenditure and profit margins. He'd done his research and after completing a business plan, had secured a start-up loan from a quango funded by the European Union.

"But don't people think the dot-com bubble will burst soon?"

"Oh, it will. Most of the new online firms are unsustainable. But the internet is growing so rapidly that the ones with a sound business plan and well-defined niche will survive. I've already spoken to dozens of manufacturers and wholesalers and the appetite for this is huge. It'll be live within the next two months."

As his eyes flickered up to mine, I realised that my concerns about him were unfounded, the idea that he could only fulfil his potential in academia misplaced. That was *my* dream, not Ed's. Far from being a consolation prize, the path he'd chosen sparked an unexpected zeal in him, something that had clear potential to make him happy. I wanted to say all this to him, to tell him I'd been wrong, but didn't know how without admitting all my prejudices in the first place.

"Sorry I haven't been to visit," he said.

"Oh, it's *fine*! I've been busy anyway. We've been focusing on applied genetic and molecular technologies recently and it's been quite hard. Plus . . . I've been seeing someone." I glanced up to see his reaction, but he gave nothing away.

"Yes, how's it going with Olivier?" So he had at least read my emails.

"Oh, I'm with someone else now actually," I said breezily. "Neil. He's a rugby player. From Exeter."

230

In the numb silence that followed I considered telling him that it *really wasn't serious* between me and Neil from Exeter. But something stopped me. There had been scores of girls in Ed's life already and I'd never heard him dismissing any of them as unimportant. I didn't like the idea of being a late developer, though I unquestionably was. By then, I'd never even had a steady boyfriend.

"Are *you* seeing anyone?" I asked.

"What? Uh, no. I mean, I *was* . . . but it didn't work out."

"How come?"

His Adam's apple rose, then fell slowly back into place. "I'm . . ." But his voice trailed away and, if he ever did come up with an answer to the question, I can't recall what it was.

"I'm really glad it's working out for you, Ed," I said.

His eyes softened and the most unusual smile appeared on his lips, one that could just as easily have indicated happiness as sadness. "I feel the same about you, Allie."

The words made my chest tighten. And for reasons that I would think about many times afterwards, emotion swept up into my throat and made the back of my eyes tingle.

We started to meet up two or three times a year after that. In between, his business grew at an unstoppable rate. Ed seemed to work like a machine, "all the hours God sends", according to his mum. He was secretive about his personal life, but once everyone started using social media, was regularly tagged on Facebook at business events in London with an Annabel or a Francesca on his arm, exquisite women whose self-assurance shone from their clear complexions and Yves Saint Laurent smiles.

All of this added to a gnawing apprehension each time I was due to meet him, a concern about how much we'd still have in common. But I came away every time with the same conclusion: life might have left us with different scrapes on our knees, but, at our core, we were the same people we'd always been. Almost the same.

As the years passed, a clear difference began to emerge and our reunions, intermittent as they were, had an increasingly significant and not entirely welcome effect on me. Namely, I couldn't stop thinking about him afterwards. I'd replay entire conversations, try to relive the same shiver down my neck that I'd felt when his hand had brushed against mine. This continued even after I finally did get my steady boyfriend.

I distinctly recall more than one occasion when I'd be sitting on the sofa with Rob and a Chinese takeaway, challenging myself to conjure up an image of each minute detail of Ed's face. The freckle under his left eye. The slight curve of his nose. The dip of his cupid's bow. When I'd hit on it, sharp as a photograph, a liquid warmth would spread right through my chest and appear on my cheeks. Then Rob would turn to me, frown, and ask: "Are you all right? I think you've had another reaction to those prawn wontons."

CHAPTER
FORTY

Ed

Ed and Julia had gone to Paris for the honeymoon and he'd taken her for lunch at L'Abeille. It more than lived up to its two Michelin stars and the glowing reviews he'd read during his careful research before the trip. The surroundings were soothing and elegant, the food refined and thoughtful. But she didn't eat. Instead, she pushed away each of the three courses she'd ordered and refused to either touch them or talk to Ed throughout.

He'd witnessed her moods before and knew she could be prone to sulking. He'd seen it first when her parents apologetically broke the news that she couldn't use their villa in Tuscany for a long weekend, because they'd already promised the dates she'd wanted for her book club to friends.

But what he experienced that lunchtime, as rain fell in sheets outside the high windows, was unlike anything that had happened before. Each time he tried to engage her in conversation or reach out for her hand, she'd snap it away. He considered everything: did she hate the restaurant? Would she have preferred New York? Had he said something offensive in his sleep? He truly didn't have a clue. Yet, tension hung in the air like a bad smell, before he could bear it no longer.

"What's the matter, Julia?"

Her slim jawline pulsed. "I'm fine."

The waiter came to take away her plate and, concerned, asked if there was a problem with the food. She refused point blank to answer him, glaring straight ahead as if he didn't exist.

"I don't think she's very hungry," Ed told him.

He nodded and as he disappeared, she leaned in, her eyes glowering. "*Do not* answer for me. I'm not a child."

"I had to say something. Julia, tell me what's the matter."

"If you don't know then there's no point in me telling you," she hissed. "I think we should just leave."

"Fine," he said, feeling more than a little pissed off. He knocked back his drink and she pulled an expression of pure disgust. Then he paid the bill and they stepped outside into the rain. Paris in springtime isn't always beautiful, it turns out. She did not hang about to talk, instead marching off towards the Arc de Triomphe. He chased after her, pleading with her to stop, until she spun around and unleashed her full fury on him, her mouth contorted into an angry grimace.

The accusations concerned a woman at the airport, someone Julia believed he'd been flirting with. As they'd flown in three days earlier and she hadn't mentioned it at all in that time, by this stage Ed

234

couldn't even work out which woman she was talking about.

"The blonde with the baby!" she shrieked. "How *dare* you try to pretend you don't know who I'm talking about. You piece of shit."

"What are you talking about?"

She just kept shouting, as tiny, watercolour blood vessels appeared on the delicate skin around her eyes. It wasn't the first time, she told him. He was *always* looking at other women, flashing his smile and turning on the charm. She'd thought after they married it would all end but Ed had proved her wrong and was as much of a bastard as she'd feared he had the capacity to be. By the end of her speech, her tears made thick, dirty tracks in her make-up and she could barely catch her breath.

She turned and fled and he chased after her, grabbing her by the arm, trying to reason with her. But a man stepped in and told Ed to leave her alone, clearly drawing unfavourable assumptions about what was going on. So he backed off and stood helplessly as his new wife ran away from him, expensive wine hummed through his system and rainwater seeped through the shoulders of his jacket.

He walked around the city for two hours after that, trying to piece together what had happened at the airport and how she could have reached the conclusion she had. The woman had been about twenty-five. She was pretty, he couldn't deny it. Yes, he'd noticed her. But had he been flirting? With a crunch of self-loathing he thought that perhaps he had.

He replayed the scene in his head, over and over. How he'd stepped in when she was struggling up the steps in the departure lounge with her baby in a pushchair. How he'd offered to carry the chair for her while she held the child in her arms. How she'd smiled and thanked him and looked at him like he was some kind of hero. How he'd liked that.

He'd told himself he hadn't tried to be anything other than decent, that he'd have done the same for anyone, skinny jeans and pretty eyes or not. But was that the truth? Perhaps Julia knew Ed better than he knew himself. Either way, why had she waited three days to mention it, before making an almighty scene?

If he was simmering with resentment and confusion about this in the beginning, all that soon dissolved in the hiss of the rain. By the time he traipsed back to the hotel, drained and exhausted, all he wanted was for this not to have happened. His marriage and everything he'd invested in it was bigger than one argument, as bad as it had been.

She was lying in bed, cleanly showered, her creamy skin naked under the sheets. She turned to look at him. Her lips were swollen and flushed from crying, but her beauty still took his breath away.

"I'm sorry," he whispered, as he'd sat on the edge of the bed.

"It's all right," she replied. Then they kissed and fell into each other's arms and had slow, tender make-up sex. By the following morning, all was forgotten.

CHAPTER
FORTY-ONE

Allie

The kind of taxis I'm used to taking have an aroma of stale tobacco, a driver delivering a party political broadcast and a potpourri of stains on the back seat you wouldn't touch without surgical gloves.

So when Ed said he would arrange "a car" to take us to the vineyard, I'd naively assumed that was the kind of thing we'd be taking. Instead, I walk down the stone steps of the hotel to find a gleaming black Mercedes S-Class purring on the gravel and a driver resembling an Armani model inviting me to slip inside. I spend most of the journey worrying about how much this is all costing — the hotel, the food, the drinks, all of which Ed has stubbornly refused any money for.

"I insist that I at least pay for this car," I say.

"Don't worry about it," he replies dismissively.

"No, but I want to. I'm the reason we're here in the first place, so there's no way I'm going to leave you to stump up for everything."

"I hate to break this to you, Allie, but I'm not only here to do your detective work. I am technically on holiday too."

Twenty minutes later, our car pulls up outside a stretching, single-storey building, painted in creamy white and with a high brick arch that leads us into the La Cavalletta estate. To the left is the glass-fronted entrance to an elegant, airy showroom, but we are directed ahead into the courtyard to wait for our guide.

We follow a pale stone path, until we find ourselves surrounded on three sides by twenty or more arches, arranged around a square lawn as green and smooth as a billiard table. Beyond that, as far as I can see, there are neat rows of thick, tumbling grapevines that ripple in the haze. Aside from the faint hum of a tractor in the distance, there is an almost monastic silence.

"*Buongiorno. Signor Holt*, I presume?"

We turn to find a short, jolly-looking man in his early forties, with ruddy cheeks, white laughter lines fanning from his eyes and a double chin that slopes all the way down to the collar of his yellow polo neck shirt.

"I am Valerio, your guide. How are you both?" He grins, delivering a vigorous handshake to each of us. "Are you enjoying your time in Italy?"

"It's absolutely beautiful," I reply.

"I'm glad you think so. And welcome to La Cavalletta, which we think is a very special place," he announces proudly, opening his arms. "Follow me and I will tell you a little bit about the winery."

We stroll along the path into the sunshine as he talks. "The winery has been in the Zenetti family for generations and in that time they have passed on, from father to daughter and son, a deep love and knowledge of the vine variety and its cultivation in this unique and diverse environment."

He invites us to follow him down to the cellars, explaining that production began more than ninety years ago, when two brothers established the vineyard. Today, it is run by the great grandchildren of one of the brothers, Giovanni, and they've invested heavily in the business since they took over.

"The other brother didn't have a family?" I ask, deliberately putting off addressing the real topic we're here for.

"Their involvement ceased a few years ago. The site has been completely modernised, using the latest advances in engineering. That way they could build a new structure with the greatest of respect for our environment. The building we are entering is less than four years old."

He unlocks a heavy oak door and invites us into the dark, where the heat dissolves instantly. Dozens of huge wooden barrels line up under a ceiling of softly lit vaulted brick arches, while a far wall is dominated by even larger copper containers.

"In here, the temperature and humidity levels are perfectly controlled so that the wine can age," he says. Valerio continues to explain how the knowledge of their grandfathers has been interpreted and refined, using modern fermentation techniques to produce the most elegant wine they could.

"It's a wonderful place," Ed says.

"And you haven't even tasted the wine yet!" Valerio laughs. "Any further questions before we move on?"

"As a matter of fact, yes," Ed replies. I lift my eyes briefly to him and can immediately tell he's not going to ask about the grapes.

CHAPTER
FORTY-TWO

Valerio invites us to step out of the cellar and pulls shut the heavy door behind him. Since we've been inside, an expanse of pale grey clouds has bruised the sky, softening the light over the vineyard.

"I wondered if you happen to know Stefano McCourt?" Ed asks casually.

"Yes, I know Stefano. But he doesn't work here anymore I'm afraid. Come, follow me," Valerio says, heading along the gravel path.

I don't think he means to be abrupt, but Ed was so convincingly nonchalant that the conversation has ended prematurely. I trail after them, as a bead of sweat trickles down my spine.

Valerio leads us into the glass-fronted showroom we passed when we came in. It's a large, uncluttered space, where natural light spills onto the polished wood floors and oak beams slice through a smooth, plastered ceiling. The only décor on the walls are blown-up black and white photographs from a bygone age, of young men smiling among twisting, sunlit vines, all Brylcreem and biceps.

There are only two other customers, browsing the freestanding shelves that display wines for purchase, some gift boxed, most neatly lined up in glossy bottles. Valerio invites us to join him round one of three barrels that stand on their ends to act as tables. He disappears behind a counter momentarily, before producing a small silver bucket and two crystal glasses. Then he pops open a bottle and pours a measure of sparkling liquid into each.

"This is our award-winning Spumante Brut. It's an elegant drink, which we produce using a slow Charmat method," Valerio tells us. "This means that the secondary fermentation — when the bubbles are made — takes place in a low-pressure steel tank, rather than in the bottle itself. We do this over a period of five months, which allows us the high level of quality control necessary for its aromatic taste. Please," he says, inviting me to take a sip.

Fragrant bubbles dissolve on my tongue. "It's delicious," I tell Ed, who lifts his glass to his lips.

We taste five wines in all — a fruity red, a grappa so strong it could fuel a Mini Cooper, and two more whites, one of which is a handmade, limited edition reserve.

"Well, I'm certainly not going to waste this by spitting it in the silver bucket," I tell Ed, taking a sip.

"You say that as if you've spat *any* into the silver bucket," he points out.

Admittedly, this might go some way to explaining my dramatic sense of well-being and relaxation, which is so pronounced that I've almost forgotten why we're here until Ed makes a second attempt at raising the subject of Stefano.

"Did you know Stefano well?" Ed asks.

"Not really, but we spent a week together. It was me who took over his job so I only met him for those few days. He showed me the ropes. Nice guy. Are you from England?"

"Yes, that's right — Liverpool."

"Ah! So that's how you know Stefano. He told me he was born somewhere near there."

Ed and I exchange a small frown, but neither of us decide to correct him.

"We heard he moved somewhere near the coast. Was it another vineyard he went to work for?" Ed asks. If the alcohol has gone to his head, he doesn't show it. "We'd love to look him up."

"No, I don't believe so. He inherited his uncle's boat yard. It's somewhere on the Ligurian coast. Portofino or Santa Margerita Ligure I think."

"Portofino?" Ed looks surprised. "I've been there. It wasn't cheap."

Valerio laughs. "He could've sold it, but from what he said, the boat yard held sentimental value, a bit of a personal passion. So, he persuaded his wife to move there. Which it's why it's *me* showing you round today and not him. Some of the others who work here are still in touch with him. If you want to leave your details, they can pass on a message?"

Ed looks at me and he can see from my expression that leaving another note for him is not my preferred option. "You don't have his email address or a number that you could give us?" I ask.

"I'm sure the office will have it. Though, perhaps it's best if you leave your details and they can send them on to Stefano. If you'd like to go and see Olivia, our new receptionist, she can contact him. It's her first week so I'll tell her to expect you."

After the tasting, we spend a little time browsing the shelves, the neat rows of amber-coloured grappa di Lugana, golden passito, ruby red Bardolinos and jars of acacia honey. They'd make lovely gifts for family and friends but that's hardly an option when everyone thinks I'm in Portugal.

"What do you think about leaving another note?" Ed asks under his breath.

I shake my head. "I don't think so. I can't just go leaving letters for him all over Lake Garda."

"Maybe this might be your chance though?"

"But if he gets both letters, it's going to look weird. It makes us look too desperate. I'm going to have to think of something else."

When it's time to head back to the hotel, I step outside into the sunshine, feeling mildly intoxicated, and am greeted by our driver, who opens the car door for me. We've settled in the back and are about to drive off, when there's a knock on the window and a young woman appears, breathlessly pushing her fine strands of dark hair out of her eyes.

Ed opens the door to talk to her and she hands him an envelope.

"I got a message that I need to give you Signor McCourt's address," she smiles eagerly. "I hope this is all you need?"

The pause that follows indicates that Ed is thinking what I'm thinking: this wasn't *quite* the message. She wasn't supposed to give away his details; it was meant to be the other way around.

"*Grazie*," I say decisively.

As the car crunches out of the driveway, I glance at Ed. "Let's hope she doesn't get into too much trouble."

CHAPTER
FORTY-THREE

Ed

In the months after the row with Julia on the honeymoon, there were times when Ed would look back and wonder if he'd hallucinated the whole thing. It didn't take long for his shock and anger to dissolve, like dirty grey clouds scudding out of view, leaving a bright horizon. And one positive had come out of it: they both now realised how much was at stake.

Julia was determined to demonstrate how much she loved him. They'd cook together on a Saturday night, when she'd slip her arms around his neck as he stirred a risotto, planting her lips on the tender spot below his ears. He'd return from work to find her waiting for him with a gift she'd picked up — cologne or a tie she'd seen and thought would suit him.

Then there were the intoxicating occasions when he'd walk in to find her draped on the staircase waiting for him, fully made up, wearing nothing but her bewitching smile and silk robe, tantalisingly loose against her freshly bathed skin. He had almost everything a man could want or need to make him happy. There was only one thing missing.

"When do you think we should start trying for a baby?"

She murmured the question as they sat in a black cab after an industry event, her thigh folded seductively over his, a chiffon ribbon of hair escaping from the clip that held it in place at the back of her head. They'd talked about children at the start of their relationship, just after they'd first met. It was one of the things they had in common, a desire to have a baby, at least two and possibly three she'd said, a thought that had made his heart swell.

"Are you serious?" he asked.

She broke into a laugh. "Of course!"

But his throat tightened. "I thought you wanted to wait a couple of years first."

She looked up at him from under her eyelashes. "I'm starting to think that there's no point in hanging around. My career is going to be there afterwards. A baby could be the making of us, don't you think?"

When Ed opened his mouth to reply, something made him hesitate.

She pulled away and a tiny wrinkle appeared between her eyebrows. "What is it?"

"I'm not . . ." A trail of breath left his lips. "You know I can't wait to have kids."

A fierce glint appeared in her eyes and her neck flushed pink. "But?"

He looked straight ahead.

"Ed. There was a definite *but* about to come there."

"I suppose I wouldn't want a baby to be a way of gluing us together, if that makes sense."

Part of Ed must have known the potentially ruinous implications of the statement. Julia's version of marital bliss had been so carefully constructed that to raise doubts about it was akin to pulling out the pin of a grenade and throwing it dead centre. After all, they'd agreed that what happened on the honeymoon was a one-off, that it was all behind them, that everything was better now. It was only once the words had escaped from Ed's mouth that he realised how strongly he felt them. That the immaculate, attentive and loving version of Julia he'd seen in the last few weeks was a thin veneer that concealed a more complex and volatile personality.

Nevertheless, he still regretted the statement immediately.

"No. It doesn't make sense."

"Sorry. Forget I said anything."

But she wasn't going to forget.

"This is about what happened on the honeymoon, isn't it?" she exploded. "That was fucking weeks ago!"

The taxi pulled in outside their house and Ed took out some cash to pay the fare as she threw open the door and marched away. He followed her inside to find her in the kitchen, pacing up and down like a caged animal.

"I cannot believe this." Her eyes were bulging, the tendons in her neck as pronounced as knives.

"Julia —"

"I've just offered to bear your child. To put the career for which I've worked my backside off on hold, so I can spend nine months of my life being fat. Putting everything that means anything to me on the back seat — for the baby YOU are apparently desperate for. And this is how you react."

"I'm sorry I —"

"You don't fucking sound it, you utter bastard."

Nothing Ed said made it better. Everything Ed said made it worse. She interpreted every sentence he attempted in the worst possible way. It was when she was shrieking about him being the shittiest husband she could possibly meet that he knew he had to get out of there. So he turned and headed towards the door.

"Don't you walk out on me, you fucker!" Her voice was raw, the rip of a chainsaw.

He stopped and closed his eyes. His heartbeat intensified. He filled his chest with air before turning around to face her. That was when she threw the bottle at his face.

Afterwards, she sat next to him in the hospital waiting room, stroking his fingers, regret etched on her slender features, in her sorrowful eyes. He stared ahead, applying gentle pressure to the wound in his forehead with a thick cloth that was now matted with blood. She gently rested the side of her head on his shoulder, her soft hair tickling his neck just like it had in the taxi.

"I feel awful," she whispered.

"It's all right," he reassured her. But it wasn't.

She looked up at him and turned down the sides of her mouth. "I wish you'd just hit me back." Her voice was higher than usual, with a childlike, petulant quality. "Why couldn't you just have hit me back?"

She seemed resentful that he hadn't, that he never would.

"What I've done . . . this is domestic violence, isn't it?" she said glumly.

"Don't." Ed was not a victim. The thought of it made him sick to his stomach. "It was just a row that got out of hand."

A thin tear made its way down her cheek and she gently turned his head towards her to kiss him on the lips. "I don't deserve you."

As she pulled away he let his eyes drift across the too-bright room to the other patients. The young woman huddled in a padded jacket, coughing fiercely. The elderly man accompanied by his daughter, his hand wrapped in an ice pack. The guy busy texting in the corner and the woman who'd been arguing with a receptionist for the last five minutes.

"I think there's a way forward here," Julia sniffed, brushing away tears. "I think we need to just try a bit harder from now on. Both of us. Don't you agree?"

Then the triage nurse announced his name and Ed tried to recall the exact details of the compendium of lies they'd agreed to tell.

CHAPTER
FORTY-FOUR

Allie

The sun has disappeared behind the lake, leaving the night air still and hot. We are back at the Hotel Villa Cortine Palace, in the garden at the rear of the building, sipping cocktails as strings of lights glow from among beds of tea roses and hydrangeas. The scent of myrtle fills the air, along with the delicate chime of running water as it cascades from the fountain of Neptune. It's a beautiful spot in the daytime, but at night, amidst the shadowy beauty of the trees, the impossible romance of the garden comes to life. Most of the guests have now retired after dinner, or are still sipping *passiti* on the terrace on the other side of the hotel. As we sit alone on the patio, the success of finding Stefano's current address shines in Ed's eyes.

"I might be wrong but you almost look relaxed," I say.

A smile creeps to his lips. "Maybe I am."

"You're sure you're not just drunk?"

"Perhaps a little. Not too much though. *I* spat out the wine."

"That was clumsy of you," I reply. "Shame I couldn't have bought any of that sparkling stuff for Grandma Peggy. It would have made a nice extra for her birthday."

"Are things back to normal between the two of you now? I mean after your argument about what you'd found in her bedroom."

"Oh, I'm not sure you could really call it an *argument* — I couldn't get a word in. I was just thoroughly reprimanded and warned off." A sigh escapes my lips. "Things aren't really normal, no. She and I haven't discussed any of it since that day she blew up at me and told me to forget all about it. She seems to want to pretend it didn't happen. I don't know how she thinks I could possibly do that."

"Perhaps this is the only way she can think of to handle it."

"Yes. The idea that I'll find out the truth, whatever that is, is obviously too unpalatable for her to even think about. She's burying her head in the sand though."

"She's trying to protect you, Allie. And your dad."

"I know," I concede. "Here's the thing though. The idea that my dad isn't my real dad is something I can't ever imagine *accepting*, but I recognise that I might not get a choice in the matter. It's silly of her to refuse to even discuss it, to try to hide it."

"That's what you're doing with your dad though, isn't it? Hiding it from him. Protecting him from the truth."

"I suppose so, but only until I know for certain. I'm finding it hard not to be a little annoyed with my grandma though. At the way she reacted, as if it was my fault I'd found the bloody thing, rather than *her* fault for hiding it."

"Well, she's always been a fairly strong-willed woman."

I snort. "That's one way of putting it. Don't get me wrong, I like the fact that she doesn't suffer fools and that she's no helpless little old lady. I like that she's so formidable. Sometimes though . . ." I shake my head.

"What?"

"I just wish she wasn't so *angry* with the world."

He fixes a serious look on me. "Wouldn't anyone be after what happened to your mum? It can't be easy for any mother to bury a child."

I feel a stab of regret and shame. "Okay, now I feel awful when you put it like that."

"Don't be silly. I know how much you adore her."

"I do," I agree. "She is the loveliest person, deep down. She's done so much for me over the years. Dad once told me she carried all kinds of guilt for Mum's death. She thought she should've realised she was sick and made her go to see a doctor earlier."

"Surely that wouldn't have made a difference with such an aggressive cancer?"

"Of course not." I take a sip of my drink. "Did I ever tell you she and Granddad met in Paris when she was working at a theatre?"

"You did," he says.

"It sounds very romantic, doesn't it? Hard to picture really."

There is something about the way Ed looks tonight that has made my heart beat wrong. The way his hair falls over his tanned forehead and the tiny lines at the side of his eyes make his whole face light up when he smiles. I find my gaze falling on his hands as he picks up his glass and I want to touch his fingers. When the breeze blows in a certain direction, I breathe in his smell and I fight an urge to lean into him, for no other reason than to feel the heat from his body.

Yet here we sit, two feet away from each other and a million miles apart. Because he is married to a woman he loves. There have been times tonight though when I've questioned my certainty about what he feels for her. When I've wondered if I've got it all wrong. Or more to the point: if I've got *her* wrong.

"Are you all right?" he asks and I snap out of it.

"Of course."

In the hush of the night, we sit for a while without saying a thing. When he finally speaks, his words feel both unexpected and overdue.

"You know, I've spent a long time trying to work out why things went awry between Julia and me. Trying to analyse it all as if it's some straightforward problem for which I can find a solution. I've come to the conclusion that the thinking, the determination, the frustration that I haven't *fixed* it . . . those things are almost as bad as anything else." He pauses then looks at me briefly. "Julia thinks we should go and see a counsellor."

I swallow. "Well . . . that works for some people."

He fixes his gaze on the fountain.

"When do you think it all started, Ed? When did you start feeling like it had reached the point where you might have to separate?"

"It's hard to say. I first thought about it a few months ago, I suppose."

"Talking about it might help," I tell him, thinking of the shrink again. But he fixes his eyes on me and says: "It already is, Allie."

A tiny muscle in my heart clenches.

"And I feel better for being here," he adds.

"Good," I say decisively.

"For being . . . around you." He looks at his drink. "Things are still complicated, I can't change that. But the point is this: I'm working them out. I might not have all the answers now but I will have. One way or another, I'll work things out."

I nod, wanting to say something else, wanting to carry on talking. Helping. But instead he takes a breath and smiles at me. "So now we have Stefano's address, we need to discuss what we're going to do about it."

I run my finger along the condensation beading on my glass. "Yes, we do."

"Well, you did come to Italy with the intention of paying him a visit."

I feel my spine stiffen.

"It's up to you, Allie," he says gently. "You can stop this whole process any time."

"Portofino's miles away."

"One hundred and six miles. A train ride or a road trip if we wanted to hire a car."

"You've checked?"

"Yes, I checked," he confesses. "But it's not up to me whether we carry on. If you want to stay here and soak up the pleasures of Lake Garda, I will not argue."

"It's so awful here though," I say, gesturing to the exquisite garden, and when he breaks into another smile it makes something in my stomach jump.

"Oh God, I don't know what to do," I say. "I really don't have the constitution of a detective. Give me a laboratory over this any day."

"Give you a laboratory over *everything* any day," he replies. "You seem excited about this thing you're working on at the university at the moment."

"I'll be excited when we've nailed it." He raises an eyebrow and I'm forced to concede a smile. "Fine. I'm *slightly* excited."

"Is this connected with that big project you were working on a few years ago?"

I shake my head. "This is gene-editing technology. That was a diagnostic tool and outcome measure we developed for use in children, called nasal potential difference."

He looks perplexed.

"Cystic fibrosis presents itself in a number of ways in the human body. It was discovered in the nineties that it changes the voltage across the cells lining the airway."

"How strange."

"We trialled a method that measures that voltage in a noninvasive way and therefore was suitable for use in children. It uses an electrode in the nose and then under the skin surface on the wrist to create a circuit,

256

from which we could then take a reading. But the gene-editing project is different. We really hope that one day it will lead to a cure."

"Are you still working with kids?"

"On a different project, but yes — a test group of about fifty. The youngest is five."

He thinks about this for a moment. "And they all have CF?"

I nod. "Sucks, doesn't it? *But* in the last ten years, things have moved on. The life expectancy of someone with CF has increased by a full decade, to nearly forty. This is what science is doing, this is what's being achieved."

"You really love it, don't you?"

"Yes. I do a job that gives people hope. And the work I'm doing now . . . if it's what we think it is, it's got so much potential, Ed."

He looks at me strangely. It's an indefinable look, a softening of his eyes, a stilling of his limbs. It's as if the energy in the atmosphere has delivered a bolt of warmth in the space between us.

"Come on, finish your drink and let's go for a walk."

"To where?"

"Follow me." He stands and offers me his hand. I look at it and hesitate, then drain my glass and reach out for it.

We walk along a cobbled pathway, the navy hue of the sky only visible in the gaps above the trees. Beyond the garden immediately outside the hotel is a whole other world of private parkland, a maze of ancient-looking columns and mysterious stone outbuildings smothered with wild roses and rampant bushes of lantana. We clamour down the natural terrace and discover unexpected coves where lovers' benches overlook the stretch of the lake.

Parts of the hotel grounds are softly lit, but there are others where it's too dark to find our step. Ed takes out his phone and turns on the torch, but even with the narrow light we slip on the stony ground every so often, laughing as we make our way. We finally reach one edge of the park, marked by a clipped row of bushes, overlooking a cliff edge, high over the moonlit ripples of the lake.

"Can we stay forever?" I sigh, but as I turn around, I lose my footing on a loose stone and stumble to the ground, landing awkwardly on my ankle.

"Are you all right?" Ed is kneeling next to me as I wince.

"I hate to be a wimp but . . . no. It hurts."

He shines the phone torch on my leg and gently slides his hand under my ankle to examine it. "I take it you got travel insurance?" he asks.

"Do you think it's broken?"

"I don't know yet. It's not swollen, so that's good. Can you move it or put any pressure on it?"

I lift my foot and move it around. "Ow! Well, it hurts when I do that, if that's what you mean."

He puts his phone into his back pocket. "It's not broken."

"But I said it hurts!" I whimper.

"I believe you. But you wouldn't be able to do that if it was broken."

I tut and he helps me to my feet, clutching my elbow as I hobble to a bench overlooking the lake. I lower myself onto it and rub my ankle, muttering. "I'll go somewhere else for sympathy next time."

But when I sit up, my eyes are drawn first to his neck, the way the short bristles on his chin divert into wild directions, then to his parted lips and eventually his eyes, in which the silver light from the moon is reflected. For a gathering of heartbeats, I imagine his mouth drawing closer to mine, until I begin to wonder if it actually is.

"Everything all right over there?"

I glance up to see the concierge, straining his eyes in the dark as I sit up straight and Ed spins round to talk to him. "Yes, fine. *Grazie.*"

"Ah. So sorry! My colleague saw on the CCTV that the lady had fallen. We weren't sure if you needed medical help."

"I'm okay now. Honestly. But thank you," I tell him.

"No problem. Apologies again for disturbing you," he says, with a cordial wave, before walking away in the direction of the building.

CHAPTER
FORTY-FIVE

In the months after Christopher was prised out of her warm arms, Peggy's anger grew and grew. There were times when it felt like the only pure thing left in her life, racing like hot mercury through her veins every time she looked at her parents.

She came to despise everything about her father, a man she'd once looked up to, adored even. When she looked at him she saw an entirely different person from the one she'd seen before. Now the stench of smoke that clung to his moustache nearly choked her. The bulge over his trousers and the gluttonous way he ate, sating his greed, disgusted her. She hated having to sit across the dinner table from him, drinking water from the same tap, breathing the same stale air in their living room.

Her simpering mother was no better. She couldn't bear the way she would hover around, hoping for a sign of forgiveness without having ever said sorry. Apparently believing that "normality" could be resumed, just like that. Not that Peggy wanted an apology from her. Sympathy, tenderness or compassion were not things she craved.

Because the person she despised most was herself. She'd signed the papers. She'd let him slip away, conscious but not fully, half-blind, half-stupid, walking through a fog. She'd never believed that it was "for the best", but after a lifetime of obedience she hadn't worked out how to fight, and for that she would never forgive herself.

She refused to go to church any longer. She couldn't bear sitting next to her parents, listening to their muttered prayers, unable to reconcile the words she heard inside those gilded walls with what had happened to her. The Christian values she'd always thought she'd been taught were goodness, humanity, love. That was what all those Bible lessons were about, wasn't it? Now, as she sat on a cold pew, every word she heard sounded as hollow and fake as a wooden egg. Because those values were wholly absent on the day her baby was handed to a stranger, as if she, his own mother, had never existed.

As the soft folds of her belly contracted, she continued to function, but she wasn't living. She'd get up every morning and sit on the bus to her new job as secretary to the manager of a match factory. He wasn't a bad boss. There was nothing wrong with him at all, as long as she was prepared to put up with him looking at her chest when she was typing.

But a few months into the job, she woke one morning and decided she wasn't going to work that day. She left the house as usual, but instead of taking her normal route, she picked up a taxi and asked the driver to go to Nightingale House.

He dropped her off outside the gates and she crunched along the same path as when she'd been pregnant, wondering if every brick of the building had always held the same grim, threatening quality. When she rang the bell, one of the nurses answered. She visibly stiffened when she recognised Peggy, before telling her to wait in the hall while she got someone to come and see to her.

Peggy caused what matron would later describe to the police as a "terrible scene". All she wanted was to find out where Christopher had gone. To get back what was rightfully hers.

"But Peggy, he isn't yours," matron argued. She'd been sympathetic at the beginning, but when Peggy wouldn't have it, she'd gripped her by the wrist and shouted for two other nurses, who dragged her out. Peggy sat on the step, refusing to move, until the police arrived and drove her home.

Mrs Bennett from next door had been scrubbing her step when they pulled up. Peggy was the talk of the street for months afterwards and her mother cried herself to sleep every night. In her eyes, this shame was far worse than anything Peggy had endured.

By the time a second summer came around after Christopher's birth, Peggy could stand it no longer. It was 1965 by then and she was twenty-four, more than old enough to leave and go as far away as her sphere of imagination went.

She thought about Jack Newman in Hollywood, blissfully ignorant of the fate of his child, a child he never knew existed — and, she suspected, wouldn't have wanted anything to do with if he had. When she considered him now, she found it difficult to remember what had so bewitched her. His glamour seemed superficial, his smile one-dimensional. But he was right about one thing: there truly was a whole wide world out there.

Armed with an O Level in French and some meagre savings, she packed a bag and took a ferry across the English Channel and then the train to Paris. She was terrified and lost, but that was fine. She had other things to dominate her mind these days than her own fear.

Her theatre experience led her to a job as a hostess in a cabaret. It didn't pay well and certainly wasn't in any of the fancy places, but she didn't care. Watching the girls dressed in feathers, evoking all the romance of the Belle Epoque, was her only joy in an otherwise joyless life, a life so filled with sadness she never thought she would smile again. She didn't deserve to.

She never wanted to numb the pain. She never wanted to stop thinking about Christopher and where they had taken him. And she never wanted to forget how it felt when his tiny hand clutched hers and her heart spilled over with love for him in those perfect and impossible few weeks they spent together.

Not knowing where he'd gone was the worst part. She tried to tell herself if two people wanted a baby enough to adopt, then they must be prepared to open their hearts to love. She hoped they spoilt him, lavished him with affection.

But as she lay on her thin mattress at night, she would feel the crawl of despair again. There were times when her insides would ripple by themselves, as if Christopher was still kicking inside her. Then she'd close her eyes and be right back in Nightingale House, watching his tiny chest rise and fall while he was sleeping, smelling the soft, sweet skin and kissing the fluff of dark hair on his head.

CHAPTER
FORTY-SIX

Ed

There have been times over their years of friendship when Ed has felt so close to Allie that she's almost been an extension of him, and others when they've been so far apart that it's made his gut ache. But has he ever been attracted to her before now? Of course. To deny her loveliness would be churlish, so he never did. But when she'd step out of a taxi to meet him, his wolf whistle would be one they both understood to be ironic. Just a joke. Not real. Only now, a fundamental realisation has come about.

Being around her makes his limbs feel lighter, the air in his chest circulate more freely. She makes that impossible gesture, smiling, so easy and natural. Every little thing about her makes him happy.

As each day in Italy passes, the greater clarity he has on an issue that has quietly troubled him most of his adult life. And yet questions remain. Has he buried his feelings for Allie until now? Or has he never had the courage to recognise them, when they both outwardly defined their relationship as platonic? Are these feelings new, or simply newly recognised? He doesn't know. Which only adds to the sensation that what he feels for his oldest friend is ready to burst right out of him, like a butterfly that's been cocooned for too long.

But Ed is married to a woman who, for all her beauty and charisma, is too often devoured by her temper. When Julia is in the mood, she can shower Ed with affection. She'll send him a message telling him how lucky she is to have him, spend hours making a meal she thinks he'll love. She's a woman who sits on the board of two charities and is capable of showing true kindness, of making anyone who is the subject of her attention feel special.

The fact that they were very different was not something he ever minded. Despite an expensive education, Julia does not read books, indeed she's almost snooty about the idea, saying a bookish type of learning was inferior to true character.

He couldn't disagree. But true character was the problem. It was not simply that Julia could not control her anger, it's that she didn't want to. So Ed found himself treading on eggshells every time he entered the house, wondering what kind of mood she would be in. Questioning himself constantly when they were out in public, firmly keeping his eyes on a menu when they'd be eating out, actively going out of his way to avoid looking in the direction of any other women. He worried if he was working late, checking the tone in her voice as he phoned her regularly to make sure she knew he wasn't having an affair.

He was permanently on his best behaviour, yet it still didn't work. The tension worsened, and that developed into rows and, frequently, violence. Though Julia's punches were by no means the worst thing about it all. At least he knew how to react then: with a stubborn refusal to fight back, even if that infuriated her further.

Weeks would go by when things went back to normal, whatever that was. They acted like people in love. But the threat of an explosion of her temper was constant, and that made him paranoid, a feeling totally alien to him.

He couldn't deny what she said was true though — she'd never had a problem with his relationship with Allie. Or if she had, she'd hidden it well. How *could* she be the jealous kind when she was happy for him to remain close friends with another woman? She used that a lot as evidence. And it was a good point, which successfully convinced him that he must be going mad.

But there are only so many times you can close your eyes and breathe freely when a woman you thought you loved leans over and tenderly kisses the bruises she herself has created. Which was why he needed time to think. To consider the serious possibility of whether he should leave her and end the marriage. If only it had been that straightforward.

Julia sank into the chair opposite him at their kitchen table, her lip trembling. "Ed please don't. I know this is my fault. I don't deserve you."

She was saying all the right things but she'd said them all before. Her words were not cynical though. At that precise moment, she meant it.

"Julia. We need to consider the possibility that this marriage isn't working and isn't ever going to work. It's making both of us unhappy."

"But that's not right!" she protested. "That's not right at all. The only times that make me unhappy are when we row and you can't surely claim that's all my fault? I mean, I know . . . it sometimes gets out of hand, but, it's rarely me who *starts* it."

He didn't answer. There really was no point.

"Listen," she continued. "How about I do something about . . . that?" She didn't put a name to her uncontrollable bursts of aggression and he was glad. "I can go to therapy."

"I think that's a good idea."

A swarm of optimism spread across her face. "We could go together. Really work at this, as a couple. Heather and James have been seeing a marriage guidance counsellor and it's been the making of them. We could make it a weekly thing, then come home for a nice dinner and lovely sex and —"

"Julia, that doesn't mean I've made my mind up to stay."

Fury started clouding behind her eyes, like dozens of times before. He was ready for her to leap towards him, to look for something to throw at him. He'd already clocked the vase on the table and prepared himself a speech to try and reason with her if she picked it up. But Julia always had been good at surprises.

"How long have your parents been married, Ed?" She spoke calmly.

"What?"

"Thirty-five, thirty-six years? And they've never rowed in that entire time?"

"Of course they have. But not like —"

"They've *made* their marriage work, Ed. I'll bet you anything there would have been times when your dad wanted to leave. Every man does. But *he's* not that kind of guy. He's the kind who sticks it out, stays loyal to his family. I thought that's the kind of man you were too."

"You and I are completely different from my parents, Julia."

"No, we're not. All marriages go through rough patches. Theirs, ours, everyone's. But you don't just bail out at the first sign of trouble to go and fuck someone else."

"There's no one else. You know that."

Then she looked at him and realised she didn't need to hit him. And that power gave her a unique kind of pleasure, one that she'd relive for many days afterwards as she played back the conversation and the words that made his mouth fall open by a small but exquisite fraction.

"You're wrong, Ed. I've got something to tell you. I found out a few days ago. It was meant to be a surprise."

"What?" he asked, but somehow he already knew.

"I'm pregnant."

★ ★ ★

269

He still hates himself for what went through his mind. The prospect of being a father, something he'd always wanted, did not bring him the joy he'd imagined it would. Instead, dread rushed up in him like a tidal wave. He considered the possibility that she was lying, but then she produced dates and times on which they'd apparently had sex, and gave him details of an appointment at the hospital when he was to turn up for their baby's first scan.

Technically, he wasn't trapped. Technically, he could've walked out of the door without a care in the world. But Julia knew Ed well enough to know how much he valued the happy, stable family life he'd been privileged enough to have. She knew he wouldn't let her down, or at the very least, he wouldn't let his child down.

"This is a big shock, I know." She slid into the seat next to him and wrapped her fingers round his hand. Her palms felt thin and clammy. "And I want you to know that the last thing I want you to feel is pressured, or anything like that. I want you to stay with us — the baby and me — because you want to. Because you love us. Because you want to make a family with us."

The thought twisted in Ed's stomach. He had so much to say but the words retreated.

"So, actually. I think you're right. I think it would be a good idea if you and I do spend a little time apart, just so you can get your head around it."

He looked up at her. "So now you *want* me to leave?"

"I want you to have some space and make the decision yourself," she said calmly. "Check into a hotel or . . . isn't Jeremy away at the moment? You could stay at his flat for a little while, I'm sure he wouldn't mind. Then hopefully you'll come to the right decision. Until then, let's keep the baby our little secret. Can I trust you to do that? Until we're both ready to tell the world, show everyone how happy we are together — you, me and our little boy or girl."

He nodded numbly.

She bent down and wiped the thread of clear liquid from her cheeks. "I want you to know this though, Ed. I'm going to change. For you and me and our baby. I promise you."

He was on autopilot from then on. He did as she suggested and moved out, logging the date of her first scan in his diary — only three weeks away. He barely remembers Allie turning up at Jeremy's flat. Julia was absolutely right though. He did need time to take stock, to work out his priorities and what he needed to do for the best.

Not just the best for her and the baby, but for him. He's always known the answer, even in his lowest moments. Because he knows that, with a child to consider, he would never be happy — he never *could* be happy — if he decided to leave. He simply couldn't live with himself. The fact that he is finally recognising what he feels for Allie, that if he's honest, he's probably loved her his entire adult life, hasn't changed anything.

His decision was made before he even left England.

At the end of the trip, he will be going back to Julia, the mother of his child. Whatever happens, he will make his marriage work.

CHAPTER
FORTY-SEVEN

Allie

The aromatic tang of coffee cuts through the sweet baked scent rising from the buffet table, as chiffon strips of light stream in from outside. There is a feast of Italian donuts and rich buns, studded with raisins and dredged with confectioners' sugar. But my appetite has left me this morning so I simply pick up a Greek yogurt and arrange some melon on a plate, before taking one of the juices lined up like potions in tiny bottles. I step outside onto the terrace and spot Ed at a table.

I feel heat blotching on my neck as I approach him, the leather soles of my sandals making too much noise as they tap along the tiles. He looks up and straightens his back.

"Morning," I say too loudly, as I pull out the chair. The legs scrape on the floor, making me wince. A waiter dashes over to push in my seat for me and ask what I'd like to drink. "An espresso please. Strong," I add.

"That could be stronger than you think," Ed tells me, as the waiter walks away.

"I need it. *Far* too much to drink yesterday," I add meaningfully, an excuse for the evening's strange events.

He lifts his cup to his lips. People are talking in whispers and I suddenly long for some music, something to make this feel a little easier.

"Our trip to Lake Garda feels as though it's gone so quick. There are still so many places we haven't seen."

"You should come back here for a proper holiday one day," he says and for some reason my spine prickles at the use of the "you" and not "we". I push the thought out of my head, appalled that it even crossed my mind.

"One coffee, strong," says the waiter as he places it in front of me.

"Thank you." I pick it up to take a sip, jolting as it hits my taste buds. "You might have been right."

When Ed smiles, the feeling it provokes in me is so unbearable that I have to lower my eyes. But it's then that I realise it's no longer enough to simply sit in front of Ed and not look at him. Just knowing he is there, the memory of last night piercing into me, turns me inside out. I don't need to look at him to know the way his lips press against his coffee cup, the gentle shift of his Adam's apple when he swallows, or the way his fingers move when he picks up a fork. I know all these mannerisms because I've seen them a million times and could see them a million more without ever tiring of them.

274

"I'm going to call Julia today," he says. "To have a proper conversation about our future."

"Oh good!" I reply. "I'm so glad."

"I'll do it when we get to Portofino."

"You're still . . . coming then?"

He looks surprised I had to ask. "Of course."

For the first time I'm not sure he *should* be coming. The thought that I should say something about last night tiptoes through my head, but I dismiss the idea immediately. I have known Ed long enough to be sure that we both prefer this civilised pretence, the one in which we can silently reassure ourselves that nothing happened. Which is of course true, or at least a version of the truth. Even the other variant is short on actual, solid happenings. A brush of skin against mine as we sat next to each other on the bench. A skipped heartbeat. A locking of eyes.

"I've made my decision, Allie," he continues. "I'm going to be telling Julia that I'm coming home. To make a go of things."

"That's wonderful, Ed." I sound like I really mean it. I *want* to mean it. "And is that what you want now?"

He hesitates. "Yes."

I think about asking him what made him change his mind, but I suspect I know. While my feelings for him were exploding last night, for him it had the opposite effect. It crystallised how important his marriage is.

"She'll be very happy." When he doesn't respond to this commentary, I add: "And so will you."

"I need to explain something though, Allie," he says. "I haven't told you everything. Julia hadn't wanted me to say anything —"

"Then *don't*," I say dismissively. "You don't need to explain anything at all."

CHAPTER
FORTY-EIGHT

I sometimes feel as though I've been powering through most of my adult life, striving, achieving, pushing the boundaries of my intellectual capabilities. This approach has made me happy, give or take the odd break-up, bereavement and punishing bout of PMS. But has something ever happened to you — something you knew would be coming sooner or later — that unravels so quickly and leaves you with so little influence upon it, that it shakes your definition of happiness to the core?

When I won my dream job at Liverpool University nearly three years ago I was ecstatic. It was everything I'd wanted professionally — to be independent, to lecture at a Russell Group university, to have my own lab. Of course, the fact that Rob reacted to the news by dumping me did take the gloss off my triumph somewhat.

"No one deserves this like you do, Allie," he said, about a minute after Alistair had phoned me to tell me I'd got the job. "You'll be amazing."

I was about to throw my arms around him, but he stiffened and something in his body language made me pull back. "We haven't talked about what this means for us, have we?"

"Oh, we'll be fine," I shrugged. "We survived a long-distance relationship when I was in the US. Cardiff and Liverpool are significantly closer together."

"Thing is, Allie, I don't think that's going to work for me," he said, as if he was referring to a faulty printer.

I spent the next twenty-four hours trying to work out how I felt about this, realising that the distress I was experiencing wasn't entirely about Rob himself. I felt oddly numb to the fact that I wouldn't share another meal with him, or lie on the sofa watching another Scandi thriller, even though we'd been together for four years and I'd always had a huge amount of respect and affection for him.

It took this rejection to make me realise how little appetite I had for being alone. That I might have work, but work wasn't everything — I don't think I'd ever believed that it was, contrary to what some people might have thought. I wanted someone to share my life with, even if that someone might not have been him. It struck me that perhaps that was the issue, what had kept us with each other for so long. Being together meant neither of us had to be lonely.

There was no point going into work to take my mind off things now that I'd handed in my notice, so instead I went shopping in St David's and emerged from Jo Malone in a cloud of sample fragrances, when Ed phoned. "You're a dark horse. I've just bumped into your dad. He told me your news about moving to Liverpool. You kept that quiet!" He sounded in an ebullient, playful mood.

"I've literally only just handed in my notice," I replied.

"Have you got an official date for your return?"

"Four weeks today."

"So we can get together on the Saturday night? Or will you have too much to do?"

"I'm technically unemployed, at least for three days. I'll have absolutely *nothing* to do."

"Great. It's a date then. Leave it with me and I'll plan something good. And, Allie?"

"Yes?"

"I can't wait to see you."

We went for small plates and cocktails at a new place in Bold Street, with exposed bricks and candles flickering on rustic-looking tables. We ate falafel and drank Whip Royales as we sat in the shadows, reminiscing.

There were times that night when I'd look at his face, at the light in his eyes, and I'd think, not just about Rob, but some of the people I'd hooked up with at university all those years earlier. The one-night stands, the flings and the flirtations. Suddenly a question that I'd tried to stop myself from asking for years pressed into the front of my mind. Why did nobody ever make me feel the way Ed did?

"Is Rob going to follow you to Liverpool?" he asked.

I froze and looked up at him from under my eyelashes. "Oh. Dad didn't tell you."

"Tell me what?"

"Well . . . we broke up."

His expression changed like a flash flood. "Oh. I'm sorry. I just assumed . . . I don't know. Do you want to talk about it?"

"No," I said quickly, stabbing my fork into my food. He frowned disapprovingly. "It's fine. Honestly. We'd grown apart," I offered, a line I hoped would satisfy him.

"I feel like an idiot, sitting here and telling you how wonderful it is for you to be back."

"It *is* wonderful. I've got my dream job."

He remained cautious. "So it was you who ended it?"

I squirmed. "No. But, honestly, I'm fine."

A strange silence hung in the air and I was keen to change the subject. "Have you done any more work on your house?" Ed had spent a fortune on his place since he'd moved into it.

But he didn't answer. Instead, he fixed his eyes on the flickering candle between us, the black dots of his pupils dilating.

"Ed?"

"Hmm? Sorry."

"How's the house? You were getting a new bathroom last time we spoke."

Then he looked up and downed the last of his drink, as I felt the heat of his eyes travelling across my face.

"It's on the market. We've been looking at a place in the Wirral."

"Very posh." Then I registered something. "We?"

He swallowed. "You remember I told you about Julia?"

It took me a moment to recall that he'd started seeing someone by that name when I'd last met up with him at Christmas. They'd got together through one of the charities he was involved with. I'd looked her up on Facebook afterwards and slotted her into the same category as the Emilys and the Annabels. I'd assumed that, just like them, she wouldn't have lasted.

"We want to get somewhere before . . . before we get married. That's the reason I wanted to see you tonight, Allie. I wanted to ask you to be my best woman."

Organising Ed's stag party felt wrong on every level and I don't mean because I have a vagina and therefore tradition says I shouldn't have even been there. Perhaps I was simply in shock, that he was marrying a woman who by this stage I'd never even met.

But I was determined to like her, I truly was.

On the morning of the festivities, I picked him up at his house, noting as I stepped into the hall that it already looked different now that she'd moved in. The dark walls had been painted in a subtle palette of stone and grey-blue. The books that had been stacked rather haphazardly from floor to ceiling had been subjected to a cull and what remained were placed in beautiful, glossy shelves. But the most striking change was the absence of clutter. There wasn't a remote control on show, nor a magazine, there were no house keys or notes stuck on the fridge.

I told myself that I wasn't apprehensive about meeting her, yet my stomach had been churning since the moment I'd woken up. But as Ed took me through to the kitchen, she greeted me warmly and, within moments, had linked her arm through mine like I was her long-lost sister.

"I think you deserve a medal, Allie," Julia said, in the kitchen, flicking on the kettle. It was the solitary item on the worktop, an Alessi polished to within an inch of its life. "There can't be many women brave enough to go on a stag party with twelve men, let alone attempt to organise them."

I remember being fascinated by her skin, which was as flawless as the surface of a satin ballet slipper, and marvelling at how her hair swept into a side bun that, unlike my disobedient locks, did exactly as it was told. "I just hope they treat you like a lady."

"Nobody else does so that'd be a first," I replied.

Ed was smiling. "Allie will cope. She's seen *The Hangover* so knows what to expect."

Julia walked over and squeezed his hand. "You're so silly," she murmured and planted a kiss on his temple.

She took the time and trouble to ask me about work and my family. She complimented me on my boots, even though they were scuffed, a little old, and I'm sure she wouldn't have been caught dead in them herself. She was generous with her small talk, refusing to give in to the temptation to discuss her own life, as fascinating as she was, at least to me.

I felt this keenly at one point, and that there was an elephant in the room that needed to be broached,

282

something I did when Ed went to collect his overnight bag from his bedroom. "I hope you don't mind the fact that Ed has chosen me to be his best woman?"

She turned around and smiled. "Allie, of *course* not. Why would I?"

"Oh, you *shouldn't*. I'm sure Ed's explained to you that in all the years we've known each other, our relationship has never been anything other than platonic."

Her eyes softened. "He did explain that. It's really good of you to say this, Allie, you're a real gem. But you don't need to worry. Ed told me the first time he even mentioned you that he's never felt the slightest attraction to you." She paused momentarily. "That sounded awful, sorry! But I'm sure the feeling is entirely mutual."

It occurred to me that from anyone else this might have been interpreted as a barbed comment, but at the time, it seemed to be an innocent remark, not intended to cause offence. So I didn't let it. Yet there have been times when I've thought about it since that have made me wonder. Julia isn't a woman prone to putting her foot in it.

I'd put a lot of thought into the perfect stag party, hoping for something with originality and style, until I realised that the only prerequisite for the twelve invitees was that it would involve lots of testosterone and alcohol. So that meant paintballing, followed by the pub. I couldn't knock their enthusiasm, bless them: I've never seen such excitement at the prospect of signing a disclaimer form waiving all rights in the event of concussion, major injuries and hospitalisation.

Still, it was easy to get into the swing of it and, during one invigorating moment, I managed to shoot Ed's brother Mike in the side. Only, when I'd stopped fist-pumping, I realised he was lying on the floor groaning and clutching his torso.

"I think I might have ruptured my liver."

I gasped, stooping down to examine him. "Oh! Mike, I'm so sorry."

"What are you talking about — this is brilliant," he grinned, before staggering to his feet and running off for more.

Afterwards, we went to the pub for the booze and debauchery part of the event. It was rather light on the latter, until Jeremy was asked to leave a club after he'd split his trousers while attempting to breakdance. Still, everyone enjoyed themselves, including Ed's dad, who came over to congratulate me near the end of the evening.

"Well done, Allie. Your first best woman duty is now done and you've done yourself proud."

"Well, I hope Mike doesn't feel put out. He is his brother after all."

"Mike would be the first to admit that he couldn't organise a piss-up in a brewery. Anyway, Ed thinks the world of you. His mother was convinced you two would end up together, you know."

"Oh. Ha! Really?" I said.

"Yeah." He chuckled. Then he caught my eye and whatever he saw in it made his laughter dissolve in his throat.

★ ★ ★

Six weeks later, I rose to my feet to deliver my speech in the magnificent dining room of Knowsley Hall. Every little touch of their big day had been perfection: the sprawling, Grade I listed mansion surrounded by blossom trees in full, delicate bloom. The vows, touching and understated, leaving barely a dry eye in the house. The wedding breakfast — succulent saddle of organic lamb and English asparagus with Jersey Royal potatoes, followed by a trio of tasteful desserts, none of which I'd been able to stomach.

I wore an exquisitely tailored suit in a rich shade of navy, to match those worn by the groomsmen. Julia had told me that I could choose peach like the bridesmaids if I'd wanted, but that hadn't felt right. Besides, the suit was so finely crafted, made just for me, that when I slipped it on with my Louboutin shoes and the singular rose pinned in the sweep of my hair, it gave me a welcome confidence boost after days of feeling fuzzy with nerves as I tried to get my speech right.

I'd known before I even stood up that it wasn't the best I could do.

Because filling it full of all the memories I had of Ed would've been impossible without laying bare what I really felt for him. The whole room would've seen it written on my face, heard it in the quiver of my voice.

So I skipped the conversations we'd have on the bus that would have us rolling with laughter until our cheeks hurt. I bypassed the hours we'd spend in his bedroom, talking about everything and nothing, and how, even at the age of fourteen, I'd somehow known that Ed was different from anybody else I would ever meet. I couldn't tell them about the time we'd considered starting a band together, or the night we spent at the bonfire party, when we planned a future that never materialised. All of that would've revealed that my relationship with this man had caused me more pleasure and pain than any other. It also would have revealed something that only then, at that precise moment, I finally admitted to myself.

I was hopelessly and irreversibly in love with him.

CHAPTER
FORTY-NINE

Peggy met Gerald after she stumbled near the waterfall in the Parc des Buttes-Chaumont and he helped her to her feet. It was mid-autumn, on a day of colliding clouds and leaves that tripped and danced in the wind.

"Mademoiselle! Ça va? Vous vous êtes fait mal?" he asked.

He spoke good French, but she could tell he wasn't a Frenchman. His accent had a familiar intonation that warmed her insides.

"I'm fine, thank you," she replied and a smile breezed onto his features, illuminating the soft grey eyes that he hid behind boxy spectacles.

"You don't look as if you're from these parts," he said and she laughed.

"Is it that obvious?"

As much as Peggy loved France, it was nice to be around an Englishman. Gerald was relatively new to Paris too — he worked for Thomson Holidays, giving rich holidaymakers from England tours of the sights and taking them to restaurants with food that "pleased English tastes".

"There aren't many of them, believe me," he'd chuckled.

She liked Gerald's kindness and humour, and the fact that he kept a jar of Branston Pickle to spread on his cheese for lunch. He was the first person she'd met since being in France who could make a proper cup of tea.

She decided early on to tell him everything. She thought it only fair that he knew what he was getting: a girl who'd got herself pregnant out of wedlock, who'd scandalised her family and allowed strangers to take away her baby.

Shame boiled inside her as she confessed every detail to him, expecting that, when she was finished, he wouldn't want anything more to do with her. But he listened in silence, then pulled her into his arms and stroked her hair, whispering, "you poor love" as she cried until her insides were raw.

Peggy didn't fall in love the way other girls do. She didn't dance around her bedroom, giddy from the thought of his touch. Instead, on her nights off, she'd sit next to Gerald in his tiny flat in Montreuil, dunking galettes into her Ovaltine as she felt the warm press of his hand in hers. Gradually, she realised that she'd found gold: a man who knew her secrets and still loved her, regardless.

One day the following spring, she found herself back in a church for the first time since she'd left England. She didn't know why she'd gone in exactly, but it was a curious and emotional experience. She sat at the back and didn't sing or pray. She just watched and listened, monitoring the doubts and uncertainty that lived between the bruises on her heart.

She walked out after the service, cursing the world, and the church, and the fact that humans are so flawed and full of contempt. But, two weeks later, she went back. Then the week after that. Gradually, she came to realise something that felt important. The church is made up of sinful people, just like her mother and father, just like Peggy herself, just like everyone who'd never set foot in heaven. But in this dark and destructive world, it could also be something else: a beacon of light.

It wasn't long after Peggy and Gerald married, in a short service in the mairie, with only his mother and two friends present, that news reached her that her father had died of throat cancer. She went home for the funeral and dutifully stood beside her mother, a timid and unhappy stranger, whose hair had been eaten away by alopecia. As Peggy reached out and briefly held her hand, her mother turned to her. The gratitude that shone in her eyes sent a surge of pity through Peggy, a feeling that would bother her for many months afterwards.

They moved back to Liverpool the following year and were happy and in love in their quiet and unshowy way. Their love was the kind that made him run a bath for her at the end of a long day, and made her never feel so safe as when wrapped in the folds of his borrowed sweater. *Soon after, an everyday miracle happened.*

Peggy became pregnant again.

Those nine months were a very different experience from the first time she'd been expecting. Her happiness was tinged with an anxiety that came from a very different place than before. Her fear was primeval, almost superstitious. And all Gerald could offer was his gentle, persistent reassurance that this time would be different: her baby was going nowhere.

Christine was born in Oxford Street Maternity Hospital in Liverpool, with the help of a jolly Glaswegian midwife called Agnes and with Gerald at her side, pretending that his fingers hadn't turned blue as she squeezed them. Afterwards, as hazy winter sunshine shone through the window, she gazed into the eyes of her new baby and for the first time allowed herself to believe that her husband might be right.

"We still haven't settled on a name, have we?" she said.

"Apart from Philip."

She chuckled. "I don't think that'll suit her somehow, do you?"

Gerald had thought of a girl's name a long time earlier, but something had stopped him from suggesting it until now. "What would you think about . . . Christine?"

Peggy froze and he immediately regretted it. He'd just thought that perhaps she might find some comfort in the name, a nod of recognition to her lost little brother Christopher. Now he felt crass and insensitive, until a tired smile appeared on his wife's lips. "I think it's a lovely idea."

As a baby, Christine had piercing blue eyes, soft, skinny legs and a rosebud mouth capable of the loudest cries Peggy had ever heard. She was permanently hungry and rarely inclined to sleep. But each time she heard Christine grizzling in the witching hour, Peggy didn't roll over and hope she'd drift off again. She'd be eager, too eager really, to lift her out of her cot and to her breast. To be a mother.

As a little girl, Christine was clever, bright and had a precocious sense of humour. She could read before any of her peers and would have Peggy and Gerald in stitches with the funny faces she'd pull, the jokes she'd make up.

By the time she hit puberty, Christine was strong, beautiful and wilful — a combination that other parents might consider a headache. She got into trouble at school a few times. Once, notably, for calling out a teacher for repeatedly referring to her friend Saiqa as "the little foreigner", despite the fact that she'd been born less than two miles from the radius of the school. After a heated debate about what constitutes racism, Peggy and Gerald were called in to see the head teacher, where they were supposed to agree that their daughter's refusal to back down was intolerable.

But the best Peggy had been able to offer was: "We'll have to agree to disagree," before Christine was suspended from school for a day. Peggy took her shopping, followed by afternoon tea and cakes. She was

291

proud that her daughter was feisty. She wanted her to be fearless and worldly, a girl who stood up for herself and others. None of the things that she'd been.

She'd always loved music and had eclectic tastes. She'd go to HMV every Saturday and spend every last bit of her pocket money on a new record, gradually building up quite a collection. She was constantly organising and reorganising it — sometimes alphabetically, other times by colour, all just an excuse to treasure each glossy sleeve.

This passion for music led to her joining a punk band at fourteen — The Rancid Peacocks. She had a romance with its chain-smoking, tattooed lead singer, a man Peggy tried to like but still couldn't shake the feeling that he needed a good wash. After the punk singer, Christine had two other short-lived romances, one with a boy whose father was a merchant banker and clearly fancied himself more than her; another with a boy who — even in Gerald's presence — couldn't stop glaring at her daughter's chest like an Alsatian eyeing up a cream bun.

Then, shortly after her sixteenth birthday, Christine did the most shocking thing of all: she met a lovely, decent boy who loved every wild contradiction about her.

The first time Peggy was introduced to Joe, he stood on her front step clutching a yellow crocus packed tightly into a ceramic pot and tied with a nylon ribbon. His young face was dappled with freckles and topped with a mop of thick, blond hair, but his shoulders were those of a man, broad and strong.

292

"Hello, Mrs Culpepper," he said, and although he didn't sound nervous, his neck turned pink when he spoke. "It's lovely to meet you."

Peggy had never been much of a cook, but she could rustle up a ham salad and a lemon drizzle cake, and if that wasn't enough there was always Marks & Spencer. "You've got a really nice house," he said.

"She's been dusting since seven this morning," Christine whispered and Peggy swiped her with her tea towel, which made Joe laugh and relax for the first time. Then the three of them chatted through a very nice lunch, if she did say so herself, even if she'd forgotten to buy salad cream and the butter was too hard to spread.

The more time Joe spent around Christine, the more obvious it became that he'd do anything for her. By this stage, she'd got a little job in a chemist on a Saturday and come rain or shine, he'd be there at the end of her shift, just so she had someone to walk home with. They'd stay for hours in Christine's room. Joe, a music lover himself, was probably the only person except her allowed to touch those records.

He'd often turn up at the house with a tatty acoustic guitar he had, a hand-me-down from his brother that he'd tried to scrape the stickers off but was still left with a gluey residue that never quite disappeared. He was shy about it at first, but eventually she coaxed a song out of him and loved listening to him.

"I will get a proper guitar one day," he used to tell Christine. "A Gibson Les Paul, or a 335, like BB King's." But it never mattered to her what he played on, just that he was playing and that, with every chord, she felt herself falling a little bit more in love with him.

Although his sweet, calming personality juxtaposed her fiery impulsiveness, somehow they worked. With this lovely boy in her life, Christine seemed to relax for the first time in her life. It was as if she could finally stop trying so hard.

That's not to say she didn't fight for the things she believed in. At seventeen, she joined a group of friends and hitchhiked to the Greenham Common Peace Camp — to protest against nuclear weapons with 70,000 other women. When she returned, just as Joe had won a job in the fire service, Peggy had wondered if there might have been a gulf between them, but the opposite was true. He was enthralled by her passion, by everything about her.

"Joe has told me he wants to marry me," Christine said soon afterwards. And when Peggy replied, "God help him," she was only half-joking. Because, for all her daughter's loveliness, Peggy always knew she had the capacity to hurt him right there in the palm of her hand.

CHAPTER
FIFTY

Allie

I was determined not to be jealous of Julia. I was not going to be that woman. But as they flew off to Paris on their honeymoon, my thoughts began eating me up from inside. It didn't feel like sadness as I'd experienced it before, more an emptiness that made my head foggy and my chest acidic.

But at least I had my job. I threw myself into work, spending hours in the lab, well beyond the point at which everyone else's lights had gone off, then returning to my new flat to polish my lecture plans until they shone. I worked most weekends too, though made time to go to the cinema or for lunch in the Georgian quarter with Petra, with whom I'd already formed a strong friendship.

Then there was Dad who, a few weekends after the wedding, I joined on a fishing afternoon. I had never fished in my life, but on that particular day, the only alternative was going into the lab again and the bags under my eyes were starting to tell me that perhaps I was overdoing it. I worked out within twenty minutes, however, that if I was looking to stay busy to stop my mind wandering to other matters, I'd picked the wrong pastime.

"There's not much *action* involved in this, is there?" I said.

"I have enough action at work," he shrugged.

"Have you saved anyone's life lately?"

"Well, I got an old lady out of a first-floor window after her electric blanket set the bed on fire."

"Seriously?"

"She was in the bathroom when it started, but thankfully had an emergency cord. We managed to get her out before the damage had spread, so the only treatment she needed was for minor smoke inhalation. And probably shock at being thrown over my shoulder while she was still in her nightie."

"Well done, Dad."

"Oh, it was a team effort."

"You always say that."

"Well, it always is."

"I can see why you'd like to just sit around when you've been doing that kind of thing," I said.

"It's just a way of slowing down sometimes. Gives you space to think and contemplate the big stuff, you know."

Precisely why it was a terrible idea for me. Because any contemplation I did these days involved the way Ed looked on his wedding day, in fact the way he always looked around Julia. It wasn't that he glowed in her presence, the way teenage boys do when the most popular, pretty girl in the school agreed to go out with them. It was subtler than that. It was as if he wanted to be better than the man he already was. His love was so big that it filled every corner of a room, it was already working so hard. But then that was Ed. He never has approached anything half-heartedly. If he was going to run a business, it was going to be the best he could make it. If he was going to be a husband, he was going to be the best it was possible to be.

"If you want action, I'll show you how to cast a fly properly," Dad said, and I snapped out of my thoughts.

"Okay."

"Once you've got the technique right for this, it'll set you up in the long run."

"What long run?"

He gave me a few instructions, and told me I needed to aim for between ten and twenty metres from the bank. After four attempts, my rod was in the water and we sat and . . . well, we just sat.

"I once tried to persuade your mother to come fishing," he told me. "She was bored stiff. She was a bit like your grandma in that sense, could never sit still."

I smiled. "So, if not this, what did you and Mum do together at weekends?"

"Oh, we went out with friends, or to gigs, or the cinema. She loved movies. 'Anything as long as it's not soppy.' That's what she always said. So, Hitchcock films, comedies . . . she loved *The Lost Boys* — we saw that twice. It helped that it had a great soundtrack. She loved her music as much as me."

"Do you think . . . you'll ever meet anyone again, Dad?"

He thought for a moment. "I don't know, really. It's not that I'm a martyr to being alone, or I'm particularly fond of cooking for one. It's just hard to envisage meeting another person who could ever mean as much to me as your mother did."

I pushed away a box of bait, hoping to get rid of the stink of what appeared to be prawns.

"Hey, have the photos come back from Ed's wedding yet? You haven't talked much about it," Dad said.

"Haven't I?" I lowered my eyes. "Well, it was swish. The venue was incredible. I don't think it would be controversial for me to say that Julia's family looked more at home in a Grade one listed Georgian mansion than anyone else." I flashed him a glance. "She's very classy."

"It must be odd for you, having not spent that much time with Ed for all these years and then, when you get back together, he gets married."

"We were never *together*, Dad."

"I know, I didn't mean that." Then I focused on the water lapping against the horizon, the orange sun shining bright in a brilliant blue sky and I realised my throat had dried up.

"All right?" Dad said gently.

Without thinking I glanced up and the look in my eyes must've been like an unfolding storybook. He didn't need me to fill in the gaps. He already knew what I felt for Ed. I suspect he'd always known.

My chin trembled and I nodded. He shuffled in and put his arm round me. I looked at his hands, the skin on his knuckles, the way they'd cracked and weathered over the years. Those were the hands that had rocked me as a baby and had helped me move house. They were the hands that had held my mother's as she was dying and the only hands that could possibly make any of this feel better, just for being folded into mine.

"You'll be all right, love."

"Of course I will," I replied, maintaining the pretence that I didn't know what he was talking about.

He pulled back and his expression changed. "The hardest thing in the world is watching someone you love lose their heart to another." I didn't reply.

"Look, Allie," he continued gently, "do you think it's wise for you to continue seeing Ed? Can you handle this friendship when he's married to someone else?"

I felt my teeth grind. "I don't know."

"I just can't stand the thought of you being unhappy around him."

I looked up. "Do you think that's what I should do? Break all ties with him?"

He sighed. "I honestly don't know. Ed is a good guy and he's been a great friend to you. And I know more than anyone that there are some people who are worth keeping in your life, even if you feel . . . they've let you down. But only you know if you can do it."

It was this speech that made me think I could.

Human beings are creatures with a unique ability to recognise that what we want is not always what is good for us, I reasoned. We have control over our actions, can identify desires as harmful and unwanted. People live with unhelpful yearnings all the time without acting on them. We might *feel* like punching that traffic warden,

299

or drinking that tenth glass of wine, succumbing to our basest instincts as we turn every one of life's corners, but we don't. We make choices, and it's those choices that define us.

I knew then, if I hadn't already, that I'd judge myself harshly if I simply called time on a life-long friendship, with absolutely no good explanation, at least not one I could share.

"I wish things were as simple as they had been with you and Mum," I continued. "You were so young when you met and yet neither of you ever had any doubts. You were unshakeable."

He picked up the rod and started winding the twine. "That's not *strictly* true, Allie," he replied.

"What do you mean?"

A lump moved slowly down his neck. "I'm just saying, if you expect fairy tales . . . you won't get them. Sometimes finding the person you're meant to be with can be a rocky path. People are complicated, Allie. Your mum was complicated. You shouldn't ever think she wasn't."

As I lie in bed on our last night in Lake Garda, the ceiling fan whirrs above me, moving hot air around the room but not really cooling it. My legs jostle under the covers, agitated as I replay that conversation until all I can do is sit up and click on the bedside lamp.

As the room floods with light, so too does a series of flashbacks. Of my mother's wedding speech. Of my dad failing to answer when the lady in hospital asked if he was my father. Of an undercurrent of a feeling that has perhaps always been there, bubbling under the surface.

A cold realisation sweeps through me.

He knew.

Dad knew that my mother had cheated on him.

CHAPTER
FIFTY-ONE

We leave Sirmione the following morning and embark on a train journey that takes most of the day. With every mile closer to the Ligurian coast, a familiar, preternatural dread begins to creep up on me. It's a feeling that goes beyond the fear of stumbling across Stefano in the street. Now I have an address where I *know* he lives.

I repeatedly glance at my mobile, my fingers hovering over Dad's name in the contact book as I contemplate simply phoning him to ask exactly what happened all those years ago. But what if I'm wrong about him knowing about Stefano McCourt and Mum? For all my suspicions, this is not a risk I can take lightly. In the absence of certainty, all I can do is stick to plan A.

Ed is immersed in his book, a collection of modern poems, the sort of thing he loves and that I'd rather eat my own forearm than read. As we zip through the Italian countryside, I watch him privately from the opposite seat as the pads of his fingers rub the corner of each page, before he turns it over, his pupils dilating as they settle onto the new words. I find myself studying the nuances of his expression, as he frowns at something he's reading, or gently raises his eyebrows in surprise.

"How many changes do we have to make on this train?" I ask.

"Three. Except I thought we could get off early for the final leg, even if it's not quite as straightforward."

"Why?"

"Because there's only one real way to arrive in Portofino. By sea."

Our boat slices through the cool water of the Ligurian sea, spraying tiny droplets on my sunburnt shoulders. A small pod of dolphins follows in our wake, playing in the bubbling surf, as the rocky coastline glows through a filter of soft pink light.

Eventually, Ed nudges me and points to our destination. Even from a distance, the sight is breathtaking: a series of painted buildings that cluster like tiny gemstones around a glistening bay. The towering valley that surrounds it is so thick with vegetation that it's impossible to work out where it starts and finishes.

As we approach the sun-warmed inlet, the colour of the sea changes to a spectacular shade of turquoise, as clear as any swimming pool. It is lined with brilliant white super-yachts, with gleaming decks built for fashionistas and film stars to lie on while the sun soaks into their skin.

The lush cliffs above us are dotted with Italianate mansions and villas, towers and steeples, all rising up from amongst the trees, as lemon blossom and sea water mingle to create a sweet-salt breeze. When we pass the narrowest point of the bay, I realise that each of the slender buildings is not simply painted in a different colour, muted shades of red and mustard-yellow, soft pinks and creamy whites. The whole stretch of architecture is a work of art, with trompe l'oeil facades that could fool any eye into believing that their windows are ornately framed with gold.

We step off the boat onto a quintessential Italian *piazzetta*, packed with stylish cafes and pretty restaurants with outdoor tables and menus dominated by catch-of-the-day fish.

"Our hotel is just up here," Ed says, taking my suitcase. I follow him up a steep street lined with chic boutiques and tiny shops, too narrow to accommodate cars even if they were allowed. He leads me through a series of interconnecting alleyways with the help of the GPS on his phone and eventually, we reach the boutique hotel in which we'll be staying, a slender building with a seashell exterior and terracotta pots filled with Moroccan daisies.

"I'm already in love with Portofino," I tell him. "Is it too late to give up my career as an academic research scientist and become an international jet-setter instead?"

He laughs. "Surely you'd be bored stiff lying around on one of those decks all day in your Chanel sunglasses?"

"Probably, but don't spoil the fantasy. Anyway, my sunglasses are M&S."

We check in and arrange to meet later for a drink before dinner, then I'm shown to an elegantly furnished room, every tiny detail of which is designed to enhance a guest's experience, from the sleek stone bathroom to the Bulgari courtesy kit. I begin unpacking when my phone beeps and a text arrives from Khalid.

Did you get my email?

I frown and type a response.

No. Why is everything okay?

I don't wait for him to answer, logging on to the hotel Wi-Fi and clicking on my inbox.

Khalid's message is at the top with the heading:

Nothing to worry about BUT . . .

I click on the email and begin reading.

Hi Allie,
A couple of the experiments yesterday did not show any chloride secretion, so the efficiency data isn't looking quite as good as it has been. I will be working on more tomorrow and the rest of the week and will get back to you as soon as I've analysed the data. Will

keep everything crossed that this isn't significant but thought you'd want to know.

Khalid.

I sit back on the bed and take this in. He's right. The latest results might not be as good as previously, but it could just be a blip. All we'd need is a couple more weeks of positive data to get back on track. Nevertheless, I begin typing:

Thanks for this. Yep, no panic. We will just keep increasing the N numbers and hope the efficiency improves again. Any other news, do let me know immediately though. Thanks, Allie.

CHAPTER
FIFTY-TWO

Our evening stroll to the legendary Hotel Splendido is more of a hike, but a leisurely one, along a tiny pathway cut into the cliff, filled with wildflowers and the sound of birdsong. Part of me is glad there were no rooms available here, because I know for sure Ed would have suggested staying and footing the bill, something I cannot in any conscience allow him to do after seeing the nightly rate. But I can live with dinner, especially as I'm paying this time.

When we arrive, we are directed to the terrace through the building, a sixteenth-century monastery decadently renovated at the turn of the last century. It is a backdrop of pure, old-world glamour, of classic cocktails and luxurious fabrics, with the finest furniture and a collection of monochrome photographs of illustrious past guests, everyone from Ava Gardner to Tom Hanks.

Outside, there are arches filled with huge potted lemon trees, a stretching saltwater pool and a myriad of sea views, framed by branches of wisteria that cascade from the cliffside gardens. It is a place of abundant flowers and Mediterranean palms that sway in the sea breeze. A place of pure Italian magic.

We take a seat and order two Bellinis, as Ed begins chatting to the waiter in Italian.

"They have quite a guest list," he says, after the waiter has left to fetch our drinks. "Apparently, Richard Burton proposed to Elizabeth Taylor — the first time — here, during a break from filming *Cleopatra*. They came back a few times afterwards. It was a favourite of theirs."

"I think it would be a favourite of anyone's," I say.

As night begins to fall and the harbour glitters with life, we dine on food that makes the most of our seaside location: seared scallops, pasta with black truffle and parmesan cream and *filetto di San Pietro* — John Dory — in a heavenly seafood broth.

"Did you finish your poetry book?" I ask.

"Yes, this evening. You can borrow it if you like?" he grins.

"Think I'll pass on that one."

"You don't know what you're missing."

"Oh, I'm sure it's all culturally important and that I should give it a chance, but poetry of any kind just isn't me. I like reading material with purpose. A beginning and an end."

"You don't think something can be worthwhile simply for being good for the soul? Words that can speak to you or explain what you're feeling better than you ever could?"

"Sure," I shrug. "I'd just prefer a thriller."

He laughs.

"So . . . what's next?" I ask.

His smile disintegrates. "What's next is . . . I've got a call to make."

My pulse falters as he realises his misinterpretation. "Oh, you just meant, what am I going to read next?"

"I did. But you're right. You *have* got a call to make."

Ed breathes deeply, as if fortifying himself with sea air, and looks at his phone. Then he nods and pushes himself out of his seat. I watch the contours of his back through his pale shirt as he dials a number and holds the mobile against his ear, slipping his other hand into his pocket as he walks to a more private part of the terrace, out of earshot, out of sight.

I focus on the tumbling hillside, swirling my drink, suddenly not in the mood to make it last much longer. I drain it quickly, sucking up every last drop of alcohol as I let it warm my chest and spread to the rest of my body. Then I order another one, craving its anaesthetising effects as I wait for Ed to return. He can't be longer than ten minutes but it feels like forever. The sight of him walking towards me makes my chest contract. The long, striding legs. The broad shoulders. His unreadable expression.

"Well?" I ask, the croak in my voice betraying me. "How did it go?"

Then he smiles a smile that could have a dozen different meanings and says: "I'm going home."

My bed that night is one of the most comfortable I've ever slipped into, yet when I look at the clock on my

309

phone, it reads 4.23 a.m. and I haven't slept for hours. I push off the sheets and pad to the window, pushing away the voile curtains to lift up the heavy frame. A high moon illuminates the sky and the harbour lights have dimmed, leaving silver threads refracting on the water.

The more I try to stop thinking about Stefano, the more impossible it is. The man in the pictures continues to push his way into my head, as I find myself imagining not only what he will look like in real life, but everything else. What he will sound like. The way he will move. Not just who this man is but the essence of him. And, more importantly, how he would react to me turning up at his house. Of all the unknowns, that is the biggest.

I find myself comparing him to my father. To Dad: those three letters that, together, make up so much more than a name. Sometimes, when I say it these days, it makes me jolt, as if I'm questioning its legitimacy already, before I have proof of anything.

I head back to bed and climb under the sheets, pulling them up to my chin. But the vacuum left in my head is only filled by Ed. I imagine him lying in the next room, his lips parted slightly, his eyelids trembling as he dreams, his chest rising and falling. And I think about how soon Julia's head will lie on it, her cheek pressed against his skin as she listens to the sound of a heart that belongs to her.

CHAPTER
FIFTY-THREE

Our taxi driver is tapping on his steering wheel and humming along to the song, "Horny, Horny, Horny," as it crackles through the radio. An elaborate set of beads dangle from the rear-view mirror. The stench of air freshener is making me queasy as I stare out of a window thick with dust, not really looking as we pass fields of tumbling vines and olive groves.

We both skipped breakfast, unable to manage anything, before I asked the hotel to call us a minicab, stressing that we didn't need anything fancy like the car that took us to La Cavalletta. Now we are on our way to the address given to us by the receptionist there. Stefano's home.

"Allie." I snap up my head and look at Ed. "You don't have to do this, you know. Not if you don't want to."

I run my tongue along the inside of my cheek and realise I've bitten into it. "We've come this far."

"It doesn't matter," he says softly.

"But it does."

Too quickly, we are winding up a dusty road that overlooks the cliffs, and the driver is talking in Italian to Ed, who tells me that we're almost there. Then he pulls in and the taxi purrs in the hot street as I feel the sweat on the back of my legs stick to the seat.

"Will you tell him to wait here, just in case there's no one in?"

Ed nods and does as I ask. Then, I click open the door and step outside feeling the sun on my shoulders as I reread the address.

I can't see much of the tiny house from the street, only the entrance to a small building with pale walls and faded green shutters. It is clearly not the main aspect of the building, but even the least inspiring side hints to the riches beyond: a view overlooking the azure sea and trails of fragrant oleander from a canopy above the door.

Ed appears next to me. "Lovely place," he says under his breath.

But I can't answer, because just the thought that Stefano could be behind this door has hampered my power of speech.

"Do you want me to knock?" Ed asks.

A bead of sweat trickles down my side. I nod. He steps forward, but glances back and looks at me. Then he rings the bell. Less than half a minute later, a door in the adjacent house opens and a woman dressed in a thin pink dress and flats steps out.

"*Buonjourno*," says Ed. She does not speak English but I listen to the conversation, anxiously trying to work out what is going on before Ed turns to me.

312

"His neighbour says he's not in." My reaction, a wash of relief and disappointment, takes me by surprise.

"Okay."

"He works a half-day at his boat yard on Wednesday."

"So should we go there?"

"She says he'll be back in an hour or so but I'll get the address. In the meantime, she suggests that you leave him a note."

"Okay," I repeat, but not because I'm agreeing to it. I don't know what to do. I look up at Ed, helplessly. "If I do that, what should I say?"

"Well . . . there's a lot to cover, isn't there? Perhaps you should simply say you're looking for him because you believe he knew your mother." A shot of anxiety makes my chest tighten: if he really is my father, this might be all he'd need to put two and two together. But what else can I do?

The neighbour tells me to wait outside while she goes to find me something to write with. When she emerges, she gestures to a small painted bench in the shade outside the house and I take a seat as Ed sits next to me. I struggle to grip the pen at first, overcome with a sense that whatever I say will be wrong. All I can do is write — and keep things simple.

Dear Mr McCourt,

My name is Allie Culpepper and I believe you may have known my mother when she was a young woman. It is very important to me to know about her

313

history because she died when I was six years old, so I am unable to ask her myself. I am on holiday in Portofino until Sunday and it would mean a great deal to me if you did find the time or inclination to speak to me. You can telephone me at the Hotel Villa Castagna or on my mobile number, below. Assuming it's not too much trouble.

Yours hopefully,
Allie Culpepper

CHAPTER
FIFTY-FOUR

Peggy noticed a subtle shift in Christine's mood, weeks before she admitted she'd met another boy. Her daughter had been distracted. And Peggy soon began to suspect why.

"Not seeing Joe tonight, love?" she asked one afternoon. Christine's eyes followed the trail of a goldfinch, as it hopped on the stretch of sill outside the kitchen window. She'd been unable to concentrate on her homework and that really wasn't like her. She was a clever girl, full of ideals, who wanted to be a journalist for all best reasons: to expose injustices and tell untold stories of people the world ought to know about. She'd been studying hard for the last few months, making sure she'd completed all her revision before Joe came over. At least, she had until recently.

"No, not tonight, Mum." Christine looked up and Peggy pretended not to notice when the apples of her cheeks flushed pink. She folded a cotton pyjama top and added it to the pile of laundry, breathing in the scent of newly washed cotton. Then she picked up the

stack to take them upstairs, when her daughter spoke up.

"Have you got a minute?"

"Of course." She returned the washing to the table and sat down.

"It's me and Joe," she said, pausing while she thought about how to say her next words. "Mum, I think the world of him. He's so sweet and kind and we have such a laugh together. He's my best friend . . ."

"But?"

"I . . . I don't know how to say this." She looked ashamed of herself.

"You've met someone else."

She lifted her chin. "How did you know?"

Peggy shrugged. "Just a hunch."

Christine's face crumpled with despair. "Oh, Mum. I am the most horrible person in the world."

Peggy tutted. "Hardly."

"Stefano — that's his name — he's completely different from Joe. Perhaps I shouldn't compare but . . . he's different from anyone I know." Her eyes focused on the blur of light through the window. "When I'm with him, it's as if I can't know enough about him or where he's from."

"Where's that?"

"Italy. But it's not just that I'm being swept off my feet by some handsome foreigner, honestly," she added hastily. "When I'm around him, I feel this . . . warmth. That's the only way I can describe it. And when I'm not with him, I can't stop thinking about him. Yet, I do love Joe. I can't imagine ever not loving Joe. How is that possible?"

Peggy wasn't sure it was. "Look, love. I think the world of Joe. And we'd all be upset if you were to split up. But, you're very young."

"What does that mean?"

"Just that you've got to follow your heart."

Christine looked up and smiled. "Mum, that's so bloody corny."

Peggy laughed. "Is it? Corny but true."

Christine split from Joe a week later and Peggy was surprised at how sad she felt about it. She worried that she'd given her daughter the wrong advice, encouraged her to do something Peggy suspected she'd regret. Still, if she'd learnt one thing in life it was that people need to make their own mistakes, that it isn't a parent's place to interfere. And, even though Christine hadn't talked much about him, there was no doubt how taken she seemed by this other boy.

For three weeks, she spent most days after school studying in the library with Stefano; at weekends they'd taken the train to Formby to picnic on the beach. She'd even gone to watch him play cricket once and, given that patience wasn't one of her daughter's greatest virtues, this felt like a small miracle.

Yet things weren't simple. Peggy supposed they never were. One afternoon when she arrived home from work, she heard a door slam in the kitchen, followed by an explosion of loud and colourful cursing. She walked in to find her daughter tipping a teaspoon of coffee grains into a cup, then reaching out for the kettle — and sending the entire jar clattering to the floor in the process.

"STUPID SODDING THING!" She threw the teaspoon down.

"Er, young lady," Peggy scolded gently. "What's that Nescafé ever done to you?"

Christine spun round and grimaced. She grabbed a piece of kitchen roll and blew her nose.

"What's going on?" Peggy persevered.

Christine's shoulders rose as she drew a breath and went to look for the dustpan and brush under the sink. "I bumped into Joe in the corner shop today."

Peggy picked up a dishcloth to help with the mess. "Well, that's going to happen, love. He doesn't live that far away."

"It was so awkward, Mum. I felt terrible."

"Joe doesn't need your pity," Peggy said.

Christine looked at her and frowned. "It wasn't that. He was telling me about some big training exercise he'd been involved in . . . and how he's planning a holiday abroad with some friends from work. And he's got tickets to see The Smiths at the Hacienda, probably with somebody else. You'd think the end of our relationship was the best thing that ever happened to him." She looked up, her lip trembling as she tried to steady her voice. "God, I miss him."

"Enough to get back with him?"

Christine closed her eyes. "How could that even be possible after what I've done?" she said furiously.

318

"What about your new boyfriend — have you gone off him?"

Christine shook her head as if Peggy didn't understand. "No," she said, slightly exasperated. "He's lovely too. Totally different but . . ." Then a thought popped into her head. "Will you meet him?"

Peggy's eyes widened. "You're not asking me to choose for you, I hope?"

"No, of course not. I've made my choice already, the least I can do now is live with it and not mess Joe about. I've hurt him enough as it is."

Peggy didn't reply.

"I just want you to meet him, that's all," Christine persisted. "And okay, I'll admit it. I want you to tell me what you think of him. I want you to let me know if you think I've done the right thing."

CHAPTER
FIFTY-FIVE

Allie

The taxi winds its way through the shimmering dust back towards Portofino, and I can't shake an unpleasant, gritty feeling that I've left myself exposed. By writing the letter, revealing my name, my hotel, giving my number. The need to run away rushes up in me, fuelling my instinct to get out of here as fast as I can.

"Do you want to try the boat yard?" Ed asks.

I shake my head. "No. Let's just leave it as it is."

Ed's presence in the seat next to mine brings with it a kaleidoscope of conflicting emotions. But above all else, it is the only thing stopping my anxiety from spinning out of control. It's not even anything he's said; it's simply the knowledge that he's there with me. My backup. My rock. No matter what the aftermath of that letter turns out to be, I don't have to face it alone, at least for the time being.

The taxi drops us off as near to the hotel as it can, but instead of going inside, we decide to wander down to the harbour.

"Fancy a gelato?" Ed asks, clearly trying to lighten the mood.

"Maybe," I shrug. I'm too agitated to be hungry, but we make our way towards the little gelateria that nestles in a stone alleyway between a fancy fashion store and a bakery.

"Did the neighbour say he'd definitely be back within an hour?" I ask, as we stand in the queue. I can't even say Stefano's name out loud anymore.

"She didn't say definitely. Just that he usually is on a Wednesday," Ed tells me.

I take my phone out of my pocket. It's 1.23p.m. Saliva gathers at the sides of my mouth and I swallow it back.

"Allie. Don't be too disappointed if he doesn't contact you."

"I won't," I reply. "In fact, right this minute, I'm desperately hoping he doesn't. Here, let me get your ice cream."

"No, it's all right," he protests, rooting in his pocket for change.

I flash him a mock warning look. "Ed, after everything you've paid for on this trip, let me buy you a gelato."

The sheerest smile appears on his lips. "Go on then. Anything but pistachio."

I choose a swirl of cream and pink, made with fresh Amareno cherries, and hand it to Ed. Then we drift back towards the harbour and along the jetty, until we're entirely out of runway. Ed lowers himself onto the wood, as I sit down next to him and slip off my sandals, dipping my toes into the water, the cold biting my ankles. With the cove behind us, it feels as though we're floating above the sea, the clear, bright sky stretching ahead.

"I haven't said thank you," he says, all of a sudden.

I look up and shield my eyes from the sun.

"That's all right. I should've got you a double scoop though. That Marsala flavour looked lovely."

"I wasn't talking about the gelato."

I can see the creases on his skin from behind his sunglasses. He lifts them up to look at me properly. "Thank you for being here when I needed someone."

Emotion throbs between us in the haze, but I can't bring myself to acknowledge it.

"No worries. Besides, you had your uses," I say lightly. "I didn't have to dig out my pocket Italian dictionary once."

He laughs and I realise how much I love that sound. He can't ever be mine but I will always have that: I was the one who made Ed laugh again.

"It's been a lovely holiday," he says.

"Are you sure it's been much of a holiday? I've had you traipsing halfway up and down Northern Italy."

"It hasn't exactly been hell. I've got to see some of the most beautiful parts of the country, with . . . with you."

The only sound is the shifting air as birds circle above us, and the chime of water as it splashes under our feet. I look away, following the lines of the lush, green cliff that rise above the harbour to a vanilla-coloured house, high above the sea. "Imagine living up there," I say. But Ed's hand is on mine, gently squeezing my knuckles. I look down and let my gaze settle on it, as heat rises up my chest. I allow myself to look up at him, at those fiercely blue eyes.

Then I become aware that my phone is ringing.

I snatch away my hand and before I even look at the screen I am gripped by panic, at the thought that this can only be Stefano. This is the first phone call I've had since I left England.

"You'll be okay," Ed says.

I turn over my mobile. But the number is from the UK and it's listed in my contacts already. I release a thin trail of breath as my adrenalin disperses.

"Hi, Grandma Peggy. You do know I'm not back from my holiday yet, don't you?"

"Allie . . . I've just had a phone call." The crack in her voice sends a rip of anxiety through me.

"What is it, Grandma? Is something the matter with Granddad? Is everything all right?"

"He's fine. We're all fine. The call . . . it was from . . . they called him Stefano."

The moments after she says his name feel like a vacuum, one that gradually fills up with an awareness that Grandma Peggy is crying. I can't think of a single occasion when I've heard her do that before.

"Grandma, what's the matter?" I whisper. "Tell me what you know about Stefano. I need to know."

It takes several moments for her to answer. "He telephoned me and told me you'd been to his house. He said you're not in Portugal. But that you tracked him down in Italy and had written a letter."

"How did he find you?"

"He . . . remembered where to look."

This entire conversation is making my head throb, as if I'm trying to work out a puzzle that's beyond my comprehension.

"I should've been honest when you found that newspaper article and the letter," she continues. "I was upset and confused and . . . I'm sorry, Allie. I never wanted to lie to you. I didn't know how to explain."

"Explain what, Grandma?"

I can hear the quickening of her breath before she finally speaks. "What happened between your mother and Stefano McCourt."

CHAPTER
FIFTY-SIX

June was always a strange month for Peggy because it was Christopher's birthday. Every year, as the days on the calendar would count down to the 16th, the memory of that day when she'd given birth on a hard hospital bed, frightened and alone, would sharpen into vivid focus.

Over the years, she'd learnt to hide her feelings as the date approached. She never did anything to mark the occasion, except for one year when she took the day off work and went to Nightingale House, just to stand outside and let memories slip over her. But it had closed a few years after Christopher was born and, after a brief spell as a children's home in the 1970s, had been bought by a businessman who planned to turn it into posh flats.

She never went back again. Mostly, she just tried to get through that date without being too quiet and pensive. But, no matter what she felt, one of the hardest lessons she'd learnt over the years was that life goes on. It has to, even on the days when you're so exhausted by the world that it's difficult to breathe.

Christopher would have been twenty this year. The intense joy Christine had brought her didn't change the fact that Peggy had had twenty years of regret burning her up from inside. Twenty years of love that was sometimes tender, sometimes so angry it was ready to burst out of her. Twenty years without a little boy who didn't even know her name.

It felt like such a terrible milestone that, when Christine announced that Peggy would finally get to meet her new boyfriend on the 15th — the day before her strange and secret anniversary — she really wanted to find an excuse to say no, to hibernate at home and not have to face the world. But Christine had it all planned. He was picking her up from home before they went off to the pictures, and she'd asked him to arrive ten minutes early so she could introduce him to her mum. Peggy's seal of approval was clearly important to both of them.

"You'll be okay for ten minutes or so, love," Gerald had said gently that morning, as he turned down Radio 2, silencing Terry Wogan. "It might just be a distraction."

Peggy nodded. "I suppose so."

"Do you think Christine's deliberately arranged to bring this lad home when I'm at work?" Gerald grinned.

"Probably," Peggy said. "She'd nearly brought him here before she went to that party with him at Allerton People's Hall at the weekend, but decided against it. Probably didn't want you casting your critical eye over the poor lad."

"Me? Critical?" Gerald protested. "I'm a softy and she knows it."

"Not when it comes to boyfriends you're not."

"I was nice to Joe," he pointed out, as he took a last mouthful of tea.

"Everyone was nice to Joe," Peggy replied. "It was impossible not to be."

"Don't say that in front of the new fellow, whatever you do," Gerald chuckled and put his warm arms round her. "You all right love?" he whispered.

His concern cracked something open in her chest but she held it in. "I'm fine," she said as he kissed her gently on the temple, grabbed the keys to his Ford Sierra and left her alone with her thoughts and the faint hum of the radio.

Peggy had to remind herself to keep an open mind about Christine's new boyfriend, though it wasn't easy given how much she'd liked Joe. But first impressions were good. He had a narrow face with serious eyes and thick, dark hair, while an exaggerated cupid's bow drew attention to the small gap in his teeth. He was polite, with a strong handshake and an easy smile.

"Can I get you a cup of tea? Or . . . what is it you drink in Italy?"

"Coffee usually. Occasionally, my parents drink wine."

"You've got some Harvey's Bristol Cream in the drinks cabinet, Mum," Christine grinned, trying her luck.

327

"Water or juice will be fine," he laughed and the ice was duly broken.

"That I can do." Peggy beckoned them through to the kitchen, where they took a seat at the table while she set about making the drinks. "Whereabouts in Italy are you from?"

"Well, I was born here, but my parents moved to Sirmione when I was very small."

"Where's that?"

"In Northern Italy, near Verona, where my mother was from. I'm half-English though. Liverpool was my father's home."

"Oh, that's right," she said, placing two tumblers of orange squash in front of them.

"Christine mentioned that your dad works at the museum now."

"He's a curator," he nodded. "My grandmother hasn't been so well, so Papà wanted to move back to the UK and be closer to her. Thanks for the juice."

"It must've been a culture shock for you and your mum though."

He hesitated while he worked out how to put this politely. "I like it in England," he said, and as he glanced at Christine it was clear why. "There are things I miss, of course. My uncle's boat yard in Portofino, for example — I've spent the last few summers working there. But I've applied for a job at the Royal Mersey Yacht Club, so who knows? In the meantime I'm working in the hospital and it's really not so bad."

"Your mum's not as keen on it here though, is she?" Christine added.

328

He took a deep breath and smiled regretfully. "Not so much, no."

"I'm sure she'll settle in eventually," Peggy replied.

"I hope so," Stefano shrugged. "Though . . . it's different for her. For me, this is where my roots are, so I have a reason to be here, other than to simply follow my father. I can find out a little about where I was born."

"Stefano was adopted," Christine told her mum, matter-of-factly.

"Not that I'm looking for my biological parents. I never wanted to do that," he continued. "I just always wanted to . . . get a feel for the place, I suppose. Understand where I was from."

A chill had run through Peggy's blood. Not because she had any idea that Stefano was her own baby — born as Christopher — before she was forced to give him up for adoption. Not yet.

For the rest of the time Stefano and Christine remained in the house, Peggy was left with a sharp reminder of her own past. Her baby was out there somewhere, she told herself. He'd be all grown up now. The idea that he might think of her in the same terms that this young man thought of his birth mother — almost as an irrelevance — sent misery spreading through her like ripening mould. Eventually, she simply had to ask Stefano something.

"You've never wondered what happened to your real mother?" The words fell from her lips before she'd had a chance to fully form her thoughts.

He shook his head vehemently. "The woman who gave birth to me gave me away. I'm sure she had her reasons, but being a parent . . . well, you already know: it isn't just about biology. That's only a fraction of it." He spoke in a measured, impassioned tone. "My mother and father were the ones who loved and raised me. They taught me to read, encouraged me to work hard, helped me stand up to the bullies at school. They're my parents, not a stranger who gave me away when I was six weeks old." Peggy felt her trembling lips try to protest, but he got there first. "She didn't even leave a note."

A thought was now ricocheting around her head: she hadn't been allowed to leave a note. Indeed, the thought of doing so had never even crossed her stupid mind.

All she'd been allowed to leave was the baby box — which she doubted his new parents would've kept anyway — and the little blanket of stars she'd knitted for him. Except that got left behind and had been gathering mildew spores upstairs in her bottom drawer for years.

There was a time when she'd spend hours holding it against her face, breathing in the warm, milky scent imbued in its fibres. But that smell had long since faded and, over the years had been replaced by musty overtones, even though she regularly wiped out the drawer with lemon juice. Eventually, she'd been forced to launder it, but the chemically produced lilac fragrance of the washing powder only made her feel as though she'd lost another little bit of him.

That thought made her eyes prick and she urgently had to say something.

"Some women were forced to give up their babies."

Christine frowned and looked at her mother, bewildered. But Peggy felt she had a duty to the poor woman who was his real mother, to let him know that she probably loved him, more than she'd ever have the privilege of telling him.

"You're right, of course, that your parents have had the hard job of raising you. But don't simply assume that your natural mother didn't want you. In the sixties, if a girl got pregnant and her parents found out, she often wasn't allowed to keep the baby."

She could feel the heat from Christine's eyes from across the table.

"I haven't put much thought into that. Maybe I will one day." He forced a smile meant to diffuse the tension and lowered his glass, clasping his hands under the table.

"Stefano, we need to go," Christine said, standing up abruptly. "The movie will be starting soon and I hate missing the trailers."

They started making their way towards the front door. Peggy felt a fool. She padded after them and tried to re-engage them in conversation so that things weren't left hanging on this strange and unexplainable note.

"What is it you're going to see?" she asked.

"An Officer and a Gentleman," Christine replied.

"Well, have a lovely time. Are you going to walk? It'll be a nice stroll through the park on an evening like this," she replied.

"Hmm. Maybe." Peggy realised her daughter was probably worried about bumping into Joe. For all Christine's enthusiasm for this new boy, Peggy knew she still had regrets about her ex-boyfriend.

"We might do that tomorrow after we've been to the new bistro at the top of the road."

Peggy raised her eyebrows as she opened the front door and they slipped out. "It's meant to be pricey, that place."

"Yes, but it's a special occasion."

"Oh?"

"Tomorrow's my birthday," Stefano said. "I'll be twenty."

As Peggy stood and watched them cross the street hand in hand, she clutched the door frame until her knuckles turned white, for fear that if she let go her own legs might not be able to hold her up.

CHAPTER
FIFTY-SEVEN

Allie

My head feels swollen in the heat as I gaze up at the vanilla house on the hill. I am woozy and confused and my heart is racing so fast that Ed appears next to me and hands me a bottle of water, placing it into my palm as he touches my back. "Everything all right?" he mouths.

But I can't answer, because everything is not all right. Everything is so far from all right that I am still hoping I've misunderstood. I must have done because my interpretation of Grandma Peggy's words is simply impossible.

"I don't understand. I don't understand any of it." I have a dozen or more questions all fighting for space in my head, but what it all comes down to is this: "Stefano McCourt was . . . *is* your son?"

After a moment of hesitation, she replies. "Yes."

The impossible implications of this rise up my chest and spill out of my mouth. "Then that makes him Mum's brother."

"Half-brother. Yes."

The sky seems to swell and undulate as I try to form my words. "Then how can he have been her *boyfriend?* That's . . . *sick.*"

"Allie, they had no idea," she interrupts. "None at all. How *could* they have known? Stefano only knew he'd been adopted and that his mother had given him up. But when his parents moved back to Liverpool, as far as they were concerned I'd just been some forgotten, anonymous girl from a mother and baby home. They thought I was long gone."

"What did you do?"

She gathers her thoughts before beginning to fill me in. "I was in shock that day. I mean, here was my lost boy. The boy I'd loved with every bone in my body, but I'd been convinced I'd never see again. And he had been standing in my kitchen, looking at me with those same eyes that had looked at me when he was a tiny baby. I wanted to reach out and hold him. I wanted to tell him, it's *me.* I'm your mum. And I love you."

"But . . . that wasn't what I meant, Grandma. I mean, once you'd discovered he was your son, you must also have realised that he was having a relationship with his sister?"

"Well, slow down," she says firmly. "It depends what you call *a relationship.*"

"You said he was her boyfriend," I argue. "She dumped Dad for him. I'd say that was a relationship."

"Let me tell you what I know, Allie," she says, her voice trembling. "As I stood at the door, watching them walk away from the house I felt . . . probably like you do now. Knowing all the pieces fit together but not wanting to accept it. I kept telling myself there must've been some other explanation. I must have got it wrong. I didn't know what to do. So I let them go off to the cinema and I sat in the living room and for a while I just looked out of the window, hoping to try and work it all out. Then your granddad came home."

"Had he known you'd had a son, before you'd met him?"

"He'd been the one person I'd told, soon after we met in Paris. He never judged, he just loved me for being me. I told him what had happened and we agreed that our only option was to find out what exactly was going on — to find the man and woman who'd raised him. His adoptive parents."

"How did you do that?"

"When they returned from the cinema, your grandfather offered to drive Christo . . . *Stefano* home. Or rather, he *insisted* on it. Your mother was mortified, as teenagers are wont to be, but that's how we found out where they lived."

"Then what happened?"

"The next day was a Saturday and Stefano's birthday. Christine had arranged to see him at lunchtime, to go to the new bistro they'd talked about. As soon as she went out, Gerald and I drove to the house he'd been to the night before. I was . . . I was scared and angry."

"Angry?"

"They'd moved to a nice house in Aigburth, less than ten miles away from the mother and baby home. What were they *thinking* coming back so close?"

"Did you ask her that? Stefano's adoptive mum, I mean."

"That and dozens more questions. She and I had a lot to discuss."

CHAPTER
FIFTY-EIGHT

The woman at the doorway of 47 Bamford Avenue wore a cashmere cardigan and slim capri pants, with neatly cut glossy hair that she pushed behind her right ear. A pair of reading glasses dangled on two fingers of one hand and a subtle shade of lipstick accentuated her pretty mouth.

Peggy noticed all of these things in the moments after she'd opened the door. But then she started speaking and the only thing she noticed after that was the horror reflected in the amber flecks of Vittoria's eyes.

"My name is Peggy Culpepper, nee Smith," she'd managed, sounding much calmer than she felt. "I was a resident at Nightingale House in 1963. I was forced to give away my baby, against my will. And I . . . I believe that that baby is Stefano."

Vittoria's knees slackened. She considered slamming shut the door, but thought better of it. "You . . . you should come in."

A tall sash window cast a hazy light on the elegant bookshelf that dominated one wall of the living room.

An intricately woven rug sat on a wooden floor with chevrons polished to the colour of honey, while a set of papers were stacked up next to the pale sofa where Vittoria had been working.

Peggy's eyes were drawn to the mantelpiece where a clutch of family pictures jostled for space. There was one of Vittoria on a pebble beach with Christopher, when he couldn't have been more than two. He was wearing a funny little hat and his chubby legs poked out of a sweet pair of trunks. Along from that was a photo of the entire family: Vittoria, her husband and Christopher, who looked about thirteen by then, his features growing into a half-man, with glowering teenage eyes that gave the impression he hadn't wanted to be pictured. In the most recent photograph Christopher was wearing cricket whites, holding up a trophy. That sat next to another taken at a party, in which Christopher's arm was draped affectionately round Vittoria's waist.

Everywhere Peggy looked, she found evidence of a close and well-educated family, who'd worked hard to make this house comfortable and homely. She'd told herself for years that all that really mattered was that her son was happy and loved; that was all she'd ever wanted for him.

Yet, looking around this room, she realised she'd been kidding herself. Now, all she could think about was how this woman — a respectable, probably very nice person — had taken something away from Peggy without ever realising she'd done it.

338

It was this woman who'd got to cheer while Christopher took his first steps as a baby. She'd got to hold his hand as he started school and run alongside as he'd ridden a bike without stabilisers, or watched proudly when he scored runs for his cricket team. It was she who'd got to bake his birthday cakes, to sew labels on his school clothes. She'd got to teach him to fly a kite, build sandcastles on the beach and read him a bedtime story every night.

They were small things, really. Nothing monumental. But, together, they felt like a hundred pieces of Peggy's broken heart.

"Excuse all the papers, I'm self-employed," Vittoria said awkwardly, gathering up her admin. "I've been working as a translator since we came back to the UK."

Peggy realised that she may have lost the ability to speak. "Please, take a seat," Vittoria added. "Can I get you something to drink?"

Peggy shook her head and gripped her bag as she perched on the sofa. "I'm sorry I turned up out of the blue," she said, the slightest crack in her voice. "I . . . I didn't really have a choice."

The sinews in Vittoria's neck tightened and Peggy pulled herself together.

"The first thing we probably need to establish is whether what I think happened is true," Peggy continued, swallowing her nerves. "So, I will tell you my story — what happened after my son was born. Perhaps we can work it out from there."

She told Vittoria how she was twenty-two in 1963 and became pregnant to a man she'd known only briefly. She told how her parents took her to Nightingale House and how she gave birth alone in the nearest hospital, before returning for six short weeks. Then she told — or at least tried to explain — how she agreed to sign the papers to have him adopted, even though that was the last thing she wanted. And how even at the very end, as she sat in the waiting room, she was hoping for a miracle, something that would keep her baby with her. But then it was too late.

The sockets of Vittoria's eyes grew hot as this stranger, a woman younger than her, sat on her sofa with more creases on her face than someone her age should have. When she and Michael had adopted Stefano all those years earlier, she hadn't allowed herself to think beyond her own childlessness and the joy he would bring. Why would she? She didn't ask any questions. She didn't want any answers, at least beyond what they'd been told.

"They said at the adoption agency that the baby's mother hadn't wanted him. They told us she was from London and that we'd never see her again."

Vittoria would never have returned to Liverpool — no matter how sick Michael's mother was, or how exciting his job offer — if she'd thought there would be the slimmest possibility of this meeting ever taking place.

"They lied to us," she whispered. "I'm so very sorry for everything you went through."

"You weren't to know," Peggy mumbled, instantly cursing this ludicrous statement. You weren't to know. That was what you said if you forgot your umbrella when it rained, or tried to make a cake when the eggs were off.

But she couldn't think of the right thing to say, so she said the thing that she'd always told herself she would if she ever found Christopher and discovered that he was safe and well looked after.

"Thank you." She tried to mean it, but as her voice began to crack, Vittoria's head snapped up in shock.

"What for?"

"For . . ." Peggy looked up at the pictures again, "for doing such a wonderful job in bringing him up."

Despite the twist in her stomach, she owed her son's adoptive mother that much. Vittoria fought a surge of tears behind her eyes, sniffing them away.

"How on earth did you find us?" she asked. "What made you come looking?"

Which brought them to the crux of the matter. Peggy drew a deep breath. "I didn't. I have a seventeen-year-old daughter. Yesterday she brought home her new boyfriend." Vittoria's hands shot up to her mouth. She already knew the rest.

"It was . . ." she nearly said Christopher, but stopped herself. "It was Stefano."

CHAPTER
FIFTY-NINE

Allie

The jagged shock in Grandma Peggy's voice has eased
but there are still so many unanswered questions.

"How did you tell my mum . . . and Stefano?"

"We agreed to do it separately, that evening. Gerald
and I would tell Christine. Vittoria and her husband
Michael would tell Stefano. It was . . . not a good
moment," she says with striking understatement. "Your
mother refused to believe us at first. She accused me of
lying and stormed out of the house. I was out of my
mind with worry. But Vittoria phoned up soon
afterwards and said she'd turned up there. We agreed
to give them an hour by themselves. To say their
goodbyes."

I'm conscious of her breathing, the distress that
resonates in her words. I've literally never heard my
Grandma Peggy like this before. "By the time your
grandfather and I pulled the car up outside the house,
your mother was there waiting on the step. She ran
towards us and, when she got in the car, put her head
in her hands and wept. I glanced up into the bedroom

window and there was Stefano. The face of my baby, all grown up. I couldn't look away from those eyes . . . that hair, still as dark as it had been when he was six weeks old."

"Oh, Grandma."

"It was the last time I saw him. Vittoria and Michael . . . they said that that was the only way. They were determined. They told us they were worried about Christine and Stefano wanting to be together, but I think . . . no, I'm sure, they wanted to keep him away from me too."

"Did they move back to Italy straight away?"

"Very soon afterwards. I got the impression Vittoria had never wanted to be in the UK in the first place and this must've been a good argument to move home. I tried writing to Stefano a few times, I couldn't not. I told him that I loved him, that he was my flesh and blood, that I'd do anything to see him again. I only got one response, the letter you read from Vittoria. As you could see, I was told in no uncertain terms to leave him alone."

"Did you?"

"What else could I have done? To persist would've made him hate me. I wrote to Vittoria again and promised I'd never be in touch again. I only broke that promise once, when Christine died. She was his half-sister, after all. I thought he ought to know. He wrote to me to thank me for informing him, to say he was sorry for my loss, but that was it. That letter was in the drawer too, but I don't think you found that one."

I become aware of Ed next to me, his expression filled with concern. "Okay?" he mouths. I nod and turn away as my eyes blur on the gently lapping water, my head rushing with questions.

"So . . . when Stefano returned to Italy, Mum got back together with Dad? Just like that?" I ask incredulously.

"Not *just like that*, no. Your mum was very upset about what had happened. And I don't only mean about her and Stefano. I mean about the fact that she'd thrown away what she had with Joe. She barely emerged from her room for a week. She wouldn't go to school, refused to see any of her friends. She was angry with me too for not telling her that she had a half-brother."

"Why hadn't you?"

"Because I was ashamed. I *am* ashamed. Not about the fact that I had him, but about the fact that I let them take him away. I'll never forgive myself."

"But you had no choice, Grandma," I say, but she doesn't respond. All I can hear is the silence of the phone line. "So . . . what happened next with Mum and Dad? How did they get back together? I mean, she'd rejected him, hadn't she?"

"She wouldn't have been the first person to make a mistake, Allie. To be dazzled by someone new when the person they love was right there in front of them. But I'll give you one thing: she was very lucky that he agreed to get back with her."

344

CHAPTER
SIXTY

In the days afterwards, disbelief hung in the air like dust beaten out of a carpet. Peggy's head was swollen with thoughts of her son's face, so close to her as he stood in her own kitchen that she could've reached out and touched it. Initially, when she'd think of him — and she was always thinking about him — she could conjure up a vivid image, picturing in detail the curl of his hair, or the movement of his lips when he spoke. But soon those details began to blur and fade, and the harder she tried to grasp for them, the more elusive they became.

Christine, meanwhile, had barely emerged from her bedroom after her departure from 47 Bamford Avenue, despite Peggy's attempts to talk about what had happened, or indeed about anything. Each time she knocked on her daughter's door to ask if she had any laundry, or to say dinner was ready, she'd mumble a response that made it clear she wasn't coming out any time soon. In the end, it was Gerald who coaxed her downstairs, with the promise of tomato soup, Cheers on the television and some gentle words about which Peggy never knew the exact nature.

It was the height of midsummer, nearly 9p.m., and with the last drop of sun still firing up the sky, when Peggy felt a touch on her shoulder. The extra light of the last week or so had made the shrubbery burst into an exuberant display and she'd been staking out the foxgloves at the time. When she turned around and saw her daughter, it was clear that there was one thing she needed above everything else. Peggy wrapped her arms around Christine and felt the tension in her shoulders melt away.

"I'm sorry I've been wallowing, Mum. I can't imagine what you must be going through. To have not seen your own baby for all these years." She shook her head. "What complete bastards. The people that made you give him away, I mean."

Despite the language, Peggy couldn't disagree.

The three of them watched television together, before Gerald disappeared to the pub for a game of crib, leaving the two women alone. It was during the long talk that followed when Peggy realised what was eating her daughter up more than anything else.

Whenever Christine had been hurt or lost before, Joe had been there for her. As much as Peggy knew that her maternal brand of tea and sympathy helped, it came down to something bigger than her need for a shoulder to cry on. It was gone midnight when Peggy suggested it was time to turn in for the night. There was a chill in the air as her daughter stood to head upstairs and, with the shadow of despair in her eyes, got to the nub of the matter, what Joe had really meant to her. "I think I've lost the love of my life, Mum."

The question was, what was she going to do about it?

Christine had never been a reticent kind of person. She could be forthright to the point of stridence and often gave the impression that she wasn't afraid of anything. Yet, the more desperate she felt about trying to patch things up with Joe, the more worried she became. Sometimes she could convince herself she was being irrational, that the worst that could happen was that she'd make a fool of herself. Except that wasn't the worst, was it?

She'd always believed that you had to be honest to build bridges. But the truth was so unpalatable. The truth was, those powerful, confusing feelings she'd had were for a man who turned out to be her half-brother. Her flesh and blood. It was a repulsive thought, but one she could neither change nor deny. The idea of confessing all this to Joe was something she could hardly contemplate.

Peggy watched twice as her daughter marched out of the house, in a cloud of Body Shop perfume and hope, before reappearing fifteen minutes later. She'd hovered at the end of his street, then lost her nerve. She tried writing him a letter, but she'd never been good with words. How could she say this terrible secret out loud, or write it down in black and white?

Another week had passed when Peggy woke early on a Saturday morning to the sound of a small commotion in Christine's bedroom. She wiped sleep from her eyes and blearily wandered in to find her daughter stacking her collection of records into three cardboard boxes.

"What are you doing?"

"I've decided to sell them. Every last one," she said.

Peggy sank onto the edge of the bed, astonished. "But why?"

Christine paused and looked up, her eyes blazing. "It's an investment."

Five hours later, having traded in her entire collection at a record shop in the city centre, Christine stood outside Joe's house. He opened the door expecting to pay the milkman. Instead, he found the girl who'd broken his heart, wearing hoop earrings and a shaky smile as she clutched a 1979 blond Gibson 335 guitar, just like BB King's.

CHAPTER
SIXTY-ONE

Allie

"She told him everything," Grandma Peggy says. "I'm sure they went through a lot of heartache than that before deciding to get back together, Allie. But I do know this. They worked it out. He loved her and she loved him."

Beads of perspiration gather at the back of my neck. Because there's one thing I still don't know and all I'm left to do now is force myself to consider the one big question I've had since I first saw that picture of Mum and Stefano all those months ago.

"Grandma: what about me?"

"What do you mean?" she asks.

"I came along nine months after all this. So, I mean . . . there's only one way to ask this: is Stefano my father?"

I can almost hear her voice harden before she speaks. "Of course not. You're your father's daughter. You're Joe's."

The swarm of relief is a temporary sensation. "But how do you *know?*"

"I just do. Anything else would be unthinkable."

"Unthinkable or not, Grandma, the timing is right. Surely it's a possibility?"

"No. Definitely not."

But this is very obviously wishful thinking. I know it and she knows it. That's why she was so determined that I shouldn't mention the letter and newspaper cutting to my dad. Because she didn't want to dredge up a question that all three of us know remains unanswered. A question that makes me feel sick to my stomach — about who I am and where exactly I've come from.

CHAPTER
SIXTY-TWO

I am shaky and overheated for the rest of the afternoon. I feel as though the world has started spinning the wrong way and that I can't stop it.

Ed tries to engage me in conversation but I can't explain to him what is going on. No matter how many times Grandma Peggy protested that she *was absolutely certain it couldn't be the case* that Stefano — her son — was my father, she is not stupid and neither am I. What she actually meant was: I can't bear the thought that it could be true. That doesn't mean it isn't.

Everything about this fits: the timing. The secrets. The fact that when I look at the picture of Stefano, at the gap in his teeth and the way his hairline traces his forehead in a high, inverted triangle, it's almost like seeing a ghost of myself.

Back in the room, I turn the shower on as hot as I can stand. The searing heat stings my skin and makes my blood vessels dilate until rosy patches bloom on my arms. I lift up my chin and water snakes down my face, before I switch it off and step out of the suffocating cloud of steam into the bedroom. I dry myself and pull on a cotton vest and pants, before walking to the window to shut it, unable to bear the heady sounds of an Italian summertime.

I slip into bed, curling my body around itself as I sink into a dreamless sleep. It must be more than an hour later when I stir, as the sun is dipping below the horizon, the cotton sheets sticking to my skin. In the moment before I open my eyes, dread spreads like black mould through me, but I can't remember why. Then Grandma's revelations prickle into my head, and I'd give anything to plunge back into unconsciousness.

A knock on the door makes my pulse jump.

"No thank you," I call out, presuming it's the maid.

"Allie, it's Ed."

I drag myself out of bed and throw on a cotton dress. Then I open up, my eyes brimming with unshed tears that I quickly sniff back. But he places his hand on my arm and it's warm and reassuring and everything it's not allowed to be.

"Hey," he whispers. "Whatever your grandma said can't be that bad."

I shake my head and feel my stoic expression collapse. He takes me by the elbow and shuts the door behind him, guiding me to sit on the bed. "Allie, what's going on?"

"I can't bear to tell you."

"Tell me what?"

The room is cast in a peach hue as sunlight slants through the voile on the window and the clean,

352

uplifting scent of pine sap drifts in with the breeze. When I look up at Ed, the tenderness that appears in his eyes moves me beyond words. Then I start talking and it all comes tumbling out, polluting everything like garbage pouring into the sea.

I find it impossible to decipher the look on Ed's face when I've finished.

"Christ." It escapes from his mouth in a croak. "Are you okay?"

I nod fiercely. Then despair engulfs me and I squeeze my eyes tight.

"Hey," he whispers and pulls me into him, his big arms around me. "It's okay to cry."

I press my cheek gently to his chest, feeling its warmth through his cotton shirt, and the throb of his heart against me.

"I'm a freak," I mumble and he tuts and tightens his embrace.

"Don't be ridiculous."

"It's true."

He pulls back and tries to make me look at him. "It's not true. Even if, for argument's sake, Grandma Peggy is wrong. Even if your mum had sex with —"

"Don't say it! Don't even say it out loud."

"Okay. Even if Stefano turns out to be your father . . . because he and your mum did something without ever knowing the consequences or implications, so what? None of it changes who you are."

"A freak."

353

He clasps my hand. I'm hyper-aware of the dry warmth of his fingers against my skin. "Do not say that. Don't ever say that."

"Why not? It's true."

"No it's not." I look away, but he moves my chin gently towards him, forcing me to look at him.

"Allie, you are brilliantly intelligent and kind and beautiful and funny. And . . . none of those words are even remotely big enough to describe how amazing you are."

His reassurance slips over me, devoid of impact. Only then he releases my hand and says, "Don't believe me then. But you know what, Allie? I'll tell you what you are. You are everything to me. Everything."

When I look up, I realise he is almost as shocked as I am. Then he rubs his head through shallow breaths and his shoulders relax as if the solution to some mystery is unfolding inside him. He silently stands up and walks to the window, breathing in the air that billows in. I am immobile, unable to know what to say. He turns around and I'm convinced he's going to walk out. But then he is on the bed next to me and he's talking again, saying things that make my head throb.

"You, Allie, are the one person on earth who can make me laugh no matter how bad I'm feeling. You are the one I can count on to be by my side, no matter what other crap is happening in my life. You are the one I want to have next to me when I'm feeling lost, as much as I do when I'm on top of the world."

I look away.

"Allie, I think I . . ." But he can't say it.

Instead, I glance up and permit myself one sweet moment when all that matters is what I feel for him and what he feels for me. He reaches up and brushes the pad of his thumb against my cheek. My belly jumps as his eyes shift to my lips. Then he slowly moves towards me and places his mouth on mine, leaving it there for a fraction of a second, before pulling away, gazing at the ghost of his kiss.

A pocket of air hovers unreleased in my chest and I close my eyes briefly. In the darkness behind my eyelids, whatever has kept us apart no longer exists, or if it does I can't remember its relevance. I move towards him and brush my lips against his. He responds instantly and we kiss, silent and soft at first, then harder and hungrier.

As he tightens his embrace, I can feel the hardness of him pressing through the fabric of my dress. I move my hand inside his shirt, feeling my way along the small of his back, before dipping it below his waistband. His palm makes its way slowly up my leg and he cups the fleshy part of my thigh, squeezing it, before his warm fingers skim the edge of my pants. His lips make their way to my neck along the burnished skin on my shoulders, before he returns to the heat of my mouth.

I touch and stroke and kiss him as if I want to devour every inch of him.

Soon I am unbuttoning his shirt, overwhelmed by a feeling that this is more like my first time than my actual first time was. The uncertainty. The new, bare flesh. But, between my silent gasps of pleasure, I become aware that his kisses begin to slow. I pretend it isn't happening at first, pulling him back towards me by his shirt, until eventually, he retreats.

I know what he's thinking, but it's me who says it out loud first. "We can't do this, can we?"

He releases a long trail of breath. "No. We really can't."

CHAPTER
SIXTY-THREE

The salty perfume of the sea drifts through the window as the light in the room intensifies to daybreak.

I turn to look at Ed's softly sleeping eyes, resting my gaze on the pores of his skin, the tiny birthmark that sits like a kiss behind his ear. I study every part of his face, at the features I've seen for so many years, but rarely this close. The curve of his eyebrows. The blurred line of his bottom lip. The tanned skin on his forehead and the faint dot-to-dot of freckles on his nose.

My unquenched desire has left me unable to sleep for most of the night. I think the same is true for him. He was restless until just before the sun rose. Now I lie next to him, not naked, but in a state of undress, only our underwear intact. His hand is clasped around mine as he sleeps. I am afraid of what will go through his head when he wakes up and sees me lying in bed with him, yet I don't want to be anywhere else except next to him right now.

It's in this strange bubble of contemplation that my belly lets out a loud, rumbling groan. I clench my stomach in an attempt to silence it, but it continues to complain cantankerously, until Ed opens one eye and smiles.

"Sorry," I mumble.

"Hungry?"

"Apparently I could eat a horse," I reply and in that small moment we roll with the pretence that we are two new lovers with nothing to worry about except making breakfast.

He turns on his side to face me and prop his head up on his elbow. For a moment we just look at each other, wondering who is going to speak first.

"So ... this happened," he says, his tone untranslatable.

"Yes. Well, nearly, anyway."

"Nearly," he agrees, because neither of us are sure what you could even call what we did last night. Not sex in the strict, biological sense of the word. But there is an exquisite kind of torment from going as far as we did, then holding someone all night, feeling the heat from their body next to yours, when you're still glowing from their illicit kisses. It's a primitive hunger that overtakes you, leaving you pulsating with frustration. The irony is, if this abstinence was supposed to make my conscience feel clear, it's done the opposite. Yet I also feel something else. Rejection. I'm trying to convince myself that the decision not to go further than we did was a joint one. But it wasn't.

He lifts up his eyebrows. "Are you okay?"

"Kind of. Are you?"

He rolls away and lies flat on his back, fixing his eyes on the ceiling. "Allie, we need to talk."

"I know," I reply. "But I don't know what to say."

He starts running his hands through his hair.

"I'm going to the bathroom," I say, reaching out for a towel to cover my body. But it's about an inch too far and as I hook the fabric under my finger, it drops again.

"I could just look away," he offers.

I nod. "Probably a good idea."

He rolls over, the curve of his shoulders facing me, as I reach out and wrestle the towel around me. I grab my mobile and a couple of random items of clothing before I dart into the bathroom and shut the door. It starts vibrating. It's only when I've already hit the answer button that I register Julia's name.

CHAPTER
SIXTY-FOUR

"I've been trying to get hold of you and Ed since last night."

"Is everything all right?" I ask.

"Everything's fantastic. What am I ever going to do to thank you?"

I close the toilet seat and sink onto it.

"What do you mean?" I mumble.

"What do I mean?" she laughs lightly. "I mean, Ed is coming back to me. I mean, whatever you did or said, you've made him come to his senses. Thank you, Allie. Seriously, thank you, thank you, thank you." Every repetition is like a knitting needle in the side of my head. "I really can't wait to see him. And you. You're wonderful."

"No. Honestly I'm not," I reply flatly.

"Did you say something, Allie?" Ed shouts through the door.

My chest clenches as I open the door and shake my head at him with flying saucer eyes. He frowns.

"Who's that?" Julia asks.

"Nobody, Julia," I reply, Ed's eyes widening meaningfully at the name. "Just . . . the window cleaner."

I close the door on Ed's dilating pupils.

"What has he said about me since he phoned yesterday?"

"Um . . . we haven't really stopped to talk. It's been a busy couple of days. Sorry."

"Allie, is everything all right?"

"Of course. Of course," I repeat.

"Are you still flying in from Verona on Sunday? Or are you going to see if you can switch your flight after moving to Portofino? I checked this morning and there's one to Manchester direct from Genoa. I can send you both the details if you like?"

"Um . . . okay. That's really good of you."

"I was trying to get hold of Ed to tell him that but his phone has gone straight to messages. Will you tell him to call me if you see him at breakfast?"

"Yes, no problem. I'll tell him as soon as I see him."

"Have you found what you were looking for in Italy, Allie?" she asks.

"What do you mean?"

"You told me you were searching for some answers about your past. I hope you've found them."

I open the door slightly and look through the crack at Ed, buttoning up his shirt.

"Yes. I think I have."

"Oh, that's great news," she says. "You know, when you get back I think we should have a big party, don't you think?"

"Sorry, Julia, the line is pretty bad in here."

"Okay. Well, I'll try Ed again. Have a wonderful final day."

I end the call, close the door and drag on the gypsy skirt I seem to have brought in with me, followed by a stripy yellow and pink T-shirt, an ensemble that makes me look as though I got dressed during an acid trip. I emerge into the room to find Ed fully dressed and standing by the window.

"Julia is trying to get hold of you."

His jaw tightens and he nods.

"What are we going to do, Ed?" I say. It's then I realise that, despite everything, despite how wrong it is, I want him to tell me he's going to leave her and be with me. I know this makes me a bitch but I don't care. I wouldn't care if it made me go to hell. I cannot get beyond my longing for him.

He turns to look at me and appears not to know what to do with himself. Then he says, "There's nothing we can do, Allie. I've got to go back to Julia."

The prick of rejection appears in my eyes and pressure builds in my stomach. I suddenly need to get out of there. I pick up a pair of slip-on sandals and quickly slide them onto my feet.

"What are you doing?" he asks.

"I need some air," I mumble, opening the door, darting out, and refusing to look back as I click it closed. I walk-run down the corridor and head down the stairs two at a time.

When I emerge into the reception, the young man at the desk attempts to wish me a "*buongiorno*" and I

362

mutter a feeble response before stepping out into the tiny street. The little boutiques are only beginning to open their shutters as I race down the steep pavement, barely registering the pain in the balls of my feet as they pound the stone. I finally reach the *piazzetta*, where the morning sunlight is already intense and the restaurants are opening.

My feet slow, as if I've lost the energy to move any further. I flop down on the stone floor of the marina, the rippling blue sea stretching out from the arc of the bay. I look up to the vegetation, the chestnut and olive trees that rise above the pastel facades of the buildings, luxuriantly green and silver. And I have never felt a stronger urge to be at home, with my dad — my REAL dad, no matter what tainted blood is running through my veins. I sit for a few minutes with my head pounding, when a shadow appears on the ground next to me.

I know it's Ed before I even look. "Allie, I need to tell you something. I need to explain." He sits down next to me but I refuse to look at him.

"There's no explaining needed," I tell him. "We both regret it. It was a huge mistake. Clearly, that's why we didn't *actually* have sex. I don't even know what I was thinking. Not only that you're married. I don't even like you anyway. Just for the record. You're not even my type. I've already told you I go for blonds and —"

"Allie, Julia is pregnant. I'm going to be a father."

A small bird with bright yellow plumage dives down to the water, before swooping off into the sky.

"What?"

"I shouldn't have let things go as far as they did. Except . . ."

"Except what?"

He sighs. "Okay, I'll just come out and say it because I have to. Then I'll never say it again, because we cannot be together. We just can't."

I swallow.

"I love you." I turn to look at him. The tremble of his lip is almost undetectable, but it's enough for me not to be able to reply. "I'm sorry, Allie. I'm so very sorry."

"What . . . what do you mean?"

"I'm sorry for what happened last night. That it's taken until now to realise it. I'm sorry that I can't be what you want me to be. Because I am about to be a parent . . . and if there's one thing I'm determined to do right, it's that."

CHAPTER
SIXTY-FIVE

Ed

Ed has everything and nothing all at once. His beautiful wife. His successful business. And now he is going to be a father.

Yet as he lies on his back on the sand, the sun glowing red through his closed eyelids, all he can think about is that he is in love with the wrong woman. He also knows he is to blame. He had a lifetime to recognise and act on his feelings for Allie, but failed to do so. Now it's too late.

But Ed isn't the same man he was before he came to Italy. He will not be pulled into a well of powerlessness. He has rediscovered his strength and he won't cave in under the weight of his sadness. He has made his decision and his life with Julia will work. He'll make sure of it. Because that is who he is. That is the gift that Allie has given him in these weeks in Italy. She's reminded him of the man he is capable of being.

Ed discovered long before he met Julia that life doesn't always go your way. He also discovered that sometimes the sacrifices are worth it. He's already feeling the power of a father's devotion. He imagines his baby as a girl for some reason, though he doesn't know why. And it's the most random things that pop into his head. Making sandcastles with her. Watching *The Goonies*. Teaching her to playing chess. Drawing and cuddling and dancing.

No matter how bad Julia is, he won't leave her. Not now that there is a child to be loved and protected. He wonders how much of that he will need to do. Because while he hopes Julia will find it in herself to be a loving and patient mother, he is realistic enough to know that she may not be capable. Which is why he will be there, by her side, stepping up to the role in which he's found himself. Ed is convinced of all of this, but there is a sharp twist in his gut that seems to exist solely to remind him of another inconvenient truth: he won't ever shake off his feelings for Allie. He will try, but he will fail.

His love for her didn't begin with the heat and affectations of romance. It began with the sweet, green shoots of friendship. Over years, their roots spread through him, mapping themselves underneath his skin, until she had filled up every corner of him. What they'd had at the start had grown into something magnificent and rare and real.

In his dreams, there will always be an alternative, impossible path. In which Allie is the mother of his baby, not Julia. In which he wakes up every morning and feels her warm breath against his neck. In which they grow together, holding their child's hand on her first day at school, letting it go as he or she leaves home.

When they are old and infirm, their house would be filled with the glow of love, and they would sit in the garden, thinking about the days on the bus years before, laughing until their cheeks hurt.

"You're going to get a dodgy tan there."

A shadow falls over his eyes and he sits up, squinting in the sun as he realises he'd left his book lying open on his chest. Allie sits down sharply next to him, sending a cloud of sand billowing.

"That novel might be a Booker Prize winner, but you'll still look stupid with a big white square on your belly. Sorry."

He's grateful for the lightness in her voice. It reassures him that she doesn't hate him, though he thinks she could be entitled. He wishes he could repeat what he feels for her, the words that he should've said so long ago. But that wouldn't be fair. So he says the only thing that's within his power to say.

"Allie, we need to discuss what happens when we return home."

Her eyes soften as she replies, "It's okay, Ed." She manages to smile. There is strength behind that smile, a resilience that is one of the many reasons why his admiration for her knows no limit. "I know what you're going to say."

He suspected she might. "We need to not see each other anymore. We need to stay away. I understand and I think it's for the best too."

He can see the torrent of pain in her eyes and he can't bear knowing he's the one who caused this, on top of everything else she's facing right now.

"I'm sorry, Allie." The breeze slips into her hair and she brushes it away. She has never looked more beautiful.

"So am I." Then she sniffs and puts on her sunglasses. "Come on. Let's go and get one gelato before we pack. I wonder if they'll do them with a Flake?"

The two friends walk side by side, as the sun beats down on their shoulders and, for one last time, they breathe in the heavenly smells of a hot, Italian summer.

CHAPTER
SIXTY-SIX

Allie

As we approach the hotel, I realise Ed's steps are slowing. I can't work out why until I follow his gaze. The man he is looking at is the same but different from the one I've seen in pictures; familiar, but not.

"Are you all right?" Ed asks.

I nod, but it feels as though I'm stepping through quicksand. He reaches out and squeezes my elbow and I am grateful for this final gesture of solidarity, before I let go and walk towards a man who is both family and stranger all at the same time. I recall the tiny, helpless baby Grandma Peggy described and try to reconcile that image with the man before me.

He is fifty-four years old now, tall, with hair that is thinning, though without a fleck of grey. His skin is tanned to the colour of a chestnut, with white smile lines sloping upwards from his eyes. He's dressed in a quintessentially Italian style, with a loose cotton shirt and stone chinos, turned up above tan leather shoes. Something about him reminds me of Cary Grant in those old romantic thrillers.

"Allison?" he asks. He looks surprisingly nervous, though somehow gives the impression he is not used to feeling like this. I accept that these are bizarre and unusual circumstances.

"Yes. But it's Allie really. Call me Allie."

The suggestion of a smile appears on his lips but I can't bring myself to return it. "Stefano."

He reaches out and shakes my hand with a firm grip. "It's good to meet you."

I perch on the edge of my chair on the terrace of the hotel and I wish that the waiter would hurry up with the coffees so I at least have something to do with my hands. I had a hundred questions and now can't recall any of them.

"It was quite a shock to hear from you," he says. He is sitting three feet away, close enough to see the weathered patterns on his hands and smell the sharp, clean scent of his aftershave.

"I haven't really been in touch with anyone from the UK since I left. I heard your mother died. But under the circumstances it wasn't appropriate for me to come to the funeral. My mother was still alive then."

It takes half a heartbeat to realise he means Vittoria.

"I didn't even know you existed until relatively recently," I tell him. "Grandma Peggy had never told me about what had happened to her. The fact that she had a baby, I mean. Did you know you were adopted?"

"Yes, I always knew that. I can't recall when I was told exactly, but that was never kept from me, nor the fact that I was born in the UK. But when you're young, you don't torment yourself with questions about your past. As far as I was concerned, Michael and Vittoria were my parents. They were the people who brought me up. The idea that I would go off searching for my real mother never occurred to me. I had nothing against her. I simply hardly thought of her. I certainly had no desire to find her."

He clasps together his hands. "The one thing I was interested in though was the fact that I was technically British, yet I didn't feel British. I was fascinated by that. That was why I wanted to come to the country when my father got a job in Liverpool and went back to see my Nonna as she was in poor health. The fact that it was a city on the coast helped too — I thought I could get a job working on boats, like I had in Italy, but that didn't quite work out."

"How long were you there before you met my mother?"

"Six months or seven months. I'd taken what I'd hoped would be a temporary job as a night porter in the hospital, but in the daytime I'd occasionally go to the library. I wanted to improve my English. Your mother was studying for exams and I'd see her on the days I went. She'd sit at the desk opposite me and would always place an apple and a bar of chocolate next to her that she'd eat during a break from her work."

The waiter arrives with two coffees, before Stefano continues. "Then one day I noticed she didn't have either, so I said: 'Where are your snacks?' She laughed and replied that she'd forgotten them. I told her to wait while I went out and bought a bar of chocolate from the shop over the road. She teased me, told me I was flirting, but she didn't ask me to leave. After that, we would talk on most days. We . . . how can I say this . . . we hit it off."

I pick up my coffee but regret it when the cup rattles against my saucer, laying bare my nerves. He studies my expression. "Do you want me to carry on?"

"Yes. Absolutely."

"I knew she had a boyfriend, but I was drawn to her. When you're nineteen years old and you're a boy who has his head turned, you don't put much thought into other people, just yourself. She'd said she loved him when we first met, but then we started seeing more of each other and . . . we got swept along with the idea. Of each other."

"So she was unfaithful to him."

"She was confused about her feelings," he says carefully. "Then, one night, she ended up confessing to him that she had met me. I don't think she'd planned it. But once it was done, it was done, and they agreed to go their separate ways."

"Then you got together?"

He frowns and picks up his coffee, bringing it to his lips as he thinks. "The first thing you need to understand, Allie . . . is this. Christine and I had no idea that we already had a connection with each other. There was no way we could've guessed we had the same mother. My poor parents had returned to Liverpool without any clue as to the identity of my birth mother. The idea that she could've been living so close to the neighbourhood they'd chosen simply to be close to my Nonna and my father's work never occurred to them. Besides, they'd been told that, as a baby, I had been unwanted and that my birth mother was from London. What *did* happen was never considered a risk."

He places his coffee cup down and continues, thinking carefully about his words. "Christine and I started to see more of each other. We had a real connection. Despite our totally different upbringings, in two separate countries, there were things about us that were so similar that I found myself wanting to know everything about her."

"What kind of things?"

"In some ways it was as basic as the fact that we would both laugh at the same things and we both loved Hitchcock movies. In other ways, it was simply that being around her made me feel at ease with myself." He looks up and says tentatively, "I interpreted this as meaning I was in love with her."

CHAPTER
SIXTY-SEVEN

Stefano's words make my stomach turn over. "It became clear however that her feelings were not as simple," he continues.

I shift forward. "In what way?"

"She missed Joe after their relationship ended. I could see that immediately. I don't believe she ever stopped loving him."

"And what about the day you met my grandma?"

He takes a slow breath. "Your grandmother will have told you that she realised quickly who I was, but I had no clue until she went to my family's house and spoke to my mother. It was agreed that Christine and I were never to see each other again." He looks up at me. "That was the right thing to do, but it was a very difficult time. To have discovered what we did that night was hard."

"I can imagine," I manage lamely.

"Until then, as far as we were concerned, we were behaving like two normal kids who'd met and started dating. Then all of a sudden we are told that we are half-brother and-sister. It was a terrible, confusing, upsetting time for everyone. For me, for my mother and father, and for Christine too. As well as all that was the realisation that there I'd been, standing in the same room as my real mother, talking to her. I'd barely thought about her before then and had never felt inclined to meet her. Having not dwelt on this much, a whole river of questions had burst its banks. The one at the front was: how could she have given up her child? Who would do that?"

"You were angry with her."

"Wouldn't you be?"

I don't answer that question. I can't even begin to try and put myself in his shoes, I'm not capable of it right now. "You ended up moving back to Italy shortly afterwards, didn't you?"

"My parents insisted and, although I didn't want to go back, I knew I had to."

"Why didn't you want to return?"

He swallows and looks at me, embarrassed at what he's about to say. "I still had feelings for Christine. I thought I was in love with her. I wish that wasn't the truth, Allie. But it was very hard to just switch off what I felt. Still, I did go back to Italy and I spent years confused about this whole thing, until finally I found the strength to put the past behind me."

"You met someone else?"

"A wonderful woman called Rosa, my wife. We have four children and a beautiful two-year-old grandson, Roberto. I was lucky enough to be able to pursue not one but two careers that I've loved. I worked in a vineyard until recently, then sadly my mother and her brother died within a year of each other and I inherited my uncle's boat yard. It was a very sad time, but Rosa and I did get to move to this lovely place. It's only small, but our own little slice of heaven. So life has been good to me and it still is. Was it difficult to find me?" he asks.

"Yes, but I'm not much of a sleuth," I confess. "I can understand why you'd be shocked to receive my letter."

"Yes. But I realised you would have some important questions and that I had a duty to address them. I know what it is like living with a history that is . . . muddled. That was why I phoned your grandmother. I still had the letters from her. Her telephone number remained the same from all those years before."

"That must've been a very strange conversation."

"It was . . . a short one." He frowns but says nothing more.

"You know she was forced to give you away?" I say.

"Yes. She made that clear in her letters to me, after we'd returned to Italy."

"But you still didn't want anything to do with her?"

He sits back in his chair and thinks before speaking. "This might be difficult to understand but I'll try my best to explain. I don't want to cause your grandmother pain. I never have. But I was very close to my mother. Vittoria wasn't just a parent to me, she was my best friend. It would've destroyed her if I'd started nurturing a relationship with Peggy. I would never have betrayed her by doing so, and I never will. That does not mean I am not sorry for what happened to your

376

grandmother." He says it as if he is talking about a complete stranger. "And I'm even more sorry about Christine. She was too young to die. A lovely girl. A wasted life." He suddenly looks up and gestures to the waiter for the bill. "Have I answered all your questions?"

"Well . . . there's still one." Anxiety prickles on the back of my neck but I know this is my only chance of addressing the one big issue that brought me here in the first place.

He takes out his wallet and places some notes on the little plate with the bill.

"What is it?"

"Okay." I take a deep breath and start talking. "My mum became pregnant very soon after you left England. So, there is a question mark over which one of you is my father. My dad — Joe — or you. That's the reason I've come here. I need you to agree to something. And I'm sorry this is a really uncomfortable thing to ask, but it's the only way. Would you have a DNA test? I need to know whether it's you or my dad or —"

"Allie," he interrupts and only then do I realise how fast I've been speaking. "It isn't necessary. You've said yourself that your father brought you up and he's the best father you could ever wish for. You said that."

"I know but —"

"And more importantly, there's this. Your mother and I . . . we never did . . ." He shakes his head meaningfully.

I study his face. "You didn't?"

"No. Not once. We spent a few weeks in what you might call a relationship, but it never resulted in that. Christine was still in love with your father. That's why they were reunited so soon afterwards. They were destined to be together. To have you."

The heat behind my eyes builds until I can't speak.

"We all make mistakes when we're young, Allie. And your mother made one. But there's one thing I can tell you categorically and without hesitation. I am not your father. It is simply not possible."

CHAPTER
SIXTY-EIGHT

I waffle on at the airport. I can't do anything else except that, and down a miniature bottle of Prosecco that costs substantially more than it's worth. I do it all under the uncomfortable, fluorescent light of the lounge, without actually looking at Ed, even though I can see from the periphery of my vision that he hasn't taken his eyes off me.

"I can't tell you how relieved I am. That Stefano and my mum never, you know . . ." I try to think of a word that doesn't make me want to bring up my lunch, "*consummated* their relationship. The reason we look alike is simply because his mum is my grandma."

Ed nods.

"And apparently," I continue, "it was Grandma Peggy's dad we both inherited the teeth gap from. She never had a picture up in the house of him so I hadn't known."

"Your grandma must have hated her father for what he made her do with the baby."

I shrug. "I don't know. Given how important her Christian values are to her, she will have tried her best to forgive him, but having his face on the wall would've been a step too far for anyone."

"So now you can go home and hug your dad — your real dad — and know that there's absolutely no doubt about your relationship with him. You're still a freak though, for the record."

"Very funny," I reply, putting down my glass. "Right, I think I'll have a browse in the Duty Free. Why don't you wait here and finish your drink?"

I grab my bag and walk away, feeling the slow release in my chest the moment I'm away from him. This pretence that everything is okay between us is proving impossible. Tension is suspended between every cheerful note in our voices and every forced laugh.

Yet, it's still easier to pretend that everything is just as it's always been, when, in fact, I unfriended him on Facebook less than an hour ago; the first step towards us landing in Manchester and slipping out of each other's lives forever.

"What's that meant to be?" I ask, peering at his in-flight meal as we're somewhere over Switzerland. "I can't tell if it's animal, mineral or vegetable."

"You mean these unidentifiable beige pellets haven't given you a clue?" he says.

"Rabbit poo?" I offer.

He chuckles. "Okay, two words, three syllables in each."

"So now we're playing airline food charades?" I ask.

"I haven't got my Travel Scrabble with me."

I peer at the dish again and narrow my eyes. "Spaghetti bolognese."

"Wow, well done."

I'm genuinely shocked. "Really? Is that *really* what it is? Does it *taste* like spaghetti bolognese?"

"No, it tastes like rat droppings basted in wallpaper paste but that's not the point."

I laugh but it fades away almost before it's released from my mouth. "You're going to be a great dad, Ed."

I detect the trace of a smile on his lips. "I'm going to do my best."

Having agreed to take separate taxis home, we collect our baggage from the carousel in Manchester Airport in ominous silence.

Then we head through the security doors and follow the tide of passengers out into Arrivals. There's a shriek of joy behind us, as two little girls run past and into the arms of their grandparents. Families reunite. Lovers embrace. And in the midst of them all are Ed and I, slowing to a halt.

"I wish things could've been different," I say under my breath, focusing hard on a newspaper stand.

His shoulders rise. "Me too."

Then I feel his hand fold into mine and the warm pressure of his fingers compels me to look up at him one last time.

"Allie! Ed!"

Our hands release, we look up and there is Julia, striding towards us.

CHAPTER
SIXTY-NINE

Julia's arms are around Ed's neck and an intense bolt of shame cracks in my chest. I hover helplessly, unable to look at them, unable to do anything except rustle in my bag, pretending to search for a lip balm, the exact location of which I already know. I eventually pull it out and smear it on my mouth redundantly. My eyes dart to the exit and I consider acting on an urge to slip outside and climb into the first taxi I can find. But I know I can't without Julia immediately questioning why.

Ed's hands find their way to her waist and sit above each hip bone, his arms tense and inflexible, like the limbs of a shop dummy that have been twisted into position. Eventually, she slides her arms down from his neck and steps back to look at him. "You look wonderful," she says.

My eyes drift to her belly and I try to locate a bulge, one that I hadn't registered when she came to my flat two weeks ago. Her frame is still so slender that you'd never guess she was pregnant if you didn't know, even with the unquestionably rosy glow to her cheeks.

382

"I can't wait to hear all about your trip. Oh, Allie, it's so good to have you back too!" Then she launches herself at me and I return her hug, hardly able to hate myself more.

"Congratulations, Julia," I say, then remember I'm not meant to know.

She narrows her eyes: "Are you talking about the baby?"

I nod stiffly. "It's wonderful news."

Her face is entirely immobile for a moment, before a tiny twitch appears on the lid of her right eye. "I made Ed promise not to reveal it to a soul until he was back, so we could do it together," she says, turning to him for some kind of explanation.

But Ed doesn't say a thing, so I find myself mumbling, "Sorry, Julia. It just . . . I won't tell anyone, obviously."

She glares at Ed again, then smiles. "Well, thank you, Allie. We're over the moon. Right, let's get you both home."

But there is simply no way I can sit in a car with the two of them. "Oh, I'm going to go straight to my dad's actually, so it's probably easier if I just get a taxi."

She looks at me as if I'm demented. "Don't be silly, Allie. I'll drop you off."

"No, honestly it's fine. It really is. I couldn't let you go out of your way and I don't want to intrude when you've got so much to catch up on."

"But your house is on the way!"

"Honestly, I think it'd be best —"

"Allie, what's the matter?" she says, fixing her gaze on me.

"Nothing!"

"Ed, tell her not to be silly."

Ed hesitates. "If . . . she wants to get a taxi, then she should."

Julia runs her eyes coldly over my expression, before doing the same to Ed. "Have you two had a row?"

I think about saying yes, that that lie would be the lesser of two evils. But Ed leaps in first. "No, everything's fine."

But she's not convinced. "What's going on?"

I panic. So all I can do is say, "Nothing at all. I just didn't want you to go out of your way, but if you're sure you don't mind, a lift would be great."

The moment that follows is suffocating.

"Let's go and pay for the parking then," she smiles.

As Julia drives out of the multistorey car park into the darkness of the street, I realise Ed and I need to pull off the performance of a lifetime. To act not only as though nothing happened between us, but also as if things are just as they should be. That we are fresh from our trip, ready to face the world, and not that we were about to part for the very last time.

Because, although Ed will have to come up with an explanation for that at some point in the future, now is most definitely not the time. The problem is, having been babbling for most of the journey since Italy, I suddenly seem to have lost the ability to speak. I sit in the back of the car, willing him to say something. But he is mute too.

"When is the baby due, Julia?" I sound so false I can barely stand to hear my own voice. I already know the answer to this question, but it's the only thing I can think of to say.

She glances at me in the rear-view mirror. "At the moment they're saying ninth of November. My first scan is next week though so they might change that date. Either way, it'll be a lovely winter baby, just in time for Christmas." She reaches over and clutches Ed's fingers. I watch his hand deliberately relax into hers. She looks over at him briefly, then returns it to the steering wheel.

"I've been really lucky so far. No sickness, just a little nausea and tiredness, nothing I can't cope with."

"You're looking really well," I say, glancing through the window and realising we've only gone past one junction on the motorway.

"Thanks. I'm not looking forward to getting so fat, though, I must admit." Julia glances at Ed. "You're very quiet, darling."

"Just tired after the flight."

She looks at him sideways. "It was only three hours, Ed. Hardly gruelling."

Nobody says anything to that. There's another unbearable silence as I slump in the back, watching the signs flick past. They are almost mesmeric, the streaming red lights, the smooth hum of the engine, the rhythm of my heart. I look up and see that Julia is looking at me through the mirror, studying my features.

385

I lower my eyes, pretending I hadn't noticed, but when I check back again she's still looking. I shift to the side of the car, pretending to make myself comfortable but really to get out of sight. I wish Ed would say something.

"Where did you go in Portofino? That's where you were when we spoke on the phone, wasn't it? Were you having dinner at a hotel?"

"Yes. The Splendido," Ed replies.

She looks through the mirror again and holds my gaze. "Nice. Very romantic. I'm surprised you could keep your hands off each other."

CHAPTER
SEVENTY

As we speed along the motorway, all I can hear in the oppressive vacuum is my thrashing heart against the thrum of the engine.

"How's work been?" Ed asks, all of a sudden.

But the energy in the car has shifted. She refuses to look at him, her eyes glowering on the road, her knuckles white as she clutches the steering wheel. Seconds tick by before she finally answers: "Fine."

He reaches over and turns on the radio.

I don't recognise the song but it is slow and melodic, dreamy almost. It lulls me into a false sense of security, a temporary distraction. Julia reaches over and snaps it off, leaving the silence beating into the car like the heat from a furnace.

Suddenly, she switches lanes, overtaking a saloon. She slams her hand on the horn violently and shouts, "Fucking idiot," even though it's not clear what he's supposed to have done wrong. Then she yanks the steering wheel and we are thundering along the fast lane, passing car after car as if on rails. Drops of rain begin to softly pelt the windscreen.

"Julia, you need to slow down," Ed says, sounding far calmer than I am.

She responds by slamming her foot down on the accelerator.

"You're going to get pulled over."

"Oh, don't be such a baby," she snaps, switching lanes again, pushing my back against the hard leather of the back seat. The rain starts to fall harder and faster, white droplets of light that thud on the glass before they're swept away by wipers that are now on full speed but still not entirely clearing the view. They're the kind of conditions that require total concentration and yet it's very clear Julia is not concentrating on her driving.

"Everybody thought I was mad for letting my husband go on holiday with another woman," she says, her voice slow and controlled. "They said it didn't matter how strong our relationship was, or that we've been married for almost two years. They said that Ed is a man and all men give in to temptation." She glances at me in the mirror. "*That's* what they said."

Neither of us reply.

"Were they right?"

The back of my neck is slick with adrenalin, my palms greased with cold sweat.

"I asked you both a question," she says, anger radiating from her. "Did anything happen between the two of you while you were away?"

Ed swallows. "Why are you asking this, Julia?" This makes him sound completely guilty. And he is.

"Why aren't you answering my question?" she presses. "Because it's perfectly reasonable to want to know if my husband has been fucking someone else, isn't it? Particularly while I'm pregnant with his child."

Guilt drips from his silence like candlewax.

"You fucking bastard," she says grimly.

"Julia, the turn-off's there," Ed says, as she's about to sail past the junction. But, at the last minute, she hurtles across three lanes, as the screech of tyres and roar of horns rings through the air.

"Julia. You really need to slow down." His voice is steady and deliberate and that only seems to exacerbate the situation.

"I don't think you're in much of a position to tell me what to do, you piece of shit," she hisses, violently diverting us onto a narrow country road, where we hurtle into slicing rain and darkness.

With each treacherous bend, the grip of the car's wheels feels more fragile. I grasp for the headrest in front of me, having given up trying to breathe and telling myself this will be okay.

"You're very quiet back there, Allie."

"Sorry," I mutter.

"Sorry for being quiet or sorry for screwing my husband?"

The glare of headlights from an oncoming car flashes through the windscreen. She tightens her grasp of the steering wheel and accelerates, until the other driver is forced to slam on her brakes and screech out of the way.

"Julia, that's enough. You need to stop the car or you're going to kill us all."

She turns and looks at Ed. "I'll tell you what, both of you — I'll make a bargain with you. I'll slow down if one of you tells me the truth. Did anything happen between you that wasn't supposed to?"

We are in an impossible place, with an impossible question. If I thought we could carry off the lie, I'd say no, for no other reason than I'm in fear for my life. But she's not stupid and everyone in the car understands that she already knows something has happened.

Ed tries one last time to reason with her. "Julia, pull in and we can talk about this. Please."

"I'm not going to do that, Ed, until you tell me that you fucked Allie. I already know it happened."

"I didn't . . . we didn't . . ." he starts saying, but how can he finish his explanation?

"Didn't what? Just tell me the truth, Ed. You only need to admit it. To say one little word: yes. Then I'll stop the car and we can all talk about this like adults."

She swings round the corner and we begin climbing up a hill, racing to the summit as the car is filled with the smell of fear and sweat. I am terrified. Ed is terrified. The only person who isn't terrified is Julia, who is pumped from the drama of it all.

We turn another corner and the car begins hurtling down a hill, gathering speed as it slides across the road. And it's then that Ed says it, in one last-ditch attempt to do something. "Okay, you win."

She glances at him. "Something happened between the two of you?"

He hesitates for a moment, before saying: "Yes."

Julia gently applies the brakes and the car begins to slow. I experience a heady and incomparable kind of relief as we finally come to a stop at the foot of the hill, which dissolves entirely when I realise that we are right in the middle of the road.

"Julia, you need to move," Ed says. "This is a blind bend."

She draws air into her chest and pushes it out again before turning to look at Ed, glowering, his betrayal burning her up. For a moment there is nothing but silence and rain coming down in sheets on the windscreen.

Then she reaches over and punches him. She throws every bit of her weight behind it, smack in his eye socket. My hands shoot to my mouth as Ed attempts to unfurl himself from the seat and I become aware of headlights reflecting on the sign on the bend.

"Julia!" I shriek.

She tries to scramble back into her seat, to fumble for the gear. But she's not fast enough. And in the next three seconds all I am aware of is the screech of brakes, my own scream and the explosion of light in the back of my head, before the world crashes to black.

CHAPTER
SEVENTY-ONE

Peggy has been up and dressed since 5.30a.m., having failed to sleep. She's exhausted, but can't keep still nor concentrate on yesterday's newspaper, which she stares at as she sits at the kitchen table. Her head is elsewhere, her thoughts rolling back to the subject that once dominated her every waking hour.

Peggy can't blame Christopher — Stefano — for feeling as he does. What sort of mother gives away her baby? He has every right to be angry, to want nothing to do with her. And although she wonders what version of events Vittoria told him, that is the undeniable crux of the matter. He was not cruel when he spoke to her. He was as polite as you'd expect any good Italian boy to be. But the distance in his voice will haunt her to her dying day.

She has allowed herself to dream of some kind of grand reconciliation over the years. She'd hoped he might soften his view, change his mind. But it's never been clearer that this would not be forthcoming. There wouldn't even be Christmas cards, or the odd email, the smallest slivers of connection.

It's only now that she realises how much she'd clung onto hope in all those years. She knew he was elsewhere in the world, but she put all her dreams into one hopeless idea — that one day he would walk back into her life. At times, it had been the single thing that kept her functioning, a vague and formless longing that, even though she wasn't allowed to reach out to him, he'd come looking for her. Only when he did, it was not the reconciliation she'd dreamt of.

So she is left again with the feeling that this is her punishment for letting Christine die. For failing to see that she looked tired and making her go to the doctor before it was too late. Peggy keeps thinking about how she probably ate all the wrong things when she was pregnant with her daughter; nobody bothered with all that in those days. There's every chance that something she did caused Christine to end up as she did, dead far too young.

So she has had to live without Christine and Christopher. For most of her life, she has been half a person, an empty version of herself. A daughter without parents. A mother without children.

She picks up the cup of tea she's microwaved three times and winces when she takes a sip, realising it's stone cold again. So she throws the liquid in the sink and opens the cupboard underneath, rummaging for a duster. Dusting is the only thing that takes her mind off things right now. She knows it's not a fashionable thing to admit to these days. She goes into the living room and sprays Mr Sheen on the mantelpiece. The

393

old-fashioned scent, half chemicals, half almonds, fills her head and hits the back of her eyes.

She rubs the cloth harder, until it squeaks against the wood and her forearm aches. But she can't polish away the twist in her stomach. Suddenly, she is unable to carry on. She drops the cloth and falls to her knees, rolling onto her back as she lies on her living-room floor, letting her eyes soften on the light shade, a cobweb dancing like a handkerchief in the breeze. She wants to sink into the ground and just keep going, tumbling below the earth.

The doorbell rings. She scrambles up to the settee and hides out of sight behind the door, not wanting the postman to peer through the front window and see her. She curses herself for even ordering a parcel, one of the blouses she got sucked into buying from the internet, another pointless distraction.

But it's insistent. And eventually she hears Joe's voice through the letterbox, raised and urgent. She frantically rises to her feet and wipes her cheeks, feigning normality, as she opens the door to find her son-in-law, gaunt with cold shock.

"It's Allie," he says. "There's been an accident."

CHAPTER
SEVENTY-TWO

Ed

There is a glinting light beyond Ed's eyelids but he cannot lift them. He imagines that he's lying on the beach with Allie by his side, a high Italian sun beating down on the pebbles under his heels. Although he has a vague memory that he travelled to Italy because he was troubled, he can't recall what those troubles were.

But he can remember the smell of her sun cream as she smoothed it on her arms. The way she would roll over and say something that made laughter tumble right out of him. How the light would reflect in her hair and she'd wiggle her painted toes in the water as the surf lapped against her ankles.

But there are certain things he can't reconcile with the idea that he is still in Italy, lying in the sun. The weight of his limbs. The clammy, cold slick of his skin. The faint beeping noises beneath his ears. The fact that his eyes are so hot and heavy that he doesn't even want to open them up. He hears voices around him, but does not have the energy to listen or interpret their distended talk about fractures and morphine and swelling on the brain. He does not try to communicate, at least not until he hears crying then recognises his mother's voice, sobbing.

"I had a dream last night that he woke up. Then we had to break the news to him that he wasn't the only victim of the crash. It was terrible . . . I just can't bear it."

He realises he wants to reach out to her, to take her hand in his and tell her it will all be okay. But he's not strong enough. So his eyes remain closed and he allows himself to slip back into a world where he can sail through time and across the Ligurian sea, with Allie by his side.

CHAPTER
SEVENTY-THREE

As the sun sets over Portofino, Stefano sits alone on his tiny terrace nursing a Rossese. But the wine, for all its aromatic intensity, is not lifting his mood. Nor is the view, usually an infinite source of fascination.

From here, he can sit and watch the gentle bustle of the harbour, the boats coming and going from the turquoise inlet, the changing light as it settles on the buildings and the rich, green forest that rises above the rooftops. His garden is small, a place for contemplation, with pungent, brightly coloured bougainvillea sweeping the walls, a modest patch of lawn and a rocky slope beyond the iron rail, lush with olive trees. A tiny paradise, high above the sea.

But not even this beauty can settle his unease.

He never had any desire to meet his birth mother and that remained as true when he rose from his bed this morning as it did when he was twelve years old.

Vittoria was his mamma in every way that counted, and more beyond. He might have been born in England, but he loved her as only an Italian man loves his mother. Their bond was unbreakable. She knew him better than anyone else, he soaked up her adoration for most of his life and would admit that in the early days of his marriage it was the source of not a little trouble.

While the two women in his life managed a reluctant truce, Rosa had to accept that his mother was more special to Stefano than any other woman would be. Growing up, he'd never argued with her — she was always right. She'd taught him everything: how to make a risotto, how to confront his bullies at school, how to be kind.

Even as she lay dying, the idea that he'd return to Peggy after she'd gone had consumed her. A stab of emotion behind his eyes makes him think about the conversation they had, three days before her death.

"I know you must have been intrigued over the years," she whispered. "You probably wondered what happened to them. But what we did . . . separating you, bringing you back to Italy, away from them. It was the only way. It was best for all of us. It still is."

He kissed her hand. "I know, Ma."

A thin smile appeared at her lips. "You asked about her once, you know. Your birth mother. You were young, about seven, I think. Do you remember?"

He shook his head.

"You wanted to know her name. I said I didn't know, but that it didn't matter anyway. Because I loved you more than any other woman could love a child because I'd wanted you so badly. I *chose* you. So you were special. I still believe that."

At that moment, his yearning to protect her, not from death but from what she feared most, filled him up. And he knew it would remain with him for as long as he had the ability to breathe.

Stefano's eyes divert to a swift in flight, its anchor silhouette arcing across the sky before disappearing behind the house. He realises that for the first time in his life he feels a discomfort about a subject upon which his views have always been crystal clear.

His brief conversation with Peggy yesterday did not involve anything beyond alerting her to the fact that her granddaughter had come looking for him. But the tone of her voice betrayed more than just shock. There was something else. Sorrow. Longing. He could hear her stretching out for dozens of unspoken words that she couldn't reach.

Then there is Allie, who appeared in his life, out of the blue. Despite her dark hair and honey skin, she reminded him so much of the young Christine. Her voice was identical to her mother's, with the softest of port city accents and all its mysterious intonations, each with a dozen or more origins. And those eyes, though not blue like Christine's, had all the same contradictory qualities: vulnerable, determined.

Yes, Allie had reminded him of so much about the past, including a single uncomfortable truth. That Peggy had never wanted to give him up.

CHAPTER
SEVENTY-FOUR

Ed

It is Julia's perfume that almost rouses Ed for the second time, eleven days after he was admitted to hospital, though he has no concept of that time passing. His only awareness is of his dream, the one in which he's waiting in a pale, sunlit room. He doesn't know what he's waiting for. It wasn't unpleasant being there, far from it. It was tranquil, leaving him in a state of deep relaxation quite unlike anything he'd experienced before.

Now the scent of his wife whispers into his head. It's a pleasant enough fragrance, with floral overtones that remind him of the penny sweets he loved as a child, though Julia wouldn't appreciate that comparison. The smell doesn't put him at ease. As he drifts halfway back to life, he doesn't think about her and feel compelled to rush into her arms. But he does think about her and remember something. He is going to be a father.

The moment that realisation explodes into his head, the idea of opening his eyes becomes a completely different prospect. But as he attempts to lift his eyelids,

400

a straightforward act he's performed every morning of his life, he can't. He tries again, but when he fails, all he can do is call out, shout for help.

"His face looks terrible," Julia replies, almost in a whisper. Then he realises she isn't replying at all. She hasn't even heard him.

"He had multiple broken bones and a fractured jaw." It's a male voice.

"Is there a chance he might not wake up from this, doctor? Tell me honestly."

There is an ominous pause. "The next few days are crucial. We're doing everything we can. He's in good hands."

Ed wonders if they teach them these clichés at medical school. Either way, he needs to protest, because he hasn't got a few days, he needs to get back to work. He's been off for too long already. He opens his mouth to talk, to give his opinion, but nothing comes out and that makes him feel suddenly as though he's suffocating. That those around him are oblivious to his distress only increases his panic.

"Well, his mother's coming back soon, so I think I'll disappear before she arrives," Julia sighs. "She's hard work at the best of times." If the doctor replies, Ed can't hear it.

He imagines Julia's profile, the neat ponytail, soft silk blouse and immaculate complexion. He opens his lips to speak again but they stick together.

Then a memory punches him in the head. Or was it a memory? It could just have been another dream, one of the strange places into which his mind plunged when he'd lost his capacity to think rationally. Either way, his mother's words are on repeat in his brain.

"He wasn't the only victim of the crash."

A chill stipples along his spine as he hears the click of Julia's shoes on the floor next to him, feels her thin, cold hand clasp his fingers. Where is Allie?

"Oh, Ed," she whispers and he realises in a blur that she is next to him, stroking his hair. "I'm sorry, sweetheart. I'm so very sorry. Please wake up, won't you? There are so many of us who want you alive." She expels a long trail of breath. "If only I had some better news to tell you."

CHAPTER
SEVENTY-FIVE

When Rosa arrives home from a shopping trip the following weekend she is in high spirits.

"New shoes?" Stefano asks.

"How often do I buy new shoes?" she hoots. "Hardly ever."

"So you don't have new shoes then?"

She tentatively walks towards him and plants a kiss on his cheek. "Not for me. Only for Roberto."

"You only bought him some a few weeks ago," Stefano protests.

"If a grandma can't spoil her only grandchild, then something's really wrong."

She is about to walk away but he grabs her by the hand and gently pulls her down into a kiss. Her thick auburn hair is swept back into a bun, but a strand falls down and brushes against his cheek as her lips find his. Her skin smells of the same bergamot soap she used when they first met, the one she still swears by.

"What was that for, you old romantic?" she laughs, pulling back.

But how does he broach the subject that has been troubling him for a week now? If he tells her about Peggy, he has to tell her about Christine and Allie. How *could* he explain to his wife that he once had a relationship with a woman who turned out to be his sister? What would that knowledge do to her, or indeed their children, if they ever found out? Do they really want to know about that side of his life, particularly as he'd kept it secret until now?

He looks back at Rosa's bemused expression and hesitates. "What's the matter?" she asks.

He squeezes her hand and the flicker of concern in her eyes confirms his decision. "Nothing, my love. Nothing at all."

CHAPTER
SEVENTY-SIX

Peggy removes the tray of roast potatoes from the oven and takes out a spoon to baste them in sizzling oil until they are golden and crunchy. It was the one thing she always knew she could cook well, a time-honoured skill she developed when Christine was a little girl, something she could do in her sleep these days.

Christine loved the way she made these every Sunday. She'd snap them open and watch as a cloud of steam rose from their fluffy centre, then wolf them down, asking for seconds and sometimes thirds. Peggy never denied her — her daughter was always as skinny as a rake and she'd be the first to admit her swell of satisfaction as she watched the potatoes disappear.

She wipes away the heat from her forehead and slides the tray into the oven, before taking out the roast chicken. As she's closing the door, she becomes aware that her hands are trembling. Her heart is racing and her chest rising, so much so that she has to keep her back turned away from the others hovering in the kitchen.

It was Gerald's idea to try and get back to normal and she's trying her best. She still can't sleep from the drama of it all. First the call from Stefano, then — just when she thought life had lost the ability to throw its worst at her — the terrible news about Allie.

She closes her eyes and pictures herself scurrying down the corridor of the hospital, trying to keep up with Joe. Turning the corner and being told by the doctors that they had to wait, that they were doing everything they could.

When she finally got to see her, her beautiful granddaughter, she entered her room and saw her lying in the dim light. She looked like a sleeping angel.

"Are you all right, Peggy?" Joe's hand is on her shoulder. She looks up and sees the creases of exhaustion around his eyes.

She sniffs herself into shape. "I'm fine."

"Shall I carve this chicken?"

She wants to answer but she can't. The best she can offer is a mumble before she goes to compose herself in the bathroom. There, she looks in the mirror and realises how old she looks. Yet, in some ways she still feels exactly the same as she did when she was twenty-two. She still loves the taste of Ovaltine. She still bristles at the feel of the wind against her cheeks on a cold spring day. She still wants to cry at unexpected moments, but swallows back her tears, another skill that has stood her in good stead over the years.

She opens the cabinet and pulls out a lipstick, twisting up the gold tube. It was a gift, never used. Then she slicks some on her lips and presses them together, edging the waxy colour to the top of her cupid's bow.

She needs to pull herself together, give herself a good talking to. She needs to stay strong, for everyone's sake.

She slams shut the cabinet and goes downstairs.

But before she enters the dining room, into which they've all now drifted, she stands at the threshold of the door for a moment and takes them in. Her husband, who would do anything for her, who has given love all her life, even in those times when she must not have been very lovable. Joe, for whom the title son-in-law feels entirely insufficient. It does nothing to describe in rich enough detail his kindness, his goodness, everything he did for her daughter and now her granddaughter.

She walks around the table and takes her seat next to Allie. Who is brave, clever, beautiful, funny and more fragile than she thinks. But, most importantly, is alive. Her brown eyes might have dulled and her arms become painfully thin, but she's living and breathing and right here now, which is more than can be said for Christine. Or indeed Ed. Poor Ed, who came out the worst of all of them.

Peggy has no idea what happened between them on their trip to Italy, but they all know that it was something. Why else would Allie stay away, even though he's now been in a coma for two weeks? The boy who was her oldest friend, the man who — her father aside — meant more to her than anyone else.

"Has the doctor said how long he wants to sign you off work, love?" Gerald asks, as Joe starts dishing up food.

Allie shakes her head. "I think it will be a while."

"I bet you're itching to get back there, aren't you?"

For the first time in her life she looks as though she doesn't know how to respond to that question. "I . . . to be honest, Granddad, I think it's probably best if I take some time to get back on my feet."

"Oh, of course! I mean, you must. I wouldn't dream of suggesting anything else." Gerald looks genuinely concerned that he's said the wrong thing.

"I know, Granddad, don't worry." She takes a sip of water, before lowering the glass. "It's not a great time at work anyway. The big project we were working on has basically all come to nothing."

Joe looks stunned. "Didn't it work?"

"Not as well as we'd hoped," she says solemnly. "All the initial signs had been that our gene-editing technique was more efficient than anything else. It was at first. Then the results started to dip and just kept dipping." She picks up her fork and gently pushes it into a carrot. "We're no further along than anybody else now."

"I'm sorry, love," Gerald says, but as she places a morsel of food in her mouth and puts down her fork again, she looks almost numb to this development, as if it hardly matters.

Peggy slides her hand across the table and clutches her granddaughter's fingers briefly, the cutlery rattling as she snatches it away. Allie looks at her and for a moment the worry in those eyes disappears.

"What was that for, Grandma?"

"I'm just glad you're here, that's all."

She smiles softly. "Me too."

Peggy picks up the bowl of potatoes and adds an extra one to Allie's plate. Then she sits back in her seat, knowing that this is her role now, to look after this girl. This is what God intended for her. Peggy might be a daughter without parents and a mother without children. But she still has this rabble. This mish-mash. This family.

CHAPTER
SEVENTY-SEVEN

Allie

My grandparents' street smells of barbecues and cut grass as Dad and I leave. Their neighbour Mrs Hopkins is in her front garden, unplugging tiny weeds from the gaps between her begonias with a trowel. There are a couple of kids skateboarding along the pavement, dodging wing mirrors. Dad clicks open the lock on his car and I slide into the passenger seat.

"When's your next hospital appointment?" he asks.

"I've got to go in again tomorrow so they can look at my shoulder. Which is good because I can't actually look at it myself, at least not without feeling queasy."

"It'll heal. The human body is surprisingly resilient." He freezes momentarily, wondering if that was the wrong thing to say, before checking in the mirror and pulling away from the kerb. "Have you heard anything more from the police about the investigation?"

"No, but I don't really know whether I'm supposed to. I haven't a great deal of experience of this kind of thing."

When I gave a police officer my initial account of the crash, at some point in the dark hours after it happened, I was still rigid with shock and can't now even recall what I told them.

It was only later when I had to give a statement that I realised that, while I could remember some of the events leading to the accident with complete clarity, I drew a blank on others. Between those two states was a strange hinterland, in which it felt as though I'd witnessed things through misted glass, unsure of whether I could trust what I thought I'd seen.

I remember Julia surprising us at the airport and us walking to her car, but only fragments of the drive on the motorway and nothing of how we ended up on the country road where the crash happened. I remember my shame and fear that she would find out about what had happened between Ed and me. But, while I'm certain that she worked something out, I can recollect nothing of what was said about it. And, while the police told me that Julia's vehicle was stationary when the other car ploughed into her, I simply can't imagine why that might be.

Oddly, it's the details from *afterwards* that are the most vivid: the low creak of the driver's door as Julia opened it and crawled out. The agonising waves of pain from deep inside my shoulder and the tufts of Ed's hair, as his head lolled to one side. When I said his name and he didn't respond, panic swept through me and I started begging for someone to phone an ambulance. By that stage, the driver of the other car already had. Like Julia, he escaped essentially unhurt.

But these pieces of the jigsaw still exist only at the back of my mind, in a place I have to scratch about to reach. I am, by all accounts, an unreliable witness.

Despite a frustrating lack of detail, every time I think of Julia, hostility bubbles under my skin. This is something I can't explain, because I've never felt that towards her before, no matter what feelings I've concealed about Ed. Just because she was at the wheel of the car doesn't mean it was her fault, though I genuinely can't imagine why she would've brought us to a complete standstill in the middle of a dark country road when weather conditions were so bad.

Nevertheless, and this is the point I keep reminding myself, she must be devastated by the whole thing. The only real explanation I have for the way I feel whenever I think about her is what happened afterwards, when I tried to go and visit Ed.

"I'm very sorry but visiting to Mr Holt has been restricted to immediate family," the nurse told me apologetically.

"Oh, but I'm his oldest friend. I'm sure if they knew it was me —"

"I'm afraid the consultant spoke with Mrs Holt only this afternoon and agreed with her that it was probably for the best."

I frowned. "His *mum* said that?"

"Mrs Holt," she repeated. "His wife."

That's how I knew for certain that Julia found out that something had happened between us in Italy. Under those circumstances, who could blame her for not wanting me there? So I slunk away and stood in the lift, filled with self-loathing, misery and a clear explanation about why she hadn't responded to any of my texts.

I am, of course, desperate to see Ed, but I have neither the fight nor the audacity to stand up for my dubious right to visit a man who is someone else's husband, and isn't even conscious anyway.

Instead, I've had to rely on Ed's mother for information about his condition, asking her to write down, word for word, exactly what his neurologist had told her. I've spent the last week scouring every published paper I could find about comas, impaired consciousness and cerebral dysfunction. I'm still signed off work, but went in on the bus yesterday, to talk to a colleague from the neurology department, Dr Isobel Franck, with whom Petra goes swimming every Tuesday.

"I need your professional opinion. I know this is difficult, but how likely is it that my friend will live?" She looked uncomfortable but not surprised by the question. "Please."

"Allie, how would this help you?" she asked me.

I couldn't give her a reason why it would, beyond the fact that my need for answers was burning me up. "I just have to know."

"It's impossible to be precise."

"A rough percentage on his chance of survival? Please."

Her forehead crumpled. "Fifteen. Twenty maybe," she said reluctantly. "But it's not —"

"Thank you," I leapt in, halting her. "I really appreciate it."

And I did, truly. Even when I ran out into the rain and wanted to keep on running until my legs couldn't carry me any further.

That's how it's been since the crash. Sometimes I feel like I'm imploding. Other times, I feel calm and methodical. There's no question which mode I prefer. And there *has* been cause for optimism. I found a research paper from London's Royal Hospital for Neuro-Disability that found that nearly a fifth of the patients who eventually woke had been in comas thought to be irreversible. Many remembered being conscious of what was going on around them but being unable to communicate. Ed, I reminded myself, *hasn't* been diagnosed with persistent vegetative state, at least not yet. So I do have hope, even if it is a fragile and vitreous force, something I've tried to construct for myself without fully feeling it.

Eventually, the only thing left was entirely unscientific sources of comfort: newspaper websites and stories of people trapped in the intermediate stage between death and recovery before they finally woke. People who spent days, weeks, sometimes *years* in a similar state. After they regained consciousness, they reported that they'd been able to feel the warmth of their loved one's hand, hear the inflections of their voice — even something as mundane as the squeeze of a nurse's tourniquet during a blood-pressure reading. I do know of course that they are the exceptions, the statistical anomalies. For every day that goes by, the likelihood of

Ed being among their number drifts further out of reach.

"Okay, sweetheart?" Dad asks, as rows of semi-detached houses pass in a blur of block paving and neatly trimmed privets.

"Yes, fine," I nod. He's always been a solid driver. Confident and vigilant, without being over-cautious. But I feel uneasy in any vehicle these days, even on a journey as short as this, when the evening is bright and clear. My mind drifts to another matter altogether.

"Can I ask you something, Dad?"

"Of course."

"Why did you take Mum back, after what she'd done?"

He doesn't flinch. He's been expecting this conversation. "Because she said she'd made a mistake and that she loved me, Allie."

I mustn't look satisfied with this answer. "I could've tortured myself forever about whether she deserved to come back. But rightly or wrongly, I chose to believe her. I had no choice. I loved her."

I look out of the window again, intending to leave the matter there. But something compels me to speak again. "Will you try the online dating again, Dad? For me."

He glances over and realises I mean it. "You really want me to?"

"I really do," I say.

He grips the steering wheel. "Okay then. I'll give it another go."

As we turn the corner into my road, I can see a BMW parked opposite my flat. Dad flicks on the indicator and it's only as he slows that I see the door open and Julia emerge, long legs first. When she spots me in the passenger seat, she clicks her lock and starts heading towards us. Her expression is bleak. It's then that I know she could only be here for one thing. Something's happened to Ed.

CHAPTER
SEVENTY-EIGHT

Coming face-to-face with Julia for the first time since the accident releases a surge of dread from somewhere inside my gut.

"What's happened?" I ask, feeling the dig of my nails into my palms. "Is Ed . . . is he still . . .?"

"He's alive," she replies, with a croak from the back of her throat. "He's still not responding."

"There's been no change at all?"

She shakes her head and her eyes glaze with tears. "None."

I heard that Julia was discharged from hospital with cuts and bruises a day after the crash and now, though her skin is a little pale, her hair remains glossy and her blue eyes clear and bright.

"Thank you for letting me know. How are you?" I ask, nodding to her bump, as my first thoughts turn to the baby that I've prayed every night Ed will live to meet.

"Coping," she replies. "Just about."

In the moments that follow, my mind begins to flicker with half-formed memories.

Streaming red lights. The hum of the engine. The rhythm of my heart.

She inhales and glances at my dad. "Is there somewhere we could talk, Allie?"

"Oh. Yes, why don't you come in." I turn to Dad. "I'll let you know how my hospital appointment goes."

"Are you sure you don't need me to come with you, love?" he asks.

"No, no, it's fine. They're just checking it over."

Eyes in the rear-view mirror. White knuckles on the steering wheel. The snap of the radio's off-switch.

Dad gently pulls me in for a hug. "Ring me if you need anything, won't you?"

I push open the door to my flat and am struck by how untidy it looks, with a crumpled pile of laundry next to the washing machine and a curling sandwich I couldn't bring myself to eat left on a plate by the sink. Flowers sent by Petra sit in the murk of days-old water, their petals beginning to drop.

I invite Julia into the living room and she lowers herself primly onto the edge of the sofa as my heart thrashes and I prepare myself to try and defend the indefensible. Or did I already do that? Yet another thing I can't remember from the night of the crash.

"I've been doing a lot of thinking while Ed has been in hospital," she says.

I try to detect anger, or sorrow, or any other emotion on her face. But, now we're inside, her demeanour is business-like and impossible to decipher. "This whole thing has forced me to come to some pretty unpalatable conclusions about my marriage. I'm sitting next to his

418

bedside and playing the part of the dutiful wife. But there's a problem with that picture . . . isn't there, Allie?"

The blare of a horn. Rain slamming against the windscreen. "Fucking idiot."

I swallow a knot in my throat and I'm gripped by a sickening déjà vu, a rush of shame exactly like the night of the accident. I consider trying to explain that we didn't actually have sex, but that would involve spelling out what we did do and it doesn't feel like much of a defence.

"I think we've already established that Ed no longer loves me." Her voice wavers as she says it. "He did once. But that love has dwindled and I don't know the reason for that. I know I haven't been perfect, but I don't think anyone is, are they?"

"Of course not. He never expected you to be."

"Well," she says dismissively, "the point is that Ed is in a coma and therefore probably unaware of anything going on around him. But, from what I hear, that's not necessarily the case. If there's even the slightest possibility that he is conscious of his surroundings, I'm not deluded enough to think that it's *me* he'd want there."

She fixes her eyes on me. "I *know* what happened between the two of you, Allie."

The flash of headlights. The roar of a horn. "Sorry for being quiet or sorry for screwing my husband?"

"I think I'd worked it out before I'd even come to pick you up from the airport."

"Julia, I'm sorry," I say.

419

"So you should be. Nevertheless, I need your help."

"What is it?"

She takes a deep breath and releases it slowly. "*Nothing* I say or do as I sit next to Ed is having any effect. He just won't wake up." There is exasperation in her voice, like she's a child who is doing everything she's been told to do but has failed to be adequately rewarded for it. "I know I'd told the medical staff that no one but immediate family should go near him, but now . . . now I think you should go and see him."

I blink at her, astonished. "Are you . . . sure?"

"Yes. Definitely. He'd want you there."

Gathering speed. An impossible question. "You piece of shit."

I lean back in my chair, silently struggling to make sense of her volte-face. She seems to interpret my reaction as meaning that I don't want to go.

"Please, Allie," she says urgently, leaning forward. "If Ed dies, I could be in a great deal of trouble."

I frown. "What do you mean?"

"Look, it's by no means cut and dried. I mean, I wasn't even *driving* at the time — I'd stopped. From what I hear you don't remember much so if it goes to court . . ." She gathers her thoughts. "But they are appealing for witnesses and if any of the other drivers come forward from the motorway, it wouldn't look good. There's forensic evidence about the position of the car when the accident happened. The other driver, *obviously*, is trying to blame me, which is ludicrous given that *he* ploughed into *me* but . . . the upshot is that, my lawyer says the worst-case scenario could be a death by dangerous driving charge. That carries fourteen years in prison, Allie. *Fourteen years.*" A quiver appears in her lower lip. "I do not deserve that. I'm not capable of it. Do you understand what I'm saying?"

As I press my palms into the surface of the sofa, the night's events begin to shuffle into place with an order and clarity that has entirely escaped me until now. How she was like a wild animal behind the wheel. How we screeched across the motorway and ended up on a narrow lane, going faster. How Ed begged her to slow down, but she kept demanding answers, determined to know if "something" had happened, until he finally said yes in an attempt to stop her. And then . . .

The weight behind a fist. The crunch of bone and flesh. Total disbelief. "You punched him," I say.

"He deserved it, Allie." She says it with such measured composure that it's clear she's rehearsed this argument many times. It makes me recall the scar on his forehead, the injury he told everyone he'd got when he was running a half-marathon.

"Had you . . . done that before, Julia?"

"Look," she says, holding my gaze fiercely as she leans forward. "I *love* Ed."

She says this as if she believes it without a shadow of a doubt. Through a new rush of adrenalin, I wonder whether I believe her myself. After all, love isn't always a wholesome, selfless force for good. "I want him alive for reasons that go beyond keeping myself out of jail, Allie. I love him. You can choose to believe that or not, I don't care either way. But you must surely see that I

421

had every right to be furious about what he'd done. About what you'd both done."

"Of course. Absolutely."

She leans back, satisfied.

"But you didn't have the right to assault him," I add. "You didn't have the right to drive your car like you did, risking at least three people's lives, your own baby's life, and possibly more. You didn't have the right to cause an accident that's left Ed fighting for survival."

My heart is now beating so hard that it feels as though it's about to burst out of my chest. Fury begins to build behind her eyes as she responds through gritted teeth.

"You are in *no* position to lecture me, Allie. Both of you are as bad as each other. Seriously, what kind of man screws another woman when he thinks his wife is expecting their baby?"

"We didn't *screw*," I plead, but am silenced by a punch of shame. Then something occurs to me. "What do you mean *thinks*?"

Pink blotches begin to blossom on Julia's neck. She straightens her back.

"We lost our little girl in the accident, Allie," she replies, placing her hand on her abdomen. "I asked Ed's mother not to tell you. It's a private matter, after all."

"I'm . . . I'm sorry," I mutter, momentarily forgetting my question.

"So am I." She takes a tissue from her bag and holds it against her nose. "You assume once you've sailed past the twelve week point and come out the other side that everything will be fine. That's one of the reasons I was quite happy to let Ed pack himself off to Italy."

"I'm really sorry," I repeat.

But I can feel the knit of my brow as I replay her sentence: *what kind of man screws another woman when he thinks his wife is expecting their baby?* Then something else entirely occurs to me. A contradiction. A slip of the tongue. Another casual statement that doesn't fully add up.

"So, you'd passed the twelve-week mark before we went to Italy?" I ask carefully.

"Yes. Why?"

"I just . . . thought you'd said your first scan was due after Ed came back. I'd understood that they could only be done between eleven and thirteen weeks, that's all. The check for Down's Syndrome can't be performed any later."

The sinews in her neck begin to protrude. "I . . . I don't think that's right."

"No, it is," I reply, standing my ground. "My colleague Gill is pregnant and —"

"So I got the dates mixed up," she snaps. "I've had rather a lot on my mind, in case you hadn't noticed." She sits forward, on the offensive again. "Listen to me, Allie. I'm not here to discuss this with you. Whether you believe there was a baby in my womb or not is a complete irrelevance to me. It's nothing to do with you *at all*."

"But *was* there a baby, Julia?" I ask. She can't look me in the eye. A tiny bead of sweat appears on her brow and begins to make its way slowly downwards.

423

She opens her mouth but closes it again quickly. It's then that I'm certain: the baby was invented, as much of an illusion as everything else about her.

"Did you make it up to persuade Ed to stay?" I continue.

The pale skin on her knuckles stretches as her fists clench into tight balls. There is a part of me that thinks I should be afraid of this woman. I've seen what she's capable of. But I'm not. Not even a bit. On the contrary, I'm pumped with adrenalin.

"What were you going to do as time went on Julia? What were you going to tell him?" My suspicion is that, in her desperation, her thinking hadn't got that far. Or perhaps she planned to wait until after his return — after she'd proven to him that they should be together — before the "miscarriage" happened.

Nevertheless, this is not something she's prepared to articulate. Instead, she picks up her bag, rises to her feet and glares at me. "Just go and visit Ed, will you? And get him to wake the fuck up."

CHAPTER
SEVENTY-NINE

I step through the hospital doors and am hit by a smell that takes me back twenty-eight years, a blend of disinfectant, food and human sickness. Saliva gathers at the sides of my mouth as I follow the signs and take the lift up to the fourth floor.

"I'm here to see Edward Holt," I tell a nurse at the reception desk.

"Sorry, it's immediate family only," she says.

"I know, but it was his wife who sent me. I was involved in the crash with him. I'm his best friend. And —"

"Ed would want her here." I turn around to see Ed's mum, wearing a pink sweatshirt that seems to highlight the colourless tone of her skin, her hair loosely tied into a topknot. "Hello, Allie love."

There is a small, unbidden moment of connection when all we can do is fall into each other's arms. "He'll be okay," I whisper and she pulls away, wiping her eyes. Her dark nail polish is chipped around the edges and there is blood around the cuticle where she's been picking at a hangnail. "Do you think?"

"I'm certain of it," I say, immediately wondering if false hope is better than no hope at all. Still, she looks grateful for my forced optimism, before looking up at the nurse.

"Well, I'll have to speak to a consultant," she says. "You might have a bit of a wait before I get an answer."

"That's fine." I turn back to Jackie. "How long have you been here?"

"Since yesterday," she sighs. "Which is why I look like the living dead. His dad and I are on our way home for a little while — he's gone ahead to get the car. I think both of us need to try and get a bit of sleep."

"You should. Definitely."

"We'll be back in the morning though. We'll be here for as long as it takes," she says, as a sob catches in the back of her throat.

I reach over to clutch her hand, as the nurse reappears, far quicker than promised, and smiles at me softly. "He's all yours."

I'd assumed Ed would be in a room by himself, but it's actually a ward with four other beds, one of which has a thin blue curtain drawn around it. There is a machine with two monitors, dozens of wires and so many buttons that looking at it would be enough to put the fear of God into anyone. The spongy silence of the room is interspersed only by the beep of a machine or laughter rising from the nurses' station.

"They reckon it helps if you talk to people in a coma," the nurse tells me.

426

I've read lots of evidence indicating that Ed might hear what's going on around him, but precisely nothing that would persuade me that that's capable of improving a patient's outcome. She obviously senses my doubt. "I've worked here sixteen years and I still haven't decided if that's true or not. But it can't do any harm, eh?"

I lower myself onto the chair next to the high orthopaedic bed as she disappears and I examine the contours of Ed's face. There is a patch around his eye in a sallow shade of yellow and a pattern of stitches along his jaw. A plastic tube extends from his mouth and there are pads on his forehead. His chest is bare, but for the thin blue sheet pulled up to his shoulders.

I'm here to talk but I haven't a clue what to say.

"Well, this is the first time in our lives I haven't got you to answer back with some wisecrack. I should be relishing this moment." My words sound silly and pointless. Yet, there's a tiny part of me that can imagine him replying, with something funny or kind. Just something.

"So, how is it in here? It looks all right, actually. Clean. A bit bare. I preferred the Villa Cortine Palace Hotel, I must admit."

There is a shot of heat behind my eyes but I decide to carry on.

"I nearly brought some grapes." His eyelids are heavy and unresponsive. "That's what you do when you visit people in hospital, isn't it? Part of me thought that if I bought you some grapes then you'd *have* to just wake up and sit here and eat them with me. I think that's what you call blind optimism. Only I remembered when I was on the way here that you don't even like grapes. Though seriously, Ed. Who doesn't like grapes? They're the most inoffensive fruit there is. They're not like . . . lychees or anything. If you'd said you didn't like lychees I could accept that. But not grapes. Grapes are . . . grapes are great."

Pressure begins to build around my temples and my throat seems to dry up. "You know what, Ed, I feel like I'm doing my first stand-up routine and I'm dying out here. Can't you just wake up and give me a little smile? Or even heckle me? I'd be very glad if you heckled me. You could give me all the abuse you wanted, I really wouldn't mind."

I open up my plastic bag and unscrew the bottle of lemonade I'd bought, wincing at the jump of sugar as I take my first mouthful. I put the lid back on again. "So. They tell you to talk but they don't tell you what to talk about. And I have no idea. I'd read to you but all they had in the shop downstairs was last week's *Take a Break*."

I sit then for what must be five minutes, failing to come up with any ideas about what to say. At one point, my failure becomes just too overwhelming to bear. So I stand up to leave and pick up my bag. But, as I start walking away, I have an idea.

I take out my mobile and head to the reception. "Excuse me, is there any Wi-Fi here?" I ask. It's a different nurse from the one I spoke to when I first came in, a man in his forties with a hangdog expression and a mop of grey hair.

"You're not meant to have a phone on in here, love," he replies. "If you need to use it, there's Wi-Fi in the cafe."

"Thanks. I'll be back in ten minutes." I take the stairs to the floor below but don't join the queue for sandwiches. Instead, I spend my time browsing the books available online, until I find exactly what I'm looking for and download it to my phone. Then I return to the ward and click on my new purchase.

"Okay, Ed, you win. Bloody poetry it is. *She Walks in Beauty* by Lord Byron. Sounds pretentious — right up your street."

When I've finished the first poem, I flick on the next page and carry on reading.

I read Emily Dickinson and Samuel Taylor Coleridge. I read Shakespeare's Sonnets and Wordsworth's Ballads. I read Shelley, Keats, Blake, Milton and John Donne. I carry on reading, all the way through the night, beyond the point when my mouth is dry and the sun has come up. I carry on reading until it is abundantly clear that my efforts are, quite simply, hopeless.

And even though I know they're hopeless, I still carry on, ignoring the invisible hammer tapping at my temple. I have two per cent battery left on my phone when I land on a passage by Mary Coleridge and read it in a whisper.

We never said farewell, nor even looked
Our last upon each other, for no sign
Was made when we the linked chain unhooked
And broke the level line.

And here we dwell together, side by side,
Our places fixed for life upon the chart.
Two islands that the roaring seas divide
Are not more far apart.

In the moments before my phone dies I recall what Ed said to me on the train to Portofino, how he loved poetry because it can express how you're feeling better than you ever could.

We never said farewell.

I look at him again. He has not moved, or shifted or shown any tiny glimmer of recognition since the moment I walked in more than ten hours ago.

"I'm sorry, Ed, but that's it for today."

I gather my belongings and settle my eyes on his pale skin. The soft fall of his hands. His lovely face, bruised and battered.

"Your mum will be here soon, then I'm going to come back later. And tomorrow."

We never said farewell.

I glance around the hospital room for one last time, feeling like I'm six years old again, at my mother's bedside. Knowing that she was going to die without fully understanding what that meant. I tried so hard that day not to cry, to tame the pain in my little broken heart. I remember how important it had felt after Grandma Peggy had taken me to the bathroom and urged me to hold it together. What she said had come from a good place, there is no doubt about that. But what did it achieve, really? Mum wouldn't have minded if I'd cried. She'd have understood. It's not as though

430

keeping my emotions tied up in a knot inside me has done any good at all in all the years since.

We never said farewell.

I look at Ed again and instinctively know that this is goodbye. I reach over and touch the skin on his knuckles with my fingertips, as I am engulfed by a tsunami of regret and grief. For the first time in my life, I need to talk. I mean, really talk, and actually *say* something.

"I can't believe I'm never going to get to swim in a lake with you again, Ed," I hear myself saying. "Or hold your hand as we go for a walk. Or listen to the sound of you laughing. I love that sound so much. I am torn apart here, Ed. I keep thinking about our lovely, messy past. And the future that . . . I don't think we're going to have together."

I lower my eyes and continue. "I had years to face up to how I felt about you. I could have told you what you meant to me. But I kept it all to myself. Buried my feelings. Now the most important person in my life is about to slip away and I have nothing to show for it except three decades of unexpressed love. Because I do love you, Ed. I really do."

The tears escape from the rims of my eyes before I'm even aware they're there and roll down my cheeks in salty streaks. I cry silently at first, but the relief of allowing noisy sobs to leave my throat is so immense that I do it until my stomach hurts and my skin stings. I don't know how long I stay there, but I rise to my feet well before my tears have dried and take out a tissue to wipe my eyes.

I am about to turn away but allow myself one last glimpse of him as I bend down to press my swollen lips against his temple, breathing him in, feeling the texture of his skin and the direction of his soft hair. Slowly, I lift up my head to leave, when a hot tear lands with a splash on his cheek. And he opens his eyes.

CHAPTER
EIGHTY

SIX MONTHS LATER

The restaurant is fancier than Peggy is used to but she's not complaining. It's not every day you celebrate fifty years of marriage, after all. And she's learnt from experience that it isn't the done thing to tell her family that she'd have been just as happy with one of Joe's roasts.

"Are you having a cocktail, Grandma? I will if you will," Allie says. Peggy's granddaughter looks especially lovely tonight, though she knows she's biased. She's in a blue dress that skims her pretty shoulders, and her eyes, with that little Audrey Hepburn flick in each corner, make her impossibly glamorous.

Peggy picks up the cocktail menu and looks at the list, at the Martinis and the Manhattans, the Boulevardiers and the Sazeracs. Such pretty names, considering they're all designed to get you smashed.

"I don't know where to start. I'm not really a cocktail kind of person."

"We had cocktails in Paris once, don't you remember?" Gerald says.

Her mind is cast back to those dark times, when the man beside her provided the first glimmers of light. "Vaguely. What were they?"

"Lethal," he says, and everyone laughs.

"How about a Cosmopolitan, Grandma?" Allie asks. "That'll get you warmed up before we go on to the karaoke bar."

Peggy knows she's joking but must look slightly worried anyway.

"Don't listen to her, Peggy," Ed says. "We won't be going to the karaoke bar. Allie was banned last time she sang 'The Wind Beneath My Wings'."

"Love me, love my bloody awful voice," Allie says.

"I do love you. But I draw the line at your bloody awful voice." She shakes her head as he leans in and plants the sheerest of kisses on her lips, before attracting the attention of a waiter. "Is there an accessible bathroom?"

"Certainly, sir, I'll show you the way," the waiter replies, as Ed takes the brake off his wheelchair. "Excuse me, folks."

Allie had gone with him to see the consultant soon after he was discharged from hospital. They sat in silence as he opened his folder and took out the most recent radiology report, pushing it towards them so they could both read the results while he talked.

There is a central fracture dislocation of the left hip joint with inward displacement of the left femoral head. Subluxation of the left sacro-iliac joint and the left side of the pelvis is asymmetrical following the fracture dislocation. A fracture in the right femoral neck with absorption of the femoral neck. United comminuted fracture of the distal tibia with separation of the fragment.

The list of injuries went on for a page and a half. Though he'd emerged from the coma and the scars on his cheek and chest had healed, the surgery to both legs hadn't been entirely successful. There were further operations planned, but the prognosis was uncertain and a full recovery unlikely. It was possible that the wheelchair was here to stay.

Ed barely flinched as he listened. It was as if he'd already known. But Allie's heartbroken silence filled the room. Then they headed outside into the waiting room and he took her by the hand, telling her with gentle but absolute certainty: "Hey. We'll be fine. Whatever happens."

Now he makes his way across the restaurant towards the disabled toilet, without any of the difficulties they faced at the place they'd tried to go to for a drink a week earlier. It was a Grade II listed former gentlemen's club, with a stunning neoclassical entrance, Doric columns and half a dozen steps none of the group had even remembered existed from their previous visits.

Allie had looked at Ed anxiously but he just shrugged. "I never liked this place anyway." A spurt of laughter erupted from somewhere inside her chest and her eyes settled on his. That was the moment when she knew that he hadn't been quite right. They were going to be better than fine. Whatever happens.

After the crash, Julia had pleaded guilty to dangerous driving and was sentenced to an eighteen-month ban and three months in prison, which the judge suspended. With her previous good character and driving record, he accepted that she had experienced a temporary breakdown and loss of control after finding out about her husband's "affair". She has lost her job and is currently living with her parents while divorce proceedings commence between her and Ed.

They only communicate through solicitors now, a request of Ed's that Julia has respected. His feelings towards her, like Allie's, have covered a whole spectrum of emotion since the crash. There have been times when he's reflected on what happened and felt angry, of course. But that isn't a state of mind he wears easily and is telling the truth when he says he refuses to be resentful, or bitter, or allow any of the rage that ate her up do the same to him. And, although there have been nights when they've talked and talked about the dark secrets of Ed's marriage, their focus now is not on the past, but their future. In that, Julia has no part.

When Ed returns to the table, Peggy is asking her granddaughter about the new clinical trial she's just been approached to lead. "It's all to do with gene-editing technology," Allie explains.

"Wasn't that the last thing you were working on?" Joe asks.

"That was gene editing too but this is different. At least, we hope it will be different. All any of us can do

436

when these things fail is to pick ourselves up and try again. That's how we'll eventually find a cure for CF. And we will find one, eventually."

As a waiter arrives to replenish their drinks, the conversation turns to what they're all here to celebrate.

"So how does it feel to have managed fifty years of marriage, you two?" Joe asks. "It is quite an achievement."

Gerald coughs. "I think I speak for my wife when I say that it's been very easy, given that I'm still such a catch and all."

Peggy rolls her eyes. "His jokes never improve, that's for sure. Honestly though, I can't entirely believe it's been this long."

Peggy has never really worried about getting older. That her skin is thinner, the flesh on her jawline lower than before. She has a heart that still pumps and a brain that tackles the quick crossword every day, albeit not quite as fast as it once did.

She won't ever be free from grief, but she never has any desire to be. Nobody who loses a child ever does. But, she is no longer drowning in the sea of intense and never-ending sadness that consumed her twice in her life. Instead, she lives with grief as her permanent companion. It accompanies her every day, when she's putting on her clothes in the morning, or when she wakes in the night and sees Gerald softly snoring next to her. When she's cooking or polishing and even when she's practicing her yoga and is supposed to be concentrating on her pranayama. She doesn't fight it. Why would she?

437

The meal is lovely, if a little on the small side, prompting Gerald and Ed to joke about stopping off for fish and chips on the way home. Peggy is showered with gifts, things she and Gerald don't really need, but that she knows it makes her family happy to give. And she must admit that she's looking forward to the posh hotel spa stay from Allie and Ed.

As they're finishing dessert, Allie's phone beeps.

"Excuse me a minute," she says, pushing her chair out from the table.

When she returns a few minutes later, she is carrying another gift. She slips into her seat again and hands it over to Peggy, a beautifully wrapped square, tied up with a dark blue ribbon.

"Just a little extra," she says.

Peggy slips her finger under the paper and gently prises it off to find a jewellery box. Inside is a necklace, with a rose gold chain and a pendant made of onyx and mother-of-pearl, with a tiny diamond set into the bail. It's exquisite and quintessentially Italian.

"Gosh . . . thank you," she says.

"It's not from me," Allie tells her.

Gerald leans in and whispers to her: "Open the note."

Peggy lifts the flap of the small envelope that accompanies it and pulls out a card.

For Peggy and all the years we have to catch up on.

"I don't understand," she mumbles.

Ed slides his hand over to Allie, clasping her fingers. Joe takes a deep breath. Gerald simply smiles at her.

It's the strangest of gestures, a look that says "I love you" and "I'm here for you" and a kaleidoscope of other things between.

"Turn around, Peggy," Joe says.

She places her napkin on the table and shuffles in her chair, until she is facing the doorway. It's the woman that Peggy notices first. She's in her mid-fifties and strikingly stylish, with generous lips and thick auburn hair swept back off her face. The woman sees Peggy and steps to the side, turning to invite someone to walk in front of her, touching him tenderly on the arm as he passes.

And suddenly there he is, right there in front of Peggy: a man dressed like Cary Grant, with a gap-toothed smile and the darkest hair she's ever seen.

Acknowledgements

Thanks first and foremost to my agent Sheila Crowley, whose unstinting energy and expertise remain perfectly unbeatable.

I've always loved working with the team at Simon & Schuster and that remains as true with this, my eleventh novel, as it did with my first back in 2008. Special thanks to Jo Dickinson, Suzanne Baboneau, Sara-Jade Virtue, Dawn Burnett, Rich Vliestra and Laura Hough.

My lovely friend, Dr Helen Wallace, taught me everything I never thought I'd need to know about physiology, life as an academic research scientist and the search for a cure for cystic fibrosis. I'm immensely grateful for the time she spent with me on this important storyline.

I'm indebted to Claire Nozieres, Abbie Greaves and Luke Speed at Curtis Brown, with a special mention for Enrichetta Frezzato, who went above and beyond the call of duty in translating the Italian passages for me.

Thanks also to Donna Smith, whose explanation of police procedure was both thorough and invaluable.

Finally, a shout out to the messy, wonderful lot that I'm lucky enough to call my family: Mark, Otis, Lucas, Isaac and my mum and dad, Jean and Phil Wolstenholme.

YOU ME EVERYTHING

Catherine Isaac

Jess and her ten-year-old son William set off to spend the summer at Chateau de Roussignol, deep in the rich, sunlit hills of the Dordogne. There, Jess's ex-boyfriend and William's father, Adam, runs a beautiful hotel in a restored castle. Jess is bowled over by what Adam has accomplished, but she's in France for a much more urgent reason: to make Adam connect with his own son. Jess can't allow Adam to let him down because she is tormented by a secret of her own, one that nobody — especially William — must discover yet. *You Me Everything* is a story about one woman's fierce determination to grab hold of the family she has and never let go, and a romance as heady as a crisp Sancerre on a summer's day.

THE NEWCOMER

Fern Britton

It's springtime in the Cornish village of Pendruggan, and as the community comes together to say a fond farewell to parish vicar Simon and his wife Penny, a newcomer causes quite a stir. Reverend Angela Whitehorn has come to Cornwall to make a difference. With her husband Robert by her side, she sets about making changes — but it seems not everyone is happy for her to shake things up in the small parish, and soon Angela starts to receive anonymous poison pen letters. Angela has always been one to fight back, and she has already brought a fresh wind into the village, supporting her female parishioners through good times and bad. But as the letters get increasingly personal, Angela learns that the biggest secrets are closer to home . . .